Praise for Jeffe Kennedy's
The Fiery Crown

"Kennedy's worldbuilding is attentive and luxurious in this middle volume of a trilogy . . . Readers looking for a well-balanced blend of romance and fantasy with a gradually building relationship and ever-increasing stakes should give the series a try." —*Booklist*

"Kennedy's second in the 'Forgotten Empires' trilogy . . . does an excellent job of setting the stage for the conclusion. . . . Readers will be fascinated by the secrets revealed." —*Library Journal*

"A thrilling tale of two strong-willed souls discovering what is truly important to them." —*Romance Junkies*

The Orchid Throne

"An enchanting world awaits in *The Orchid Throne* . . . With detailed worldbuilding and an intriguing cast of characters—especially a warrior woman and an enigmatic and amusing wizard—this captivating story will have readers holding their breath." —*BookPage*

"I highly recommend this for lovers of fantasy romance who like intricate but not overly complicated worldbuilding, strong characters, and exciting action-packed scenes to go along with a sexy love story." —*Harlequin Junkie* (Top Pick)

Also by
Jeffe Kennedy

The Orchid Throne
The Fiery Crown

THE
PROMISED
QUEEN

Jeffe Kennedy

St. Martin's Paperbacks

This is a work of fiction. All of the characters, organizations, and events portrayed in this novel are either products of the author's imagination or are used fictitiously.

First published in the United States by St. Martin's Paperbacks, an imprint of St. Martin's Publishing Group

THE PROMISED QUEEN

For information, address St. Martin's Publishing Group, 120 Broadway, New York, NY 10271.

www.stmartins.com

ISBN: 978-1-250-19435-0

Our books may be purchased in bulk for promotional, educational, or business use. Please contact your local bookseller or the Macmillan Corporate and Premium Sales Department at 1-800-221-7945, ext. 5442, or by email at MacmillanSpecialMarkets@macmillan.com.

Printed in the United States of America

St. Martin's Paperbacks edition 2021

10 9 8 7 6 5 4 3 2 1

To Kev—first cheerleader, forever friend.
(I can't believe I haven't dedicated a book
to you yet!)

"Lia? Wake up."

The voice reached me deep in the dreamthink, where I slept wrapped in the verdant cloak of Calanthe's maternal embrace. For a moment, I thought all was well, that my realm was at peace, safe and protected—and that I was, too. That my world was as it had always been, and my ladies had arrived to wake me for the morning rituals.

But no . . . that wasn't true at all. Calanthe roiled with restless anger and furious hunger. All that blood, violently spilled in battle, saturating the waters and soaking into the very bedrock of my island kingdom, had woken Her. And that same ravenous rage filled me. Rage, pain, and death. So much death, including my own.

I screamed. The bloodcurdling shriek ripped itself from Calanthe's bones to rise from my stomach and rake my throat with rending claws as it tore from me.

"Lia. Lia, no." Con wrapped himself around me—a man, not an island—human, made of sinews, muscle, and hot skin, stilling my thrashing limbs with his overpowering strength. "It's me. You're home. You're safe. It's all right now."

I nearly laughed at how wrong he was, but it came out

as a moan. None of us was safe and nothing would be all right ever again.

"Lia, please wake up."

"I'm awake," I said, cutting off any further empty reassurances and opening my eyes.

Con held me on his lap, cradling me there. Beyond the wind-ripped awning that stretched overhead, full night had fallen, blackness severed by lightning-streaked skies. Rain poured, the wind howled, and waves rose white-tipped in the torchlight. Calanthe had tasted blood and wanted more. Her longing was mine, intertwined. The insatiable craving filled me. The orchid burned on my arm, drawing life from me, the spindly new fingers of my regenerating hand clicking as I flexed them. They itched and needed flesh.

I had lost my ring finger, and then my hand. Suffered torture. Then, drained of blood, I'd died . . .

No, I couldn't think about that. I needed to feed. Or Calanthe did. It didn't matter which—no other thought could withstand that ravening appetite.

"Lia?" Con sounded uncertain, shadows haunting his face from the last few, eternally long days. He'd come for me and saved me—and he'd never looked more beautiful to my eye. Longing for him filled me, and I *wanted*. Mine. I was famished for him. I'd died thinking of him and here he was, for the taking.

His eyes caught the golden light of the torches as he studied me, concern turning to wariness. A blast of wind-blown rain shattered over him, but he didn't seem to notice. I laid my intact hand on Con's cheek, his pitted skin rough over his snarled beard, and I trailed my nails over the water droplets on his skin. He flinched slightly. That's right. My nails had all broken. Untended, they'd been reduced to brittle nothingness, all ragged, sharp edges.

Just like me. An orchid can't live on its own. I needed . . . something. Whatever it was, I would have it.

"Kiss Me," I commanded him.

Con might have hesitated, his keen instincts whispering of danger, but I wound my fingers in the hair that trailed over his shoulder, pulling him to me. He lowered his head, arms easily lifting me at the same time, brushing my lips with his. Sweet, hot, so tender. Alive.

I bit. Like a snake striking, I had his lower lip in my teeth, hot blood flowing into my throat. He jerked, but I had him, holding him tight as I drank his life-giving vigor.

Then, instead of fighting me off, he growled deep in his throat and moved into me. Tongue coaxing me to open to him, he kissed me, sending salt and heat into the damp chill that lay deathly still in the marrow of my bones, the heat a melting caress. Needing me in return, he kissed me like a man desperate for a deep breath of air only I could give. His arms powerful around me, he held me against the furnace of his body, kissing me as if our lives depended on it. Maybe they did. Because somewhere in there, sanity returned—and I remembered who I was.

Euthalia, queen of Calanthe. I was Euthalia, not Calanthe. A flesh-and-blood woman, not an island made of soil and sea.

"Enough, Lia," Con murmured against my lips. His big, rough hand gripped my jaw, gently but insistently coaxing me away from my prize.

Reeling into humanity again, I unclamped my teeth and broke the kiss. Con pulled back enough to search my face. Blood ran from his lip—swelling rapidly—and smeared in his beard. Abruptly, astonishingly, he grinned at me. "They warned me you were a man-eater, but I never thought they meant it literally."

"Bringing the dead back to life can be a tricky proposi-tion," Ambrose observed, leaning over Con's broad shoul-der to peer at me. The wizard's sunny curls were plastered with rain around his face, making him look even younger than usual. That deceptive youth made for an odd contrast with his eyes, which held the wisdom—and sorrow— of centuries. The clinical interest in them reminded me of the four wizards who'd tortured me so cheerfully in their pursuit of knowledge, and a shudder of animal terror shook me. "I do hope that there won't be a problem with— well, no sense worrying about it now."

"Explain," Con demanded.

Ambrose smiled wistfully. "We'll see if such explana-tions become necessary—or useful. Suffice to say, Your Highness, that it will take time for Your spirit to recali-brate to being in flesh again."

"Unfortunately, time is what we don't have at the mo-ment." General Kara, dark and lean, stepped into my line of sight and bowed from the waist. "Your Highness, we need Your assistance." He grimaced, looking away to something. "Rather urgently," he added.

A startling lurch threw us to the side, another wave splattering us with chilly salt water, though Kara, a long-time sailor, absorbed the motion easily. That's right: We were on a boat. The name came into my mind. The *Last Resort*. Percy's yacht that they'd sailed to Yekpehr to res-cue Sondra and me. Though I only recalled waking on a couch under this awning, to sunset skies and Calanthe's flower-scented breezes.

Now waves tossed the ship about, a storm raging. I frowned in puzzlement. There shouldn't be a storm this violent near Calanthe, should there? But we *were* near Calanthe's shores; I knew that like I knew my hand moved at the end of my arm.

"We might be fucked." Sondra strode into view, her smile nearly gleeful. "It's total chaos out there. Your Highness—good to see You awake. And alive," she added as an afterthought. Self-consciously, she ran a hand over her shorn head, the tufts of pale hair uneven, fine as puffs of cloud. I didn't know how she'd come to lose her beautiful hair.

I couldn't remember much at all, except the pain, and that dreadful, nauseating weakness as my blood and very life drained away. And dying. Remembering that *nothingness*, the sense of my self dissipating, had me spinning down and away, the clammy claws of death reaching for me . . .

"Stay with me, Lia." Con's hand still on my jaw, he turned my face toward his. "We need you to get us home."

Home. To Calanthe. I should never have left.

"What's going on?" I asked, my thoughts clearing as I levered myself up. I had a duty, a responsibility. There should *not* be a storm like this. Con helped steady and support me as I tried to see past the pitching deck that filled most of the scene, but couldn't. "I need to stand."

I pushed to my feet but my legs gave way like wilted flower stems, and I collapsed back against Con. How humiliating. I hated being weak in any way, and now I was nothing but that.

"Let me," Con said, sweeping one arm under my knees and lifting me as if I weighed nothing. Probably I did, after all I'd been through. He tucked me against his chest—a comforting place to be—and braced against a pole that held up the awning sheltering us from the storm. I scanned the night-dark sea. Our torches made a pitifully small circle of flame in the swirl of wind, seawater, and sideways rain.

In the distance, Calanthe shone with drenched light,

crowned by the glittering jewel of my palace high on the cliffs. The home I thought I'd never see again.

Lightning forked through the sky with an immediate *crack!* of pulse-jumping sound, illuminating everything in a harsh, ruthless glare, thunder rolling after as Calanthe groaned her pain and hunger. Not far away—entirely too close—sea spray fountained dramatically from the waves churned into fury by the massive coral reef that protected Calanthe.

"*That* is our problem," Kara shouted over the wind, pointing, in case I'd failed to notice.

"Why are we so close?" I demanded. "Your boat will damage My coral reef."

Con snorted out a sound suspiciously like a laugh. Kara looked pained but inclined his head. "My apologies, Your Highness, but it's true. Unfortunately, *we* may not survive the encounter, either."

"I thought you said you knew the trick of navigating My reef and harbor." I could remember at least that much.

He grimaced, wiping rain from his face. "It seems to have . . . shifted, Your Highness. And the wind is driving us straight for it."

Oh. Of course. Calanthe had changed the conformation of the barrier reef. Not only was the coral a living entity, but so was the entire island, though in a different way. And where I'd thought of my connection to Calanthe before as trying to coax a sleeping cat to do my bidding, now She was awake and beyond my control, a raging lion savaging all in Her quest for more blood.

The storm was like a living thing, too, ravening and full of inchoate rage. Even when I understood little else of my abilities, I'd always been able to steer the worst storms around my island kingdom. Allowing the gentle, nourishing rains and sending the rending winds and waves out to sea had been as natural as breathing.

This, however, was no normal storm. Birthed by the thrashing of Calanthe's abrupt awakening, the ferocious surf and driving winds ignored my call. And . . . something else contributed here. A magic not my own. But one I recognized. Anure's wizards.

"I need to see the other direction," I told Con.

He turned, stepping out from our dubious shelter, his body flexing, briefly shifting me in his arms as he looped an arm around the post and braced against the pitching of the ship. I peered into the gloom, seeking through the violent chatter of Calanthe's ravings for what disturbed Her waters.

"Lia, I don't know what—" A flash of lightning cracked, illuminating the night. "Great green Ejarat," he breathed in horror.

Rearing against the horizon, an enormous wave rose against the stormy sky. Kara and Sondra shouted orders and—absurdly—Ambrose laughed. "Now, *that* took some doing!" he exclaimed.

Yes, Anure's wizards were throwing power at us from the other direction, seeking me. Sick terror, rising like that enormous wave, wanted to swamp me. I battled it back with determined rage. At least Calanthe provided plenty of that to work with.

"We have to get below," Con shouted in my ear.

"No." I loaded my voice with all the authority I could, ridiculous as it might be from a bald, barely clothed, and sodden heap who couldn't stand on her own. "I can stop it." I had to.

"Then do it fast," he answered without further argument, then shouted something back to Kara and Sondra.

I concentrated, feeling my way, the orchid ring stirring to life with brilliant connection to Calanthe. These were my waters, mine by birth, responsibility, and long familiarity. This sea belonged to me as much as my own blood did. Not a great analogy, as those wizards had tried to steal that, too. But it had done them no good. They'd ultimately failed to take the orchid ring, and they'd fail in this, too.

The waters were mine, but the wave that shaped them came from elsewhere. As wizards, they couldn't bend my elemental magic to their will; they could only try to disturb it. Like dropping a rock in a still pond. The rock wouldn't change the water, only displace it. The wizards no longer powered this wave. They'd started it—dropped the rock to swamp us—but it traveled on its own now.

The yacht plummeted down a slope, following the irresistible current as the powerful wave sucked the sea toward it. A roar of the tumbling water filled my ears. Con's arms tightened on me, and he shouted some kind of prayer or exhortation.

Be still, I told my sea. *Shh. Lie down.*

The wave stalled, shifted, and simmered, blacker than the sky as it reared above us. Then, like a shattering bowl of water, it *splooshed* down and outward. The swell caught us, lifting us high and tossing the yacht down again. Con bent over me, holding us against the post as the ship hurled up one wave and down another—and shuddered to a screeching, bone-jarring stop.

We'd hit the coral reef.

Another swell—smaller, but still huge—hit, and the boat leaned to one side, grinding against the rocks ominously. The *Last Resort* shuddered, as did my bones, the living coral beneath us screaming their small deaths as the yacht crushed them.

The boat lurched again. Something broke beneath us with a loud bang, the *Last Resort* tilting precipitously. Agatha and Ibolya had joined us on deck, clutching each other for support, their faces pale, but calmly turned to me, trusting in me to save them.

"We need to get off this boat, now," Con barked in his rough voice. Not so much trust there. "Can you swim?"

I needed to be firm, and I couldn't do that while cradled like an injured babe in arms.

"No, but I don't need to. Take Me to the prow."

"What? No. We'll be swept over onto those rocks."

"Take Me now or put Me down so I can walk," I commanded coolly.

Con muttered something but began forging uphill toward the leaning prow, powerful muscles working against the incline. Sondra came up beside him, using an odd-looking walking stick to dig into the wooden planking of the deck, steadying herself and then Con with a grip on his arm.

"Close enough, Your Highness, or would you prefer I dangle you overboard?"

I ignored Con's sarcasm, concentrating on reaching through the tempest to the waters of Calanthe.

"I have to stand," I told Con.

He huffed out a sigh but set me down, bracing me between his bulk and the railing, one arm around my waist—and pretty much supporting my entire weight—his other hand gripping the rail. "Whatever you're going to do, do it now. If the ship breaks apart, it will get ugly."

A smile stretched my lips, the dry skin cracking painfully. Being dead left a body in less-than-ideal condition. Layering metal into my spine, I reached out to Calanthe's churning seas once more. They responded less sluggishly this time, and I directed the currents to calm, to follow my bidding. With a mental twist, I reversed the direction of the waves. *No need to be anything you are not. Simply flow the other direction.*

The *Last Resort* lifted, shifted, then shot off the coral reef. A wave curled over us, dousing the spontaneous cheers as we hit a trough. I had the sea catch us, encircling the yacht in a pool of calmer water. Con laughed, a belly-deep howl of relief and delight.

"We're on the wrong side of the reef still!" Kara shouted over the wind as he clutched the rail on our left.

"Shut up. She knows what She's doing," Sondra, on our right, yelled back.

I wouldn't put it that strongly, but I did have a plan. During my abduction and imprisonment, I'd spent so much time and effort trying to reconnect to my lost Calanthe that She roared into me now, as if in trying to reach Her again, I'd given up all reservation to Her will. The orchid ring fluttered on my wrist as the dreamthink flowed like blood, infusing my lungs like air, and the coral reef spoke to me. Millions of small voices created a symphony of information, singing of their place, the movement of the water around them. I let them inform the waves, who then took us around and between the crevices.

Calanthe wanted me home as much as I wanted to be there, hurrying us along. With the sea carrying us into the harbor, I diverted my attention to the storm, inviting it to turn its savagery on the open water, away from land.

The fury of it lessened. Not abating entirely, but the rain no longer slanted sideways, and the wind no longer howled. The *Last Resort* glided into the harbor without sails, more or less upright, though with a definite list to one side.

"We're still taking on water," Kara reported, "but we should make it before she sinks."

Percy would never forgive me if I sank his boat, so I encouraged the sea to flow back out again. Slowly, the yacht righted. Kara glanced my way but said nothing.

The harbor sat quiet in the drumming rain, the docked ships tossing in their berths, lights on in only a few houses that wended their way in spirals up the hill. No one waited to greet us. Not surprising, I supposed, as the hour was late and everyone would be hunkered down to wait out the storm. Still, returning from the dead seemed like it should be an occasion for a bit of celebration.

"Your Highness." Lady Ibolya stepped into the place Sondra vacated, curtsying deeply. "I brought a cloak for You, in case You wanted to return without fanfare." The cloak had a deep cowl and long sleeves with draping cuffs that would cover my hands—and lack thereof. My nobles and courtiers often wore that sort of thing to secret assignations, and I'd worn this one before to sneak out and visit Con in the map tower, back in my previous life.

"They don't know, do they?" I asked Ibolya, then tipped my chin up to Con. "What did you tell everyone?"

"We kept the news as quiet as we could," he told me gravely, a hint of doubt in his face. "I know how hard you've worked to keep your—our—people from panicking. Not many know you disappeared from the Battle at Cradysica."

"What do they think happened to Me?"

"That you were injured and needed time to recover," Con replied.

"Your other ladies went to the temple, Your Highness," Ibolya added. "They've gone into seclusion, and we let everyone believe You went with them. To heal."

The way she added that last, so tenderly and hopefully, sorely tested my precarious poise. *To heal.* It sounded as far beyond me as the sky.

"Lia." Con at last let go of the rail and gazed down at me very seriously as he ran a gentle hand over my bald scalp. "You should know—Tertulyn is with them."

I nearly staggered. Would have, if Con hadn't been supporting me still. "I didn't see her," I managed to say, "at Yekpehr. I looked for her in Anure's court, but she was here all along."

Con nodded, then shook his head. "It's a long story, and you're weaving on your feet. Let's get you inside and take this slowly."

I looked past him to the horizon I couldn't see, the night and storm obscuring it all. But I felt the gazes of those wizards streaming through the distance, the hot glare of their obsession following me. I'd vanquished their wave, but they'd be back with more and better.

"Taking things slowly isn't an option," I observed. Ambrose stepped into my line of sight and inclined his head in apparent agreement. "Unfortunately," I added with a nod to Kara, "time is what we don't have."

~ 2 ~

Lia at last agreed to let me carry her into the palace, conceding only because no one was awake to witness her weakness. Not that she had much of a choice about it. The woman might possess the courage and will—and the obstinate pride—of a person ten times her size, but her ordeal had weakened her to the point that she couldn't stand without me holding her up. I hadn't gone twenty steps carrying her before she'd slipped back into sleep. Or unconsciousness. A fine line there, but the flesh only responds to will so far as physical laws of the universe allow.

Though if anyone could bend those laws, Lia could.

Ibolya, wearing a cloak like Lia's that hid all vestiges of the woman beneath, led us up to the palace via a path that was little more than a deer trail through the woods. The storm had escalated again. Lightning snaked through the sky, rattling us with sudden, intense cracks of nearby strikes, thunder shaking my bones. At least the canopy of broad, tropical leaves blocked most of the rain and tearing wind. Orchids danced in the waving limbs, trailing lush and luminous in the shadows. Vesno, at first delighted to be freed from the small cabin we'd stuck him in to keep the wolfhound from being swept overboard by the storm, whined at every boom and huddled so close to my leg I kept nearly tripping on him.

Runoff streamed down the trail from above, making the sometimes steep path treacherously slick. Rain lashed in a downpour through breaks in the canopy, startlingly chill. Still, I'd tromped through worse, with heavier loads. Lia weighed basically nothing—something I tried not to worry about.

I had zero experience with the dead coming back to life. I had no idea how to cope with this fresh terror that she might die all over again. Could I survive Lia's death twice? I doubted it.

And then Rhéiane . . . I'd thought my long-lost sister dead, too. I'd lived all these years with that grief, had hardened myself to that reality along with everything else that lay in dust at the bottom of my burnt-coal heart. If Agatha's "Lady Rhéiane" at Yekpehr was truly my sister, she'd have been Anure's prisoner and probably his plaything all these years. If she was really alive, that meant what she'd endured . . . I shook that thought away.

I hope she's dead, because the alternative doesn't bear contemplating, Sondra had said. I didn't know what I wanted, but "hope" didn't enter into it.

When I'd thought Lia dead, yeah, there had been a restfulness to that loss of all hope. I shifted her in my arms so I could better see her face, so pale, luminous as her orchids in the thrashing trees. Her petal-thin skin had sunk over the hollows of her fragile skull, and shadows pooled there, giving her the uncanny aspect of a skull. She lay so still, lax and limp as death. Was she even breathing? I lowered my head to check, wary lest she bite me again.

Relieved to feel her breath, I studied her parted lips. Had she truly been drinking my blood? The intensity of her animal reaction had taken me by surprise. It had been like wrestling a spitting cat, all claws and fury. Those teeth she hid behind close-lipped smiles—they were sharp as any predator's. *A force of nature*, Ambrose had once called her.

No, surely that attack had been a fluke. Wounded soldiers woke like that sometimes—like part of their brain thought they should still be fighting whatever took them down. It had to be that. Better to settle on that explanation than suffer this grinding worry that Lia had lost too much of herself. That she'd come back as something other than who she'd been.

Because if she had . . . what then?

"It's not easy to know what to wish for," Ambrose commented, walking beside me with apparent ease despite the rough going and his withered leg, seeming not to notice the raging storm. He used his tall staff as an aid, digging it into the mud and rocks, but also moving without any visible limp. I'd pretty much given up on wondering about it. "Thus the traditional caution," he added cheerfully.

"What's that?" I asked, though I was too wrung out to care. When Ambrose wanted to tell you something, he couldn't be shaken from it.

"Be careful what you wish for," he said, as if every schoolchild knew that one.

I pondered that for as long as my exhausted brain and battered heart would allow—which was about five steps—then shook my head. "Seems to me it's better not to wish for anything at all."

"A reasonable conclusion on the face of it, but a false correlation when you examine it more deeply. Not to mention cowardly."

"Conrí is no coward," Sondra called from behind us.

Ambrose glanced back at her and winced as if in pain. "Lady Sondra—I must caution you about using your new acquisition as a walking stick in that manner. The results could be most unpleasant."

"You use yours like this," she replied stubbornly.

"Yes, but I understand that mine is more than a simple staff *and* I know how to use it. Whatever you do, just don't drop it."

"Huh." From her tone—and knowing Sondra—that information had only whetted her interest in the knobbed cane she'd grabbed as a makeshift weapon from the wizards' horrific dungeon where we'd found Lia's corpse. "Anyway, I must caution *you* about calling Conrí a coward when he risked his life infiltrating Yekpehr to rescue us. While you were noticeably absent, I might add."

Ibolya halted abruptly enough that I nearly ran into her. Tipping her cowl back, she gave us all a strained smile. "Conrí, my lords and ladies, I must ask for silence if we wish to enter the palace unremarked."

"No one can fail to observe Conrí," Sondra pointed out. "One look and they'll know who he is, and from there it won't be hard to figure out who he's carrying, even if they believed Her Highness was sequestered in some temple."

"I can get us in unobserved," Ibolya explained patiently, "but only if you're silent. At least quieter than the storm."

"You all heard her," I told them. "Everyone be quiet, even the wizard." *Especially the wizard*, I thought wryly to myself.

Ambrose made a soft snorting sound but subsided. Ibolya and Agatha led us out of the woods and into a maze of night-blooming flowers thrashing in the tumultuous wind like the raging sea behind us. Beside me, Ambrose bent his head to the onslaught of wind and rain, Sondra bringing up the rear. Kara had stayed with the *Last Resort*, hoping to shore up the damage enough to keep the yacht from sinking where it sat. That wasn't all for Percy's sensibilities, either. After the devastating Battle at Cradysica, we had pitifully few seaworthy vessels left on all of Calanthe. If the *Last Resort* could be saved, then that was a priority.

I'd also ordered Kara to close the harbors as soon as the sun rose and people were available to do it. We didn't need anyone chasing us to Calanthe. Though if Lia had been right about the wizards sending that wave . . . *One crisis at a time*, I told myself grimly.

We ducked out of the punishing weather and into a courtyard I realized led into the kitchens. Calanthe had no slave gates, as Yekpehr did, but I couldn't escape the unsettling parallel of entering Lia's palace as we'd snuck into Anure's: in disguise and through the doorways used by those who served. This time, however, I carried Lia's body *in* rather than stealing her away.

Not her body. Lia is alive. Get that through your thick head.

Those short, horrifying hours of carrying Lia's leaf-dry corpse through the halls of Yekpehr had left their mark on me. I jumped at every scrape of boot against stone, every click of doors as Ibolya opened and closed them. Even the click of Vesno's claws on marble had me flinching.

With a quiet wave, Agatha went off in another direction, disappearing into the shadows. The rest of us followed Ibolya up some winding stairs, emerging into a side hallway that led to Lia's rooms, the double doors closed and locked but unguarded. Ibolya produced a key to unlock the doors and stepped aside for us to enter. The lamps and candles leapt with flame, filling the rooms with golden light, and Ibolya hastily closed and locked the doors again. The windows usually open to Calanthe's gentle weather were now tightly boarded against the storm, giving the normally airy rooms a claustrophobic staleness.

Ibolya assessed the unconscious Lia in my arms.

"Should I summon Healer Jeaneth?" We both looked at Ambrose.

"What? Oh." He frowned. "No. There's not much of human healing to be done here, if you understand me."

Of course, we didn't understand, but Ibolya nodded anyway. "Perhaps some food and water for Her Highness, then? Though I hate to wake Her."

"Her body can't assimilate much yet," Ambrose said, and fished something out of the pocket of his robe. He held up a glass vial of shimmering green liquid, then handed it to Ibolya. "Let Her Highness sleep until She wakes on Her own, then have Her drink this."

"What is it?" I demanded.

"Stardust and moonbeams," Ambrose answered, rolling his eyes. "She's alive again, isn't She? Trust me on this one."

"Conrí." Ibolya gestured for me to precede her. "If you would lay Her Highness on Her bed, I can help Her from there."

I nodded to Vesno, obediently sitting at my heel. "Let's go, boy."

Released, the wolfhound sprang into enthusiastic action, proceeding to sniff every possible surface en route. I carried Lia into her—our—bedchamber. I hadn't slept in the bed when I returned from Cradysica without her, and though it hadn't been all that long, the room had a musty, unused quality. Possibly because the grand circle of windows overlooking the sea had also been boarded up. Ibolya, wrinkling her nose at the stale damp, muttered unhappily.

"At least the bed is dry," I told her as I eased Lia onto it. I couldn't get past the notion that she might break if I jostled her too roughly.

"Thank you, Conrí." Ibolya began unfastening the ties

of Lia's cloak while I stood back awkwardly. The darker cloth parted over her thin shift—and the many stains on it showed clearly in the light. Blood, dirt, and other substances I couldn't bear to think about.

"I can help with this," Sondra said, shouldering past me. "Maybe you should step out, Conrí. Keep Ambrose company," she added, giving me a jaundiced look. "You're no lady's maid."

"Since when are you one?" I retorted, venting some of the frustration that had no other target.

She straightened. "Since I was the only one to tend Her these last days."

"Oh. Right." I was an idiot. "Sorry."

"Just go away, Conrí." She sounded unbearably weary. Sondra had been through hell, too, and had yet to sleep since we'd rescued her. "Give Her some privacy."

I knew Lia's body better than my own, but left without saying so. In the outer chambers, Ambrose had stepped out onto the small balcony where he'd married Lia and me. The rain still fell in torrents beyond its slight protection. Lightning stalked across the open ocean on flickering legs, distant thunder booming ominously.

Vesno came to me, nosing his muzzle under my hand, his drenched fur tangled. "This storm," I said, "it seems unnatural."

"Yes," Ambrose mused. "A fascinating combination of Calanthe's unraveling and bombardment by distant wizardry."

"Like that huge wave." When Ambrose only nodded thoughtfully, I tried again. "Lia settled that."

"An effective use of her elemental magic, yes. And She calmed Calanthe somewhat, too—though that faltered once She fell unconscious again." He tipped the staff at the storm, as if I hadn't noticed it. "It's a privilege to witness that sort of thing in action. I only wish Merle were here to see it."

"Where *is* Merle?"

"Otherwise occupied," Ambrose replied absently. A crack of lightning jabbed from the sky, striking a nearby cliff outcropping and illuminating it in harsh blue-white light. Rocks tumbled into the roaring sea below, punctuated by the roll of immediate thunder. "Hmm." Ambrose chewed his lip. "That can't be good."

"Then . . ." I waved a fist at the raging sky. "Do something. Fix it."

"I can't. Calanthe belongs to Her Highness. For various reasons, I have little power here. We'll have to wait for Her to wake up."

"When will that be?"

He eyed me askance. "How should I know?"

"You are supposed to be giving wisdom, and guidance, and . . . *help*, Sawehl take it. But you've done nothing."

Ambrose gave me a cool look. "How quickly you seem to have forgotten that I did extract you from Yekpehr—no easy feat, given the poor planning involved."

"That plan worked." Mostly. We achieved the goal, and that's what mattered.

"Only because I stepped in at the last moment. It would never have worked otherwise." Ambrose actually sniffed in disdain.

"It was a hell of a lot better plan than *you* came up with, since you weren't even there," I snarled, curling my hands into fists. Great Sawehl, how I wanted to break something. All that waiting, planning, skulking, and sneaking. I wasn't built for this crap. All I knew was how to smash, rend, kill, and tear. I'd gotten Lia killed. Lost my chance to kill Anure twice over. I could've rescued Rhéiane and hadn't. I'd fucked up everything imaginable and now Calanthe was falling apart. "Where *were* you anyway?" I demanded, regretting it instantly when I ended up sounding like a kid who lost his mom at the festival. Raking my hands through my hair, I found it as wet, snarled, and filthy as Vesno's coat.

"Conrí." Ambrose sounded uncharacteristically gentle, even setting a hand on my shoulder. Though I wanted to shrug it off, I didn't. I didn't punch the wizard in the face, either. Points for me. "It couldn't be helped. I promised Her Highness that I'd secure Calanthe if She was taken."

I lowered my hands to stare at the wizard as the import of his words sank in. "She knew. Lia knew Anure would abduct her."

Ambrose patted my shoulder—somewhat awkwardly—and reached for his staff, leaning on it heavily as he hobbled inside. "She knew it was possible."

And I'd served her up to him. How could she ever forgive me? I started to sit, then thought better of getting my filthy self on Lia's pretty furnishings. Vesno sprawled on a cream rug, mud circling him. I should wash him, but where—my bathtub? Maybe outside somewhere . . . Not in the storm, though. Why couldn't I solve a stupidly simple problem?

"When did you last eat, Conrí? Or sleep, for that matter?"

I stared at Ambrose in bemusement, pretty sure he'd never expressed interest in my physical well-being before. Had it been days? "I have no idea."

"I'll arrange for food, Conrí," Ibolya said, entering the room and closing the door behind her. "You all need to eat, including you, noble but filthy Syr Vesno."

"Lia?" I asked, looking past her, as if I could see through the stout door.

"Sleeping. I left the elixir on the bedside table for when She wakes. The Lady Sondra is sitting with Her Highness."

"Sondra needs to eat and sleep, too."

"I don't think she will yet, Conrí," Ibolya replied with firm compassion. "Give her this time to assure herself that Her Highness is safe and well. She needs that."

Yeah, so did I. We all flinched at another crack of nearby lightning. "What about the storm?" I demanded of Ambrose.

"Pray it doesn't worsen," he suggested.

"That won't do us much good if the cliff falls into the sea, taking the palace and us with it."

"True." Ambrose pointed a finger at me. "As we can't stop that from happening, we might as well rest and hope it doesn't."

I growled incoherently.

"A bath and food, Conrí," Ibolya said firmly. "Then you can relieve Lady Sondra and sleep."

"Why are you so determined on that?" I snarled, rounding on her.

Her pleasant smile faded. "Please, let me do this for you, Conrí, for Lady Sondra and for Her Highness. It's . . . it's what I can do." Her voice wobbled a bit, the first hint of strong emotion I'd seen from the composed young woman. Ashamed by my rudeness, I nodded in agreement.

"Syr Wizard?" Ibolya offered him a cloth-wrapped bundle. Lia's severed hand and finger, I realized, that we'd retrieved from the wizards' workroom. "Lady Sondra said to give you this."

Ambrose didn't take it. "Conrí claimed that. It's his."

Ibolya glanced at me but hesitated. "Shall I keep it for you, Conrí?"

"Please," I replied with a rush of relief. Ambrose watched me knowingly, though with amusement, contempt, or sympathy, I wasn't sure.

"Syr Wizard, will you eat here or shall I have something sent to your tower?"

"The tower," Ambrose answered with a nod and a sigh. "My cauldrons have not been stirred or cackled over these many days." Though he'd said that last to poke at me, he didn't look my way, instead hobbling toward the doors as if greatly pained.

"Ambrose," I called after him. When he turned, cocking his head like his raven familiar would, I realized I didn't know what I wanted to say. *I'm an ass. I'm sorry. What are we going to do now? How do I fix this?*

He smiled, as if hearing my unspoken thoughts. "You're a good man, Conrí. Bathe. Eat. Sleep. In my great wisdom, I recommend you do so in that order. Be there when Lia wakes up. She'll need you." He left, and I stood there, in the empty room, not sure what to do with my hands.

Ibolya returned and handed me one of two mugs she carried. "Bone broth, Conrí," she said. "Food is coming, but this will hold you until then. Your bath is ready, so I suggest drinking it there. I'll give this to Lady Sondra, then take Vesno to be cared for. When I return, I'll come help you with shaving and so forth."

I huffed a laugh. "Is that necessary?"

"You'll feel better for it, Conrí," she replied gently. "And Her Highness will be reassured on waking to see you groomed. I promise: no jewels or flowers. Syr Vesno, would you like some breakfast?"

I drank the broth in gulps as I sank into the tub. Hot, salty, and robust, the nourishment filled the aching, exhausted pit inside me. Groaning, truly feeling the last grueling week now, I let my head fall back, the fury of the storm dimmed in this inside room. As with everything in Calanthe, the ceiling had been lavishly decorated. In this case, colorful pebbles swirled in a pattern like birds flying in a vast flock. As my eyes blurred, they almost seemed to move, flipping in mid-flight to alter their course in a flickering cloud.

Ibolya entered with quiet discretion, but not so silently as to startle me. I dunked my head to wet my hair, and she sat behind me to wash it. "It might be easier to cut it all off," I remarked.

"Oh, but Her Highness loves it so."

"She does?" An odd thought, to imagine Lia liking much about me at all—much less commenting on it.

"She does," Ibolya said firmly. "And putting it in order won't take much. Let me tend you, if only for Her sake."

Slathering something warm over my head, she worked it through, using her fingertips to massage my scalp. Another groan escaped me, this one of pure pleasure as I relaxed. It took her a while to comb through all the snarls, along with several rinses of warm, scented water. But I didn't mind the perfumes and fussing. After Yekpehr, it all seemed so . . . human. Nourishing in another way.

Ibolya cleaned the blood from my beard, dabbing something soothing on the lip wound I'd forgotten about. Then she lathered my skin above and below my beard, face a picture of concentration as she shaved me with smooth precision.

"Why is this what you do?" I asked her. When she raised a brow in polite question, I searched for the words. "You said before that this is what you can do. And you came with us to Yekpehr, a dangerous mission."

"I stayed on the yacht, not exactly a hardship," she replied, using a warm cloth to remove the last of the suds.

"Dangerous," I repeated, "to the point of suicidal, and you knew it. Yet you asked to come along so you could tend Lia. Now you're missing your own food and rest, doing the same for me. And after this, I bet you will for Sondra."

"I doubt Lady Sondra will allow it," Ibolya said with a rueful smile, "though I wish she would."

"You're clearly intelligent," I persisted, "and can do magic, since it seems you have to be able to, in order to be one of Lia's ladies. So why is *this* what you say you can do?"

She picked up a comb and silver scissors, setting to trimming my beard. "Taking care of Her Highness—and now you, Conrí—is hardly an easy or lowering task. I am not a queen, nor do I wish to be. I'm not the sort to pick up a sword or solve knotty problems of government." She paused, turning my head gently so she could survey her work, began trimming again. "But I can tend those of you who are. In my own way, I like to think I have a hand in making Calanthe what it is—if indirectly."

"I didn't mean to imply . . ." Abashed that I'd insulted her, I groped for an explanation.

"You didn't, Conrí." She handed me a towel. "But you did give me something to think about. I'll check on the food while you dry off. There's a warmed robe for you by the door. I'd leave you to soak, but I'm afraid you'd fall asleep and you need to be in a bed for that or you'll be bent over like an old grandpa."

Fed, clean, and feeling like I could sleep for a week, I found the bedchamber much fresher also. Ibolya had somehow worked her magic to clean up the room without disturbing Lia's sleep. Or Sondra's, as my lieutenant and old friend had passed out cold in the chair beside Lia's bed, her head bent at an angle painful to look at.

There'd be no way to wake her without scaring her to death, but so it went. I put a hand on her shoulder, ready for it when she leapt to her feet, dagger in her hand.

"Easy," I said quietly, and waited for her brain to catch up.

She looked at my grip on her wrist, where I held her knife well away from my throat, and shook her head, relaxing. "Sorry, Conrí."

"Nah. I was quiet." We both glanced at Lia, but she slept like the dead. *Bad analogy*.

"Ibolya has food and a bath for you. She's waiting." I cocked my head at the other room.

"I don't need—"

"Let her help you. She's a good hand with a razor. Maybe she can do something about that tufty shit on your head."

Sondra ran a hand over her badly shorn scalp and scowled at me. "Too bad there's nothing even her magic can do for your ugly face."

"True." I grinned at her. "It's good to see you again, if I didn't say so."

"Thank you, for coming after us," she replied soberly. "I knew you would."

"Yeah."

"And we're going back, to get Rhéiane."

One day the sound of her name wouldn't feel like a knife to the gut. "Yeah," I said again. Thunder boomed, and in the distance rocks tumbled in an answering roar. "Go sleep."

"Back at you."

She left and I crawled onto my side of Lia's big bed, easing myself closer to her as best I could without bouncing her around or disturbing the covers. She lay on her back, barely more than a white blur in the dimness. They'd lightly bandaged her regenerating hand again, and both lay crossed over her belly, too much like how some buried their dead.

I watched until I could be sure her breast rose and fell, if ever so slightly. I really wanted to put an arm around her, but that might wake her. So I rested my hand next to her on the sheet, a brown, scarred paw compared to her bruised and fragile loveliness. A strange wistfulness that felt kind of like grief and kind of like happiness drifted through me on the mists of exhaustion. Hope, maybe, but not attached to anything. Maybe hope could be a general thing.

Just plain hope.

~ 3 ~

The dreamthink grabbed me by the throat and roared into my mind with brutal force, nightmares blending with the tumult of reality. They were one and the same: full of death and chaos.

The wolf fighting its chains, howling in hoarse rage, shedding fire and ash. The sea churning, bloodred and crimson dark, bones tossed in the waves, white as foam. Cliffs, towers, and villages collapsing into piles of rubble. Entire islands falling into the sea. Rain poured, mudslides following after. Cracks opened in the ground, people and animals alike shrieking as they fell, calling for me to save them. I reached out, but I had no hands—only bleeding stumps at my wrists. A whirlpool roared beneath, swirling and drinking up the blood, crying for more and more and more . . .

I woke with a choked gasp, a storm raging outside, pain racking my body inside. Hunger in both. Calanthe's hunger, demanding and full of frightened rage, my own body echoing that craving, even as I cowered before the strident volume of Her demands.

"Lia?" Con murmured my name sleepily. He was draped heavily on and around me, his body tensing as he came awake, hands running over me as if checking for injury. "What's wrong?"

"I'm starving." I nearly snarled the words, Calanthe's ferocious need echoing in my voice.

"Right." He rolled over, broad shoulders flexing in the dim light as he reached for something on the bedside table. "You're supposed to drink this," he said, showing me a glass vial. "Do you need help sitting up?"

"Don't be ridiculous." I pushed myself up on one elbow, somewhat astonished when it gave beneath me, dumping me ignominiously onto the pillow. How had I come to this? I was so confused, and the grinding hunger made it hard to think. There were things—important things—that I should be remembering.

"Let me," Con said, sliding an arm beneath me and easily lifting me to lie against his chest. He uncorked the vial with his thumb and held it to my lips.

"I can do *that*," I said, reaching for it, but he moved it away.

"Other hand."

I looked and saw my hand swathed in a filmy bandage, the spindly green twigs of my growing fingers spidering against the cloth. "My hand . . ." The bleeding stumps. That hadn't been the nightmare?

"Your hand is growing back, yes," Con replied firmly.

"What happened to . . ." I recoiled from the rush of remembered terror.

"Shh, Lia. Don't think about it. Drink this and you'll feel better." He held the cool vial against my lips and I drank, more from lack of will to resist than anything else. The liquid tasted like sunshine on green leaves, and my stomach leapt with gladness. I seized the vial from Con with the hand I still had and drained it, tipping my head to get every drop.

The din of Calanthe's need receded somewhat. Where was I?

My own bedchamber, but the windows had been boarded up, a storm lashing rain to leak around the edges. Calanthe prowled along my nerves, howling of Her starvation, snarling and struggling to break free, the land shedding from Her back like dirt off a dog. The elixir, at least, had sated some of my body's insane hunger, but Hers raged on. "What was this?" I asked, holding up the vial.

"Something Ambrose came up with. He said it would help—did it? You seem better."

He said that cautiously enough that I turned to look at him. A bit of blood dribbled into his beard from his swollen lower lip. It looked like it had been chewed. "What happened to your lip?"

He fingered the wound thoughtfully. "An accident."

He was lying, I could tell, but I couldn't remember the truth. "Why do I feel all wrong?"

Con's face creased with emotion, and he seemed to be struggling for words. Pushing himself up, he shoved a hand through his hair. "There's time enough to explain—"

"What requires explanation? Am I sick?"

"Not exactly." He sounded strangled, gesturing to my hand. "You were injured."

I tried to think back, dredging up memories that felt thin, ragged, stagnant. All finishing with that horrible feeling of my life draining away, the blackness overtaking me. "And I was unconscious."

He blew out a short breath, looking away. "Yes."

Another lie. "Don't coddle Me. Tell Me the truth."

Swallowing hard, Con pressed a hand over his face. "You were dead, Lia. That's why you feel wrong. But you're getting better."

I stared at him, uncomprehending. "Actually dead," I clarified. "You saw My corpse?"

He dropped his hand, curling it on the sheet, and met my gaze levelly. "I did. I carried your—you—out of Yekpehr, so I can verify."

"If I was dead, why am I alive now?" *If* I was alive. Maybe the dead had nightmares of being alive.

"I don't even know. Ambrose did something, but your own magic had something to do with it, too. I'd say ask Ambrose but we both know he won't give a straight answer."

His smile faded, unreturned, as I struggled to pull the memories together. My mind felt spongy, eroded at the edges. I pressed a finger to the stabbing pain in my head, ruthlessly suppressing the scream that wanted to well up from the black terror of those memories.

"Maybe it's better not to think about it just yet." Con slid a rough-skinned hand to the back of my neck, squeezing and steadying. "What's important is that you are alive. We should be happy that—"

"Happy?" I ground out, forcing my voice past the scream I'd squelched, but that remained trapped somewhere around my heart. "You want Me to be *happy*? Look at Me. I'm a wreck. I can't even sit up."

"You'll get stronger," he replied stubbornly.

"How do you know?" I shot back, then nodded at the look on his face. "See? You don't."

He set his jaw. "I know you're doing a hell of a lot better than you were at this time yesterday."

Yesterday . . . when I was *dead*. The scream trapped in my chest shattered into a sob, and I gasped for breath. What a weak and sniveling mess I was.

"Lia . . ." Con tried to pull me into his arms, but I pushed him away.

"How long was I dead?" I demanded. "A few minutes?" Like someone drowned who seemed dead, but was revived. No, Con was frowning, searching for words to soothe me. "Longer, then. Hours?"

"Lia . . ."

"Just tell Me, Con," I grated out.

He shook his head, then set his jaw. "Nearly a full day and night. You passed away about four hours before midnight and came back to life when we hit Calanthe's waters the next evening, right as the sun was going down."

So long. "You weren't there, though, when I died." I'd been alone, wishing for him. I remembered that, the sorrow and regret.

"No." His face contorted with emotion, and he put his arms around me. "I'm so sorry I wasn't there. Sorry for so much that—"

"I don't need comforting," I snapped, pushing him away. "I need answers. How do you know what time I died if you weren't there?"

He sat up, releasing me and curling into himself, elbows on drawn-up knees, face in his hands. "I know what time you died because I felt it. The marriage bond, or whatever, went *poof!* Vesno lost his shit and I knew you were gone." His voice thick and grating, he lifted his head to glare at me, seeming unaware of the tears leaking over the pitted skin of his cheeks. "It was the worst fucking thing I've ever gone through—including holding my father when he died—so don't you dare tell me not to want to hold you, to want to be glad for a few damn minutes that you're here and alive, even if you are snarling and spiteful."

I stared at him, taken aback by the passion of his speech—and realizing the truth of what he'd said. The marriage bond indeed had shattered, and I was no longer the woman he'd married. I was . . . something else. He stared back, defying me to argue with him, eyes molten gold, new lines around them, carved there by grief and despair. I needed to get ahold of myself, regain some poise and control.

"I'm sorry you went through that." I sagged, lifting my hands to my own face—remembered, and dropped the amputated one to my lap. The orchid on my wrist above the bandage stirred, less colorful and robust than usual. "I didn't know you'd feel it when I—" No, not going to be able to say it that time. I took a breath, marveling at the way my lungs expanded, my heart pounded. If I reached for it, there was a memory of when my breath had been still, unmoving. I'd found myself pulled back into my own body, but it had become an alien thing to me, a lifeless slab of meat, inert with the dank chill of death. I shivered, thrusting that memory away. Maybe I didn't want to remember everything after all.

"You don't have to be sorry," Con said when I failed to finish that sentence. "I once thought having to watch my father die was the hardest thing I could do. But feeling you die and not being with you was much worse."

I met his eyes, the rawness in them a mirror to my own. "I felt so alone, you know, at the end."

He nodded, as if he knew that. "You remember now?"

"That part." I touched the orchid's petals, so velvety soft. "The wizards had been trying to find the secret of transferring the orchid, so they'd decided to get Me to the brink of death, hoping the orchid would release. They had Me on this table, with gutters for My blood, so they could catch it in these . . . urns, and . . ."

"I saw it," Con said quietly when I faltered.

Ah. That's where I'd died and that's where he'd found me. "When I got near death, they put My blood back in me, adding magic to it, and then drained Me again. Over and over. I don't know how many times."

"Oh, Lia . . ." He sounded as broken as I felt.

"It was awful," I whispered, taking his hand in my good one, savoring the warrior roughness of it, the warmth and realness of human skin. "You know what I thought about, when I felt death coming?"

He searched my face. "Tell me." The request came so hoarsely, it was almost without sound.

"You," I said simply. That memory came back with vivid clarity. At the end, I'd longed for death, welcomed it, only regretting that I wouldn't see Con again, that I hadn't kissed him goodbye. And here, already, I'd tried to push him away. I extracted my hand from his grip and lifted it to brush the wetness from his cheeks. "It gave Me comfort, to think about you and the time we'd spent together. And I thought about how you'd laugh, knowing I'd finally put you first."

He firmed his lips. "I would never laugh at that."

"I was comforted, because it felt like you *were* there, that I wasn't alone." I was shaking my head. "But if I had realized that it would . . . affect you, that you'd feel Me, I wouldn't have done it. I'd have tried to—"

"I'm glad you did," he said fiercely, wrapping my hand in both of his. "It was my fault, what happened to you, so I deserve to suffer. Nothing that can happen to me would be worse than what you endured, but I'll take it. I don't expect you to forgive me, but—"

I stroked his cheek, stilled and held it, cupping his face as he leaned into my touch. "You came for us."

"There was never a question."

"No. Even Sondra said so. If only to pursue your vengeance."

"That's not why."

"No?"

"I should have told you, Lia—that night before the

battle. I nearly did say so, and I've regretted a thousand times that I failed to—but you should know that I . . . I love you." He closed his eyes briefly, turning to press a kiss to my palm, then drew in a ragged breath. "I don't know why that's so hard to say."

I wasn't surprised, not exactly, but somehow I'd never imagined such soft words from this wild wolf of a man. *He loved me.* I hadn't expected anyone to love me—not for myself—but I believed he meant it. It felt like a precious gift—and one I didn't deserve, didn't know how to reciprocate. I'd spent my entire life navigating tricky political waters, always knowing the right response to give, the exact value of a tribute and how to balance the giving and receiving. But I didn't know how to handle Con saying he loved me.

I did know, however, that I couldn't say it back, for so many reasons.

"You and I, we're not so good at being vulnerable," I said instead, pushing the words through my tight throat.

He breathed a laugh, lips still against my palm, carefully not looking at me. "No, we've learned better, haven't we? And don't think that I expect anything different from you because of my . . . feelings. I just regretted not telling you before, and then you were gone and I couldn't. I know it's kind of breaking the rules between us, that our marriage was never supposed to be about emotions."

"We're not, anymore, you realize. Married," I clarified when he frowned in confusion. "You felt the marriage bond break when I died," I prompted. "You're absolved of your vows. Besides, the prophecy lied. You claimed My hand, but the empire didn't fall. We lost."

His frown deepened. "But I do have your hand still."

"My hand?" I glanced at the bandaged one, weirdly

regrowing. When I managed to get alone, I'd unwrap it and take a good long look.

"Your original hand—and finger—that the wizards . . . removed. We took it from their workroom. I know that sounds macabre, but your Lord Dearsley kept insisting we bring your body back, no matter what, so I figured that meant all of you. And Ambrose said something about it. Then Sondra said you'd made her promise to burn your body rather than let it remain in Yekpehr. So we brought it."

"I'm glad." I remembered some of that, how the wizards had discussed burying my body and harvesting orchids from it, how I'd exacted that promise from Sondra. "So you've quite literally claimed the hand that wore the orchid ring and escaped a marriage you never wanted. Cleverly done."

"What? No, that's not—"

"Oh, come now, Conrí." I extracted my hand from his hold. "We both know you hated being My husband. Court life felt like a cage to you."

"No—you don't get to do that." He folded his hands around my head, holding me there and staring intently into my eyes. "Did you hear me when I said I love you?"

"Yes, but that doesn't mean—"

"It *does* mean," he interrupted. "I don't care about the rest of it. I'd wear salt-encrusted armor made of rusty blades if it meant I could stay with you. I was never happier in my life than I was being your husband."

I nearly laughed, but he looked far too serious. "Con, please. You were miserable."

"I was too stupid to know what I had," he insisted. "And now I have a second chance. At least, I hope you'll give me one. We'll get married again. If you want to," he added with less confidence, searching my face.

"It's not necessary," I said, feeling my way through it.

Not succeeding, because his face hardened into disappointment.

"You *don't* want to," he said, not exactly a question.

"I don't know *what* I want right now. I can't think." I really couldn't. I pressed fingers to my temple, willing the dizziness away.

He relaxed, smiling ruefully. "Sorry—stupid of me to push. We'll talk about that when you're stronger."

"Do you really think I will get stronger?" I asked hesitantly. It seemed impossible right then.

"You? Absolutely."

"I don't feel like it, Con. I'm not the same as I was before."

"You are queen of Calanthe and more powerful than anyone I've ever met."

"Con." I hesitated to give voice to this, too. "Calanthe is crumbling, out of control."

"I know. It's a bad storm, but you're back now and everything will be fine."

I was shaking my head as he spoke. "No. You can't understand. All that blood at Cradysica, and Me ripped from Her. And those wizards—I can feel their magic tearing at Her, making it worse. It will not be fine."

"Then we'll fix it. Ambrose and Merle will help you. And the orchid. It's a powerful magical thing, right? That's why the wizards wanted it. But they don't have it. *You* do."

"Con, you just don't—"

"Isn't this what you were born to do?" He interrupted, gripping my shoulders and staring me down. "How many times have you told me that protecting Calanthe and your people is your sacred duty and you'd die before you failed in that?"

"I *did* die," I pointed out, a bit taken aback by his ferocity—and that he was exactly right.

His mouth cocked up on one side in a half grin. "Yeah, but you're not dead anymore, so that's no excuse."

"I'm not making excuses! I'm explaining that I face impossible odds."

"Hey." Con curled his fingers under my chin, lifting it. "We'll figure it out. Step by step, all right?"

I managed a nod, mostly to make him happy.

"How about we start with food?" he suggested.

"I need to bathe and dress." Get out of this bed and find out what was going on, try to *do* something.

He cocked his head dubiously. "I was thinking you eat and go back to sleep."

"How can I sleep when Calanthe might dissolve beneath us? I have to try, Con."

With a sigh of resignation, he threw off the covers and strode naked to the stand where he'd left his robe. "I'll get Ibolya."

Gathering up his bagiroca and rock hammer, but with no place to put them, he stood awkwardly a moment, holding them and gazing at me. "You'll be all right for a bit if I go?"

"Conrí." I managed a hint of an imperious tone. "I've been alone all My life. Yes, I can manage for a few moments."

He smiled wryly, a shadow behind it. "Yeah."

The door clicked closed, and I sank back into the pillows, closing my eyes a moment, the fatigue dragging at me. I forced my eyelids up so I wouldn't fall asleep again and unwrapped the light bandage around my left hand, making myself look at it. The pale skin of my forearm below the wilted orchid ended in furious reds and purples at my wrist. The skin there furled in ridged waves of angry flesh. Five twiggy fingers emerged from it, like saplings sprung from bloody soil. Wispy green tendrils connected them below the first joint, but otherwise each was a long extension broken into four segments. I wiggled them and they flexed with spidery grace, clicking softly.

Curious, unsettled, I touched the tip of one with the index finger of my other hand. No sensation in the twig finger. I tried plucking at the sheet with the twig fingers, and though they obeyed my intent, closing on the silk as they should, they lacked grip and the cloth slid away again. Lifting the hand to my cheek, I stroked my skin with the pointed end of one twig finger. It felt like exactly that: plant not human.

Deciding not to wrap my monstrous hand again, I lay there for a long time, staring unseeing at the shadowed ceiling, listening to the sounds of anguished life dying all over Calanthe. Feeling my own body die around me.

4

"How is She?" Sondra shot at me, leaping at me from the dim shadows of a sofa in the darkened outer chamber. With my bagiroca in one hand and rock hammer in the other, I nearly brained her. I still might.

"Why aren't you asleep?" I asked, setting my weapons down. With all the frustration I'd concealed from Lia, I yanked the bell string that would summon Ibolya. Spying the silver coffeepot some thoughtful soul—probably also Ibolya—had left for us, I headed straight for it. Calanthe's coffee couldn't be beat, and I mixed a large mug with healthy portions of fresh cream and sweet honey.

"One thing about genteel imprisonment, there wasn't much to do but eat and sleep," Sondra said wryly. "I'm better off than most of you. The question is, why aren't *you* still asleep?" By the light of the lanterns she'd begun lighting, I saw someone had indeed trimmed her hair, removing the awkward tufts and sculpting it to one length, but so short that it mostly stood on end. I supposed we couldn't regret any of the choices that had gotten us safely out of Yekpehr, but the sight of Sondra with shorn hair reminded me of being back at Vurgmun, and—particularly after that gut-wrenching conversation with Lia—I couldn't quite look at her. I took a bracing gulp of coffee, willing myself to wake up.

"I'm awake because Lia is. She wants to get up, but I'm hoping if we get some food into her, she'll sleep some more."

Sondra nodded but didn't move. "But how is She?"

I added more honey, then more coffee. Clearly I needed more kick. "She's weak and you know how she hates that. And she's . . ." *Depressed. In despair.* "Sad."

"No surprise there. You can't expect a person to just bounce back from a trauma like that."

"I didn't say I thought she should."

"You didn't *not* say it—and you can be a prick that way, Conrí. You kind of do expect everyone to just soldier on, to get back up and fight even harder."

I set my teeth. "Did you want something," I asked as mildly as I could, which wasn't very, "or were you just in the mood to kick me around?"

She grinned, briefly and toothily. "I'm always in the mood to kick your ass, Conrí, but no—I told Ibolya I'd keep an ear out for Her Highness in case She needed anything."

"I was with Lia," I replied, unreasonably irritated, "so there was no need to hover."

Sondra eyed me. "Like I said, you're not the most sensitive guy, Conrí."

"I can be sensitive," I snapped.

Sondra huffed out a sigh. "Don't look like a kicked puppy. Sawehl knows you're in bad shape yourself. Ibolya said you've barely slept since Cradysica. We were worried about you both, all right?"

"I'm fine. You're the one who was imprisoned at Yekpehr. You can pretend it was genteel, but I know that had to have been hard on you."

"I'm fine," she retorted, mimicking me. "Let's not compete for who's more fucked up. Besides, I—" She broke off as the outer doors opened, admitting Ibolya, two servants with platters of food, and an excited Vesno.

The wolfhound bounded straight for me, and I crouched with open arms, bracing myself not to fall over at the impact of the wriggling mass of large—and thankfully clean—dog. "Hey boy, hey." I laughed as he licked my face, spinning and twisting to get the best angles. At least someone was happy to see me around here. And wasn't that a self-pitying thought.

"Vesno was terribly put out to be locked away from you, Conrí," Ibolya said, a smile in her voice. "But he made for an effective alarm. I knew you must be up and about from his determination to get to you, even before I heard the bell." Ibolya had dressed in a bright gown, though not in full court regalia. Not wearing a wig, she'd fixed her dark hair in loose waves decorated with fresh flowers.

"Thanks for looking after him," I said, giving Vesno another brisk rub and standing. "Lia's awake and wanting food. I gave her the potion, but she's still hungry."

"That sounds encouraging."

"Yeah. She also wants to bathe and dress. She's worried about the storm and the state of Calanthe, but she's weak still."

Ibolya grimaced. "Not as encouraging. I'll see to Her."

Leaving a loaded plate for me, Ibolya dismissed the servants and took the other platter with her into Lia's bedroom. I nearly followed, then thought better of it. Lia might let her lady-in-waiting assist her in ways she'd be too proud to say in front of me.

I dug into the food, not particularly hungry, but aware that I needed to eat. Vesno sat politely on his haunches next to me, and I rewarded him with a slice of ham.

"Speaking of the state of Calanthe, any status reports?" I asked Sondra.

She gestured to the boarded-over windows, the wind shrieking past as the rain pounded against the wood like angry fists. "The storm is obviously as bad or worse. Dearsley is still acting regent. He's been holding court today and doesn't seem to suspect that Her Highness has returned. We'll have to think about how to announce that news, show Her to the people and stuff."

I grunted, shaking my head as I swallowed. "Not yet. She's not up to a public appearance."

Sondra poured herself a cup of tea and sat. "How long, do you think?"

Maybe never. I hated the traitorous thought, but if Lia couldn't stand on her own, she might refuse to be seen. Despite my assurances that she'd get stronger, I couldn't be sure. She seemed so changed—and how did a body recover from being dead a night and a day?

"Conrí?"

"Weren't you the one scolding me not to push her too soon?"

She scowled at me. "The mood out there is uncertain at best. There's been a lot of damage to the island, and it's ongoing. Natural disasters like mudslides, cliffs shearing off, sinkholes opening up, floods, and fires. The weather is dreadful. Villages have been sending people here to ask for Her Highness's help. Dearsley is sticking to the story that Lia is at the temple, but people are starting to doubt—and panic."

Hmm. "Anything from Anure?"

"Not that I know of. Do you think the toad even knows he lost Her?"

I stared at Sondra. "Why wouldn't he?"

She shrugged a little, snagged a piece of toast off my

plate, and chewed thoughtfully. "After that first audience, Anure pretty much washed his hands of Lia. He turned Her over to the wizards and—sorry."

I stroked Vesno's silky head. If they'd endured it, I could hear about it. "Go on."

"Well, after that, we never saw him again. The wizards had Lia—trying to get that orchid off Her—but I think they weren't supposed to kill Her. Could be that they haven't told Anure any of it: that they accidentally offed Her, and then lost Her corpse. I'm betting the wizards don't know She's alive, and Anure thinks She's still his prisoner somewhere in the bowels of Yekpehr."

"The wizards sent that huge wave," I pointed out. "And both Lia and Ambrose think they're still launching magical attacks."

"Yeah, but that could be about getting Her Highness's corpse—and the orchid—back. That could be all from the wizards, not Anure."

I nodded. "It's good thinking. But what do we do with it?"

"You're the strategist, Conrí. But surely we can use this to our advantage when we return to Yekpehr."

To rescue Rhéiane, but could I leave Lia in such a state? Abandon her in her hour of need. Again. "We can think about that later."

"What?" Sondra thunked her head with the heel of her hand. "Did I hear wrong? We have to go back."

"We will. There's a lot to consider first."

"Who *are* you?" Sondra banged her fist on the table, and Vesno jumped to his feet, wagging his tail in excitement. "I'm going back for Rhéiane, whether you are or not!"

"Would you be quiet?" I hissed. "Down, boy. Sit. Yes, of course I'm going back for Rhéiane, but Lia doesn't need to know about it."

"What? She knows. We talked about it on the *Last Resort*, when Agatha told us."

I shook my head, raking a hand through my hair. "Lia doesn't remember much about when she first woke up. Or the second time."

Sondra set her cup down, lips parted in dismay. "How bad is it?"

I shrugged, unwilling to go into it—or to admit to myself how crazed Lia seemed.

"Brains rot first, you know," Sondra commented thoughtfully, cupping her tea in her hands.

Staring at her, I had no words.

"You know that," Sondra continued remorselessly. "You kill an animal, or a person, and the brains go to mush way before the other organs. It makes sense that, even if Lia isn't entirely human, Her body is still flesh and blood. It had to start decomposing some and the—"

"Enough!" I snarled it way too loudly, but I couldn't take anymore.

The door to the connecting chambers opened, and I spun to look, but it was only Ibolya slipping through and closing the door again behind her. She smiled at us with her Calanthean serenity that prettified all things, but her dark eyes held worry. "Her Highness ate and now She is sleeping some more."

Instead of reassuring me, that news was only worrisome. Lia had been so determined to get up. Was she feeling weaker? "I'll go check on her," I said.

Ibolya put a gently restraining hand on my arm. "If you please, Conrí, Her Highness asked not to be disturbed. She'd like some time to Herself."

Oh. The door stood forbiddingly closed, but I stared at it as if I could see through the ornately carved wood.

"I'll stay close, Conrí," Ibolya added, squeezing my

forearm. "I set out clothes for you in your bathing chamber, so you can go ahead with your tasks. I'm sure a great deal awaits your attention."

I realized I still wore the bright-red robe I'd put on not to be naked. Sondra must've been going easier on me than I thought, that she hadn't commented on the fancily embroidered silk. Apparently I wasn't going back to bed, so I might as well dress and deal with stuff. Disasters, the people panicking. Lia would expect me to handle things. Nobody else had figured out she and I weren't married anymore, I hoped. Calantheans had been able to see the marriage bond before, but maybe they wouldn't notice its absence. Ibolya hadn't said anything.

No matter—I was still officially Lia's consort and she'd wanted me to help with Calanthe. I'd go check in with Dearsley. And maybe I could pry Ambrose out of his tower to help Lia.

"You coming or staying?" I asked Sondra.

"Staying. Keeping a low profile, since I'm supposedly with Her Highness at the temple."

"How'd you find out so much already then?"

She shrugged. "I'm a good skulker."

"What about you?" I asked Vesno. The wolfhound wagged his tail, gazing at me with canine worship. There's a true friend for you. With a last glance at Lia's closed door, I grabbed my rock hammer and bagiroca, then headed to get dressed, Vesno a faithful presence at my heel.

Not many people were around in the public areas, since court was still in session, and the usually airy main halls were dark and gloomy with everything blockaded against the storm. A small army of servants worked feverishly to clean up a deluge of mud that had apparently poured in from one of the flooding ponds—and to set sandbags to prevent more encroachment.

A bit farther on, a group of courtiers marked my passage with excited whispers behind fluttering fans. I hadn't figured yet how to explain my absence—and renewed presence—but having a reputation for being a taciturn brute had its advantages. No one had the courage to question me, especially as I wore a black scowl along with forbiddingly elaborate court gear. With my bagiroca hanging heavily from my belt, sword at the other hip, and rock hammer at my back, I felt at least something like in control. I wouldn't ever be the Slave King again. I might never make a king of Calanthe—imagine me being called the Flower King—but I could at least be the guy with a bag of rocks and a big hammer. It's good to know your strengths. And limitations.

I didn't go the back way, the one Lia used to access her throne like a street magician in a show sneaking through the curtains in a puff of smoke to magically appear. On my previous rare, and abortive, court appearances with her, I'd gone along with her traditions. Even my own people had used showmanship to dress up the Slave King's speeches. But I was coming to grips with the idea that whatever life I'd led before this, it was over.

So I went around to the great double doors, easily three times my height, that opened into the great court of Calanthe. Unlike on my first "visit," the doors stood open, the sleekly groomed guards snapping to attention, then bowing. I waved a hand at them to relax, and I strode up the main aisle, Vesno alert beside me, nose lifted to sample the thick scents of flowers, perfume, and the sour sweat of frightened people.

A ripple of reaction rolled through the assembly, the

courtiers closest to the aisle widening their eyes and frantically scribbling notes while passing the news back to their neighbors with less advantageous views. Like Vesno sniffing for scents, I tested the atmosphere of the court. Lia could assess that kind of thing like a connoisseur of fine wine, instantly identifying the subtle notes. I could tell you basically red or white—and yeah, the court thrummed with incipient panic. More petitioners than usual lined up with their noble patrons, the folk from the outlying villages standing out in their simpler clothing, many sporting injuries and other signs of hard times.

Taking it all in with one sweeping glance, I returned my gaze to Dearsley. The elderly man sat in a chair only a couple of levels up the steps to Lia's throne. A lover of protocol, of course Dearsley wouldn't presume to sit on the throne, or to even take one of the stools positioned for Lia's ladies. Until that moment, I hadn't figured what I'd say to Dearsley, who watched my approach with a pained expression torn equally between hope and despair.

I knew that feeling well.

And I guessed I'd wing this. For all that I loved to plan a battle strategy, politics made me want to hurl things through the windows. Lia would probably say that politics and battles are the same, both equally deserving of careful strategy, and she'd be right. Maybe someday I'd get it.

"Conrí." Lord Dearsley stood, with the help of a handsome lad at his elbow, and bowed to me. "I yield the Throne of Calanthe to You. Welcome back."

Sawehl smite me, that was not what I'd intended. That's what I got for not planning better. The court politely applauded, some sending up cheers and I turned to wave and smile, just as Lia would expect. How she'd feel about me still claiming a right to her throne, though . . . I winced internally.

"Do You bring news, Conrí?" Dearsley asked tentatively, leaving me plenty of room to maneuver around the truth.

I couldn't lie to the old man, who'd practically raised Lia. "Her Highness has returned to the palace," I said, deciding on the spot that secrecy would be not only pointless, but impossible in this hive of gossips.

Dearsley's polite expression crumbled, a real smile wobbling into place as tears filled his eyes. The lad at his elbow firmed his grip, keeping Dearsley from swaying. "It's true?" Dearsley asked in a quiet voice that wouldn't carry even to the nearest courtiers, who leaned forward in their eagerness to catch every sound. "I thought I felt, but . . . Sometimes hope deceives."

I clasped him on the shoulder, adding my strength to keep him upright. "It's true. Your queen has returned. But she remains in seclusion for the moment, and sent me to address anything urgent." A mix of truth and lies there, but it served to satisfy our audience, who swiftly passed back the news.

"Where to start?" he said with a humorless laugh and bowed again. "We are grateful for Your help, Conrí. If You will take Your throne, we can commence."

I winced again, internally, as Dearsley employed the honorific. Just digging myself in deeper. Fortunately the chair Lia had added for me to sit beside her remained in place, though I'd only sat in it twice. It saved me taking her ornate and flowery throne. Mine was simple black and silver, another example of her consideration for my taste.

I sat, gesturing for Vesno to sit also, and he settled on his haunches beside my chair with grave ceremony. At least one of us looked regal. I surveyed the sea of faces, all turned hopefully up to me like I could do something for them. I'd never quite figured how to explain to Lia how sitting up here made me feel like a fraud. Shifting on the hard seat, I unslung the rock hammer and set it, heavy-end down, between my chair and Lia's empty one.

"So," I said to Dearsley, "I hear there are damage reports."

"Indeed, Conrí." Dearsley had sat as soon as I had—I needed to remember that he wouldn't until I did—and sent his lad up with a long scroll. "The current list, Conrí."

I took it with a nod, pretended to scan the list. Oh, I could pick out words here and there if I really worked at it, but mostly it looked like spider tracks tangling across the page. If I needed to know exactly what it said, I'd get Ibolya to read it for me. Or Sondra. But I was practiced in working around this particular limitation.

"What, in your estimation, Lord Dearsley, are the most critical concerns?" I asked, rolling up the scroll and tapping it on my knee.

The court erupted into a din of sound, different factions and delegations yelling all at once about their disasters.

"Silence!" I roared, the volume making my voice harsher than usual, the strain biting painfully. It worked, though. The room fell silent, everyone staring at me in shock and more than a little fear. I nearly ruined it by smiling. "There is *one* person in this room named Lord Dearsley," I continued in a more reasonable tone. I stroked Vesno's head to give the impression of calm. "Now then, Lord Dearsley? And remain seated. I can hear you fine."

Dearsley cleared his throat. "As You say, Conrí. The chief concerns arise from the intensifying earth tremors and the ongoing storm. All seagoing traffic has halted, with a number of fishing ships lost at sea with no way to search for them. Three bridges have collapsed, isolating a number of communities. Two villages have been buried under mudslides, and the rain and earth tremors are preventing rescue efforts. Numerous coastal towns are so flooded their entire populations have evacuated to high ground, where they're now stranded with sick and injured and no supplies. Plus a string of islands off the north shore seem to have sunk entirely. Those are the disasters involving the largest clusters of population, but there is suffering across all of Calanthe—children lost in swollen rivers, families missing, structures collapsing. It's difficult to know where to start." He smiled hopefully at me. "What do You think?"

I wished I'd never gotten out of bed.

Hours later, we'd made stopgap plans to address the most critical disasters, but I felt like I'd been running flat out only to slide back. For every decision we made—and I hustled those along as fast as I could—to fix what had already broken, three more reports arrived of additional disasters.

Lia hadn't been exaggerating when she said Calanthe was unraveling. From what I'd learned in the past hours, the situation was accelerating at a daunting rate, and we could only slap a few bandages on it. We really needed to get Lia on the job of fixing the problem at the source. I could only hope some real food and more sleep had worked a miracle. When Vesno and I got to our rooms, however, Ibolya sweetly deflected me from checking on Lia.

"I just looked in on Her Highness, Conrí," Ibolya said with a respectful curtsy. "She's sleeping. It would be best not to disturb Her."

"I won't wake her."

"Nevertheless, I can't let You in."

"Is she any better?"

Ibolya hesitated. "I can't say."

That meant no. From the look on Ibolya's face, Lia was worse. "Did Healer Jeaneth look at her?"

"Yes. But . . ." Ibolya bit her lip, firmed it. "As Ambrose said, there's nothing she can do. Her Highness needs food and rest."

"Lia *did* eat, though?"

Ibolya knotted her fingers together. "She wasn't able to keep it down," she admitted.

Curse it all. I strained with the need to be with her. "I'd like to see Lia for myself."

"For Her sake, Conrí—or Yours?"

For mine, of course. In my mind's eye, I kept seeing her on that slab, white as death, cold as stone, lost to me forever. I needed to see the flush of life in her skin, to listen to her breathing. "For Calanthe's," I said, Vesno shoving his nose under my hand in comfort. "Things are getting worse."

"Her Highness is not up to doing anything for us right now. We must let Her recover first."

I shifted on my feet, tempted to shove the slight woman aside. Ibolya cocked her head, reading my intention—and I recalled Lia's warning that all her ladies possessed thorns. The last thing I needed was to be knocked out and wake up hours from now with a headache worthy of a three-day bender.

I took a calming breath, deep enough that the scar tissue in my lungs twinged. "What's the problem, Ibolya? I want to see my wife. That should be enough."

"Conrí," she said, very gently. "Her Highness specifically asked that I keep You away. I'm sorry, but I must obey Her command. It's my duty."

What? I jerked my gaze over Ibolya's head—she barely reached my shoulder anyway—and glared at the door. A low grinding noise rose up, and I realized the growl came from me. It had been a mistake to tell Lia I loved her. Now that she was free of me, she clearly wanted nothing to do with me anymore. Well, she wasn't getting rid of me that easily, especially when I knew she needed me. I hadn't saved her to let her wither away and die now. "Has Ambrose examined her?"

Ibolya shook her head. "I've sent multiple messages to the tower, as You requested, Conrí, but he has yet to respond."

Oh, the wizard was going to respond all right. This I could do. I gave Ibolya a last glare and she smiled politely, still not budging. "I'll be back, and I *will* see Lia."

"I will give Her Highness Your message, Conrí," Ibolya replied with formal courtesy.

"Come on, Vesno." I turned on my heel and strode out of the rooms again, the door guard saluting as I departed. Sondra jumped up from her post on the sofa and followed, extending her stride on my other side to keep up with my pace.

"Where are you going?"

"To get Ambrose."

"Will he admit you?"

I curled my fingers into a tighter fist. What was with everyone locking me out? I might have to start bashing heads with the rock hammer after all. "I'm going to make sure of it."

Sondra didn't immediately reply, still flanking me. "Conrí, maybe you need more recovery time, too. You're still running on, what? A few hours of sleep after a week or longer of practically nothing?"

"I thought about sleeping, but I'm not allowed into my own bed, am I?"

"There are other beds, Conrí," Sondra said in a careful voice.

"Don't," I growled.

She subsided again, probably needing her breath as we climbed the stairs to Ambrose's tower, Vesno galloping ahead with enviable energy. Vesno happily explored the bare, circular room at the top, devoid of furniture but apparently not interesting smells. Sondra wiped the sweat from her forehead and I frowned at her. "You all right?"

"Yeah. Yekpehr—" She drew a deep breath, deliberately holding, then releasing. "That fucker Anure burns vurgsten on the walls, night and day."

"I saw."

She rolled her shoulders. "You know how it is. Worked my lungs over to breathe that shit."

I did know. "Thank you," I said, feeling awkward and, yeah, like an idiot. "For sticking with Lia," I explained.

"I promised you. Besides," Sondra added with a snort, equally uncomfortable. "She's worth sticking with."

"I'm just sorry it came to that."

"What in Ejarat's bountiful tits are you talking about, Conrí?"

"We both know that it was all my fault," I said, not looking at her but at the sealed trapdoor in the high ceiling. There used to be a ladder for guards and servants to climb up to Ambrose's chamber, but no longer. We'd have to get him to let one down. "If I hadn't been such a hotheaded, shortsighted, stubborn fool, you and Lia would never—"

"Stop already!" Sondra shouted, surprising me and bringing Vesno running to nose her inquiringly. She patted his head, gaze on me. "The fact that Anure abducted us is Anure's fault. The fact that the wizards tortured Lia is the wizards' fault. Despite your delusions of grandeur, Con, you are not the master of the universe. Get over yourself."

I eyed her. "Was that supposed to be a pep talk?"

She bared her teeth in a flesh-eating grin. "Yes. Now, how are we getting Ambrose to let down his golden hair?"

Snorting in turn, I studied the ceiling, then cupped my hands to my mouth to focus my shout. "Ambrose!" My

voice ran around the windowless chamber in a mockery
of echoes. *Ambrose . . . mbrose . . . brose . . . sss.* "Ambrose, let us in!" *Us in sin sin nnn . . .* "You'd think he'd
have a bell pull or something," I commented sourly.

"But then people could reach him," Sondra pointed out.

I set my jaw. "This is ridiculous. I'm getting up to that
trap."

"As you say, Conrí." Sondra snapped me a salute. "I
shall locate a ladder."

While she was gone, I shouted for Ambrose some more,
even inciting Vesno into a spate of barking, which made
him wildly gleeful. I was jumping up and down, encouraging Vesno to leap ever higher on his hind legs—the
wolfhound could clear some serious height—both of us
barking at top volume, when Sondra returned with two
servants carrying a long ladder.

She eyed me dubiously, but simply instructed the servants to put the ladder in place. I crouched down to calm
Vesno, both of us panting. Oddly enough, I felt a little better. Less roilingly frustrated, anyway.

The servants disappeared immediately, both casting
wary glances at the ceiling, as if a monster lurked up
there. I climbed the ladder, finding a midway point where
I could stand and still reach the trap. "It should push up
and in," I remembered.

"Unless Ambrose is sitting on it."

"He's not heavy."

"Are you sure?"

I grunted, not willing to debate that. How Ambrose appeared and how he actually was didn't always match up.
I pushed, and it felt like pushing on the ceiling. Nothing
gave. "Ambrose!" I shouted. Vesno circled the bottom of
the ladder, adding his howls. Sondra leaned against the
wall, calmly putting her hands over her ears.

I slammed the meat of my hand against the trap, yelling for Ambrose. Going up another rung took me a bit out of center but let me coil my legs, giving me spring to pound on the stone in steady thumps that bounced the ladder.

"Con!" Sondra shouted. "Give it up! This is insanity."

"No," I snarled, keeping up the pounding. Ambrose was supposed to be Lia's wizard and she needed him, so he could dammed well step up and be accessible. I'd blast the trap open with vurgsten if I had to. If we had any left after squandering everything we'd painstakingly saved, all on that one battle that should've ended Anure forever and had instead left us crippled and broken, Lia and her realm shattered—both continuing to erode beyond recognition or repair.

The rage returning, I unslung the rock hammer from my back with the other and swung it. The leverage was wrong—and the ladder tilted precariously away from the wall with the change in balance—but I heaved the heavy mallet against the stone with a small *clang*.

"Conrí, *please*!"

I swung the hammer again, my shoulder protesting the awkward position, but managed to hit the stone harder. *Clang.*

"Conrí!"

I ignored Sondra, winding up to hit the door again, fury lending me additional strength.

"Con! Listen, you fucking idiot!" Sondra screamed.

Pausing, I glanced down. Sondra stood there, pointing ostentatiously at Ambrose beside her. Vesno sat on his haunches, tongue lolling happily. Ambrose cocked his head at me, his smile very like Vesno's. "Why, Conrí," he said mildly. "What an unexpected pleasure. Would you care to come in for tea?"

5

"Is he gone?" I asked Ibolya when she slipped into the darkened room.

"For the moment, Your Highness. But he'll be back before long. Conrí was most distraught."

"I heard."

"When he returns, as he undoubtedly will, if Your Highness still wishes to keep him out, I might have to use power to deflect him."

"You have My permission."

"Truly, Your Highness? This is Conrí." She carried her lit candle to light one on a far table, then moved to the lanterns. "He simply wishes to see You."

Well, I couldn't bear to see him. Couldn't bear to see him worry for me and be unable to do anything to help. No one could. "No, don't light the lamps. And blow out that candle. I prefer the dark."

"Yes, Your Highness. Can I bring You anything?"

"No. Leave Me."

Ibolya poured a glass of water anyway, setting it within reach, and replaced the cooled teapot with a warm one. Then she slipped out the doors, finally leaving me in blessed silence.

Except for Calanthe. As much as I tried to block out

Her rage and savage hunger, the din of it roared through my mind, my heart frantically beating to keep up. In the dark, I listened to the raging storm. It only seemed to be growing wilder, tearing at my palace, my island and ripping pieces away. Once it had been second nature for me to steer storms around Calanthe. Though I tried to send this storm out to sea, I had as little strength to do that as to lift my own arm. Ibolya had sponged me clean and assisted me into a fresh sleeping gown, but I was weak as a babe, needing help to use the toilet. And what had come out of me . . .

I didn't know what all the wizards had added to my blood, but it was gone now. I hoped. Expelling it all had left me shuddering in a cold sweat, and dizzy to the point of fainting.

All I could do was stare at the shrouded ceiling. My twig fingers caressed the skin of my good hand, tickling and not like a part of myself. I'd never been a person to dwell on death. I'd certainly never longed for death until those last moments on the wizards' sacrificial altar, but when I'd resigned myself to the inevitability of it, when I'd actively embraced death and welcomed Her in . . . I couldn't seem to stop. There might be no coming back from that.

It could be that was one invitation I couldn't rescind, and those final thoughts clung to everything else I tried to consider, a cobwebbing of death that cast a shroud over my soul. Perhaps my body had only *seemed* to come back to life—animated by a ghost of my former self.

Unable to summon the will to fight it, I succumbed to the drugging sleep—and the nightmares that awaited me.

"What's wrong with Lia?" I demanded.

Ambrose raised an eyebrow. He wore the robes that Lia had given him as court wizard of Calanthe, the dark velvety material studded with constellations of jeweled stars. "Drink your tea, Con, and consider phrasing your questions better. Cookie?"

"No," I bit out, but I drained the teacup and set it aside. Ambrose never could be rushed along. I fed a cookie to Vesno who'd lifted his tufted ears at the invitation. Sondra stood at the open window, gazing out at something, unflinching though cold rain spattered her face and the fierce wind tore at her clothing. Ambrose reclined on a wine-red sofa with gold tassels. That was new. In fact, everything was new since we'd unwillingly stayed in that tower, the room much larger than seemed possible. It had been divided into work areas, some screened off, others openly cluttered, some I couldn't seem to get my eyes to focus on. A large bed poked out from behind a curtain, while chairs and more fancy sofas clustered in conversational groupings like a ladies' salon.

How Ambrose had gotten everything in there defied rational explanation. Which shouldn't surprise me, as everything about Ambrose defied rational explanation. I raked my hands through my hair, digging my fingers into my scalp. It didn't help dredge up better questions, whatever the fuck that meant.

"Sondra," Ambrose called, "would you like a cookie? They're excellent."

She waved a hand in dismissal without turning. Ambrose sighed, then fed a cookie to Vesno, who took it with delicate precision, munching happily.

"She's locked me out," I said. Not a question, but it helped to think it through. "Literally, by having Ibolya bar my way, but effectively before that. At first she seemed to be talking to me—" Pretending to care, but maybe she'd been trying to say goodbye? "—but all along she was edging me out the door. She's messed up, not like she was before. I mean, I don't expect her to be magically better, but . . ." But that would be *useful* magic. I lifted my head to stare at Ambrose. "I think she's dying. Or not fully alive. I don't *know*. What can I do to help her?"

"Ah. That's a better question." He wagged a cookie at me, then popped it in his mouth, munching thoughtfully. I waited while he chewed, swallowed. When he reached for another cookie, my hand shot out of its own accord to seize the wizard's wrist.

"And the answer?" I prompted.

He smiled sadly, then was no longer in my grasp, instead sitting back some distance, cookie in hand. "A better question helps to elicit a useful answer, but is no guarantee of one," he remarked. "I might return the question to you. What *can* you do to help Lia?"

Sondra might have made a snorting sound, but she didn't turn around. No help there. I set my teeth. "This is what I'm trying to find out."

"Or, to put it another way, can you give Her what She needs?"

"Yes." I'd give Lia anything, whatever she needed. "If I know what it is," I amended.

"Ah, and that can be the sticking point. Very often we need the people who love us to give us what we need before we know what that is ourselves."

"Which means those of us with no one to love us are pretty much fucked," Sondra muttered darkly.

"How do I figure out what Lia needs if she can't tell me herself?" I asked. I agreed with Sondra, in theory, but I couldn't dwell just then on the painful truth that Lia didn't love me in return. I'd gone over half my life with no one loving me—I could hardly start dwelling on it now.

Ambrose sat up, poured tea into a fresh cup, handed it to

me, then reclined again. "You are a man of action, Conrí, which is your strength and your weakness."

"Yeah. And?"

"You can't force Lia into full health. You can't make Her want to live. Some things are beyond even your might."

"This is what I've been trying to tell him," Sondra muttered.

"Of course Lia wants to live," I said, ignoring Sondra.

"Does she?" Ambrose asked Sondra, who shrugged but looked grim.

"So what are you saying?" I looked between them. "I should do nothing?"

"Oh." Ambrose waved a hand vaguely. "Did I say that? I really don't think I did."

"Lia is a woman driven by duty and responsibility," I explained carefully, reining in my temper. "She wants to live, if only to protect Calanthe." I knew that much about her. But . . . did I? *Calanthe is crumbling, out of control—it will not be fine.* I dropped my face in my hands, groaning. What if she couldn't repair Calanthe? She'd never forgive herself. "I need her, and so do her people. Calanthe is coming apart at the seams, just as she warned us."

"Oh, I know," Ambrose said. "The situation is probably even worse than you realize."

Wonderful. Just fantastic. Never go to a wizard for reassurance.

"Did you find Merle?" Sondra asked. She'd turned around, finally, and leaned against the sill, apparently uncaring of the cold rain blowing against her back.

"It's never been a question of *finding* Merle, so much," Ambrose replied with a rare frown. "That's where I was when you dropped by to visit. But Merle is the only thing holding Calanthe back right now—and will be unless and until Her Highness can take over." He shook his head. "I'm afraid his strength won't hold much longer. And that's not including other complications."

"How much longer?"

"That's difficult to put in human terms," Ambrose mused. "You see, Calanthe exists in several dimensions of reality at once. In some, She is a goddess; in others, a monster; in others, a landmass."

Sondra and I exchanged glances, and she shrugged in her confusion. That left me to take a stab at it. "I'm going to say Calanthe is a landmass in this reality."

Ambrose wagged a finger in the air. "Aha! Not so fast. These realities are not separated by impermeable barriers. They're more like . . . colors in a rainbow, ever shifting, leaking into one another, blurring the lines."

"Sounds like magic—dragging stuff from one reality into the other."

Ambrose turned his head and smiled at me, beaming as if I were a prize pupil. "Conrí! At last you begin to understand how magic works. I'd rather despaired of you."

I decided not to touch that one. "So: How long do we have before this goddess-monster-landmass sinks into the sea?"

"From the tales I've studied and what Her Highness confided, it might be more of an erupting and rampaging than a sinking," Ambrose corrected. When I growled, he hastened to continue. "Regardless, we're talking about a combination of metaphysical and geologic time scales, which have very different linear functions than time as humans understand it. Putting it in terms you'll understand is an approximation, at best."

"Try," I said drily.

"Minutes, hours, days, weeks, months, years, centuries, eons. They're all arbitrary measures." Ambrose sat up, warming to his subject. "If you theorize that metaphysical time operates on a logarithmic scale, then—"

"Ambrose," I interrupted, "from what we're seeing out in human reality, it's looking closer to weeks than eons. Can we narrow it to one end of the spectrum or the other?"

"Did you know," Ambrose said, tapping his oddly long fingers together, eyes bright, "that some propose that we should think of time as a circle, rather than as a spectrum? So eons would at some point merge into nanoseconds, which means—"

"Ambrose." This time Sondra interrupted him, a wary eye on my twitching fingers, which I'd seriously been considering wrapping around the wizard's throat, if only to stop the flow of words making my brain ache.

"Point taken," Ambrose conceded. "It helps to have Her Highness present on the island, so things aren't progressing as fast as when She was gone. I'd say days. No more than a week."

There. Was that so fucking difficult? I throttled back the accusation, however. "Can *you* do anything?" I asked bluntly.

"Not with Merle in between, no."

For some reason I imagined the raven stuck between two giant wheels, holding them back with his wings—and they would crush him if anyone tried to shoulder in to help.

"Close enough," Ambrose said, nodding at me, as if he'd plucked the thought from my head.

"What about Anure's wizards?"

Ambrose poured himself more tea. "What about them?"

"You said they're worsening the situation, so is there anything we can do to stop them?"

"'We'? Oh no. You shouldn't take that on yourself,

Conrí," Ambrose assured me. "More tea?" The tower trembled slightly, the ground shifting far below, and Ambrose cocked his head at the ripples in his tea. "Definitely a sign," he announced, "that you should focus on the immediate problem, which is Calanthe."

"If you can't do anything about Calanthe," I replied, "then we need Lia. And we need her healthy and strong."

"Conrí," Sondra said, "you can't just—"

I held up a hand to stop her, concentrating on Ambrose. "*You* can't save Calanthe. Merle can't keep doing whatever he's doing, which isn't enough anyway. Is there anybody else who can save Calanthe and all the people on it, besides Lia? Yes or no, Ambrose."

He met my gaze soberly. "If you insist on a dichotomy, then no."

Good enough. By eliminating options, we at least narrowed our focus. "Your elixir seemed to help Lia. Is there anything else you can do for her?"

"Oh, I'm sure there is." He looked vaguely toward one of the workbenches I couldn't quite make out, as if it remained in shadow, though parts of the room next to and beyond it were well lit by lanterns. "The death part is tricky, but in general what a wizard has done, a wizard may undo. That's not a hard-and-fast rule, but it gets the point across."

"What?" Sondra burst out, advancing a step, hand going to her sword. "You can help Her Highness and you haven't done it?"

Ambrose didn't even look at her, still focused on the shadowy work area. "She hasn't asked."

"She isn't even strong enough to *get out of bed*, you numbskull!" Sondra shouted. Vesno jumped to his feet and barked in agreement.

Giving the two of us a hurt and puzzled frown, Ambrose

fed Vesno a cookie. "Well, why didn't you say so? I've never brought anyone back from the dead before, so I can't know these things. Really, Conrí, I don't know why you didn't ask me that in the first place."

Sondra threw up her hands and paced away, muttering how she should've let me pitch him out the window. Ambrose wandered over to the bench, disappearing into the shadows, even the lamplight glittering off the stars and jewels on his wizard's robes dimming. "Of course what I do depends on what She asks for," he called out, sounding as if he stood at the bottom of a well. "It won't do anyone any good to give Her something She hasn't asked for."

Giving me a *look*, Sondra circled her hand with impatient prompting, wanting me to say something. Wonderful. What had Lia actually asked for? "She wants to be stronger. And she says her mind isn't sharp. Her memory is full of holes and she says she can't think."

"No?" Ambrose stuck his head out of the gloom, his face a floating bright spot. "That's not good. Not good at all. Brains rot first, you know."

Sondra shot up a finger in vindication, leveling a grim look at me, as Ambrose vanished again. Then we waited. Sondra paced while I ate cookies, which felt like throwing crumbs into an empty pit. Maybe feeling hungry for real food was a good sign. Finally Ambrose emerged, arms full of jugs, vials, and various other implements—all piled up so that it seemed impossible they'd stayed balanced this long, let along another second.

"Can I help you carry some of that?" Sondra asked him, starting forward, hands outstretched.

"No, child, no," he answered vaguely as he juggled. "These things aren't for you to touch."

She dropped her hands helplessly, exchanging a glance with me. "But how will you get down the ladder?"

"Oh, I'll meet you there in a bit. After all, you two still have to figure out how to gain an audience with Her Highness. It *is* quite late, and—"

"Oh, I'll get in to see her," I said. It was my own bedroom, too. I wasn't relinquishing that hard-won territory without a fight. "It's for her own dammed good."

"The queen has to *ask* for help," Ambrose cautioned me, no longer vague at all. "Especially mine. That's a critical point, for very good reasons."

I waited, but he didn't explain. "I'll see to it," I promised. When they both looked dubious, I headed for the trapdoor and opened it. "I'm a man of action, right? I might not be able to force Lia into full health or make her want to live, but I *can* make her listen to me." *Maybe*.

When Sondra, Vesno, and I reached the royal chambers, the guards admitted us—though I'd been braced for a refusal there—and Ibolya rose gracefully, gliding to intercept me as I strode purposefully for Lia's private chambers.

"Welcome back, Conrí. I've ordered food for you, if you'd care to—"

"Later." I reached the door and put my hand on the knob.

Ibolya put her slender hand on mine, staying me. I might've imagined the light prickle, like a static spark, but continuous. Probably not, as her pretty dark eyes took on a determined gleam. "I'm sorry, Conrí, but Her Highness's orders have not changed. I cannot admit you."

"You don't have to *admit* me. I'm going into *my* rooms on my own."

"Please, Conrí. I don't wish to harm you." The prickle increased in clear warning.

"Have you been in to see her since I was here last?"

"I checked on Her Highness several times. She's sleeping." Though her serene face didn't so much as twitch the wrong way, she didn't quite meet my eye.

"I smell a lie," I said softly enough that it came out like a low growl.

Her eyes widened slightly. "I'm not lying. Her Highness is . . ." Ibolya sagged ever so slightly. "She is not well. I wish the other ladies were here. I don't know what to do for Her."

"I'll take the responsibility," I told her gently, but adding the firmness of command. "I know what to do for Lia. She's not in her right mind. Let me help her."

Ibolya searched my face for an endless moment. "If you harm Her, or if She calls for me, I will take action to remove you, Conrí. I can do it."

"I love Lia. I'm trying to save her life."

With one last searching look, Ibolya nodded in decision. Stepping back, she decorously folded her hands. "I'll keep Vesno," Sondra said. "Good luck."

I opened the door and went to confront Lia.

"Your Highness, I do hope You will pay attention. I have no doubt You'll find this as instructive as we do." The red wizard lowered the knife, sliding it deftly through the space between my ribs. The cold metal poked uncomfortably inside my empty chest cavity, not painful but disconcerting. What had happened to my heart? "You must understand, Your Highness, Your kind aren't truly human at all, thus You lack the capability to feel emotion. Otherwise, You wouldn't be so heartless, if You'll pardon the word play." He smiled, gentle and dispassionate.

"I have a heart," I protested weakly, then wondered at my lapse. I'd resolved not to speak to the wizards, not to give them the least thing. Anything they took from me had to be wrested away. It didn't stop them, but at least I had pride to cling to.

He began prying my ribs apart with the blade. "Allow me to demonstrate. I know Your Highness is a student of sciences, and thus fond of empirical evidence." With a *crack!* my ribs gave. The wizard clucked in satisfaction. The smell of fetid swamp water rose up, tinged with algal bitterness. "If You will observe."

The red wizard gestured, and the wizard in black stepped up, bowing to me. "Your Highness is looking most lovely today." He held up a mirror the height of a man, with an ornate frame and a perfectly liquid silver reflective surface. My ladies used to do that—hold up the full-length mirror so I could approve my appearance for court.

I gazed unwillingly at the image of myself. A gnarled oak tree, bark knobbed and ancient, limbs broken and leaves wilted, stood cleaved nearly in two with a vertical hole running down the center of its trunk. A gaping cavity oozed blood and entrails, green water gushing out, leaving the interior hollow and depthless.

"That's not Me," I protested, but my voice was small. I tried to make it louder. "That's not Me. I have a heart."

"But it is You. Demonstrably so." The wizard in the blue robe stepped up beside the large mirror. Using a slender wand, he indicated the leaking hollow of the tree. "Observe the rotting interior, the lack of turgor pressure in the limbs. Death lingers at the core."

The black wizard took the wand. "Death is merely a transition. By removing the vestigial flesh and other animal artifacts such as blood from Your Highness's corporeal form, we've revealed a refined, more pristine version of Your true self."

"No. I have a heart. I've felt it."

"But have You?" The wizard in purple robes came into

view, Merle perched on his shoulder. The raven croaked a hello at me, bobbing his head in greeting. "If Your Highness had a heart, then people would actually love You. And You would be capable of love, which You clearly are not."

"Tertulyn could never have betrayed Your Highness, in that case."

"Con couldn't have sacrificed a woman he truly loved simply to win a battle."

"It was all a lie."

"Do You see now?"

"I have a heart!" I protested, forcing the words past my numb lips. "I do! I'm not dead. That isn't Me."

The oak tree in the mirror flailed, wilted orchids falling like rain to shower onto the swirling green water that rose around the base of the trunk. The tree began to lean to one side, the orchids a sodden mass of dying petals, pale rose and violet, sinking into the current that swirled in a huge whirlpool of ravening hunger.

"No, please—that isn't Me." The dark maw of the starving sea drowned my words. "That isn't Me . . ."

"Lia." The whirlpool called my name, night-dark voice hoarse as the growl of a wolf. "Lia. Come to me."

"I won't." I pushed at it. "I won't go!"

"Lia!" The sea lashed waves of black, unyielding, demanding. "You come back to me right now. Wake up."

"No no no no . . ."

"Do it, Lia. I'm not giving up on you."

A sharp pain made me gasp. Flesh and blood. I had a body, a living, flesh-and-blood one. Furious golden eyes pierced me, Con's pitted face contorted with blazing anger. I lifted a hand to my stinging cheek, the twig fingers tapping a light pattern against my skin. Not flesh, not entirely. "You slapped me." I meant to sound imperious, indignant, but it came out a soft cry of distress.

Con gripped my shoulders, searching my face, then his fierce expression relaxed, and he pulled me into his arms, wrapping his strength around me. "I know. I'm sorry, Lia, please forgive me." He buried his face into the crook of my neck and shoulder. "You were raving in your sleep. Then you stopped breathing and I couldn't get you to wake up. I didn't know what else to do."

"The wizards had Me again."

"No, Lia. No. It was only a dream. A nightmare."

"They were . . . experimenting on Me."

"No." Con said it firmly, lifting his head and cupping my face in his hands. "They weren't. They'll never have you again. I promise you that. It was a dream, nothing more."

A dream? Scraps of images came back. The hollow tree. The rain of dying orchids. My dreams had always been of the future, not the past. "Some promises you can't keep, no matter how hard you try," I whispered, the heart I didn't have feeling like it might crack apart at the haunted look on his face.

"I failed you before, Lia," he replied, voice creaking like old floorboards, "but I *will* keep this promise. Believe that, if nothing else."

"Where is Ibolya? I distinctly recall commanding her to keep you out."

"Yeah, she tried. No luck there. We'll discuss that later. Right now I'm here and I'm not letting you die again, no matter how much you might think you want to."

I gazed back at him, aghast. "I don't want to die." I might not want to die, but death was reaching for me. The orchid lay limp on my arm, like the sodden orchids falling from the dying oak tree.

"Good." He let me go and went to the lantern on the bedside table, lighting it with the clicker there. I hissed at the sudden brightness and he glanced at me, assessing, then continued on, lighting all the lamps until the room blazed with light. He paused, surveying the table laden with food, all untouched. "Here's an easy place to start. You need to eat, Lia."

6

I fought the immediate revulsion at even the thought of food, barely managing not to gag. "I can't." Instead of snapping out imperiously, the denial came out with a hint of a whimper.

He eyed me, the stubborn wolf in his gaze. "Can't? Or won't?"

Dizziness swamped me—did I imagine the odor of fetid swamp water?—and I lay back against the pillows, weak as a wilted petal. *Orchids can't live on their own . . .*

"Lia, answer me." Con had started to fill a plate, clearly intending to force me to eat. He probably would, too, even if he had to hold my nose and cram food down my throat. How charming that would be.

"You don't order Me, wolf," I replied archly, though my voice was thready and weak.

He smiled, showing his teeth. "Fair enough, blossom— but you don't order me, either. If you don't give me an answer, I'll take matters into my own hands."

"Can't," I said flatly, managing enough certainty to make him pause. "I tried. I really did. I couldn't keep it down. Ib- olya had to clean up the mess. I'm so hungry, Con. I really did try and—" I had to stop talking lest I start weeping.

"Shh, Lia. I believe you." Abandoning the plate, he

came to sit on the side of the bed, enfolding my good hand in his with infinite tenderness. Under the concern, fear lurked. Not for himself, but for me. "Ambrose is coming. He can give you more of that elixir. That helped you before. Just remember that, when he gets here, you have to ask him for it."

Ambrose the wizard. Had he been in my dream? "The wizards are wrong."

"About what?"

Oh, that's right. The wizards weren't real. I'd dreamed them, so Con didn't know. But Con did love me. He'd said so. Hadn't he? The memory got dark and swampy. "It's so dark. Why did you put out the lamps again?"

"I didn't." He patted my cheeks. "Lia? Stay with me. Ambrose will bring the elixir."

"It's so dark," I whispered.

"Where the fuck is Ambrose?" Con snarled. He was no longer there, and I groped for the loss of his anchoring touch. He was shouting in the distance, his harsh voice suited to the burr of command. Other voices answered, some rising stridently. A shattering crash echoed, and I imagined Con bashing something with his rock hammer. A dog barked in excitement. Vesno. I smiled vaguely. Even my ferocious wolf couldn't fight death. He should know that it always won in the end.

"Here now, Euthalia. Conrí is only a man—a stalwart hero to be sure, and Sawehl's chosen son, but only a man—so we can't expect him to battle the Goddess of Death." Ambrose smiled at me when I opened my eyes, the being hidden behind his wizard's illusions more apparent than usual.

"What are you?" I asked, the curiosity getting the better of me in my weak condition. Normally I was too cagey to ask the wizard directly, but this might be my last chance.

"Ah ah ah." Ambrose waggled a finger at me. "You know the rules. A question for a question, and You're in no condition to fulfill Your end of the bargain. You'll have to live to find out."

"I don't know if I can," I confessed. "My roots—they shriveled away while I was gone."

"I see that. Hmm. Quite the riddle and not one we have the luxury of pondering for long."

Just remember . . . you have to ask him for it. "Would you help Me?" I asked.

He gazed at me soberly. "Are You certain You want my help?"

"Why wouldn't I?"

Searching my face, he grimaced and sighed. "I had to make sure. If You hated me, You would instinctively reject my magic."

"I could never hate you, Ambrose. You're My wizard."

"I'm my own wizard," he replied with a sad smile, "which I haven't been very good at."

Con barreled back into the room. "Where in Sawehl's balls have you been! How did you get in here?"

"The windows," Ambrose replied brightly. "Easiest way, of course."

I glanced at the windows, but the wooden coverings to keep out the storm were still in place.

Con snarled in frustration. "Lia is dying."

"Yes, I see that. We have to do something."

If I'd had the strength, I would've laughed at the incandescent rage on Con's face as he reached for the smaller man. Sondra appeared, inserting herself between them. "Don't. Kill. The. Wizard," she said, clearly and distinctly.

"Give her the elixir," Con demanded as if Sondra weren't there.

Ambrose shook his head with regret. "It's done what it could. More can't do what the first one didn't."

"My roots," I whispered, trying to explain, and Ambrose nodded, patting my hand.

Con looked wild, the whites of his eyes showing. "I don't care what it takes. I'll pay any price, promise anything. Just . . . *do something*. Please."

"Con, no." I summoned some strength for that. "Never promise a wizard any price."

"I do promise it. I don't care. Anything, Ambrose. Just . . . help her." He sagged, then dropped to his knees, burying his face against my legs under the blanket. "Please. I can't survive her death again."

I lifted a hand, reaching to touch his hair, but he was too far away. "My roots," I said again.

"Why does She keep saying that?" Sondra asked. She'd come to the head of the bed, stroking my forehead.

"She's starving," Ambrose replied.

"Because she won't eat," Con said, voice muffled in the blankets.

"Can't," I corrected. I was hollow inside. So hungry, so emptied.

"Without roots, She cannot absorb nutrients," Ambrose explained.

Con had lifted his head. "No riddles, wizard. Just give me a plain answer for once."

"Some things don't translate," Ambrose replied with unusual heat. "Her Highness is an elemental, not exactly human."

"I *am* human," I protested. "I have a heart."

"Of course You do," Sondra said soothingly.

"You are *part* human," Ambrose corrected. "Like the magical artifacts You showed me in the garden at Cradysica, You are a creation of human flesh, the floral body

of Calanthe, and an extension of the goddess. Does that
sound about right?"

I considered that. I'd never quite thought of myself that
way, but considering how I'd been born, that did make
sense, so I nodded.

"Flower made flesh," Con said, testing out the words.
His molten gold gaze met mine. "Orchids can't live on
their own."

I'd forgotten I'd told him that once, in a summer-
blossoming garden, forever ago. "True," I said, on a sigh
of regret. "Ambrose, please help Me."

"With all my heart, Your Highness." He laid hands on
my forehead, his forest-deep magic infusing me, banish-
ing the stagnant waters of death. It felt so much better to
be finally cleansed of that clinging dank filth.

"What did you do?" Con demanded, and I realized Ambrose had stood and stepped back.

"I made it so Her body can absorb nutrients again."

Con frowned blackly. "She doesn't look any better."

I wanted to say something snide to that, but wit eluded
me.

"She can absorb nutrients," Ambrose explained patiently, "but She must have them first."

"Feed her then!" Con snarled.

"Alas. I cannot." Ambrose looked at Con expectantly.

"I'll feed Her," Sondra declared. She smiled at me.
"Tick tick tick."

I smiled back, feebly. "Not food. I . . . can't."

"No," Con said slowly. "Not food. I understand now.
I know what you've been asking for. Everyone out." He
got to his feet, unstrapping his rock hammer from his
back and shrugging off his fine jacket. Black trimmed in
silver. Court garb. Had he been conducting court without
me?

"Con." Sondra sounded suspicious, not budging from her station. "What are you going to do?"

"Feed Lia. Get out."

Ambrose patted my hand, smiling beatifically, and rose. "Lady Ibolya, I wonder if I might trouble you for some cookies and tea? They're really quite excellent."

"But Her Highness—"

"Will be fine, dear. Let's leave Her to Conrí's tender ministrations, eh?"

Con had rolled up his cuffs, revealing his corded, scarred forearms, and held a dagger in his hand. Sondra stared at the blade. "Conrí. I can't let you—"

"It's all right, Lady Sondra," I said, lifting my hand to touch hers on my forehead. She flinched, blue eyes startled, and I realized I'd touched her with the twig fingers. "Thank you for all you've done for Me. I'd like to be alone with Con."

"I don't think—"

"*Don't* think. Go." Con pointed the knife at the door.

"Come along, child," Ambrose called cheerfully. "Tea and cookies will do you good, as well."

Looking unconvinced, she went, leaving the door ajar. Con shut it firmly behind her, throwing the bolt I rarely used. I wasn't a person who'd spent much time alone. All my life I'd been surrounded by people, but none that truly cared for me, the person. Even when I'd died, I'd been alone, except for the company of my murderers.

Con came back to the bed, standing over me with the knife, expression set with determination.

"Are you going to kill Me?" I asked the question with vague interest.

His face melted into blank shock. "No. How can you ask that?"

"Put Me out of My misery and so forth." I waved the

twig hand as I said it, then became absorbed in the strange flickering clicking of the green filaments.

"Lia. No." Con caught my hand, releasing it just as quickly.

"Horrifying, isn't it?" I waved the twiggy appendage he'd dropped so abruptly.

"Not at all," he replied, going over to his side of the bed, sitting, and toeing off his boots. "I was afraid I'd hurt you. The new fingers seem so fragile, like I could break them." He turned back the covers and crawled across the big bed to me, black shirt hanging open where he'd loosened the ties, dark hair falling around his intent face, eyes the gold of the setting sun. Settling himself against the pillows, he set the knife aside and slid his arms under me.

I grasped for balance. "What are you doing?"

"Feeding you," he replied calmly and in a tone that brooked no argument. Lying back against the pillows, he adjusted me so I sat mostly reclined against him. The heat of his body melted through me, and I doubted I could've mustered the desire to resist, even if I'd had the ability. "We'll start with a wrist and see how that does."

"I don't understand."

"You don't have to. Let me handle this for you." Picking up the knife, arms in a circle around me, he precisely placed the edge of the blade against the pulse point of his wrist and sliced. Bright blood welled up and, before the cry of shock passed my lips, he'd pressed his wrist to my mouth. "Drink," he ordered me. "It's what you asked for."

His blood filled my mouth, hot and salty sweet. It reminded me of the flavor of his seed, which I'd gladly swallowed before. But this was his blood. In horror, I tried to refuse, but he held it there in an implacable grip, staring me down. "Try, Lia. Just try this. One swallow."

I couldn't. How bestial and monstrous and yet . . . The hunger took over and I swallowed. Then again.

"That's it," he coaxed. "Calanthe wants blood, and so do you." His eyes closed in satisfaction, relaxing as I willingly drank now, like a babe at her mother's breast. "I wondered, you know, how you could be both flesh and flower. Now we know, huh?"

The lifeblood filled me, heating that persistent damp chill in my bones, filling the aching hollows where there had been stagnant pools in my death-riddled flesh. I drank until the blood slowed, and it wasn't nearly enough. The savage need for more drove me and I bit down, drawing hard. Con made a sound part pain, part laugh, and levered me away with his superior strength, gentle but inexorable. "No teeth, blossom. I don't want my arm in shreds. Hold still a moment." He contained my thrashing. "You're already stronger," he noted, pressing a cloth to his seeping wrist. "Now the other side."

With equal dexterity, he held up the uncut wrist near my face, sliced it, and pressed it to my mouth. He held me in that embrace as I drank with less desperation, gazing at the ceiling mosaic with my head resting near his heart. It thumped, loud and steady, and my own heart slowed its frantic race, evening out to match his. *See? I do have one.*

When that wound, too, slowed in its seeping, I let it go, licking the sluggish creep of blood. He levered up to study my face, relief smoothing away the worry. "Your color is much better. And your eyes are brighter. How do you feel?"

Less like I was going to die. The sarcastic thought felt more like myself, and the starving rage had backed off. "Better."

"Still hungry?"

Yes. But I didn't say so. At least my mind had sharpened enough that I could control the animal desperation. I wouldn't drain him to save myself. "No."

"Yes, you are. Don't lie." He shifted me, picked up the blade again.

"You're out of wrists," I protested.

"But not blood." Lifting his chin to expose the clean-shaven skin beneath his beard, he set the point of the knife against his throat. "You'll have to place this one since I can't see."

"Con . . ."

He looked down at me, chin still raised. "Do it, Lia. Let me do this for you. Please."

I'll pay any price. He would, too. With a sigh of resignation, I lifted my fleshly hand and guided the point of the blade to a place where the pulsing blood rose to the surface. "There."

He grunted and pressed, but the leverage was wrong, the skin giving without parting. "Can you help?"

"I don't want to hurt you."

"Those sharp teeth of yours hurt more, but if we have to do it that way, we will."

Maybe I was still asleep and all of this was a continuation of the dream. Gathering my determination and courage—how funny that it took bravery to hurt someone else—I pushed the knife into his skin. It took more pressure than I'd expected, but his skin finally parted and the blood gushed out. I made a sound of dismay, and he laughed as he cupped my head and guided me to his throat.

"That's why I like black," he said, his hoarse voice vibrating under my lips. "Hides blood well. Can't say the same for your sheets, but we'll change them."

I lay splayed against him, face buried against his skin, his flesh and lifeblood in my mouth, like kissing him but at a more profound level. Sex, even the brutal unraveling pleasure Con had brought to me, hadn't felt this . . . intimate. He was feeding me from his own body, out of selfless love, and my heart—so shredded and lonely—flowered in his nourishing heat. My sex swelled, growing slick, and Con's cock hardened against my belly. Aroused and needy, I shifted, parting my legs to straddle one muscular thigh, my sleeping gown riding up so the leather of his pants provided delightful friction against my naked sex.

I rubbed against him as I fed, in a slow rhythm that echoed our heartbeats. I sucked harder on his throat, a parody and deepening of the love bites that came with sex, and he shuddered under me. Groaning, the sound thrumming through me like distant thunder, Con murmured my name, his arms vising to hold me tighter against him. He flexed his hips, moving beneath me, a sensual undulation that rocked us both. I reached with my intact hand for his cock to free it, but he caught my wrist, stopping me.

"You need to feed and rest."

I needed *this*, needed even more of him inside me. But I couldn't say so with my mouth full of his blood. So I cheated, using the magic of Calanthe to reverse his intention so his hand released its grip on my wrist and fell away. He uttered an oath of surprise as I tugged at the laces of his pants. The pressure of his erection and the slide of our bodies had him springing free of the confining leather. I wrapped his shaft in my hand, working him hard, and his head fell back in abandonment. "Lia," he moaned. "How I love you. Have me then. Have everything."

I slid up his body—my mouth still fixed on his throat—and impaled myself on him. The convulsion took us both, twin cries of need climbing from our bodies. Pressing down, I sheathed him in the glove of my body, releasing the pressure of my mouth. Then I rose up, slowly, titillating us both, and I sucked hard, fresh blood filling me. He moved with me, flexing and filling, giving me everything.

And I reversed the flow to give back to him. All the verdant, fertile daylight pleasures of Calanthe as I remembered them. The sounds of bees in the blossoms so heavy with pollen and nectar their heads drooped with it. The scent of sea air and sunshine-heated leaves. The blue of the sky and the soil-dark richness below. The song of birds and the caress of petals on naked skin, the bite of thorns and the pain of birth. I rolled over him like gentle thunder before the downpour lets loose. His hand cupped my head against him, the other bracing my hip, helping me to work the plunging rhythm as old as the tides that surged onto land.

He stiffened as I did, the impending climax seizing us both in a grip as relentless as time. Tighter the tension coiled, our hearts racing in tandem, the magic of life and death pounding in cycle of blood and sex and love. A keening sound filled my ears and I realized it was me, the cry building to unbearable heights, and he thrust into me chanting my name like a prayer to his own personal goddess.

And we came together. The climax rent and sealed us, bound together by my mouth drawing his blood from his heart, my sex drinking the seed from his balls, and all of my skin sending life, and gratitude, and love back into him.

We rode that point of impossible ecstasy together, then crashed, falling into a long spiral of light and darkness, the dense fertile soil of Calanthe catching us, salt and sea, blood and flowers.

Lia went lax against me, lissome and fragrant. The sweet scent of blossoms rose from her skin, softly new, like springtime in Oriel when the snows first began to melt, withdrawing in patches to reveal those white and purple star-shaped flowers my mother had loved.

Lia nuzzled my neck, making a sleepy sound, and I stroked her head and back, soothing her. It seemed the fuzz on her scalp had grown, which surely was a good sign. I cradled that hope tenderly, unsure how to properly coax it into being.

Instead of succumbing to sleep, however, Lia shifted, giving my neck a last kiss that both stung and soothed. Pushing herself up, she sat over me, and I anchored her there. Her flimsy sleep gown had parted over lush breasts, nipples tight as rosebuds, and her tilted eyes dominated her delicately boned face. Devoid of her elaborate masks of makeup and jewels, her beauty took on an unearthly cast. It went beyond the bicolored eyes, one bright green, one deep blue, or the blood reddening her full lips. For the first time, I understood how easily she'd be spotted as someone not entirely human. In that moment, it amazed me that I—or anyone—could ever have seen her otherwise.

She took a corner of the sheet and wiped my lips with it, tenderly and carefully, not meeting my gaze. "Thank you, Conrí," she murmured.

"You're more than welcome, Your Highness," I replied in turn, and her brilliant eyes lifted to mine, her faintly green brows rising with a glint of her dry humor.

"Is that what this was, service to a queen?"

"You ask me that with my body still joined to yours?"

"Many have serviced their kings and queens so," she reminded me, dropping the sheet to run a fingertip over my lower lip.

"With the blood of their veins and the lust of their groins," I replied, feeling as if I quoted something.

She smiled, her former wicked humor blossoming. "There's a song I haven't heard in a long time."

"Is that what it is? Hmm." My own memory seemed to be serving up patchy offerings of its own lately. I'd gone so long remembering nothing of before the mines, thinking of nothing but the vengeance that fueled me, that having memories of spring flowers and ballads made me feel like a different person.

"At any rate, I meant to thank you for . . . feeding Me." She seemed tentative, fragile in some indefinable way.

I flexed my hands on her slender thighs. "Anytime. As often as you need it."

"That might get unsustainable."

I shrugged against the pillows. "I'm a big guy. I have a lot of blood, and I can make more."

"Even you aren't invincible, wolf," she pointed out with some asperity. "What if I take too much?"

"I'm stronger than you are. I won't let you."

"I can use My magic."

"You won't, because you'd have to think about it and once you did, you wouldn't."

I wasn't sure that chain of words made sense, but she considered them, head tilted as she trailed a finger through my beard, dropping to my chest, tracing the skin where my shirt had parted. "Maybe so. Though I seem to have the upper hand now." She flexed her internal muscles, rocking on me, and I rode the wave of almost too-intense sensation.

"Because I'm allowing it."

"We'll pretend that's true," she answered with a soft smile, then she sobered. "Con—how did you know what to do?"

"The wizard told me."

"Did he?" She pursed her lips, thinking. "I don't think that's true."

"What do you know," I mock-growled, "you were out of your head." *Dying.* I didn't say it, but she met my gaze, the troubling knowledge in it.

"I think this makes twice you've saved My life. At least."

"Since I'm the reason you nearly lost your life in the first place, that seems only fair."

She considered that seriously. "I don't believe this sort of thing comes down to accounting."

I cast about for an answer to that, feeling oddly exposed. The orchid caught my eye. "Look, Lia. The orchid ring."

"Bracelet, gauntlet, armband," she corrected idly, without bite, as she held up her hand, turning it, surveying the orchid growing from the narrow part of her forearm, just above the stump of her wrist. Green vines twined in an intricate pattern worthy of any court jeweler, wrapping around her arm with curlicues and forming the dense pad her twig fingers sprouted from. The blossom itself had sprung to life along with Lia, flushed a deep red with shades of blue and purple. The scalloped petals billowed, wafting a rich, sweet scent. "Does it draw life from Me or do I draw life from it?" she mused.

"Maybe you both draw life from the same source."

She cocked her head at me. "How philosophical My snapping wolf has become."

"I had a lot of time to think," I commented, my voice rough as I recalled those dark days and sleepless nights.

"Hmm. So how did you really know how to heal Me?"

I shifted restlessly, but she had me pinned, had me—quite literally—by the cock. So I lifted her off me and settled her against my side, turning to face her.

"Ambrose did say it, and so did you," I told her. "He said you're a fusion of flesh and flower. And you bit me, on the boat, asked for my blood then. You said Calanthe was hungry, and you were hungry. You're some kind of extension of Calanthe. Calanthe was awakened by blood, and you needed to be revived. Those fucking wizards drained you of your blood, so I gave it back to you."

A smile curved her lips, delight illuminating her eyes. "You have the intuition of a king, Conrí. Who'd have guessed?"

"I'm no king." But the denial was reflexive. Kara had said that to me as we stood in the ruins of the temple at Cradysica, in a rare burst of sentiment. *You are Conrí. Our king. My king. Now these people's king.*

"But you are. I think you knew what to do for Me because you are a true king, and you know intuitively how to tend the land."

"Are you the land in this equation?" I teased.

"Obviously," she breathed. She kissed me, and I tasted the salt of my blood on her lips, along with nectar, like the honeysuckle blossoms Rhéiane and I would pick, sucking the plucked tips of their sweetness. "Tend to Me, Con."

"Always," I said into her mouth. It didn't matter if she wanted to be married to me. I was married to her the same way I belonged to lost Oriel. Something in me shifted and settled, the rightness of it glowing with surety. The king loved the land; the land didn't necessarily love him back. But it did belong to him, and Lia was mine.

She'd been holding her injured hand carefully away, the twig fingers flexing like she wanted to touch me with them. I kissed her, feeling her open to my mouth, then touched my hand to the regrowing one. She tensed, pausing in her lush pleasuring.

"Does it hurt?" I asked, pulling back to see her face.

"No." She searched my eyes. "You don't mind?"

"Not at all." We both turned our heads to watch as I threaded my fingers with the slender twigs of hers. They felt both delicate and strong, like the new limbs of a willow tree. Our hands joined, I brought them closer, brushing one of the slender fronds with a kiss. It smelled green, the leafy scent that was Lia. "I love all of you," I told her.

She smiled and drew me into a kiss, opening like a blossom, heated and redolent of life. Much later, as I drifted into sleep, I realized the storm no longer howled.

7

When I woke, it was all at once, and I felt singingly alive. Con, his big body lax in exhausted slumber, lay curled around me, protecting me even in sleep. Bloodstains dotted the white sheets like crushed roses, the color vivid in the bright late-afternoon sunshine leaking through the cracks in the boards over the windows.

Sunshine. The storm had abated, at last heeding my wishes. That boded well for me getting a grip on Calanthe again. She still roared in the background of my mind but no longer felt entirely beyond my control. I could separate myself from Her again—a relief as visceral as being released from her grinding hunger. I still wasn't sure how to pacify Her, or if I even could. Anure's wizards, too, nibbled at Calanthe's wards, searching for the orchid ring. I could feel their magic needles, poking at Her. I'd have to destroy them before they devoured me.

At least I felt finally able to face the possibility of trying.

All thanks to Con and his extraordinary actions. I studied his face, so much younger-looking in sleep. He'd come after me in Yekpehr, saved my life at least twice, declared his love for me—and shown it in so many ways. My heart wrung itself, full of so many raw emotions. As always,

Con had a way of turning everything upside down. I didn't know what to do about him.

But I did know I needed to get up and save my realm—if possible—so first things first.

Moving as silently as I could, I eased myself from his embrace, sliding out of the bed. I was so focused on not waking Con that I was standing before I thought to test my legs. They held me easily, vitality coursing through my veins. The orchid rustled in agreement, and even my twig fingers looked thicker, the vine webbing from the orchid's band weaving through the lower part, forming a hand, the hint of a palm.

You are a creation of human flesh, the floral body of Calanthe, and an extension of the goddess. Ambrose had pinpointed a truth I'd only guessed at, perhaps half remembered. Had my father even known the origin of the infant crown princess the priestesses gave into his care? I thought not. He'd only known to protect me, to hide me from the sight of those who'd know me for what I was.

And now the wizards knew perhaps more than I knew about myself. I would have to change that. At least I no longer needed to hide.

My sleeping gown was spattered with blood—and no faithful lady-in-waiting had left a robe for me. So I put on Con's black shirt, large enough on me to fall to my knees. When I reached the door, I discovered how we'd slept so long unbothered, and slid open the bolt. Con didn't stir, so I eased open the door and slipped out. He'd been nearly gaunt with exhaustion, and hopefully would sleep himself out.

I padded silently on the thick carpets, seeing my beautifully appointed rooms as if for the first time. The windows out here weren't boarded over, and flower-scented breezes wafted in filled with sunshine and birdsong, blue skies beyond. The graceful architecture, the works of art on the walls and gleaming in niches, all of it seemed new. When had I last truly looked at any of it? I would now. Pausing, I smoothed my fingertips over a marble sculpture of a bird taking flight. Drawn by a painting of a shrouded woman with a snake's skeleton at her feet, I admired that, too.

I'd been granted a reprieve, a second chance. I'd returned to my home, my sanctuary and the refuge of so many. I *would* find a way to save Calanthe, and everything and everyone on Her.

When I opened the door into the outer sitting room, Vesno spotted me first, the wolfhound lifting his head from an afternoon drowse. He bounded for me, waking Sondra who'd been draped over a sofa—boots on and sword in hand, an ugly walking stick lying on the floor beside her. She was on her feet nearly as fast as the dog, lowering her sword soon after and gaping at me.

Ibolya dashed in from an adjoining chamber, most indecorously, skirts lifted high to allow herself to run. She slid to an astonished stop, then threw herself at my feet, pressing her forehead to them. I coaxed Vesno to the side—not easy, as he seemed determined to lick me everywhere—and Sondra came over to urge the wolfhound away.

I crouched down, placed my hands on Ibolya's shoulders. She was sobbing, shaking with it. "Your Highness," she gasped. "I—I apologize. I was so afraid."

"But look," I said, gathering my poise around me as if I wore my crown and full regalia, "here I am. All is well. Or will be," I amended.

She lifted her tear-streaked face and nodded. "So many terrible things have happened, Your Highness. Do You truly think it will be right again?"

"Yes," I told her with all the confidence she required

of her queen. "I'll see to it. But first, I need to bathe and dress, hmm?"

"Oh, blessed Ejarat, what am I thinking?" She scrambled to her feet, assisting me to rise at the same time, then curtsied. "Allow me to summon a bath for You." She curtsied again, paused as if tempted to do so yet another time, then hurried out to take care of it.

"It was hard on her," Sondra said, sitting again on her sofa, rubbing Vesno's ears, "being locked out all this time. Especially after Conrí acted so crazed, waving that knife around and kicking everyone out. I did manage to talk them out of knocking the door down. You're welcome."

"How long has it been?"

"A little over eighteen hours. But hey, You look considerably less like a corpse now."

"Thank you, Lady Sondra. I wish I could say the same for you," I replied with a lift of my nose.

She snorted, surveying her bedraggled appearance. "Yeah, holding vigil and all. Maybe I'll go have a bath now, too." She stood and cast a glance in the direction of the bedroom. "Conrí *is* still alive, also?"

"Yes. Sleeping hard. I think he missed a lot of sleep."

"No doubt. He was out of his mind worrying about You."

She seemed to be asking a question, but I didn't have an answer, so I nodded. "Thank you, Sondra," I said instead, "for being there, in that place, with Me."

"I didn't exactly have any more choice than You did."

"Nevertheless, I appreciated your . . . companionship."

She gave me a crooked grin. "Is that what we're calling it?"

"For lack of a better term."

"Fair enough." She swept a gallant bow. "It was an honor. But let's not do it again, shall we?"

I had to laugh. "Agreed."

"Your Highness?" Ibolya, makeup repaired and composure restored, glided in. "Your bath is ready."

Sondra gave me a cheerful salute. "And I'm off to mine."

"One moment," I told Ibolya, and with a thought to Vesno, I took him to sit with Con, easing open the door to the bedchamber. Vesno, heeding my mental instructions, climbed gently onto the bed to lie next to Con, so he wouldn't wake alone.

Finding Ibolya in my bathing chamber, I shed Con's shirt, stepped into the steaming tub, and sank in, sighing at the bliss of hot water. It seemed so quiet, to bathe with only Ibolya there and no Morning Glory, none of my other ladies. Good thing I had no intention of donning my normal costume, as the two of us would never have been able to manage without more help.

"Does Your Highness have a preference in gowns today?" Ibolya asked, her thoughts clearly going in the same direction. "I have not yet sent for Lady Calla and the others, but I can."

"No, don't bother." I rolled my neck on the edge of the tub, watching her bustle about. "I'll be going to the temple as soon as possible."

"You will—I mean, we will, Your Highness?"

"Yes." To Calanthe's center, the wellspring and the vortex of Her power and the rapidly collapsing ties that bound Her to the physical world. I sensed them keenly now, as if my time away—the brutal ripping of my roots and blood-fueled grafting of myself back into Her—had made me consciously aware of what I'd always taken for granted. Now that I knew myself as a person away from Calanthe, I recognized where I ended and She began. Though it wasn't a clear demarcation, so perhaps grafting was the wrong analogy. *An extension of the goddess.*

Our connection flowed in a circle, and I was both part of Calanthe and my own person.

"Yes," I said again, recalling myself from riddles I might never fully resolve, "I must travel to the temple immediately."

"Surely not today, Your Highness?"

"The sooner the better. I have to address the problems with Calanthe, and I can't do it from here."

"Will a night make that much difference, Your Highness? It will be sunset in another hour or so. And You've only just arisen from Your sickbed and a terrible trial. You look so much better, but . . . perhaps go a bit slowly?"

She had a point. "Tomorrow morning, then. Tonight I'll show Myself to the court." If Ibolya had been that distressed at thinking me dead, when she had better reason to hope than many, then I needed to reassure everyone. Calanthe's thrashing wouldn't be helped by the people's panic.

"Conrí held court yesterday and let it be known that Your Highness had returned to the palace."

"Ah." That's right—even in my near-death delirium I'd noticed his handsome clothing, wondering if he'd appeared formally. Would wonders never cease. "I'll meet with Dearsley, too, do what I can to set things to rights. I'll require a gown, but not underpinnings. Something unstructured—no corset or other padding. I shall go as Myself."

"Of course, Your Highness," Ibolya murmured. "The black wig?"

"Did you bring it from Cradysica?" I asked, startled by the thought.

"Yes, Your Highness. None of Your things were damaged."

No, just me. *Don't think about it.*

"No wig," I declared. I intended to grow out my own hair—vines or flowers or sticks, or whatever it would be—and until then, I'd go bald proudly. *If I were You, I'd just wear my crown on my bald head and let the critics go fuck themselves,* Sondra had said. Unfortunately, I lacked a crown to put on my bald head, actually now quite fuzzy with soft green growth. I'd last seen the crown of Calanthe with my other jewels, tossed onto the heaps of treasure piled on the steps of Anure's obscene throne, as if he were a dragon of old, hoarding every bit of glitter and keeping it from the world. "We'll have to devise a crown."

"I have ideas, Your Highness."

"You always do."

Ibolya seemed unsurprised when I refused the body makeup. The patterns of petals, leaves, bark, and thorns shimmered over my skin in subtle counterpoint to the dramatic crimson-black of the gown Ibolya brought out. Scarlet as fresh roses—or new blood—the pleated gauzy silk fanned over my breasts from narrow straps that otherwise left my shoulders bare. A crisscross of silver-edged strips of silk gathered the fabric over my ribs and waist asymmetrically, cupping my hips on one side.

From there, panels of bloodred, sheer black, and crimson silk swirled around my legs, parting to my hips as I walked. Gauzier scarves in the same colors floated from one shoulder, balancing the asymmetry of the gown. The fine silk floated around me like a mist of sunset fire, backed by the surcease of night. Yes, it suited my mood exactly. Perfect for someone arisen from the dead.

Ibolya did my makeup in rose and charcoal, mild and smoky. We discussed my feathery, flowery lashes and brows at some length, and finally elected to emphasize their natural colors in deeper shades of the same. We decided against false lashes, and added only a few small jewels, mostly as a nod to what my people expected to see.

"We just need jewelry and something of a crown," Ibolya mused. "Let me—"

The door flew open, a shirtless Con glowering in the doorway, barefoot and wearing only his black leather pants, rock hammer in his hands. Vesno charged past him, far more cheerful, blazing a joyful circle around me and then setting to sniffing out every corner.

"Really, Conrí." I lifted a brow. "Must you?"

His snarling gaze raked me, then traveled over me again. "You're dressed."

"Indeed. Preferable when one makes public appearances."

He blinked at me, and I decided he wasn't up to being teased yet. "I thought you'd sleep longer," I said more gently. He clearly still needed it, judging by the shadows under his eyes. The dried blood flaking off his chest and the angry-looking wound at his throat didn't help. Bruises radiated from it where I'd sucked, drawing his blood as I rode him through that astonishing interlude. Feeling my cheeks heat with an unaccustomed blush, I tore my gaze away.

He snorted, then shook his head. Dragged his fingers through his wildly mussed hair. "I woke up alone." He sagged a little, looking around at the tub still waiting to be emptied, at Ibolya's discreetly retreating back as she slipped out of the room.

"I left Vesno to keep you company."

At the sound of his name, the wolfhound trotted over, nudging his head under Con's hand and gazing at him with rapt adoration. Con ruffled the dog's ears. "Yes. Thank you for that. When I saw you were gone, I . . . I overreacted."

I held out my good hand to him. After a moment's

hesitation, he came over and threaded his fingers through mine. "I'm fine, Con."

"It might take me a while to feel confident in that," he confessed.

For me, too. "I'm feeling like Myself again—and there's a great deal that needs My attention."

He grimaced ruefully. "There is. There's a lot of news I should probably tell you."

"Yes, I understand you held court the other day."

Narrowing his gaze, he assessed me. "Are you pissed about that?"

I laughed, squeezed his hand, and let go. Ibolya had set out several pairs of heels for me, and I gestured to them. "Which ones, do you think?"

"Stand up and let me see," he answered, surprising me when I'd expected a gruff disinterest.

Bemused, I stood, then turned when he circled a finger. "No wig?" he asked.

"You said I didn't need to?" I sighed at myself for making it a question, but it still felt odd to go without that weight, that layer of armor that provided protection and disguise. Checking myself in the mirror, I ran my good hand over the soft shoots of spring colors. "I told Ibolya not to shave it, but she still can."

"No, don't." Con put his hands on my bare shoulders, standing behind me, easily looking over my head with me barefoot. He made a darkly masculine frame for my colorful and slender form. The flesh-and-blood man to my . . . exotic orchid self. He pressed a kiss to my scalp. "I meant it when I said you should let it grow."

"It will be very strange," I warned him.

"Spectacular and unique," he corrected with a grin. Then he bent and picked up a pair of shoes. "These."

They were not the ones I would've picked. Unobtrusive, with narrow straps nearly the same shade as my skin, only the stiletto heels themselves were striking, a gleaming deep crimson that looked nearly black.

"They'll show off your gorgeous legs," Con explained, kneeling to slip one onto my foot, "and that dress. Which is something, by the way."

Well pleased with Con's sincere, if gruff compliment, I stepped into the shoe, balancing myself on his broad, naked shoulders while he deftly laced the straps and buckled them, then repeated the process with the other heel. Taking a moment, he rubbed a thumb over my bare toes and glanced up at me. "Nothing to cover your toes, either?"

"No. Nor My nails. It seemed silly with this." I flicked my twig fingers, which still moved more like a wooden doll's than human ones. "We thought about trying a glove, but that would just look odd and not really hide anything anyway."

Nodding, he stroked his rough hands up my calves to my thighs under the filmy skirts. "If you're going to show yourself as you are, then do it all the way."

"I was thinking that there's no point in hiding My nature any longer," I ventured.

He shook his head in grim agreement. "Hiding won't do either of us any good."

"What will?"

He considered me. "I think we have to be prepared to fight." He said it with some hesitation, the knowledge that we'd argued bitterly about this before in his eyes. Along with guilt that his winning that argument had led to disaster.

"I think we have no choice," I agreed, smiling at the ghost of surprise crossing his face. "I can acknowledge

now that we never did have a choice. And no, Conrí, I'm
not at all pissed that you held court. I'm grateful that you
handled things when I could not. It's a great comfort to Me
to know that . . ." So much I couldn't quite put into words.
That I couldn't afford to say aloud. "That I'm not alone in
this."

A crooked smile lifted one side of his mouth, and he
caressed my cheek with a callused knuckle. "Not as long
as I'm alive."

Uneasy, well aware I couldn't make a similar promise,
not with the choices that lay ahead of us, I touched a finger
to the wound in his throat. He didn't flinch, exactly, but
definitely twitched. "Does this pain you?"

"Nope."

"Liar," I said softly, then took up one wrist to examine,
then the other. "These look much better."

"The neck one got chewed on more," he replied with
an intimate rumble, the heated look in his eyes and slow
smile reminding me again of that incandescent sex, unlike
anything I'd imagined, much less experienced. "Lia—are
you blushing?"

I resisted the urge to clap my hands to my warming
cheeks. A great disadvantage of wearing only light makeup.
The heavier creams would've hidden such a traitorous response. "Obviously not, as I never blush."

"Obviously not," he agreed with a widening grin and
brushed his fingers over the blush, cupping my cheek.
"If we're making an appearance, I should probably get
dressed, too."

I smiled and kissed his finger, beyond glad that he
planned to go with me to face the wilds of my frantic
courtiers. "You could always go shirtless," I said, sliding
my palm over his impressive chest. "I went bare-breasted
to our wedding ball, after all."

"As if I could forget. I thought my brains might fall out of my skull." He feathered his fingers down my jaw and throat, the tenderness in the gesture at odds with the fierce desire in his eyes. The fire burned hotter than ever between us, but born of something different now. Before it had flared like this when we fought. Now it seemed to come from a deeper place, something raw and needy. "Lia," he breathed. "I—I'm so happy to have you back." He grimaced, shaking his head. "That's not what I mean. I wish I had better words for you."

"It's all right, Con," I whispered. I knew what words he'd swallowed back. I wished that I knew how to handle the tumult of emotions he stirred in me, but I didn't.

"Shirtless would be easier, but I think I'll wear actual clothes," he said, breaking the spell. "Preferable when one makes public appearances," he added in a posh accent completely incompatible with his hoarse voice.

"I do *not* sound like that."

"Sometimes you do," he said, as if confiding a secret.

I swatted at him, and he caught my hand, laughing.

"Your Highness, Conrí, I beg Your pardon," Ibolya said, carrying a chest into the room, quite heavy by the look of it. Con immediately stepped to relieve her of it, raising his brows as he tested the considerable weight, then eyed Ibolya's slight frame. She smiled sunnily at him. "Your Highness, there's something here that might work for a crown. I'll return in a moment."

"A crown?" Con frowned.

"Anure kept Mine," I said as Con set the chest on the vanity under the mirror. The dress swirled and flamed around me as I walked to it, the heels making me feel tall and powerful. Most satisfying.

"I'm sorry, Lia." Con looked stricken. "I didn't think about your crown."

"Why would you?" I opened the chest, which was cleverly wrought with springs, the many trays within spiraling open to display their glittering treasures.

"I could've gotten it for you."

"The way I heard it, you were occupied with rescuing Sondra, retrieving My corpse, and smuggling the lot of us out of Yekpehr."

"Agatha, too." He raised his brows when I looked up sharply. "Maybe you don't remember that bit."

I frowned, thinking. Oh yes, Agatha had been on the *Last Resort.* "Agatha," I said, musing over that oddity.

"She'd been a prisoner—or a servant—or both, at Yekpehr before. She volunteered to guide me, use her contacts there to locate you. I couldn't have found you without her help."

The memory pieces fell together into a full picture. "One of her contacts was Rhéiane."

Con nodded, watching me carefully.

"You're sure it's *your* Rhéiane?"

"It's not a common name, but no—how can I be sure?"

"How indeed," I murmured, turning my gaze to the glittering jewels but not seeing them as I processed the implications. "We never saw anyone else after that initial audience. Sondra and I were always locked in our prison chamber or I was—" My heart clenched. Ah. Apparently I wasn't so recovered as to be able to speak *those* words.

Con's fingers trailed down the exposed skin of my back. "I know," he said, more hoarse than usual. "Sondra told me."

I nodded. Swallowed. Focused on the jewels, though they made a glittering blur.

"I can't ignore the possibility that it's her," Con continued matter-of-factly, though his voice was rough. "You were the one to speculate that the Imperial Toad is holding royals hostage to maintain control of their lands. Even before Cradysica, you thought Anure might have my sister."

More than speculated, I'd known it must be the case. The information from my spies had been too consistent for false rumor, and my intuition too certain. "You'll be wanting to go back for her," I said, marveling at how well I modulated my tone to sound as if we discussed plans to walk in the garden.

"I—" He cleared his throat and traced my spine with one finger. "I think I have to."

I nodded. Of course he had to.

"You don't have to think about it, though," he said, still tracing my spine, up and down. "I can only imagine how difficult that is for you." He was right. The very thought of Con going to Yekpehr brought back the stink of the burning walls, the sulfur sticking in my throat, the fetid taste of despair and metallic shiver of terror and pain. "Lia?"

"I'm fine." I even managed to make it sound like not a lie. Blindly, through the blur of unshed tears, I picked up something pure and glittering with white light. "I plan to go to the temple tomorrow morning. When will you leave for Yekpehr?"

"Not yet. I'll go with you to the temple."

I glanced up at him, surprised, unbearably relieved. "You will?"

"I wouldn't leave you to face that alone." He hesitated. "You remember that Tertulyn is there?"

"Of course," I replied tartly. "I'm not an imbecile."

"No, you're not." His grin at my attitude faded. "You should know that we found her in the aftermath of Cradysica, on one of Anure's ships."

That shouldn't sting. I'd accustomed myself to the likelihood of Tertulyn's betrayal. And I'd clearly suffered far worse wounds in the interim, physical and emotional. Amazing that I could still feel any pain on top of the rest. "I'm surprised you didn't kill her."

"I wanted to," he replied with blunt honesty. "I would have, but Calla and your other ladies begged me to spare her life. Besides, it would've been like putting down a rabid dog. Tertulyn is . . . She's not right in the head."

"How so?"

"Some kind of magic. Nobody knows. She can barely speak, can't care for herself."

"I see. I'll handle it." Though how? With a mental sigh, I added it to my list of problems to solve.

"Tomorrow is soon enough." Tugging the sparkly crown from my hands, Con held it up. "This is pretty."

It was. Formed of gold instead of silver and platinum, this crown nevertheless had a lighter look. A twelve-pointed sunburst sat at the apex, glittering with diamonds. Beneath it, a crescent curved upward, like Ejarat cradling and receiving Sawehl's brilliant light. A star flanked either side of the crescent, all of it shining with the pure clarity of perfect diamonds. It spoke less of Calanthe than of all the world, of the land flourishing under the benevolent fire of the sun and stars.

"It is pretty," I echoed Con with a teasing smile, "but does it go with My gown?"

He didn't tease back, turning it in his big hands, unexpectedly grave. With an almost reverent mien, he raised it and fitted it gently onto my head, the metal cool but warming rapidly. "I'd say it goes with the woman. It's perfect for you."

Looking in the mirror to check the position, I found

it needed no adjusting. A perfect fit, indeed, as if it had been made for me. Ibolya with her finely honed timing returned then and clasped her hands at the sight, smiling in triumph.

"Where did you find this?" I asked her.

She shrugged a little. "It must've arrived in a smuggled shipment at some point, Your Highness. It's been in storage for some time, I believe."

Ah. A treasure hidden from Anure's looting, painstakingly transferred from hand to hand until it found refuge on Calanthe, as so many works of art—and the people who created them—had over the years. Who knew what realm it had once belonged to, whose brow it had once graced. Likely we would never know.

I took it as an omen, however, of what I needed to do.

As much as I'd tried to cling to a relatively small responsibility—the island I'd been born of and had sworn to die for—the many forgotten and orphaned lands had still cried to me in the night. I *had* died for Calanthe, and now I must face that I couldn't pretend to owing a duty only to my realm. All the kingdoms suffered and slowly died under Anure's uncaring, rapacious rule. Con and I were the only ones free to help them, so help them we would.

"So," I said, lifting my eyes from the crown to Con's intent gaze, "any plan we devise to rescue your sister should include rescuing all of them."

"That . . . we devise? Lia, you don't have to—"

"I want to. I can't go with you, but you'll let Me help you plan this one."

He capitulated immediately, surprising me. "I would be grateful for your help. But . . . all of who?"

"All of the captive rulers," I explained patiently. "Anure

can't be allowed to keep them captive any longer. This has gone on far too long already."

He studied me, clearly bemused. "I didn't realize we'd been allowing it."

"We haven't stopped it, either. It's time we did."

"Oh." His mouth quirked in a half smile then went serious. "It won't be easy."

"No, but we can do it."

"How do you know?"

"You told Me," I replied with just a bit of impatience. I quoted, "*Take the Tower of the Sun, Claim the hand that wears the Abiding Ring, And the empire falls.* We're two-thirds of the way there. We're going to bring down this cursed government before it grows even more powerful, more depraved, and destructive enough to take the world down. And now I see the way to doing it."

"You do?" He still seemed bemused, struggling to wrap his head around me not resisting him every step of the way, perhaps.

"Yes. All this time, I've played Anure's game, and I paid the price."

He winced. "Lia, I'm so—"

"That's not what I mean," I said, cutting off his apology. "*We* paid the price. Because Anure's been a step ahead of us all along."

"He played me at Cradysica," Con admitted, folding his arms. "He knew exactly how to do it."

I nodded. "But now I know how to defeat him. We're going to use what *he* cares about to undermine his grip on the empire."

Con shook his head. "That's what makes the Imperial Toad such a difficult foe. He cares about nothing. I tried to be like that, and I couldn't do it." His gaze burned into me as he again swallowed back the words. That I hadn't reciprocated, couldn't tell him I loved him in return, lay between us, huge and invisible, with sharp edges I had to avoid, lest I carelessly cut either of us.

"That's not true," I said, using the deflection ruthlessly. "Anure *does* care about something. One thing."

"The land," Ibolya murmured, and I nodded at her.

"Yes. Anure cares about power, and control, and possession. It's all he lives for." I'd looked into his florid face and soulless, empty gaze, and known it. "He's a man so bereft of anything meaningful in his life that he hoards everything he can grasp, trying to fill that pit inside. The land gives him some of that, so he cares about the one thing that allows him to keep it."

Con stared at me with dawning understanding. "The captive royals."

"Precisely. If we liberate them, then we take away Anure's power."

"*And the empire falls,*" he breathed. Then he frowned. "I hate to mention it, but what about his wizards?"

"I'm working on that," I said with cool poise that covered the quaking fear in my heart. "Suffice to say that they must be dealt with."

"You make it sound easy," he commented, expression grave and not in the least fooled by my bravado.

"Not easy, no. But necessary."

Abruptly, he grinned. "Well, you know me—I love nothing better than a potentially catastrophic plan."

I rolled my eyes at him but couldn't help the smile. "If we succeed, we'll also have to restore the rulers to their lands," I pointed out. "It won't do the world any good if we destroy the empire and leave nothing in its place."

"Restore the lands," he mused with a hint of awe.

"Restore Oriel." The cautious, wary hope flickered in his face that he could perhaps reclaim the realm he'd been ripped from. A feeling I now knew well. Con hadn't been king, so he hadn't experienced the same level of profound loss as I had in being bereft of Calanthe, but part of him—the intuitive king in him—longed for that connection. More, I wanted that for him.

The consuming love I felt for him swelled in me, pressing to be spoken, but I pushed the words down with all the ruthlessness I'd practiced all these long, lonely years. For if the Rhéiane at Yekpehr wasn't his sister, or, even more likely, if it was and she'd suffered too greatly, was too far gone to be recovered, then Con would have to return to Oriel and take his place there as king. Even if Rhéiane could be recovered, he would have to do that. He was Conrí, rightful king of Oriel, and everything in him would long to make that a reality.

Con couldn't be king of both Oriel and Calanthe. If we managed to defeat Anure and free the royals, then there would be years of rebuilding. I couldn't leave Calanthe again, and Con couldn't stay here and let Oriel go to dust when his realm could be saved.

It was meant to be that our marriage bonds had dissolved. I could see that clearly now, also. All part of the cascade of the prophecy. The marriage had served its purpose—if it had even been needed in the first place, since Con had claimed my hand regardless—and we'd both eventually go our own ways. I loved Con with all my heart, and fiercely enough to spare him the agony of deciding between his love for me and his true destiny. If he believed I didn't love him, he'd feel better about choosing Oriel.

That choice would be inevitable for us both. After all, kings and queens were born to sacrifice themselves for the land. The form that sacrifice took wasn't always to bleed their lives away.

Sometimes the sacrifice required far more lasting suffering than mere death.

8

Lia dazzled them, naturally. She'd elected not to forewarn the court and palace at large of her plan to make an appearance. She wanted to simply appear, as if she'd never forsaken her duties as their queen.

No fanfare, no heartfelt welcome speeches that sound like hastily rewritten memorials, she'd said crisply.

I knew what she hadn't said—that she feared she might not have the stamina to withstand a formal affair she couldn't easily vanish from. Though her recovery from where she'd been the day before—or, far worse, the day before that—was remarkable, she was still far too thin, her skin pale and translucent, haunted shadows in her startlingly vivid eyes.

She also had to know what an impact her changed costume would have. No more hiding for her, though the revelation might be shocking to some. Even when she'd appeared greatly altered after our wedding, she'd still been in makeup and the wig of black hair, her eyes magically disguised to look human. No longer.

Court had adjourned for the day, but the people of the palace lingered to exclaim over the vistas revealed as workers removed the boards from the windows and arched galleries, the golden evening light streaming in. Enjoying the balmy weather, people filled the battered gardens and damp salons, breaking out the wine and liquor, nibbling on dainty delights as they exchanged the most valuable currency on Calanthe: gossip.

Also, despite Lia's determination to avoid a formal celebration, the news of her return and recovery had clearly run like wildfire ahead of us. Between her reappearance and the storm breaking, a vast party seemed to be in the making.

As I escorted Lia—Ibolya demurely trailing in our wake and Sondra stalking not at all demurely, but more or less gracefully at the rear—I watched as people glanced our way, then did a double take. First shocked into bobble-eyed silence, they then burst into whispers that grew rapidly to louder exclamations, the ripples widening out until more people came literally running to see.

Lia observed it, too, her expression smooth and remote, but her keen mind nearly audible as she filed away how each person reacted—both initially and when they thought better of it.

She graciously accepted their greetings and well wishes, ignored their subtle inquiries about her health—and their attempts to get a good look at her regenerating hand—and crisply cut those bold enough to ask blatant questions or launch into petitions. Only when Lord Dearsley approached, spine straight and chin high, the same young man escorting him with a solid grip, did Lia truly smile.

Slipping her arm from mine—as she would only use her good hand with me, even though I kept telling her the twig hand, as she called it, didn't bother me—she let Dearsley take her hand in both of his. He bent over it, kissing the back with reverence, a fine tremor running through him. When he straightened, tears brightened his pale eyes.

"Your Highness, we celebrate Your return to Your rightful place."

"Thank you, Dearsley," she murmured. "I am overjoyed to be back where I belong, and forever grateful to Conrí for all his service."

I nearly choked at the layered meaning there, and she cast me a mildly curious glance through her lashes. Her innocent expression might've fooled me into thinking I was the one with the dirty mind, if her eyes hadn't sparkled with mischief. Now that I knew her tells, I could detect her wicked humor at work. Not that I had much hope of combating it.

"The storm has passed," Dearsley said, waving at the clear skies, "and Calanthe is . . . ?" He trailed off delicately.

She shook her head minutely. "I must travel to the temple in the morning, to retrieve My ladies and complete a few tasks I left undone." Her face a mask of polite regret, she fed Dearsley the proper cues.

"Ah yes." He nodded vigorously, half bowing over the hand he still held, clutching her in his palpable relief. "All else can wait for Your Highness to tend to Mother Calanthe."

"Not all," she corrected. "Conrí has briefed Me on the situation, and I know it's evening, but I'd like to sit down with you—perhaps in an hour?—to discuss and review everything."

"I'm at Your Highness's disposal, naturally."

The news spread through the people lingering nearby, though they pretended to be conducting their own conversations rather than shamelessly eavesdropping. A few even scribbled notes and handed them to fancily dressed children who took off running. Hopefully we wouldn't face a mob of her admiring people at the temple.

Dearsley departed, promising to meet in an hour, and we moved on.

"Where to next?" I asked under my breath.

"I'd like to take a stroll in My gardens," she replied as we entered the lavish, though soggy, gardens.

"Stroll?" I echoed, wondering if I could get her to sit down somewhere. She looked paler than she had, but I doubted she'd take the suggestion to rest very well.

"Amble, Conrí," she replied in a dry tone. "It means to walk slowly, without particular direction."

"I know what it means," I growled, though without rancor. If she felt well enough to needle me, then that was a good sign. "I just wondered what your goal is."

She turned down a curving path that glowed with its own light. Night was falling swiftly and fully, as it did on Calanthe, but lanterns hung in the trees, small starry lights shone sprinkled over shrubs, and people reclined around firepits in jeweled colors, or enjoyed parties in lamplit gazebos, wine and food spilling over the tables. They raised glasses to their queen, cheering her, and she inclined her head, though not waving as she would've before. Instead she kept her twig hand entangled in the shrouds of her filmy skirts.

"Must I have a goal?"

"You always do. Besides, I don't see you putting off Dearsley just to stroll in the gardens."

She laughed, and the warm sound of true amusement from her warmed me like a kiss. "To see and be seen," she murmured. "Nothing more complicated than that."

"Your Highness!" Lord Percy sashayed in our direction, arm linked through Brenda's, both beaming. Percy wore a shirt like mine, though in white, and with a vest embroidered lavishly with flowers that matched the full skirt billowing beneath. In contrast, Brenda seemed to be in uniform, though of no military or guard of any kingdom that had ever existed. The top looked like fanciful chain mail, made of gold scales like a dragon would have, with metallic spikes that curled up to frame her square jaw and short silver hair.

They both bowed from the waist, Percy with a lavish flutter of his green-and-gold nails. "I must say, Your Highness, while it's delightful to see You looking so, well, *alive*, I do believe Your new fashion statement has already caused a great deal of difficulty." He cocked his head, eyeing Lia's revealing gown with envy. "We don't all have the figure to carry off the sexy naiad thing."

Brenda huffed out a short breath. "Wear what you want to, Percy. It isn't that fucking hard."

"Well," he simpered, flipping open a fan painted with the same huge flowers as on his skirt, "not yet. But it will be! Ooh, stop," he exclaimed when she elbowed him sharply. Then he leaned in, speaking behind the fan. "I absolutely forgive you two for what you did to my life raft. Kara darling is adding a few extras during the repairs, to make up for it."

To my surprise, Kara appeared then, wearing somber clothing but carrying a colorful cocktail. He lifted it in a silent toast, acknowledging us, a slight smile on his thin lips. Sondra eased around us, taking his elbow to talk with him quietly.

"So," Brenda interjected, "any further initiatives we should know about?"

Lia glanced at me expectantly. Great. How was I supposed to know what Lia wanted me to keep secret? Though I guessed she wouldn't leave it to me if she thought I'd screw it up.

Or she trusted me. The thought hit me with more force than I could've imagined. She'd made it clear, but I just hadn't quite gotten it through my thick skull, that we'd be planning this venture together. Lia trusted me to say what I needed to. It shouldn't have hit me so hard, but it did. Lia believed in me. Even now, when she had less reason than ever. I put my hand over hers on my arm and squeezed lightly, rewarded by the warmth in her gaze.

"There will be something," I told them, catching and holding Kara and Sondra's eyes, too, so they sidled closer. "Her Highness needs to visit a temple first, but upon our return, we'll need a strategy."

"Any hints?" Percy yawned dramatically, fluttering his fan over his mouth. "A riddle, perhaps, to enliven the otherwise dull evenings."

I didn't bother glancing around at the elaborate festivities. The oppressed people outside of Calanthe would likely give anything to savor just one of Percy's dull evenings. We all had our masks, I figured, and Percy's pose of frivolous boredom hadn't fooled me for long.

"Is Agatha around?" I asked.

Brenda and Percy exchanged interested glances, and Percy snapped his jeweled nails. A young man wearing only a strategically placed garland dashed up and kissed Percy's hand. At Percy's whisper, he trotted off again— his naked behind twitching and gleaming with oil.

"It's after hours," Lia murmured to me. "While we're not fully in the Night Court, the lines become . . . blurred."

I yanked my attention back, realizing I'd been staring in shock. That explained a great deal. I'd known about the nighttime revels at Lia's palace, in theory, but hadn't witnessed them. Clearly I needed to recalibrate my head to Calanthe's excesses, even more strange to my eye after the starkness of Yekpehr. And if it felt that way to me, after being in Anure's fortress only a few hours, what was Lia going through?

I studied her face, still turned up to me, and saw the acknowledgment there. "It's good to see your people happy and enjoying the delights of Calanthe," I said, and she smiled. A soft, closed-lipped smile with sadness in it, but also gratitude, maybe.

Agatha drifted up on the half-naked guy's arm. Kissing her cheek, he handed her over to Percy with a saucy wink. "Your Highness." Agatha curtsied. Wrapped in a shawl as usual, Agatha nevertheless looked dressed up, too. She wore flowers in her hair, and the shawl gleamed like peacock feathers.

"I haven't thanked you yet, Lady Agatha," Lia said, "for your enormous service to Me."

Agatha looked anywhere but at us. "A small favor compared with all Your Highness has done for me and mine."

"I think we both know it was no small favor," Lia replied gently, but she let it go, glancing at me again.

I weighed what to say. "After Lia and I return from the temple, we'll meet to thrash out a plan, but to give yourselves time to think: I'm going back for what was left behind."

Percy fanned himself, his expression deadly serious, and Brenda put a supporting hand on Agatha's back. Sondra and Kara looked unsurprised but grim.

"For *all* of them," Lia clarified with an arched brow.

The group contemplated that. Brenda snagged a short glass of amber liquid from a passing serving girl—also wearing nothing more than some fluttering blossoms— and drank it in one gulp. "Do we have any idea how many people that might be?" she asked, turning the empty glass with blunt fingers, glancing obliquely at Agatha.

"I don't, not exactly," Agatha said in a clear, thin voice, drawing her peacock feathers around her as she spoke, though the tropical night remained warm, even stifling in these gardens sheltered from the coastal breezes and lit with so many fires. "I don't know if anyone but *he* knows how many there are. People die," she added bleakly. "And he moves them around frequently, keeping them divided."

Hmm. I'd been picturing royal prisoners all gathered in one big cell, but I could see how that kind of thing wouldn't work long-term. And Anure would have to be sure they didn't conspire. Even beaten and broken people begin talking to one another after a while, devising impossible plans to escape from terrible captivity. I should know. "Agatha," I said slowly, hoping I wouldn't spook her too much, "would you give us information on your contact there, so we can find out more?"

"Yes," she said, eyes darting to the shadows as if someone might leap out at her. "First let me see what I can find out."

"I'll help. We'll put our pretty heads together," Percy declared, drawing Agatha between him and Brenda. "It will be fun!"

Agatha gave him such a sour look that Brenda laughed. "Your Highness, Conrí—we have a table in the grape arbor. Would you care to join us for supper?"

"Alas," Lia replied immediately, "I have meetings. But Sondra and Ibolya can join you."

Sondra looked startled. "I couldn't."

Kara handed her the cocktail, looking relieved to be rid of it. "You could," he said darkly. "In fact, you really should."

She looked to me with a hint of panic. "Conrí and Her Highness need me."

"We don't," I replied immediately, and Lia squeezed my arm, a tremor of laughter running through her, though her composed expression showed nothing. "Go play with the other kids," I told Sondra, grinning when she gave me a betrayed scowl.

"I'll attend Conrí and Her Highness," Ibolya said with quiet assurance.

"No need," Lia declared airily. "You may be dismissed for the evening, Lady Ibolya."

"Your Highness, I—"

"Have been on duty all on your own, nonstop for days," Lia finished gently, but with the firmness of command. "Do as you wish, but you will not be needed by Me until morning."

Ibolya looked like she dearly wanted to argue, but she curtsied, inclining her head.

"Come on, Ibolya," Sondra said. "We've been dismissed by the grown-ups apparently. Why not get drunk with us? I bet you could stand a good drunk."

"I," Agatha put in pointedly, "will not be getting drunk."

"Nor I," Kara agreed in his gravelly voice.

"More for us!" Percy declared gaily, swishing over to take Ibolya's arm. "The inimitable Lady Sondra is so clever. You *must* drink with us, Lady Ibolya, and tell us all of Her Highness's secrets. Is the rumor true about that one little mole of Hers?"

"Oh, I couldn't possibly . . ." Ibolya protested as Percy led her briskly away.

"So, what was your purpose in sending them all away?" I asked as Lia surveyed the festivities.

She slid me a glance. "You seem to be under the impression that I have a reason for everything."

"Because you always do," I countered, "which is why I helped."

"Thank you for that." She chose her direction and started that way. I followed along, taking in the sights with fresh eyes. Much of the celebrating looked like the sort

I'd spied on as a boy in Oriel, but here and there I caught glimpses of more. Bare skin. Sensual dances. Alcoves lit only by candles with lurid movements flickering. So odd to go from discussing a dangerous rescue attempt to this level of frivolity.

But I supposed that very tension encapsulated all that was Calanthe.

"I wanted some time alone," Lia said, and I had to think back to what I'd asked her. "Just to look around. Without people . . . hovering."

"Should I go?" I slowed my steps, preparing to be dismissed also.

"No." She glanced at me with some surprise, eyes glittering with faceted light even in the shadowed gardens, and squeezed my arm. "You don't count."

As pleased as if she'd declared her undying love for me, I smiled at her. "I'm glad."

She took us down another path, one that skirted a large, shallow lake. Small boats glided aimlessly, brilliantly lit with lamps, and groups of people reclined on them, laughing, talking, and indulging. "That looks fun," I commented.

"Why, Conrí." She widened her eyes and made an O of her pretty mouth. "I do believe that's the first time I've ever heard you mention the concept of fun, much less an interest in a specific activity."

"That's not true," I grumbled. "Sex is fun, and I'm always interested in that."

"Besides sex. Name one thing. And don't you dare say killing people."

"I wasn't going to," I retorted, stung. Though, to be fair, that was the first thing that sprang to mind. Not fun, exactly, but satisfying to dispatch my enemies. All right, something else that sounded fun. What could I say?

"If you have to think about it this long . . ." Lia drawled teasingly.

"Fine. You have me." I scowled at her and she laughed, a happy sound that did me more good than any amount of fun would. "So *are* those dining boats fun?"

She glanced over, a thoughtful line between her brows. "I imagine so. I've never done it."

"You haven't?"

"No." She breathed a laugh. "You forget, wolf, that before you arrived to ravage Me, I was the virgin queen, the innocent and pure betrothed of the false emperor. If I attended evening events, they were formal affairs inside the palace salons. Afterward, I retired to My rooms, allowing this night garden to blossom."

I understood then. *See and be seen.* "That's what you're up to. You wanted to see the Night Court."

She glanced up at me, that new vulnerability in her face. It could be that it showed now, without the heavy makeup and jewels to mask her feelings, but I thought it was something more. The time in Yekpehr had torn away her shields and icy protections. Her body might be healing, but her heart and soul had yet to even scab over. I remembered that feeling very well—though by the time I'd escaped Vurgmun, my scar tissue was so thick I thought I'd never feel anything again.

"Is that foolish?" she asked. "I know there are pressing matters to deal with, but I thought—just until I meet with Dearsley—that I'd like to stroll the Night Court with you."

"Not foolish at all," I answered gravely, putting my hand over hers. "Though you deserve more than a measly hour to enjoy all that you created."

"I didn't create it. The traditions of Calanthe are very old."

"But it's all here because of you, because of the sacrifices you made."

She flinched, ever so slightly, when I mentioned sacrifice—if I hadn't been touching her, I'd have missed it—but she spoke before I could ask about it. "When I was . . . a prisoner, I couldn't feel Calanthe anymore. Did I tell you that already?"

I shook my head. "That must have been terrible for you."

"It was." Her soft voice held a world of dark pain. "I was bereft in every possible way. And I kept thinking about all the things I hadn't done."

"I think regrets are natural, when you're in a place like that." We'd rounded the lake and entered a shadowed maze of tall shrubs dripping with red and purple flowers. Even here the rocks in the path glowed, and some kind of lights inside the dense foliage illuminated them from the inside. But the glow didn't go far, even in the narrow aisles, giving the whole place a mysterious, even eerie cast. Above, the night sky shone with a glitter of stars, brighter than I'd ever seen them.

A cloaked couple passed us, bowing to their queen but moving on without addressing her, as everyone had started doing. Since we'd parted from our escort, no one had approached us, as if they somehow knew she was off duty.

"What did you regret," Lia asked, "when you were at Vurgmun?"

In the night-muffled maze of shadows, the subtle glows soothing, making it seem as if everything spoken inside its tall walls and under that starry sky would be kept forever secret, even held with a kind of compassion, I could think back—as I almost never did—to those days of toiling in the stinking, stifling mines. The boy I'd been there, the laborer I'd grown into—they were almost unrecognizable to me now. More desperate, savage animal than a person. A monster in a human skin.

Lia didn't need to hear that, with her own monstrosity so vividly haunting her at the moment. I'd recognized that skittish, wary way she'd looked at herself in the mirror, the way she kept the twig hand hidden in her skirts.

"You'll laugh," I said, "but—"

"I would never laugh," she interrupted, voice solemn as a vow in the shrouded silence, the only other sounds the crunch of our steps on the sparkling gravel and the distant music of gaiety.

"My father would've laughed then," I corrected, "but I regretted screwing off on my lessons. I was a bad kid, you know."

She did laugh then, but with affection. "This does not surprise Me."

"Yeah. Rhéiane . . . she was the scholar, but I drove our tutors crazy. And that's when they caught me. Half the time, I'd skip out on lessons and they couldn't find me."

"Not at all?"

"They didn't have your trick of seeing me through bats and bees," I teased her, and she tipped her shadowy profile in acknowledgment.

"Where would you hide?"

"See, that's where I was clever: I changed it up. Every day, someplace new. Unless I got caught in one of them, then I'd go back to it, because I figured they wouldn't expect me to return to a spot they knew about."

"Practicing your strategy even then."

"I guess." I hadn't thought of it that way. "But yeah, once I was in those mines, I regretted that I'd spent more time and effort avoiding lessons than I did learning anything. Sometimes, at night, in the bunks, people would talk about books they'd read, and music and art. Or they'd debate politics or argue about the composition and uses of vurgsten—and I realized I'd never have any of that. That I'd been too stubborn and willfully ignorant when I had all the world offered to me. Instead I'd be an uneducated oaf for the rest of my life."

We walked in silence for a few steps, Lia turning us at a four-way intersection where all the paths looked the same to me. "Do you know where you're going?" I asked.

"Metaphorically in My life, or literally in this maze?" she replied lightly.

"Now you sound like Ambrose."

"He has his moments. The answer is yes to both."

"You know where you're going in life?"

"That has never been a question for Me. My life belongs to Calanthe." Before I could say anything to that, she continued. "And there's a pattern to the turns in the maze, which everyone knows, even if they never come this way. The maze is here primarily to prevent anyone from stumbling into the heart of the Night Court by accident."

"Am I going to be shocked by what I see?" I blurted out, figuring I'd better ask.

She gave me an assessing look, eyes glowing with color, like the decorative lanterns did. "You might be. Do you mind? We can turn back."

"No way. Not after I just confessed to regretting not learning what I could when I had the opportunity." Besides, maybe I'd get some ideas about pleasing Lia. If I could figure out how to be a better lover for her, she might want to marry me again.

"You could still learn, you know," she offered. "It's never too late."

For a pained moment, I thought she'd read that thought—then I realized she meant reading and stuff. "I'd feel like an idiot." I could just picture it, sitting there like a hulk in some schoolroom, painstakingly reading aloud from a kid's book.

"You said you feel like an idiot most of the time anyway," she countered.

"Good point." We turned twice more, and I began to get the pattern now. "Two lefts, then a right, and repeat?"

"Exactly. Now you know."

"Not that I'd come this way without you."

"You could. The Night Court would—"

"I know, I know. You offered this before and I said I didn't want it. Quit bringing it up."

"No need to growl, grumpy bear."

I laughed, a hoarse, grating sound. "I thought I was a wolf."

"It changes moment-to-moment," she replied. "And you're not, you know."

"A wolf or a bear?"

"An idiot. You're a very intelligent man. One of the smartest men I've been privileged to meet."

That struck me dumb, for sure. And humbled me. "I can't even read a kid's book, Lia."

She shrugged, the movement wisping silk and the warm curve of her breast against my bare arm. "Intelligence is more than reading. Or knowing the composition of vurgsten. How many people have devised a way to infiltrate Yekpehr and rescue captives there?"

"I had a lot of help, and good luck."

"You have a talent for picking good people, and we make our own luck."

"You definitely sound like Ambrose now."

She laughed, a warm purr of delight. An archway ahead

glowed with brighter light streaming through blossoming vines hanging over the opening. "Are you ready?" she asked.

"As I'll ever be." When she gave me a dubious look, I patted her hand. "It'll be fun."

Laughing together, we parted the vines and stepped through into the Night Court of Calanthe.

9

Though I'd never before set foot into the Night Court, I'd heard plenty. My ladies had regaled me with salacious stories, partly to give context to gossip they imparted, partly to entertain and educate me. If worse had come to worst—and at that time we'd thought the worst would be me marrying Anure. Ha!—then no one wanted the queen of Calanthe to be ignorant of the basic elements of human sexuality.

As much as I'd teased Con about being shy about what we'd see, I surprised myself with a hint of nerves. Ridiculous, after what I'd been through, but I supposed I was as innocent in some ways as Con was. Both of us had been locked away from the normal explorations that young people engaged in. An unlikely pair of virtual virgins, we were—and out for an evening of pleasure for the first time in our lives.

"This is like a date," Con said with some surprise, and echoing my own thoughts.

"I suppose that's true. Though we've gone about it entirely backward."

He stopped in the arcade draped with white lilies and fairy lights, turning to face me. He held my good hand in both of his. "I would've wooed you, Lia, if I could have. If we'd been born to a different world."

"I've thought about that," I confessed. "That there's another time line where Anure never happened, and Crown Prince Conrí of Oriel came to Calanthe to court Me."

"You told me once that, in that time line, you might have said yes." He seemed to be holding his breath, this big, rough man with the soft heart, who fretted over being unable to read.

"I might have," I answered airily. "After I strung you along for a while, and made you suffer to prove your undying passion for Me."

"Seems like I've been doing exactly that," he said, not joking at all.

I sobered. "Unfortunately true. I shouldn't have made light of it."

"I don't mind. You know I love that wicked sense of humor of yours." He didn't move, his face very serious. "I love *you*, Lia."

My mouth went dry. "I know."

"Marry me again. We'll do it right this time."

At least he hadn't waited for me to say the words back to him. "I don't think there was anything wrong with the way we did it last time. Marriage bonds aren't meant to outlast death."

He shook that off. "I mean a big deal, with actual guests, and a celebration afterward."

"Guests like your sister?"

He cleared his throat, nodded. "Yeah. That would be nice."

Nice, perhaps—and an unlikely fantasy. "Let's talk about it after all this is done."

Giving me a long look, not at all deceived by my deflection, he turned and tucked my good hand in the crook of his arm, holding it there where I could feel the flex and play of his muscle, the heated skin, wiry hairs, and occasional rough scar. Real flesh and blood. Mine . . . for the moment.

"Your Highness, Conrí." Lady Delilah, queen—though not officially—of the Night Court, spoke to greet us. She'd been waiting at the entrance. No doubt her network had informed her the moment I stepped into the guardian maze. Delilah curtsied deeply, an impressive feat, given what she wore. Structured like a gown of the sort I used to wear regularly, this had the steel boning of a corset, panniers, and a bustle, all on display over her otherwise naked body. A fine network of chains draped from her shoulders, linking to rings through her prominent nipples, then gathered to a post through her belly button, creating a nipped-in waist. The chains draped artfully from the panniers and bustle, the fine silver links hiding nothing. The high-heeled black leather boots she wore rose to thigh-high, with higher silver tips at her hips, all framing her lush sex.

I could practically feel Con quiver with trying not to stare at her, and I somehow managed not to laugh.

"We of the Night Court are honored by Your visit," Delilah purred. "If You wish to participate, there are customs to observe. You will need to register passwords."

"Not necessary tonight," I told her.

She frowned, tapping the short whip she carried against her boot, stirring the skirt of chains so they sang with a dark whisper. "I suppose no one would fail to heed any word from Your Highness, regardless. But for Conrí . . ."

I ignored her snide tone. "We'll confine ourselves to observing," I replied, feeling Con relax under my hand.

"Then the only custom we ask You to observe is the privacy sign." She indicated an example nearby: a white ribbon painted with small images of closed eyes. "Otherwise You are welcome to go anywhere You wish."

I eyed her, appreciating that she "ruled" here and did it well—something I'd never interfered with, at first because I was only a girl, and later because it suited my strategic disguise—but I also found her ever-so-slightly disdainful of my authority. Understandable, I supposed, as she did govern her small realm with absolute discipline, and yet . . .

"I would certainly hope so," I replied in a deliberately and icily imperious tone, "as it is My palace, and My realm. The Night Court exists under My benevolent hand, as do all the people in it."

Delilah's face tightened, but she managed to incline her head in something like humble obedience. "Of course, my queen. I apologize if I misspoke. As You command, always."

After we'd gone a bit farther, Con chuckled, a deep, quiet sound. "Is it wrong that I love it when you do that?"

"What, pull rank?"

"Yes. You do it so effortlessly. Just ease the pins out from under them until they collapse without knowing how it happened. It's like you hit them with this magic queen power you have. Your own invisible rock hammer."

I laughed at the analogy, glancing up at him. He'd worn his crown, because I'd insisted, and Ibolya had combed and oiled his hair into a sleek shine, tying it at the base of his neck so it trailed down his back—unfettered since I'd also persuaded him to leave his very visible rock hammer behind. In his black sleeveless shirt and vest, his arms bulged with physical power, the black leather pants fitting tightly over his muscled thighs and narrow hips. Con might be oblivious to his own charisma, but no one else was.

Certainly not me—and he was something else I wanted to be sure to enjoy while I could.

We strolled along the path that wended through a wildly groomed garden as lushly overgrown as a jungle. Beds, sofas, and divans were strewn throughout, however, lending a sensual luxury that no jungle had ever seen. In other places, groups gathered in lit gazebos, enjoying food and wine as they did outside the Night Court, but here waited on by naked servants, who sometimes served as furniture or serving platters.

Beyond the next curve in the path, we came upon a startlingly familiar scene. A throne, so similar to mine it could be the very one, sat on a dais under a bower of orchids. A woman perched regally upon it, wearing a gown I recognized as a copy of one I'd worn several months ago. At least, I hoped it was a copy. It had been altered considerably, leaving her full breasts exposed, and the skirts divided over her bared and parted legs in a way I could personally vouch that particular gown would never do. She wore a black wig and heavy makeup, all decorated with flowers and jewels in close mimicry of my style, though fortunately the crown she had perched upon it was clearly a tinny fake. Deliberately so, I thought, as she wouldn't dare take the imitation too far. No orchid graced her left hand, either, though she did wear a pretty ring there.

A man groveled at her feet—licking the high and graceful heels she wore—and she allowed it, her expression imperiously bored. Con made a choking noise and I glanced at him with narrowed eyes. The sound caught the woman's attention, her eyes flying wide with chagrin as she recognized me. I shook my head slightly, smiling to let her know I wasn't offended. Or all that surprised, really, as I'd heard about similar scenes—and others far more extreme.

She inclined her head regally, really a perfect imitation

of me, and I smiled more widely. As we moved to go, I saw her carefully studying my current look, and I wondered how fast she'd come up with a copy.

"I like your fancy shoes," Con commented quietly, "but I don't see my way to licking them."

I smothered a laugh. "I'll grant an exemption. It's a specific fetish," I added, "and I've heard of that courtesan. She's apparently highly sought."

"Hmm. Does that bother you?"

"No. She's not the only one who dresses like Me. As with everything in the Night Court, it provides a much-needed outlet for . . ." I trailed off, unable to settle on the word I wanted.

"For the poor sods who can never hope to have the real thing," Con replied smugly, patting my hand, making me laugh in truth.

"You have your own imitators," I mentioned oh so casually.

He jumped as if I'd poked him with a needle, then glowered at me. "You're making that up."

"I am not. Shall we go look for them?"

"Definitely not." No hesitation there, his expression set. "Unless you want to," he conceded, though his lips twisted as if he'd tasted something bad.

"Not at all. That's for the poor sods who can never hope to have the real thing," I replied, enjoying his answering smile.

The next clearing held a large four-poster bed where a woman lay spread-eagled, blindfolded and tied to the posts with thick crimson ribbons. She moaned and twisted, her gold-painted lips gasping as she sobbed in frustration as two other women in half masks slowly licked her body. Her open sex showed wet and swollen, her nether mouth flushed as her hips pumped in helpless abandon. I glanced at Con to see if he liked what he saw, but he was staring steadfastly into the shadows, jaw tight and flexing.

"You can look," I told him, and he dropped his chin to meet my gaze, his golden eyes fulgent.

"I saw," he murmured, more roughly than usual.

"But you didn't like what you saw?"

"Are you asking if it made me hot?" His gaze went to my mouth. "It did. Does. But I'm not sure it should. It . . . seems like an invasion to look."

My darling Con. How he'd survived witnessing so many terrible things with such a tender conscience was beyond me. "She wants to be seen. It's part of the pleasure for her. Or she wouldn't be here."

He searched my face. "You're certain she's willing?"

Ah, it hadn't occurred to me that he'd worry about that, though it should have. I slid my hand down his forearm to twine my fingers with his. "Absolutely certain. Lady Delilah is many things, but she is unyielding in her rule of the Night Court. The passwords she mentioned? Everyone who enters must have a code phrase or gesture to indicate if they need to stop. That allows people to dance the line of power and helplessness without losing true autonomy."

He smiled, a bit rueful and a lot relieved. "I should've known that you wouldn't allow anything else here."

"I wouldn't, it's true. But this ritual goes beyond me— and it's a true freedom that anyone can come here and indulge their wildest fantasies, where they'll find willing partners to enjoy with them, and where no one will judge."

He nodded, a short jerk of his chin. Then he pulled me in front of him, turning us both to watch. Settling his hands on my hips, he pressed against me, the bulk of him warm and reassuring. One of the masked women had moved between the bound woman's spread thighs and, using a feather dipped in oil, lightly stroked her engorged sex. It was like lightning struck. The bound woman convulsed, body arching as she wailed.

My own sex clenched in sympathy, my nipples tightening under the silk of my gown.

"Why do you suppose she likes this?" Con murmured in my ear, lips caressing the sensitive shell as he spoke, making me shiver.

"She's bound and can't control what they do to her. Even though this is a torment, all of it is for her sensual pleasure and eventual release. For someone who can't otherwise set down the burdens of their responsibilities, these hours of giving themselves over to someone else's control are a blissful reprieve, a release on every level. Of course, I'm only guessing." With a smile at him, I tucked my hand in the crook of his arm again and we walked on.

"Why only guessing?" he asked. "You haven't done that?"

I laughed, but it came out wistful. "No. When would I have?"

"With your ladies," he supplied, surprising me a little. He arched a brow at my expression. "Did you think I hadn't guessed that you had sex with them before me?"

I did think that, because I'd never told him as much, at least not directly. While it wasn't exactly a closely guarded secret, my reputation as a chaste virgin queen awaiting the emperor's touch to truly make me a woman—such a bilious thought—had meant that my ladies and I never openly discussed the many ways they tended me.

"Not all my ladies," I replied, "and we never played games like that." In truth, while I'd enjoyed their ministrations, it had been a pleasure on the level of a good massage. Deeply relaxing, but without the emotional component I had with Con. Not even with Tertulyn, though I'd thought we'd shared a certain affection. Perhaps not.

"Why not?"

I thought he meant Tertulyn at first, then realized he meant the sexual games. We'd come to a brightly lit arena where naked men wrestled one another, the winners pinning the losers and taking them with masculine roars of triumph. Pausing on the outskirts, I cast a coy glance at Con. "I've heard a number of whispers speculating that you would be especially well suited to this game. A champion, even."

Con looked momentarily startled, a rabbit facing the sudden appearance of a predator, then he laughed softly, shaking his head. "I can safely say no to that one."

"Because you're not interested in men?"

"I'm not, it's true." He pulled me under a nearby tree, its weeping limbs blossoming with white trumpet flowers that made a veil all around. Under the soft globes of golden light hanging from the interior branches, he pressed my back against the trunk. "I'm not much interested in anything that doesn't involve you, Lia."

He bent his head and kissed me, the sweet heat moving through and dissolving into my blood and bones. When I'd drunk his blood, he'd become part of me in a fundamental way. I slid my good hand around his neck, under the queue of hair, clinging to him as he kissed me even more deeply. He cupped my breast through the silk, thumbing my taut nipple, and I groaned.

"You didn't answer my question," he said against my cheek, his lips moving hot to my ear, taking the lobe in his teeth and gently nibbling.

I had to think, which wasn't easy with my body yearning for more. "With My ladies, it wasn't like that. And besides, I can't do that sort of thing."

"Not even in the Night Court, where anything goes?"

I sighed, and not only for the delightful trail of his lips coursing down my throat. "It's not for Me."

"Because you don't want to?" He slid the narrow strap of my gown down my arm, easing the silk over my nipple, teasing so I shuddered with the sparking need. "You could've been speaking of yourself—the person who can never set down her responsibilities, who's always in control, who maybe craves a release from that, if only for a few short hours." His hot mouth closed over my nipple.

"Ohhh . . ." I let my head fall back against the smooth green trunk, grateful the light, close fit of the new crown allowed for that, moaning for the feelings his words stirred in me as much as for the delight of his mouth on me.

He lifted his head, replacing his mouth with rough fingers, brushing my temple with a kiss. "I think you want to."

"I can't." I sounded like I was begging, though I wasn't sure what for. "It would be irresponsible."

"Even a queen deserves time for herself."

"It wouldn't work, anyway. Delilah is right that everyone must obey Me, games or no."

He kissed me, harder than usual, then broke away to stare into my eyes, fixing me with that hot golden gaze of the predator. "I don't have to obey you."

The intensity of his expression had me catching my breath.

"And you trust me," he continued. Taking my hand from the back of his neck, he lifted it and pinned it high above my head against the tree. My breathing quickened, tightened, and I shuddered, rubbing against him, my one bare breast tweaking against the leather vest.

"I don't know . . ."

"You don't know if you trust me?" But he was teasing,

not annoyed. He dropped his other hand to my hip, easily finding a slit in the flowing silk panels, sliding his rough fingers up my inner thigh, then cupping my sex in his hand. "Oh, Lia," he breathed, dropping his forehead to mine as I shuddered under his touch. "You're drenched. You want this badly."

"Yes," I confessed. "And I do trust you."

"I hear a *but* in there."

"I have to go meet Dearsley, remember? Ejarat take Me, I'm probably late."

He laughed, a rough rumble that made me arch against him in frank longing. "You are the queen. We'll send a message that you are indisposed and will meet him early in the morning before we go."

"We will?" I'd gone for arch, but he slipped a blunt finger inside my lingerie at that moment, pushing inside me, so I nearly climbed his body, my voice coming out breathless.

"Yes." He withdrew his finger, and I nearly cried for its loss. "I'll decide for you. I'll send the message and you won't have a choice. That's what you want, isn't it?"

I gazed at him, unbearably aroused but terribly uncertain. "But what about the damage reports?"

"They'll be there in the morning," he replied with a grimness I understood. "One hour's delay tomorrow won't change anything. For tonight, you wanted to taste the pleasures of Calanthe. I do, too. We deserve this. What's the point of surviving if we don't enjoy life? Let me give you this. Say yes."

"I think it would be strange, with Ibolya and maybe Sondra hovering outside the door. Or Ambrose flying in through closed windows."

Con chuckled. "You remember that, huh? But I agree. That's why we'll do it here."

"In the Night Court?" People might afford me the courtesy of the appearance of anonymity, but the orchid bound to me would always reveal my identity. I didn't think I could allow that kind of intimate exposure.

"That's what it's here for, right? We'll use the privacy thing."

Hmm. He had a point. Did I dare? Perhaps I would. I'd died without tasting this particular fantasy, and I might not survive the next day.

"All right."

He let out a long breath, turning his head to press a kiss to the exposed skin of my inner elbow, where he pinned it against the tree. That, too, arced through me. Heat and lightning. "Pick a password." Now that I'd agreed, he began tracing lazy circles on my inner thigh again, tantalizing, teasing.

"I don't want to register—"

He bit my earlobe, more sharply, making me squeal. "Only you and I will know it."

Oh, I liked that idea. But what? I wanted something I associated with Con, but that I wouldn't normally say to him. And nothing alarming, in case I needed to give warning. Con was nibbling along my throat, making it difficult to think, the sweet rush of heat winding with the scent of night-blooming flowers. "Jasmine," I breathed.

"Got it." He released my hand, and lifted my dress to cover my breast again. "If I hear that, we stop immediately. From now on, though, you don't speak unless I ask you a direct question, and you do everything I say."

Taken aback, my heart hammering, I nodded, the sensation of giving over control as exciting as it was liberating.

"I love you, Lia," he said, taking my chin in his hand and holding it firmly while he kissed me breathless. He tucked my good hand in the crook of his arm. "Come with me."

Parting the weeping branches of the tree, he led me back out to the path and glanced around. I watched with some amusement as he tried to divine how to summon someone, then had to suppress a giggle when he raised a hand and snapped his fingers as he'd seen Percy do. It worked, and a young woman who worked the Night Court appeared immediately. She knelt, pressing her forehead to his boots.

"I am Hyacinth. How may I serve You, Conrí?" she asked.

It disconcerted Con—both that she knew him and her kneeling, I thought—but he recovered quickly, telling her to stand. "I need to send a message to Lord Dearsley, and I'll need a private alcove."

"Of course, Conrí." Hyacinth carefully averted her gaze from me, a discretion I appreciated. A good reminder of why I tolerated Delilah's cheek: She did know her business. I was also impressed by how quickly and well they'd restored the Night Court gardens. Signs of damage lingered here and there, but overall this section was in better shape than closer to the palace.

Hyacinth summoned a page, who ran off with the message, then she led us through several barely lit winding paths. "The usual equipment, Conrí?" she asked, glancing coyly over her shoulder, swaying her naked bottom— reddened from a recent spanking—enticingly.

Con glanced at me and I shrugged. I didn't know what they considered usual, either. Besides, I wasn't supposed to speak.

Noting it, Hyacinth said, "You can always ring for something if You need it, Conrí. Or I can remain with You."

"That won't be necessary," Con replied, seeming not to notice her disappointed pout.

She stopped at a turn, nimbly unhooking the privacy ribbon that crossed the entrance, dropping to her knees to allow us to pass.

"How do you know it's unoccupied?" Con asked.

"This alcove is expressly set aside for our king and queen, Conrí. It hasn't been used for many years." She kept her gaze demurely cast down. "But we always keep it ready, as is our sacred duty."

"Thank you."

"There's a bell pull with a red cord, Conrí. I'll listen for You, should You need anything."

Without reply, he escorted me down the winding path, densely lined with impenetrable foliage. We rounded a corner to find a candlelit alcove with a gorgeously appointed bed—with the requisite four posts—made of living wood, orchids growing from the surfaces. Several tables held a variety of supplies, such as the expected oils and cloths, while a number of chests held other tools for exploring pleasure and pain.

It occurred to me that my father had likely used this place—an image I absolutely didn't want in my head—but then I recalled a distant memory of being told when I took the throne that this alcove existed, ready for my pleasure. And that it had been completely refurbished at that time. Calanthe and her rituals, handling even these intimate details.

Con had left me to my thoughts, prowling the space in wolf mode, first checking the periphery and, yes, even under the bed. Satisfied, he turned his attention to the bed itself, testing the golden rings embedded in the various surfaces, then taking up a crimson ribbon from a cluster hanging conveniently from a hook on the wall.

"Turn around and cross your wrists," he ordered, and I obeyed with a burst of rising excitement. He wrapped the ribbon snugly and expertly around my wrists, binding them. With heady awareness, I realized that Con would know very well how to secure a prisoner. Pressing a kiss to the back of my neck, he lifted the crown off my head and set it on a nearby table, following it with his own. Then he slid the straps of my gown down my arms, letting them dangle there as he kissed his way down my naked spine. The dress fell away from my breasts, but only so far as the bodice that hugged my waist. I shivered with need, my bare breasts tightening with the erotic sensation of being out of control, but also safe and cherished.

Con sank to his knees, sliding his hands up my thighs to hook his thumbs in my lace panties, drawing them slowly down my legs. With one strong hand on my waist to balance me, he eased the lingerie over one heel then the other. "Turn around," he told me, holding my waist with both hands, arousal gruff in his voice.

I did and he placed a soft kiss on each nipple, sweet, nearly reverent. The tenderness and—yes—love in his touch undid me, and I trembled violently. He lifted his face to study mine. "Do you want what we saw—being tied to the bed like that?"

I swallowed against a suddenly dry mouth and nodded, though technically I could've spoken. He nodded with me, then wrapped his arms around me, laying his cheek against my belly. "I keep thinking," he said, "not that I want to bring up bad stuff, but I think we have to talk about it. That stone slab, they tied you down. I saw the chains and . . . And I don't want you to—"

"Con," I interrupted. Had my hands been free, I'd have combed them through his hair. "That's part of why I want this." Something I hadn't realized until this moment, that maybe this was part of why I'd wanted to visit the Night Court, to exorcise my own demons. "I need to . . . replace all that. With you." *With someone who loves me.* I didn't—couldn't, shouldn't—speak those words, but he lifted his face again to meet my gaze. "Because I trust you."

He grinned, his dimple flashing into existence, as it did only when he was relaxed and happy. "You are so fucking beautiful, Lia. I'm going to eat you alive."

Surging to his feet, he lifted me in his arms and carried me to the bed.

With everything in me, I surrendered to him, letting the wolf finally and fully devour me.

10

While Lia met with Dearsley in the map tower, so she could *see* the damage, she said—Sondra and Ibolya acting as her escort—Vesno and I went to find Kara. He was down at the shipyard, still working on the repairs to the *Last Resort*. Boats of all kinds crowded the working harbor, unfortunately making the place look like a ship's graveyard, given the sorry condition of most of them.

The dreadful fallout of the Battle at Cradysica continued to rain down, along with the more recent ravages to other parts of the island, and ever more broken boats had been towed to the busy shipyard near the palace. While we'd been off at Yekpehr on the rescue mission, the ship builders had triaged the wreckage. The most salvageable ships had been dry-docked and swarmed with workers—many of them my own people assisting the Calantheans—while other vessels had been drawn up on the long beach or floated nearby. I spotted only one of the three battleships we'd taken to Cradysica—not surprising, as the other two had seemed irredeemably sunk—and that one looked pretty beat up.

Another tier of boats that could still float were anchored a short distance out. Most of those had little left of the upper decks, and it looked like staying above the waterline was about all they could do.

Beyond that, on a long spit of flat rocks, hundreds of other boats of all sizes had been piled up, clearly junked and intended for salvage. The immensity of that pile loomed as large as my guilt.

You wrought this, they seemed to scream. *All for your ego.*

"Conrí!"

I started at the shout, for a moment hearing it as yet another accusation, then shook myself out of the daze, Vesno nudging his head under my hand. I was still running on far too little sleep, and while the mind-blowing sexual adventure with Lia the night before had been absolutely worth it, we hadn't gone to sleep until very late. Or very early, more like. But we'd both slept hard and peacefully.

A blessing from Ejarat right there. I'd never imagined sex like that could be so cathartic. It had been for her, too. At least I'd done that right, given Lia what she needed. I'd never felt so powerful as when I'd had her trembling at my mercy. The way she'd looked at me when I finally carried her to our bed in the palace in the wee hours . . . She might not love me—Sawehl knew I'd given her no reason to—but she did trust me, and had some kind of affection for me. That could be enough. I hardly deserved more.

"Conrí." Kara's hand clapped my shoulder. "Didn't you hear me calling you?" He narrowed his dark eyes. "You're not drunk, are you?"

Drunk on fantastic sex, maybe. I shook him off. "Still catching up on sleep. How are repairs on the *Last Resort*?"

As we walked the short distance to the dry-docked yacht, a worker popped up from the deck and, seeing me, strode down the gangplank. Vesno dashed up to greet him like a friend. Realizing it must be Percy, I eyed him with some bemusement. He wore rough coveralls and thick-soled boots, and had his hair tied back in a functional club. With none of his usual finery, he looked efficient and almost plain—and when he stripped off his leather gloves, no jeweled nails graced his blunt fingers.

He raised a brow at my perusal. "Did you think I'd waste good clothes on the shipyard, or risk breaking a nail?"

I grinned at him. "I guess I did."

He sniffed in disdain. "You're such a brute, Conrí. Did you enjoy your adventure in the Night Court?"

Taken aback, I hesitated too long and Percy pounced.

"Oh," he crooned. "You *did*. You're blushing."

No way was I blushing. Sawehl take me for an idiot.

"You went *into* the Night Court?" Kara asked. "The actual Night Court, itself—past the maze?"

"Yeah, what of it?" I made sure to sound absent about it, studying the *Last Resort* as Vesno charged ahead up the gangplank.

"Nothing, Conrí. Just . . . surprised."

"Clearly *you* know about the maze and how to get there," I noted, heading around the side of the ship to where the worst damage had been.

"Because I was warned away," Kara replied stiffly, pacing beside me.

"Uh-huh."

"Did Her Highness go with you?"

"None of your business."

"Yes!" Percy crowed at the same time. "She did, for the first time, *ever*. Everyone is talking about it. But information is sadly scarce on what you two got up to. So spill."

"How are the repairs coming?" I asked.

"They're nearly complete," Percy answered. "And *my* lifeboat will be ready as soon as tomorrow to be put in the water and sailed for a test run."

"Good," I grunted, peering up at the underside and the new planking that had been sealed and awaited a final coat of paint. "If all goes well at the temple, we could sail for Yekpehr in a few days."

"Did you hear me, Conrí?" Percy's voice rose. "I will not let you borrow my lifeboat again unless I receive some quid pro quo."

"I thought you wanted to destroy Anure as much as any of us."

"I do. But I can't just twiddle my thumbs in the meantime. You are in possession of valuable gossip. I want it."

I straightened and looked the smaller man in the eye. "No."

He wasn't intimidated in the least. Folding his arms, he didn't budge. "Don't be such a prude, Conrí. This is Calanthe. It's hardly a big deal. We all talk about this sort of thing."

"Then you'll easily find someone to tell you."

He unfolded a hand to wave it in disgust. "Those Night Court servants. So closed-lipped. Their sacred duty, blah blah blah. You have to give me *something*."

Clearly I should send Hyacinth that something. A reward for her discretion. "Don't have to. Not going to."

"Then find another boat."

I put a possessive hand on the keel of his, baring my teeth in a grin. "I like this one."

"Besides the fact that it's still our only seaworthy ship of any size," Kara put in.

Percy lifted his nose. "Too bad you can't have it."

"Her Highness will simply commandeer it," I pointed out, very reasonably.

"She would *never*," he retorted. "Clearly, Conrí, you are unfamiliar with the Calanthean laws that assure sanctuary to asylum seekers, *including* the goods they bring with them."

Really? I glanced at Kara, who shrugged his ignorance.

"Her Highness has no interest in looting the possessions of Her subjects," Percy filled in archly. "*She* is a good and noble queen."

"True," I agreed ruefully. Lia and I would discuss this law of hers. "Too bad for you that I'm a rapacious brute with no regard for niceties." I patted the boat. "Consider your yacht commandeered, Percy."

He dropped his folded arms, opening and closing his mouth like a stranded fish. "You wouldn't dare!"

"Already done. Kara, what supplies do you need?" I whistled for Vesno, who came bounding up, soaking wet from a romp in the bay. We walked away, leaving Percy fuming behind us. "You might keep an eye on him," I said quietly. "Make sure he doesn't sabotage the yacht."

"He did us a favor lending us the *Last Resort*, Conrí."

"Yeah, I know. But I'm not trading Lia's privacy for his favors."

"For your sake or hers?"

"Same thing." As I said it, I knew it was true. What had happened between us was too . . . precious to expose to gossip. "We'll need more ships than the *Last Resort*," I said, "depending on how many royal captives there are."

Kara looked taken aback. "You think there are more than a dozen or so?"

"I don't know, but I was thinking—if Lia's theory is right that Anure has at least one captive for every kingdom, including the tiny ones . . ."

Kara whistled low and long, squinting at the listing

battleships, then scanning some of the fishing boats we'd
stolen from Hertaq. "I'll see what else I can scrounge up."

I clapped his shoulder. "Thank you."

I returned to the palace via the gardens, passing by Dearsley's offices and noting they were empty—which meant
Lia was still at the map tower with her adviser. Since
she'd given me a pass on the meeting—I knew most of it
already, and she could fill me in on anything new—I decided to make a quick side trip while she was still occupied.

"Come on, Vesno. Want to see some pictures?"

The wolfhound woofed doubtfully but still faithfully
followed at my heel as I turned down the quiet hallway to
the portrait gallery. Not many people came this way—
and the ones I did encounter acted a lot like they did in
the Night Court, offering distant greetings and plenty of
privacy.

I doubted that Lia—or her father, who'd started the
collection—had meant for the gallery to become a kind
of shrine, but for those of us refugees from the forgotten
empires and scattered kingdoms, it was the one place we
could go to see something of our homelands. I'd made
a number of visits to the gallery before Cradysica, but
hadn't been back since. When I'd haunted the place before,
though, I'd come to recognize a few of the other frequent
visitors, all of us going to our own personal collection of
portraits.

The gallery probably wasn't meant to feel like a tomb,
but the dim light—to protect the art—and profound silence
gave it that feel. They'd packed the walls with portraits,
landscapes, and other paintings, drawings, etchings, and
renderings. Not arranged to please the eye, but grouped by

cities within kingdoms. One wall held art that couldn't be traced to any particular place, orphaned works like Lia's new crown.

I always went straight to one portrait, dominating the center of the wall that held Oriel's art. The royal family. My family. Lia's words on regrets had been on my mind, and one of my many regrets at Cradysica had been that, as often as I'd visited this portrait, I'd never been able to bring myself to look at Rhéiane's face. I'd assumed her dead, and in the most horrific way, but now that I knew she might be alive . . . Well, I wasn't sure I remembered what she looked like, and if I was going to rescue her, I'd dammed well better be able to recognize her.

Not giving myself the opportunity to lose my nerve, I strode up to the painting, pointed at Vesno to sit, and looked right at Rhéiane.

It felt like a punch to the gut.

I *had* forgotten, far too much. I should've looked at Rhéiane's portrait long before this, because I realized in that moment that I'd been carrying around the last image I'd had of her. The blood, and tears, and screaming . . . I shook that away and determinedly stared at this version of my sister. Painted not long before Anure began his campaign of terror and destruction, Rhéiane had been about sixteen, and beautiful with the first blossoming of womanhood.

With hair dark as a raven's wing, like mine, but glossy and waving to the backs of her knees, she smiled impishly, full of merriment and vitality, her tawny eyes seeming to sparkle. She and Sondra had been fast friends, and I'd remembered Sondra as the beauty, but that had clearly been a little brother's blindness. For Rhéiane had a radiance to her of intelligence and personality. And the sight of her face brought back a rush of memories, of her teasing me, reading to me—even yelling at me not to mess with her stuff. Which I always had anyway.

Some deep place in me stirred, like a seed putting up a shoot in soil long since dried and cracked. I remembered Rhéiane, and it was good.

Stepping back, I surveyed the wall full of images I'd previously ignored. Paintings of the crown city of Oriel, with the palace high on a craggy hill, tumbling in tiers to the buildings of the town. The seven walls circling in rings marking the various sections of the city, then opening to the rich pastureland below. Low stone walls wended through field and orchard, making designs.

There were more—paintings of famous people of Oriel I barely recalled learning about—and other scenes I didn't recognize. A mirror-bright lake with snowcapped mountains beyond. Another city, bounded by three rivers, arched bridges spanning them. I had no idea where that might've been.

What did Oriel look like now? I guessed I'd pictured it like a scoured wasteland of ash and bare rock, much like Vurgmun. Probably the beat-up, grief-ridden boy I'd been had seen the mines at Vurgmun and painted all the world in those colors. Past time, probably, to rethink all kinds of things.

As I left, Vesno happy to escape the boring place I wouldn't even let him investigate, I passed someone in a violet cloak, kneeling before another grouping of portraits. They made the sign of Yilkay's blessing and stood as I came abreast, tipped back the cowled hood to reveal short silver hair.

"Good morning, Conrí," Brenda said.

"Brenda." I nodded at her, then looked curiously at the wall.

"Derten," she offered, turning to look, too.

"Your homeland?" I asked. I was uncertain of polite manners in the best of circumstances, and among my people we observed the tacit courtesy of not asking about the past. It was easier that way, but maybe not better. I should've tried to remember the good things a long time ago.

"Yes. Next to fall to Anure after Oriel." She tipped her head to me apologetically.

"I remember Derten," I said, realizing I did. So many memories returning, as if by allowing a few, I'd opened a crack that kept widening. "You were allies of ours."

"Bad ones. Derten failed to come to the aid of Oriel when your father called. Or maybe you don't remember that."

I shook my head. "I was a boy still, and a wayward one. My parents had decided to give me a few years before they tried to get me to sit still and listen to politics." When she snorted, I smiled wryly. "Unfortunately, I think Lia faces the same frustration today."

"Her Highness has a canny mind for politics," Brenda acknowledged, "but you bring other talents to the table. You make a good team that way."

With nothing to say to that—too much hope and too much regret there to touch—I studied the portraits. "Are you up here?"

"Me? No." She shook her head for emphasis, then laughed without humor. "I was wayward myself. And a sixth child, after three brothers and two sisters. I hung out in the armory most of the time, decided I must've been adopted, the way I didn't fit in, then ran off with a traveling mercenary group when I was fourteen. Thought I'd show them all." She nodded at a portrait of a large royal family. "Missed the sitting for that one."

"You were a princess?" I asked with too much surprise, because she barked out a laugh and wagged a finger at me.

"We come in all types, Conrí."

"I apologize."

"No need. As I said, I never fit the princess mold. When Anure took Oriel, I went home. My father immediately put me in charge of our military." She turned and faced me, expression set. "If I'd stayed home, I might've been general when Oriel called—and I would've come. If we'd stopped Anure then . . ." She shook her head, then unfastened the clasp of the violet mourning cloak at her throat and bundled it under her arm. "So you see. It's me who owes you the apology." She bowed, low and formal.

I gripped her shoulder, levering her up. "You can't think that way. The *if-onlys* will make you crazy."

Her eyes unexpectedly filled with tears, an odd sight in her tough warrior's face. "I know. But I keep thinking, if I'd just stuck it out, I could've made a difference—and maybe gotten to know my brothers and sisters. As it was, I lost them all and became an actual orphan. A bitter joke."

I had no answer to that, so I just squeezed her shoulder. "But you're alive now to make a difference."

"Yeah, about that . . ." She turned and started walking, Vesno bounding up from his patient sitting to trot between us. "According to your theory, Anure has one of my siblings."

"It's really Lia's theory."

"I keep trying to figure who."

"You didn't see any bodies?"

"Dertens cremate their dead. And I was at the front lines fighting Anure's army when a strike team went to da'Derten. Our primary fortified city," she added when she saw I didn't know it. "The entire ruling family was killed. By the time I got back, they'd all been burned and committed to the sea. Or so I'd always thought."

I nodded, understanding all the things she didn't say, and we walked on in silence.

"Hey, want to see something?" Brenda stopped at the collection of orphaned art near the entrance. Sunshine, birdsong, and the flower-scented air of Calanthe streamed through the giant open doors, three times my height, dispelling some of the funereal gloom of the gallery. She pointed at a life-sized portrait of an elaborately gowned woman. Perfectly coifed and wearing a crown, she smiled serenely out at the viewer. "Recognize her?"

"Should I? I don't—wait. *Agatha?*"

"I think it has to be. The likeness is uncanny."

"A princess, or a queen?"

"That looks like a queen's crown to me, though I don't know."

"You never asked?"

She shook her head, grimacing. "We don't ask, do we? And I don't know that she even realizes this portrait is here. You know how it is—some of us visit here religiously and others can't bear to. She's one who doesn't, and I've never quite brought myself to mention it to her—I just happened to glance at it one day and *boom!* That's Agatha, or a twin sister. Could be her mother, I guess, but I think it's her. The dress style isn't that old."

I studied the image, finding it hard to reconcile the plump, even merry woman in the painting with thin, enervated Agatha the weaver. Brenda was right, though: The resemblance was too perfect to be coincidence. "And she was captive in Yekpehr, but escaped."

"Yeah. I was surprised as you all to discover that tidbit."

"Have you spoken with her since we returned from the citadel?"

"Last night was the first time she came out of her rooms since you got back. She only stayed for a little while."

"Think she'll go back with us?"

"Hard to say—but I'll find out."

"Thanks, General."

She smiled a little at that, though sadly. "By the way, *I* will go with you."

"You sure?"

"Never been more sure. If one or more of my brothers and sisters are in there, I owe it to them to do this."

I couldn't argue with that.

I made it back to our rooms ahead of Lia, but just barely. I'd just poured some fresh water for Vesno from a pitcher into a bowl at the station Ibolya had thoughtfully set up for him when the doors opened and Lia glided in.

Even though Lia still hadn't resumed the ritual of entertaining the Morning Glories, I'd vacated her bed at Ibolya's knock and left the ladies to their grooming. So aside from a sleepy wake-up kiss, I hadn't seen Lia yet that day.

She'd continued in the same vein as the night before, wearing a slinky gown that looked almost like a dressing robe to me. Except fancy. A pretty coppery color that matched some of the dark gold in her new crown and brought out her pale skin and jewel-like eyes, the robe had long sleeves that ended in huge cuffs bordered with a black angular pattern. The deep vee in front, bordered with the same pattern, showed off a lot of her breasts—which were obviously otherwise naked—and then a big black sash twice the width of my hand cinched her waist, tied off to the side in a giant, intricate bow. The robe divided over her long, lovely thighs, skimming to her sleek black heels. Along the bottom hem, stylized figures danced along the angular border, as if in worship. Hard to blame them.

Spotting me, she blushed, a pretty pinking of her high cheekbones. I grinned at her and she rolled her eyes. Yeah, the pair of us. You'd think we were kids.

Sondra muttered something and stalked over to flop on a sofa while Ibolya started to greet me, then cried out in dismay. "Oh, Conrí, I'd *just* had him bathed."

I followed her gaze to Vesno, currently lapping up water and shedding sand with equal enthusiasm. He'd probably tracked it all through the portrait gallery and palace, too. Oops. "Sorry, Ibolya."

She gave me an exasperated look, and I couldn't help smiling. I'd rather she treated me like a pain-in-the-ass brother than the formal bowing and scraping. Of course, that made me think of Rhéiane, and her brilliant smile, her youth and innocence. Would any of that girl remain? I pushed that thought aside. I was going after her as soon as I could. I had to help Lia wrestle Calanthe first. Since it was my fault she had to do this in the first place, I owed her that.

"I'll have to see him bathed if he's going to ride in the carriage with You, Your Highness."

Lia looked up from a scroll she'd been reading, one of a number that had been piled on her private desk in the short few hours we'd been gone. "No need. He'll just get dirty again, since we'll be riding to the temple."

"Ride, Your Highness?" Ibolya repeated, somewhat faintly.

"Yes, on horseback," Lia clarified unnecessarily, sliding me a serene look, her eyes dancing with mischief. "Conrí prefers it."

"Ambrose is not fond of riding horses," Sondra commented.

"But he can do it, and has," I supplied. "Is Ambrose coming with us, though?"

"Yes." Lia tossed the scroll aside, rubbing her twig hand with the good one. It must be itching or aching. Both, maybe. Her face darkened with concern. "I'll need him to reach Merle before I attempt anything else. More disaster reports have come in. Abating the storm helped, but the earth tremors are worsening. I don't want to delay any longer."

"How soon do you want to leave?"

"Immediately. I can leave as soon as we pack some things. The path isn't long or arduous. We should be able to reach the temple in a few hours."

"I'll roust out Ambrose while you do that," I said. This time I'd be prepared and grab a ladder along the way.

"I'll help you," Sondra offered, sounding resigned as she stood. "Ejarat only knows how long it will take, though."

"No time at all," Ambrose declared, breezing through the double doors that opened of their own accord, the surprised guards still reaching for the handles. "Really, Conrí. You should know I'm never late. And I love horses. I live to ride. Get your facts straight."

I shook my head, catching Lia's amused smile. "I don't know what I was thinking."

In less than half an hour, we'd mounted and were riding out. Lia had planned that outfit with this in mind, it turned out—no surprise there—and wore close-fitting silk pants under the robe, in a matching copper color. She'd traded the heels for soft black leather boots that hugged her calves and chimed with copper chains. She also wore a matching black glove on her good hand, which held the reins, while she tucked the twig hand into a loose pocket, the orchid above it lush in similar shades of copper and purple.

Though a crowd had gathered to see us off, showering us with flower petals, once we left the palace grounds, we turned onto a quiet trail through the forest that went inland. "This is the Pilgrims' Path to the temple," Lia explained as we rode side by side.

Ambrose and Ibolya rode behind us, chatting amiably about flower varieties, by the sound of it. Sondra brought up the rear, sulking because Ambrose had dodged teaching her to use the stolen walking stick, which she'd brought along, thinking to have the wizard's undivided attention for a few hours. Vesno, naturally, raced ahead—periodically returning to check on our sadly slow progress.

"Does that mean no parade party?" I asked.

She slid me a tolerant smile. "It does. The journey is intended to be a time of reflection, an opportunity to meditate on Calanthe's verdant beauty and to commune with Her."

"Ah. Is that a hint for me to be quiet?"

"No." A faint line drew her brows together. "I have no intention of communing with Calanthe before I have to."

"That bad?"

She blew out a breath, glancing at me with a rueful grimace. "That might be overstating things. I'm keeping the communication minimal, regardless."

I considered that. Lia was no coward, and she'd never shirked from a perceived duty. "I know it's not because you're afraid or lazy," I said, deciding going with that thought was a start anyway.

"But I *am* afraid," she replied softly enough that she couldn't be overheard.

"What are you afraid of, exactly?"

She frowned at me. "Isn't it obvious?"

I shook my head. "When I'm worked up and worrying about some battle or something, I—"

"You?" she interrupted. "The great and terrible Conrí, worried and afraid?" A teasing smile danced on her pretty lips, but I gazed back at her somberly.

"More than you know, Lia," I answered. I didn't say that the most afraid I'd ever been, though, was when I realized Anure had taken her. "Anyway, I ask myself, what exactly am I afraid of? What's the worst thing that can happen?"

She chewed her lower lip, sharp teeth flashing in lethal contrast to the soft pink. "The worst that can happen is Calanthe will shrug off My grip, rise from the sea—killing us and the entire population of the island in the process—and rampage around the world in an unstoppable destructive frenzy."

"Well, we won't care about that part if we're dead, right?" I pointed out.

She laughed, catching it back as if she hadn't meant to. "I suppose that's true. Grim, but true."

"And if you don't attempt this thing at the temple, what's the worst that can happen?"

Tipping her chin as if I'd scored a point, she took a long breath. "The same."

"There you are."

She slid me a look. "My feral wolf: warrior king and philosopher."

I snorted. "Do you really allow asylum seekers to keep everything they bring with them to Calanthe? No tithing or required gifts?"

"There's a change of subject," she noted, arching a brow.

"Did you still want to talk worst-case scenarios?"

"No," she agreed fervently. "And yes, that is My law. Why do you ask?"

"Eh—Percy and I had a disagreement. I ended it by commandeering the *Last Resort*."

"Oh yes. He came to Me about that."

"He did? That was fast." The little shit must've found her while I lingered in the portrait gallery.

"Yes. He pounced on Me outside of the meeting with Dearsley. He was most put out."

Huh. I eyed her. "What did you say?"

She shrugged, eyes on the path ahead. "I told him that I don't hold your leash, and that if he wanted to appeal your decision, he'd have to take it up with you."

I laughed, appreciating her ever more. "Cagey of you, to sidestep your own laws that way."

"It's not sidestepping. There are simply certain loopholes introduced by your presence."

"Meaning you find it useful to let me be the bad guy."

"Why, Conrí." She managed to look shocked and offended at once, one of her deliberately exaggerated expressions. "I can't imagine how you'd come to such a conclusion. I am but a simple woman. How can you expect me to wield influence over the terrible and terrifying Conqueror of Keiost?"

I burst out into a hearty guffaw, enjoying the sly twinkle in her eyes—and that she'd forgotten to be afraid for a few minutes. "We make a good team."

Something dimmed in her, even as she nodded vaguely. Well, shit. I'd been so pleased when Brenda said that, but Lia apparently not so much. "What's that look for?" I asked.

She deliberately brightened, smoothing her face. "I beg your pardon?"

"Why did that bother you that I said we make a good team?"

Gaze steadfastly on the path ahead, she lifted her chin and firmed her lips. Stiffening her spine with regal resolve. "It didn't."

"Lia, talk to me."

Sighing, she shook her head. "This isn't the time or place for this conversation."

"We have a few hours, right? And no one is listening to us, so this seems like the perfect time and place. You know we never get anywhere when we don't communicate."

"Well, you won't like this *communication*," she said, curling sarcasm around the word.

"Try me."

"Fine." She didn't sound annoyed, though. She sounded . . . sad. "Con, it doesn't matter what kind of team we make. We both know that you can't stay on Calanthe. Let's not pretend otherwise."

Wait. What? I shook my head, tempted to thump my ear to check my hearing. "What under Sawehl's gaze are you talking about, Lia? Where else would I go?"

She faced me with a long and resolute look. "Oriel."

I stared back, feeling like I'd hit myself in the head with my own rock hammer. Stunned, I tried to process that, while she watched me think it through, compassion in her eyes, though nothing could disturb the impassive mask she wore.

"Oriel," I breathed. Somehow, despite everything, it hadn't occurred to me that *I* would go there. *Home*, some deep, long forgotten part of me murmured. Maybe Oriel Herself, calling out to me, like the voice of my mother.

Lia tilted her head, smiling wryly, as if she sensed me hearing that call. For all I knew, she could. She'd said she heard the voices of all the orphaned realms crying in her dreams. Oriel would be one of them. The land I'd been born to rule and had abandoned. Sure, Anure had ripped me from it, but when we escaped Vurgmun, it had never once occurred to me to go home to Oriel. But now, as if she'd pulled stuffing from my ears, I heard the siren song of home. Those paintings in the gallery had been calling, too. That lake, the city of bridges I didn't even know the name of. They were Mine.

"See?" Lia's smile turned sorrowful. "You have to go, Con. Oriel needs you. You are a king; that's not something you can walk away from, even if you wanted to. I would never stand in the way of that."

"Even if I go to Oriel, you can come with me."

"I can't. I cannot survive leaving Calanthe again. I have to be here, just as you have to be in Oriel. Only more extreme, because I draw life from Calanthe. Orchids can't live on their own," she reminded me with an attempt at a smile that failed miserably.

"Maybe I don't have to be in Oriel," I argued, feeling desperate. "What would we have done in that other time line of yours, if I'd come to court you and convinced you to be my wife?"

"Probably it would've been a condition of marriage that you stay here with Me on Calanthe." She shrugged. "We'll never know."

"No, that makes sense." I seized on that idea. "Rhéiane was crown princess—and older than me—so she can be queen of Oriel."

"*If* it's your Rhéiane in Yekpehr. *If* we can rescue her. *If* we can destroy Anure's power. *If* we can elude the wizards. *If* I can return the nobles to their lands. That's a tremendous amount of uncertainty, Con."

I filled in the condition she'd been too circumspect to say aloud. *If Rhéiane hasn't lost her mind.* "And all of that is if we don't all die and slide into the sea by tomorrow," I countered grimly.

She laughed, though I hadn't meant it as a joke. "An excellent point."

"A critical point. If we manage all of that, then yes, I'll go home to Oriel—just to see if anything is even left of the land, maybe help Rhéiane get her footing—but then I'll come back here, to Calanthe. Home," I added belatedly, but not quickly enough to deceive her.

"When did you start thinking of Calanthe as home?" she challenged, those bicolored eyes so brilliant in their ability to see through me. "Be honest, Con. You don't. And you shouldn't need to pretend you do. You'd never set foot on My island until a few weeks ago. This is not a place that demands your fealty. Oriel does. We both know that."

I struggled to find the argument to counter that. "My home is with you."

She smiled, but it wobbled with heartbreak. "That's a lovely sentiment, but you and I are not people who can indulge sentiment. If you gave up Oriel for Me, you would be forever second place here on Calanthe, a land that isn't Yours. And in time any affection you have for Me would turn bitter and resentful. I don't think I could bear that."

"Can't we just savor the moment then?" I pressed. "We're alive now, together now."

She managed a small smile. "I thought that's what we had been doing."

"All right then."

"But Con—no more talk of marriage, please. Or being a team, or of a future that might never come to be. I can't—" She firmed her jaw, lifting it and drawing her cloak of regal indifference around her. Not that it fooled me, not anymore.

"What can't you do, Lia?" I asked quietly, the burr in my voice harsh. "Love me?"

Her eyes flashed as she glanced at me, quickly gone again as she focused on the path ahead. And didn't answer. She didn't have to.

11

Con looked so wounded by what I'd said that I felt as bad as if I'd kicked Vesno on his tender muzzle. I didn't want to be cruel, but I wasn't as strong as I'd once been. Or maybe I'd never been truly strong—I'd just naively believed a brittle shell of poise and intimidating makeup made me invincible. Then layer by layer, I'd lost all of it. First Con had blasted into my life and cracked open the shell of ice I'd used to protect my heart—all of his passion, ferocity, and unlikely charm thawing me in a way I'd never thought possible—and then Yekpehr had happened. The events there had stripped me to the core. Ripped from Calanthe, from everything I'd thought valuable about myself, I'd been reduced to nothing.

And Con had come for me. He'd saved me at the risk of everything. No one should be that noble. He saw himself as some ignorant brute, but he was the best of men. Not perfect, but a shining example of selflessness. A true hero who I now believed could save the world from Anure's death grip, and restore the forgotten empires, including and especially Oriel. He owed it to his land and his birthright. He owed me nothing.

Even before the wizards broke me on their altar to

knowledge, greed, and power, I'd suspected I'd never be a good custodian of Con's heart. That night before the Battle at Cradysica, I'd stopped him from declaring his love without fully understanding my own impulse. I had known, without consciously knowing, that we could never last. We'd been thrust together by dire circumstance, and now even more dire events had cut those bonds.

Con could be free of me, and should be. Maybe that girl in the other time line, in that world where Anure never happened, maybe she could've loved Con as he deserved. But the woman I'd become, the icy queen and incipient monster, she didn't have it in her to love anyone. I'd become that hollowed-out tree, with no real life in me. *Your kind aren't truly human at all, thus You lack the capability to feel emotion.*

Even my connection to Calanthe had changed. Where Her glorious voice once succored me, a strange and awful hole gnawed away, sucking everything good into it, like the whirlpool at Cradysica. And this trial ahead—I didn't know what kind of thing I'd be when I emerged. I'd drunk blood to live, and there might be no coming back from that. I still was not able to stomach any food—something I'd managed to hide from Con, though Ibolya suspected.

If I could only live on human blood now . . . Well, it didn't bear thinking of. Except that I refused to feed off Con for the rest of my life.

For a while the night before, for those few glorious hours with Con, I'd been able to forget all that. But with the morning light and Ibolya's call for me to arise and tend my realm, that had faded into perspective. I could give Con sex, but that wouldn't be enough to replace Oriel. He'd seen right through me to the truth: I couldn't let myself love him—if I was even capable of that generous emotion—and then be broken when he inevitably had to leave. Or worse, if I had to watch his love turn brittle and sour while he fought the collar of being tied to me, in a land far from the one he'd been born to.

Call me weak. I hated being weak, but I had to confront the harsh reality of that truth. I wasn't strong at all. Just a fragile orchid, I'd be a parasite on the strength of something that truly lived, blooming while the core of Con's strength rotted from the inside.

The Pilgrims' Path angled steeply now, winding the last loops to the top of the ridge behind the palace. Truly, it wasn't that far as Merle would fly it. Most of the effort went into the climb, which was another reason—besides the meditative aspects—to take the journey slowly.

My mind and heart were far too unruly for meditation. Following my impulse the night before, visiting the Night Court, and then letting Con take over to act out my fantasies . . . That might not have been a good idea. I'd thought to excise the wizards—and that had worked—but in doing so I'd also lost a last and vital barrier between Con and myself.

He'd seen me at my most vulnerable—dead, broken, dying, starving until he fed me with his own body. But nothing had exposed me on every level as willingly submitting to his bonds and desires had. The night before had been revelatory, transformative, exquisitely cathartic beyond my imaginings, and . . .

And what in Ejarat had I been thinking? I should have been building walls between us, not tearing down the final ones.

I was thinking in circles. At least Con had fallen silent, dropping the topic of our heartbreaking, doomed future, as I'd demanded. Or he was brooding.

I should maybe apologize. Except—would that blur the clarity of the boundary I'd drawn between us? I glanced at him, to gauge his current mood. Con was staring fixedly ahead, a look of puzzlement on his face.

I followed his gaze and saw the temple in view, framed in a break in the tree-lined path.

"Is that it?" Con asked, noticing my attention.

He had been deliberately staying quiet then. Letting *me* brood. Ejarat take him and his considerate tending of me. Maybe I should pick a fight with him. I knew how to handle a pissed-off Con. And if he made me mad enough, perhaps I'd stop feeling this terrible tenderness toward him, this desperate yearning for more, and more, and more.

"Lia?" He frowned a little. "Are you feeling all right?"

"I'm fine," I bit out, far more harshly than necessary. "And yes, that's the temple. Not what you were expecting?"

He narrowed his eyes, studying me, assessing my change of mood, then glanced at the temple again. "Well, yeah. Everything on Calanthe is so pretty. I guess I expected the temple to be all spun-sugar spires and altars carved of single, giant gemstones. Not . . . What is that? It looks like a cave. A big fucking damp, dark *cave*."

I tried not to laugh, I really did. And not only because I knew he was trying to lift my dour mood. So I rolled my eyes at him and assumed my most sanctimonious manner. "You dare mock the sacred womb of Calanthe?"

"The . . . *womb*?" The look of faint horror on his face wasn't manufactured this time. "Please tell me that's figurative and not literal."

"Well, the cave is obviously formed of rock." I gestured at it, twig fingers clicking, before I remembered and tucked that hand in the pocket of my wrap tunic. "And Calanthe is an island."

Con narrowed his eyes at me, the tawny gold of them striking in the dappled sunlight. "Don't give me that shit, Lia. You're the one always telling me Calanthe is alive and could stand up and start walking around. Why wouldn't She have a literal womb? And don't smile all mysteriously like that, either."

"That was a smile of amusement," I retorted. "And yes, I was born here, so I suppose calling the temple a womb isn't a bad metaphor."

"You were born *here* . . . Does that mean your mother lived here, not at the palace?"

"In a manner of speaking," I replied drily.

"You haven't been paying attention, Conrí," Ambrose chided from behind us. "You're the one who intuited the cure to restore Her Highness to health, so you should also be able to guess who Lia's mother is."

Con seemed to be wrestling with accepting that concept.

"A creation of human flesh and the floral body of Calanthe," I reminded him.

"Yeah, but I thought that meant . . . well, a woman still had to give birth to you. And you told me your mother had been married to your father, then died."

I gave him a cool look. "I lied." When he narrowed his eyes at me, frowning, I nearly rolled mine. "You were the enemy, holding Me captive and forcing Me into an unwanted marriage. You're surprised I didn't answer your questions honestly?"

He snorted but held up his hands in peace. "So what *is* the truth, now that you've agreed not to lie to me anymore?"

Aware that Ibolya—who had been at least raised on this mythology—and Sondra were listening intently, I asked our horses to halt on the last landing before we emerged onto the greensward before the temple. "My father provided the seed, which mixed with the fertility of the maidens who volunteered themselves for the rites. But the priestesses then extracted that mixture and planted it to be incubated in large blossoms. Calanthe chose which of us would emerge to be Her daughter." I watched Con carefully for signs of disgust.

"So you were . . . hatched?" he ventured, trying to sound neutral and not quite succeeding.

"In My head it looks more like a seedpod with a tough hide that had to be sliced open," I replied.

He started to smile, then sobered. "I can't tell if you're joking this time."

Feeling weary of it all, I shook my head. "I've never actually seen the process. It's sacred knowledge belonging only to Mother Ascendant, the high priestess. Besides, it really isn't relevant, except that you should understand even more clearly now that you and I are different in more than temperament. I am truly not human."

"I know that, Lia," he said softly.

"You think you know, but you pretend I'm a woman anyway."

"Because you are a woman," he argued. "I've been as close to you as anyone can be and—"

"And you're deluding yourself. Open your eyes, Conrí. I'm a monster, just like Calanthe."

A strained silence descended, our entourage no doubt embarrassed by the lovers' quarrel. I asked our horses to continue. As they stepped onto the emerald moss, Sondra rode up beside me. "Can I ask a question, Your Highness?"

"Why stop now?" I replied, flicking a quelling glance at Con, who glowered blackly.

"Great." Sondra grinned, undaunted. "So if the Calantheans can essentially grow their own nobility, why was old King Gul a fully human guy? I mean, he was, wasn't he? And then, when You were gone, why didn't they just harvest a new queen? Or, you know, have some podlings ready to go before this?"

I laughed at the image, which was maybe Sondra's intent. For all her brusque ways and sarcastic mutters, she had a knack for relieving the tension of heightened emotion.

"Yeah," Con put in darkly. "If you could just grow a new daughter, why were you concerned about getting an heir with me?"

My breath caught at that reminder. I'd been so concerned with simply clawing my way back to life and health that I hadn't been paying attention. Ambrose had promised Con would give me a true heir, and perhaps he had. I'd felt a seed of life bursting into being when I'd fed on Con's blood, making love to him at the same time, but I thought it had been my own life. Could it be that . . . Something to think about later. Much later. Like, after we knew if we would survive.

"It's not that simple," I told Sondra. "The previous queen died without an heir—I understand it's preferable to produce heirs through human birth." Probably so they wouldn't be saprophytic monsters. "Calling for surrogates and creating a new heir via ritual and Calanthe's intervention is an extreme process. Besides which, I'm human enough that I was an infant, then a child, an adolescent, and so forth. Any podling would have to do the same. I didn't leap full-grown from a flower with a crown on My head."

Con muttered something about not being so sure about that, but I ignored him. While they pondered, I quickened the pace of our horses. Mother Ascendant had emerged from the temple, along with my other four ladies. My heart leapt with gladness to see them again.

"My question, Your Highness," Ambrose said mildly,

"is why You told me that you knew a ritual was involved, but not the specifics You described just now."

I frowned, realizing the wizard was correct. "That wasn't a lie. I *didn't* know then. Why do I now?"

"Because You're coming into the fullness of Your knowledge, Your Highness," Mother Ascendant said, taking point to greet me. She wore her thick silver hair in a long braid, woven with orchids. "Your communion with the orchid ring has grown tremendously. It's there to give You access to the answers You need. Welcome home, Euthalia."

"Thank you. It's good to be home." I began to dismount and somehow Con was already magically there, lifting me down with his big hands around my waist.

"Allow me," he said, well after the fact, then released me.

"Mother Ascendant, may I present Conrí." I did not call him my husband, and he caught the careful omission, giving me a sardonic side eye. But then he went down on one knee, lifted the hem of Mother Ascendant's robe, and kissed it.

"All bright blessings to you, Mother Ascendant," he murmured.

She looked amused but placed her hands on his bowed head. "Blessings to You, Conrí," she intoned. "But please rise. I am no priestess of Ejarat. And call me Mother. Everyone does."

Con flowed to his feet, his grace always surprising given his bulk and raw appearance. "Forgive me, Mother." He gave her a crooked grin, glanced at me, and back to her. "I'm not clear on where Calanthe stands in the pantheon of gods and goddesses."

She smiled warmly, the laugh lines crowding her dark eyes. "I believe it is a fallacy to expect deities to follow a hierarchy. That's a construct of human hubris. A trait You are familiar with, yes, Conrí?"

I braced myself for his bristling anger, but Con shook his head in chagrin. "A humbling lesson, and a harsh one," he agreed.

The world must certainly be coming to an end if Con had developed self-awareness and humility, though I stopped myself from acidly saying as much. He didn't deserve my scathing anger—I didn't even understand why I wanted to rail at him. At the same time, I wanted to weep and cling to him.

I needed to get this over with and move on.

"Lady Calla," I called, holding out my good hand and keeping the twig hand firmly in my pocket. "Lady Orvyki, Lady Nahua, and Lady Zariah. It's so good to see you."

Given permission, they ran to me with glad cries and happy tears. They all sank to the ground around me in billows of colorful skirts. Being at the temple, they had forgone wigs and wore their natural hair loose, decorated only with flowers. They took turns kissing my hand, voices overlapping as they exclaimed over their fear for me and rejoicing that their prayers had been answered.

"Praise to Calanthe, who protected Your Highness and brought You home to us," Calla intoned.

I barely restrained myself from looking at Con, wanting to point out that the escaped slave and rebel she'd disdained had more to do with my survival. Along with a wizard and a brusque warrior woman.

"May I, Your Highness?" Calla asked, looking to the orchid on my wrist, a puzzled frown for my hand in my pocket.

Of course, I would have always offered them the hand that wore the orchid ring. With some reluctance—ridiculous, as these ladies knew me nearly as intimately as Con did, and for far longer—I withdrew the twig hand and proffered the orchid to them. I caught Ibolya edging into the periphery of my vision, concern in every line of her body as the other four ladies stared at my monstrous hand, aghast.

They all began speaking at once and, suddenly exhausted, I waved them to silence. "Lady Ibolya, would you please give your sisters the tale?"

"I'd be happy to, Your Highness." She curtsied and began walking away, leaving the others to scramble to rise and scurry after her.

Con set a hand at the small of my back. "They were simply surprised," he murmured. "Give them time to adjust."

I let out a sigh, not at all sure how to analyze the mix of emotions that plagued me. "I thought seeing My ladies again would feel more . . . natural." I'd thought I'd feel like my old self with them, not even more monstrous.

Before Con could reply, Mother stepped up, holding out her hands as if ready to receive a gift. Hesitantly, I laid the twig hand in her cupped ones. It had regenerated even more, though it still looked more like plant than flesh, and a webbing of vines and spongy tissue like the center of a flower stem had filled out the lower twigs, forming the shape of a hand again.

Mother held it with gentle reverence, bending over the orchid itself to inhale its otherworldly fragrance. "They tried to take the orchid."

"Yes. First by cutting off My finger. Then, when the orchid moved to the next finger, by cutting off My hand."

Con made a soft sound, like a protest.

"Will I—will My hand be like this always?" I felt ungrateful even asking, when I should be giving thanks that my severed hand was regrowing at all.

Mother smiled at me with understanding. "It should look fully human again in time. After all, the rest of You does."

Con shifted beside me—subtly withdrawing? That might be for the best. Tempted to ask if that meant I looked like all of this inside, a conglomeration of animated twigs and plant tissue, I decided against it. Perhaps that's why I hadn't remembered the circumstances of my birth until now. If I'd known all that when I was younger . . . a shiver of revulsion ran through me. I'd felt wrong and ugly enough as it was.

"What's most important is that You kept the orchid from them," Mother continued. "Well done, my brave girl."

I felt my composure crumple and scrabbled to recover. How I hated being this weak and weeping thing. "I didn't do anything," I told her, shame in my voice. "The orchid did it all."

"Oh, child." She placed a soft kiss on the twig that had been my ring finger, then drew me into her embrace. I burrowed into her like I was that child again, inhaling her scent of fresh soil and clear, cold springwater. "You simply don't realize Your own power," she said, holding me with maternal warmth. "Not many could withstand one wizard, let alone four. Isn't that so, Syr Wizard?" She released me and gave him a stern look, one I recalled from my early childhood, when I'd been naughty.

Ambrose edged up, seeming apprehensive, as he never was. He held his emerald-topped staff rather conspicuously between himself and Mother. "I would hesitate to speak for all wizards, Learned One. We are not a homogeneous group—in power, training, or purpose."

"Hmm." She eyed him as if unconvinced. "It's difficult to accept the assurances of one who disguises himself by existing in several realities simultaneously."

Sweeping a bow, Ambrose beamed. "For that I must apologize. However, I can promise that deceiving you is not the reason for my current . . . manifestation."

She gave his twisted leg a considering look. "I see that. Your fellow wizard finds himself in a similar predicament." She turned her disappointed frown on me. "That was quite a risk You took, daughter, leaving such as these to hold Calanthe."

"I apologize, Mother," I said, bowing my head. "It was an act of desperation, and not at all how I hoped things would turn out. But I'm here now."

"Yes, You certainly are. We can only hope it's not too late."

"Perhaps we should get to it then," Con prompted, "instead of standing around, talking."

Mother cast him an exasperated look. "So the rumors have that much right—he has more ferocity than patience to temper it."

"Conrí's determination and decisiveness have saved us a number of times," I countered, before I realized I was defending Con—and against an accusation I'd leveled against him more than once. He noticed, too, giving me a bemused look from the corner of an eye.

Mother sighed and finally released my hand. "Well, we always knew it would come to this. Enter the temple and be welcome, all of you. Except you, Syr Wolfhound." She raised a finger to Vesno, then pointed away. "You shall wait outside. And you, Syr Wizard—are you equal to what you will find within?"

"We shall know soon!" he replied, his cheer a thin veneer over grim purpose.

I walked beside Mother, Sondra and Con falling in behind us. Ambrose brought up the rear, muttering something to himself—or engaging in a one-sided conversation.

"What was *that* all about?" Sondra hissed to Con, quite audibly.

"You're asking *me*?" Con muttered back. "Ask them."

Sondra snorted at the likelihood of that, and I suppressed a smile, imagining their expressions.

"Tertulyn," I said to Mother, "is she . . . ?" I stumbled over how to finish that question.

Mother waited, raising a brow at me as we stepped into the cooler interior of the cave mouth. Finally she took pity on my inability to put words to my fears. "She is here. She is not herself. What is to be done? That is not mine to say. You will know." The ground trembled beneath us, the sound of rocks grating against one another from deep below, roaring in a groan more felt than heard. Mother's serenity cracked, too, revealing her anxiety and concern. "*After* You appeal to Calanthe and settle Her again."

"And will you be able to guide Me in that?" I asked hopefully.

She cast me a startled look, then laughed. "Me? No, Your Highness. I am but a humble priestess. This falls to You. This is Your sacred duty—and knowledge—not mine."

I'd been afraid of that. In silence, we all proceeded deeper into the temple. It was a cave, yes, formed of an opening in the bedrock of Calanthe, but also a window into the wellspring of all life on my island. Occasional breaks in the rough ceiling allowed light to stream in, and lush emerald moss lined every surface, muffling our footsteps into silence, like the thickest of carpets. Water dripped and trickled, echoing in the quiet, the melodies overlapping like singers chanting in rounds.

Tunnels branched off to the sides, leading to prayer rooms and living quarters. Tertulyn would be in one, along with other people who sought the temple's healing solitude to cure them of ills physical, mental, emotional, and spiritual. I felt somewhat better, surrounded by the harmonies of my early childhood. A taste of the coming home I'd longed for.

We reached the sacred spring, where a waterfall splashed from solid rock above, filling a still pool below. A vent in the ceiling admitted sunlight, which wound and danced in the falling water, but the pool lay in deep shadow, glossy and black as obsidian.

"The waters of truth," Mother informed the others. "You may taste of it after we do, if you dare, then remain here to meditate on what Calanthe chooses to reveal. Euthalia and I will go on alone from here."

"I promised Lia I'd stay with her," Con protested, hand on his bagiroca, as if he'd attempt to bash her over the head with it. He might try—and then he'd discover that my abilities to reverse his intention paled in comparison with Mother's. Between the warning in my eyes and Mother's serene smile, Con reconsidered. But he still looked to me, the question in every line of him.

"Where I'm going, you cannot come along," I told him as gently as I could.

"I hope that's not a metaphor for our lives," he answered, bitterness in his voice and yearning in his face.

I didn't have a good answer for him, as it was probably the perfect metaphor, except in the reverse. I was the one who ultimately could not go where he went. "Wait for me?"

"Forever." He wanted to kiss me, I could see that much, but I moved away and he didn't follow, except with his eyes.

I turned to Mother. "I'm ready, but Ambrose should also accompany us."

"Why does Ambrose get to go?" Con snarled, fingers twitching.

"Because I need him to extract Merle before I can step into the place he's occupying," I explained. When Con frowned, I tried again. "Imagine a person holding a huge rock on their shoulders. If you want to take the rock onto your own shoulders, the other person must step out from under it and let you take their place."

Ambrose nodded, as if he'd seen this coming. Likely he had. Con still frowned.

"What are the odds of you being crushed by this huge rock?" he wanted to know.

I sighed. "Con, it's a metaphor."

"The *metaphorical* rock then."

"I don't know, all right? I haven't done this before. But I have to, so can you just let Me go?"

In two strides he was on me, lifting me easily and holding me tightly against him, so fiercely and with such swiftness that my head spun. "Never," he muttered hoarsely in my ear. "I'll never let you go. Not willingly, and no matter how you try to push me away." He pulled back and stared into my eyes, his the molten gold of the wolf, all the ferocity and determination of the man he'd made himself into set in the lines of his face. I parted my lips, though I had no idea what I'd say, and he closed his mouth over mine, kissing me with drugging dominance and heartbreaking tenderness. He'd kissed me like that the night before, when I'd been bound naked to that bed under the rustling leaves. Kissing me endlessly as he crouched over me, refusing to touch me until I begged for him.

As abruptly as he seized me, he set me down, all satisfied male as he took in my dazed expression, probably knowing exactly how helpless with desire he'd made me. "I promised myself I wouldn't fail to kiss you goodbye ever again," he said, a hint of unsteadiness in his voice. "Good luck. Don't let that huge rock crush you." He nodded at

Ambrose. "Take care of her or I *will* finally strangle you, wizard."

"You won't need to," Ambrose replied cheerfully. "If Her Highness doesn't make it through, none of us will." He winked, though it lacked his usual insouciance.

"If Her Highness and Syr Ambrose are ready," Mother said serenely, though I heard the unspoken *finally* in there, "drink of the waters and come with me."

"Is it safe?" Con asked, fingers flexing as if he'd still rather be bashing something.

"This part I've done before," I reassured him. "Many times." It wasn't pleasant, but repeated encounters with one's own truth made it at least a familiar ordeal. And I learned something new every time, always useful, which mitigated the discomfort.

I sat on a boulder, slipped off my glove and boots, leaving them there, along with the crown. Then I unfastened the thick satin sash and shrugged out of the wrap tunic, discarding it so I wore only my leggings and a sleeveless camisole. Con and Sondra observed silently. I waded barefoot into the pool, the cold water always a shock no matter how often I'd done this, until I stood under the fall of water, the chill from deep inside Calanthe shivering over my skin. I tipped back my head, allowing the water to splash over my face, opening my mouth to drink.

The pure life of Calanthe bubbled through me, effervescent and vital. Distantly I wondered how this aspect of Calanthe could feel so peaceful and nurturing, while another face of her continually snarled in the background of my mind, raging for blood and death.

The same way, I supposed, that I'd been behaving—going from feeling radiant with love to snarling rage. *You are a creation of human flesh, the floral body of Calanthe, and an extension of the goddess.*

The truth hit me hard, cold and clean. I'd been fooling myself that I'd had any distance from Calanthe. I *was* Calanthe, an aspect of Her, made in Her image and animating a form created of Her body. I saw in a way I hadn't before understood that, though I existed via magic, I could also wield magic. The orchid ring couldn't be parted from me, because it had become an extension of my magic, just as I was of Calanthe's. And I'd been lax and irresponsible in not learning how to wield that magic.

Because, though I was an extension of the goddess, I possessed all the flaws and failings of human flesh. Con was correct that I was a human woman, however bizarrely birthed. And I'd made so many mistakes.

They paraded themselves for me, all the errors in judgment, passion, pride, and vanity. This moment could indeed eviscerate a person, those unwilling to face the ugly reflection of their full selves. But I'd been here before, and while I indulged various foibles in myself, I'd always tried my utmost to be honest about my flaws, about the truth of my life. Denial was a luxury I'd never been able to afford.

And so I couldn't deny that I had indeed conceived a child, one that could be a True Heir, to one day take the orchid ring. I also had to face the truth of my own heart. Of course I'd fallen in love with Con. That wasn't something that would change or dissipate. It didn't matter if I fought it, pushed him away, tried to resurrect the walls between us. I loved him utterly and always would. No denying it. And it had been pride and fear that kept me from telling him, not any sort of wisdom as I'd been pretending to myself.

I did have a heart, and it loved as desperately and unwisely as any human heart did. I had to face the truth of that. I'd never been cold. I'd only isolated myself, a tactic that had worked all too well.

So—humbled a bit more than usual, but thankfully not entirely hollowed out—I stepped out from under the spring still not resolved on whether to tell Con I loved him in return. Or whether to tell him about my pregnancy. Drinking the waters gives you the truth, but no guidance on what to do with it. It's one thing to recognize that your own pride and fear have gotten in the way—and something else entirely to overcome them.

All things I could think about later, if I managed to tame Calanthe.

I waded across the pool to the dark mouth on the far side, the soaked clothing clinging like the flaws I had yet to polish away. They served as a reminder that I carried them with me always, unless I found a way to do better, to shed myself of my failings. Folding my hands, I cleared my mind and waited.

Taking a visibly deep breath, Ambrose—barefoot already, as always—waded into the pool, leaning heavily on his staff. He wore his court wizard robes, and the jeweled stars, planets, and moons seemed to leap into life as the sun motes hit, whirling into a vast waltz as the wizard's magic and Calanthe's collided.

He shuddered, clinging to the staff with both hands, then—clearly forcing himself to do it—he tipped back his head, opened his mouth, and drank. For an endless moment, he froze. Even the galaxy on his robe halted its mad dance. Then he fell to his knees and screamed.

Sondra leapt forward, hands outstretched to drag him out of the pool, but Mother glanced her way and sent Sondra flying backward with equivalent force. Con caught her with an *oomph* of expelled breath, wrapping his arms around her and restraining her fierce struggles as she fought him with the wildness of an enraged lion.

"You must not interfere," Mother explained smoothly,

returning her attention to Ambrose, who—still clinging to his staff—nevertheless sagged in the water, sobbing and writhing in pain. Con nodded at Mother, tightening his grip on the still-flailing Sondra, then met my eyes across the pool. His gaze held a question, and I wondered if he thought of all the times he'd wished suffering on Ambrose.

I have an old debt to repay, restitution to make for unforgivable crimes, and labor of deepest love before me, Ambrose had once said to me. I'd always figured he'd seen more of what the future held than he'd shared. With Calanthe's lifeblood surging through me, Her crystalline truth in my veins, I knew Ambrose had foreseen this moment—and had faced it willingly.

Ambrose's shuddering had subsided, his sobbing moans receding like the surf gentling at low tide. His hands tightened on the staff, using the leverage to climb to his feet. He stood there, shuddering, then turned and staggered toward me, leaning heavily on his staff and dragging the one leg. His forest-green gaze met mine, the ancient being I sometimes glimpsed in him bent over even more, face lined with centuries of grief. But he gave me a rueful half smile, a faint glimmer of humor in it.

"That will teach me to wait so long to face my many uncomfortable truths," he said. "Good thing I was already on a path to expiate my crimes, or I don't think I'd be standing now."

I smiled in perfect understanding, offering him a hand on impulse—realizing too late that I'd offered the twig hand. But he took it, bending over the orchid on my wrist to inhale its scent with grateful reverence. The orchid always responded to the wizard with flirtatious flutterings of its petals, and it did so now, but more gently than usual. When Ambrose lifted his face, something of peace had been restored. "Thank you, Euthalia," he said, using my full name with the confidence of friendship. "I apologize for what happened to You in Yekpehr. If I could've suffered in Your place, I would have."

So fresh from the spring, Calanthe's clear truth still rattling me with my own failings, I couldn't summon any anger that Ambrose had obviously seen my fate. He'd known about Con needing to bring my hand home from Yekpehr, and the wizard had been prepared to bring me back from death. He hadn't warned me, but I believed he'd had good reason not to.

"There's no need for you to apologize," I said. "You couldn't have—"

He held up a finger, stopping me. "The apology stands, even if the explanation must wait."

"Then I forgive you," I told him.

He shook his head. "You cannot, not until You know what You would be forgiving."

"I don't understand." A curl of distress wormed through me.

"I know, child. I know." He patted my hand, then released me. "Let's go rescue Merle and settle Calanthe down, yes?"

"Yes." As we'd been speaking, Mother had drunk of the waters, and now approached us beaming with radiant truth. She drank from the spring daily and so had purified herself to the point that she emerged perfectly dry and with no weight of regret.

"Follow me," she said, and entered the tunnel.

12

I watched Lia until the last glimmer of her pale skin disappeared into the deep shadows. Her crown, glittering in the bits of sunshine that leaked into the shadowed cave, abandoned to perch on a bed of moss, seemed like a bad omen. No sense reading into it, though. I couldn't go with her, so I'd wait. I unstrapped the rock hammer and set it aside, along with the bagiroca, and settled myself on the ground, back against a boulder. The thick, weirdly bright-green moss covering everything—which I tried not to find too creepy, though it was—made the seat as comfortable as a bed.

"You going to drink the water?" Sondra asked, standing at the edge of the pool and scuffing the toe of her boot through the gravel.

"I don't know," I answered honestly. I could see this going either way. Whether I gambled on drinking that water might depend on how bored I got—which was probably not the best reason to elect to examine the dark corners of my psyche. "Are you?"

"Asked you first," she retorted, then came to sit next to me.

"On the one hand, we have nothing better to do, and it could be a long wait." I stared at the water. The fall from the spring barely stirred the mirror-still blackness of the surface. It made a pretty tinkling sound, but it seemed Ambrose's screams still echoed from the deep tunnels. "On the other hand, there's a lot of shit in my head I'm pretty sure I don't want to dredge up."

"Yeah," she agreed glumly, drawing up her knees and dangling her hands between them. "Look what happened to Ambrose. For a few minutes there I thought it was going to kill him."

"I think it nearly did." I'd never expected to see the wizard brought so low. "I think Ambrose is really old," I said, mulling it over as I spoke. "And it could be he paid a heavy price to be a wizard. He might be paying it still."

"Do you think that's why he doesn't use his magic much?"

I glanced at her, surprised. Sondra still stared intently at the water, like she hoped to catch a glimpse ahead of time of what she might see. "Could be. I hadn't thought of it that way."

"Yeah. You know, like maybe he pays a price every time he uses it. Like that old tale of the minstrel who snuck into Sawehl's golden palace and stole the magic harp. He got to keep it, play it, and write those songs we still sing— but his fingers bled every time, and he wept from the pain."

"I don't think I ever heard that story," I finally said.

She grinned at me. "You were a naughty kid—you never paid attention to any of the songs and stories."

"I listened to some," I protested. "I remember hearing *you* sing," I added on impulse. Maybe the truth of the place had snuck into me anyway, just by breathing the mist in the air. Though Sondra stiffened, I plunged on. "Your voice impressed even this snot-nosed kid. It was like . . .

magic. And the way you sang those old songs—I could see the stories in my head. I've never heard anything like it since."

She didn't reply right away, and I hoped I hadn't pissed her off—or hurt her too much by bringing up old wounds. "Thank you," she finally said, her voice thick with emotion. "I miss singing. I miss the music, giving voice to it."

"You could still sing."

She gave me a baleful stare, blue eyes catching the light. "I croak like a frog."

"Frogs sing and don't care if someone thinks it sounds pretty."

She laughed, shaking her head. "I sure hope you say nicer things than that to your wife."

"I'm working at it. And you don't know how you sound singing, because you haven't tried. Maybe you can relearn. It won't sound exactly the same, but . . ." I waved a hand, trying to think of the right words. "You have that musical talent still, right?"

She considered that. "Hard to say. I can't fall back on training, that's for sure. Singing was so effortless back then that I never worked at it like my voice tutor wanted me to. I didn't appreciate what a gift it was. Maybe that's why Ejarat took it back, you know?" She swiped a fist under her nose, clearing the thickness from her throat.

"I don't believe that," I said, surprised at my own certainty. "I don't think the gods punish us. We do that to each other well enough."

She snorted a laugh. "Don't we, though."

"If not for Anure, you would've had time to mature, to appreciate your gift and work at it." I stared at my own hands, so gnarled and permanently stained black in the creases, and thought of Brenda's tale, how she never had the chance to repair the foolish decisions of her youth.

"I guess we both turned out different than we would have, for sure." She eyed the spring. "You know, Conrí. I've killed a *lot* of men."

I had no trouble following her thoughts. "We both have. Men and women." If Calanthe planned to parade their faces in front of me, I didn't want to see that, either.

"I mean that I made them suffer. I wanted to hurt them, and I did. Nothing to say?" she asked when I didn't reply.

"What am I, your confessor? Find a priest of Sawehl for that."

"No, you are my king, Conrí," she replied slowly. "If I appeared before you in the court of Oriel, what sentence would you pass upon me?"

"None. Full pardon. There you go."

"That won't work. If Lia's plan works, you'll be king of Oriel and you'll be dealing with rafts of this shit. What about the nobles that colluded with Anure? They'll have all kinds of war crimes to answer for. You won't be able to just pardon me—you'll have precedents to set."

I pinched the bridge of my nose. "I thought you wanted me to take Anure's place, to be emperor."

She was so quiet that I glanced at her, but she was still staring at the pool, as if something might rise out of it, grab her by the ankle, and drag her in. "Not anymore. If you'd seen Yekpehr, the citadel . . . They paraded us through the streets and crowds gathered, but . . . they all looked dead inside. And Anure's throne room—it's like a monument to greed. No one person should have that much power. I don't wish that on you."

"You could say the same about me being king," I felt I had to say.

But she considered me, expression canny in the speck-led shadows. "I think . . . this whole thing about serving the land, maybe it keeps you honest, you know? Lia, She's suffered for Calanthe. It's not all jewels and waving Her pinkie for the least little thing." She gazed off down the tunnel. "Who knows what She'll have to carve out of Herself this time, to tame Calanthe again."

The prickle of doom crawled over my scalp, my gaze drawn to Lia's sparkling crown, settled into its niche like some artifact of old, waiting for a true ruler to come claim it again.

"I'm drinking the water," Sondra declared, prying off her boots.

"You sure?" I hadn't really thought she would, despite my poking at her.

"Seems cowardly not to," she replied, standing to unbuckle her sword belt, then shucking off her reinforced leather vest and her leather pants, so she stood in just a thin undershirt and shorts. "I'm thinking maybe that there's something to facing the truth. It doesn't change anything I've done, and even though I can guess what I'll see, there might be something I can learn just by making myself do it."

She walked to the pond, waded in. "Shit, that's cold. Why didn't they tell us it was so fucking cold?"

"Probably because that's the least of it?" I suggested. "If you can't take a little cold water, you sure aren't going to be able to handle the truth."

"Fair point." She waded in farther, stopping shy of the fall of water. "That girl I was—she never faced anything difficult. Never worked at anything."

"I think you've faced plenty of difficult stuff since."

She glanced over her shoulder, the mist making her look younger, hiding the toughness and scars. "Because I had to. I was forced into that. This is something *I* am choosing." With that, she stepped under the fall of water, tipped back her head, and drank.

It was a lonely vigil, and an uncomfortable one, watching Sondra sit in the pool and weep. She didn't scream like Ambrose had, but she stayed in much longer, her tears almost invisible under the fall of water. Only the occasional soft sob betrayed her.

Feeling more impotent than I had since before we escaped the mines, I sat there while Sondra faced her truth, while Lia tamed her monsters, while Ambrose fought his own demons. I kind of expected one of the priestesses—or Lia's ladies—to arrive and chastise me for my idleness. But no one did. I didn't even have Vesno to keep me company.

When Sondra finally crawled out of the pond on her hands and knees, she went to the stick she'd taken from the wizards' workroom, wrapping her hand around it thoughtfully before sprawling back onto the moss. She lay there, staring at the cave ceiling, holding that ugly stick and staying nothing.

By then I'd about had enough of sitting around. Why had I come along, if I was just going to waste time getting soft, accomplishing nothing? I could've gone to the shipyard and at least lent another pair of hands to repairing a ship. Or I could be meeting with Brenda—Percy probably wasn't speaking to me—about our strategy to free the captives from Yekpehr. I could be getting Agatha to tell me everything she knew about Yekpehr and the royal captives. I knew I damn well wasn't drinking that water.

"You should do it, Conrí," Sondra said, like the voice of my conscience, as she'd always been. The first to swear loyalty to me. *Long live the king.*

"Why," I grated out, "because you had so much fun?"

She rolled her head to look at me. "Don't be a baby and just do it."

"No, thanks." I adjusted my seat. Maybe I'd take a nap.

"It's the furthest thing from fun," she said, rolling her head back and closing her eyes, "but it's . . . informative. Freeing. Cleansing, maybe, like purging a festering wound. It wasn't what I expected. You'll be glad you did."

"Maybe after Anure is dead and Rhéiane is on the throne of Oriel," I said. "Time enough for spiritual awakenings then."

"Your choice, of course," she replied drowsily. "But you might need to do this, if we're going to win."

That odd sense of premonition prickled over me again. "Why? What do you think I'll need to face?"

She shrugged a little, snuggling deeper into the moss. "Dunno. That's your shit to figure out. But I have this feeling that we might not get to leave until you do it."

"What?" I reached for my rock hammer, other hand going to the bagiroca at my hip. "Is there—"

"The magic, Conrí." Sondra didn't even open her eyes. "Think about it. We've been here hours and hours and the light hasn't changed."

I squinted at the sun angling in. It looked the same as when we'd arrived, but . . . "That's just a trick of the cave vents. It probably always looks like this, unless it's night." But even as I said the words, I knew they weren't true. This place sure made you aware of untruths; even a little bit of wishful thinking sounded like an outright lie.

"If you say," Sondra agreed sleepily, then yawned. "Are you hungry?"

"No."

"See? You should be. And no one has come to check on us. Maybe we're in a time bubble."

"A time bubble," I echoed with scorn. "That isn't a thing."

She shrugged again, less movement this time. "Guess you'll find out." And she dropped off to sleep, snoring softly.

Tempted to head out of the cave, just to prove nothing would stop me, I didn't even get up to try. Though I'd argued with Sondra, I suspected she'd nailed it. Something about the cave, the pool, the endlessly falling water, the sunbeams that danced but never changed angle—it did feel timeless. Sondra had stopped snoring and slept very still, barely a sign of breathing.

Probably if I tried to leave, I'd find myself just circling back to this same place, like in the old stories. Like the one about the guy trapped in the labyrinth chased by the monster, and him forever looping back and finding himself facing it again and again. See? I'd listened to *that* story.

Hopefully Calanthe wouldn't send a monster to drive me into the pool.

Though I guessed She wouldn't have to. The advantage of immortal beings who wielded time bubbles was they could wait you out. And if Lia was some kind of extension of whatever spirit inhabited this island, then Calanthe knew everything that Lia knew about me. Which I already knew about myself, right? I mean, I didn't need to drink some water of truth to be very aware of my many crimes and failings. I'd fucked up over and over. I'd killed countless people, either by my own hand or through orders to others—and all out of arrogance and hubris. I carried the weight of those deaths willingly, as a punishment I deserved. There wouldn't be any surprises in the water.

Especially Lia's death. I might as well have handed her over to Anure personally, I'd been so determined to kill him myself. I wasn't kidding myself about that reality. Even if she said she didn't blame me, I knew it was true. I could feed her on my blood for the rest of my forsaken life and never make up for that failure.

Or the fact that she clearly still believed I'd inevitably leave her. Oh, she said it was because she figured I'd have to answer the call of Oriel, but I knew better. I'd broken my promises to keep her safe—had offered her up on the platter of my vengeance—and now Lia understood better than ever that I simply couldn't be trusted with her heart.

I had to face that I'd failed everyone I'd ever loved. My mother who died in front of me. My father, drowning on dry land, his lungs filling with his own blood as he died in my arms. Rhéiane, captive all this time while I wandered free. Sondra and Lia. And all the people who'd followed me, giving their hope and their lives to me so that I'd rid the world of Anure.

I'd failed all of them. Of course Lia couldn't love a man like that. She deserved better.

There: I'd faced the truth. And on my own, too, without that stinking truth water.

I glowered at the tinkling waterfall, so pretty with the mist and the filtered sunlight. "I get it, all right?" I said aloud, my voice startlingly gruff in the sacred space. I was the ill-mannered dog fouling up the place. "Start up time again or whatever. I'm not drinking. I don't need it."

Musical water answered me. Lia's crown glinted on the mossy boulder a thousand leagues away. "Sondra, wake up. Let's get out of here," I said loudly, but she didn't move.

Just great. I got to my feet and went to her, nudging her with the toe of my boot. Her breathing didn't even change. I crouched down to shake her awake, but she stayed deep asleep. Fuck me.

"I thought this was an optional thing," I shouted at the waterfall, my voice echoing back all around, like the distant howling of wolves.

I turned to go back to my seat, to wait Calanthe out. Lia would emerge eventually. She had magic, or *was* magic, and Calanthe would have to obey her and let me go. Dammed if I'd let some temple force me to, what? Relive the worst moments of my life? No, thanks.

But I couldn't go back to my seat. My feet wouldn't move. I tried taking a step sideways and just stood there like an idiot. Unless I took a step toward the pool. Oh right—*that* worked just fine.

"Fuck you!" I yelled at the waterfall, shaking my fist at it. "I refuse to be cowed by you. Enough already." Twisting and snarling, I fought whatever kept me from moving backward, but it felt like fighting myself. I reached for my rock hammer, but I'd left it out of my reach. Unhooking the bagiroca from my belt, I swung it wildly, hoping to break the invisible bonds.

But I only ended up closer to the pool, my gyrations moving me forward by increments, the magic preventing me from going back at all. My shouts and curses echoed, overlapping and making a mocking chorus of my ruined voice, of my fundamental impotence.

What will you do, wolf? Lia's voice seemed to rise from the chiming water. *You can't just bash them all over the head.*

At last, exhausted, lungs straining for air, sweating like I'd fought a battle, I stood at the edge of the pool, bagiroca hanging limply by my side. Sondra slept on. And as the echoes of my raging faded, the pretty melody of the tinkling water took over. The sunlight wove through the falling droplets. So peaceful. So deceptive.

"Is this *truth*?" I roared. The question bounced back to me. *Truth? Truth? Truth?*

So that was the deal. Either I drank the water or I lost my mind in this cave. Maybe *I* would become the monster charging out to drive people to doing what they couldn't make themselves do.

"Fine," I snarled and put the bagiroca down. I lifted one foot to yank off my boot, then the other. I tossed them aside, then ditched the leather vest and shirt. No way I was standing there stark naked, so the pants would just have to get soaked. I already felt naked enough without weapons in this uncanny place. Stepping into the water, I managed not to flinch—but only because Sondra had warned me. It *was* cold, like snowmelt cold. I didn't get how that could be on an island that I'd bet had never seen a snowfall. "Guess that's part of the torture," I muttered, stomping to the fall. "Can't have the water of truth be *comfortable*."

The water splashed over me, instantly soaking my hair and beard, cold on my bare chest—more like a deluge than what looked like a little trickle. "Just get it over with," I ordered myself, and threw back my head and drank.

It tasted delicious, like the purest water ever—which maybe it was. And for a minute nothing happened. Just a cold shower and a long drink of water.

It would just figure if I was the only one to drink the water of truth and not see a dammed thing. The gods always had the last laugh. Here I was, wet and shivering, and just as much an idiot brute as when I stepped into the pool.

A hoarse laugh escaped me. I would suspect the others of putting on a show to fool me, if I didn't know Ambrose and Sondra's pain had been truly felt. Lia hadn't shown as much emotion, but then she never did. And her gaze across the pool had been thoughtful, as if what she'd seen had to do with me. That might be vain of me to think so. She had much bigger things to deal with than whatever relationship we had. "So much for truth," I muttered.

"Still my hotheaded and impatient son, I see."

I whirled, water flying. My mother. Standing right there. "Mama?" I croaked, sounding five years old again.

She smiled, full of indulgent love. "My Conrí. It's so good to see you. And look how you've grown up. You're even taller than your father, broader in the shoulder, too."

I scanned the cavern. Everything looked the same, including the sleeping Sondra—except my mother was now standing beside the pool, wearing a gown I remembered from when I was a kid. "You're not real," I said.

She cocked her head. "What is real?"

"You're not my mother. You're a figment of my memories."

"If that was the case, then you would've known already that you're taller than your father," she said gently, then smiled at my confusion. "You didn't, and why would you? Not many other people besides me would be in a position to know."

"The others didn't get a visitor," I pointed out. At least, none of them had seemed to be talking to anyone else.

"Everyone has their own truth, my son," she reminded me. "I am part of yours."

"How are you here then?" I demanded, burying the burst of debilitating emotion under the gruff demand.

"This place is between realms, so it's easier for those of us existing in other forms to meet with the living."

"You still . . . exist?"

She gestured at herself. "Clearly. Though usually we only watch, not speak."

"You've been watching over me?" The thought both pained and warmed me.

"Always, my son. I like Lia. Bright and noble, with a generous heart. You chose well."

"I didn't choose her," I replied reflexively.

"Didn't you?" She gave me a reproving look, like when she'd caught me in a lie.

Was it a lie? It seemed the truth water should've stopped me from saying it, if so. Then I realized both things were true. "I didn't, and then I did."

She nodded. "Everything in our lives is a choice, even if it doesn't seem like it at the time. Even love."

I laughed, a little bitterly. "Yeah, well, falling in love with Lia was an accident."

"Love is never an accident. We choose to love. It's not a wave that overtakes us and sweeps us along. Love comes from our deepest selves, not some outside force. Love is active, something we *do*."

"Even if it's not returned?" I asked, sounding hollow.

"Does Sawehl's sun cease to shine if Ejarat's earth ignores him? No. Love as the sun shines, and you will be warmed by it, too."

"Love can be a weakness," I argued. "Anure uses it against people."

"It can also be a strength. Again, these are choices that belong to you."

"I didn't choose Anure," I retorted harshly. "Or choose to lose you, and Oriel, and Father, and Rhéiane. I didn't choose those stinking mines." At the thought of all that, the helpless black rage rose up, the bloody thirst for vengeance.

"We can't choose what the world does to us, but we can and do choose what to make of all those things," she replied sternly. "You're not a little boy anymore, Conrí."

"I know that," I bit out. "Are you telling me I shouldn't be angry? That I shouldn't want Anure dead?"

"I think you should ask yourself the price of anger, of vengeance."

"I gave up on vengeance. I know my blind need to kill Anure with my own hands got Lia captured and killed. I learned my lesson."

"Have you? You no longer wish to destroy Anure and his empire?"

"I know that freeing Rhéiane and the other captives is more important." There, I'd said it under the influence of the waters, so it must be true.

"Knowing a truth and acting on it are two different things." My mother shook a finger at me, fond exasperation in it. "You are willing to rescue the royal captives because you also hope to kill Anure. There are no secrets here, not even from yourself. Especially from yourself."

"Killing Anure will destroy the empire and liberate everyone. That's why I'm doing this," I answered stubbornly, ignoring the false ring to it.

"And what if restoring the many orphaned kingdoms requires you to let Anure live—will you be able to do that?"

"Are you saying that's what it will come to?" I demanded. Ejarat take me, how I hated the vagueness of prophecies. Either tell me a solid prediction or don't tell me anything. "Because I don't see Anure just walking away. We have to destroy him if we have any hope of a lasting peace."

"Do you? I would carefully consider what you hope to accomplish—and the cost to yourself. You'd be risking your own life."

"Maybe my life is worth that," I answered bleakly. I'd never planned to survive killing Anure. "Killing Anure is what I've lived for all these years."

"Maybe you should change that," she countered. "Dying for vengeance changes nothing, but living well, giving your life to creating a world worth living in, that changes everything."

"I don't know how to do that." I thought of how I'd felt, sitting beside Lia's throne, pretending to be a king and knowing myself for a fraud. "I know how to kill. Not how to make things live."

"Dealing death is easier," she agreed. "Just as it's easier to destroy than to create. Death is always there, waiting for us, but life is not. Which is more precious?"

"You want me to say life," I answered when she paused expectantly. "But I still don't get what you're telling me."

She shrugged a little. "Think it over. Maybe you will. And now I must go."

"Wait!" I reached for her but couldn't move. Figured. "Sondra thought—I thought that I'd learn something I needed to know to win this battle. What is it?"

She shook her head, smiling still, but with that exasperation. "So like your father. It's not always about winning. Sometimes enduring, surviving, is enough. Hasn't your Lia taught you that yet?"

"I guess I thought this truth thing would bring more clarity."

She laughed. "Clarity. Ah, yes. I'm not sure anyone gets to have that, much as it seems desirable. There are layers beneath layers, and it takes a great deal of scrubbing away to get to the core. Consider this a first layer. I love you, Conrí. Give my love to Rhéiane when you see her."

"Then I *will* see her? She *is* in Yekpehr?" I felt like I was yelling down a long hallway as my mother's image faded. "Don't go yet! Mama, I love you, too."

Love you too. Love you too. Love you too. Our voices, intertwined, echoed around, making a harmony with the endlessly tinkling fall of water.

~ 13 ~

I'd been past the waterfall to the inner temple any number of times, but never down the passage Mother led us through. The path sloped down, going in spirals that tunneled ever deeper. Formed initially of smooth polished stone, the tunnel had no moss, as we'd left sunlight far behind. After a while, the stone began to look more organic, with ripples that seemed to pulse rhythmically. Though I'd always understood Calanthe was both an island and a living being, depending upon which reality you viewed Her from, the feeling that we moved through the veins—or intestines— of some enormous creature was unsettling.

It's fucking creepy, Con's voice said in my mind, making me smile. Would he and Sondra drink from the water and see their truths? I put my wager that they would, if only because neither of them could stomach backing down from a challenge.

Ambrose walked beside me, dragging the bad leg and leaning heavily on his staff. He managed to keep up, though Mother never slowed her pace.

"Does your leg pain you?" I asked him, wishing I could offer assistance, though I didn't know what I could do.

"Not pain, exactly," he replied. "All that truth has made it more difficult to ignore the weight dragging at it."

"Weight?" I recalled what Mother had said, about Ambrose existing in several realities at once. That certainly explained how he looked different to me, depending on what kind of vision I used—and perhaps on his own magic. I focused on the leg, looking for magic or trying to see through to another layer. It changed with each lens of attention—sometimes looking like a young man's healthy leg, sometimes withered to skin and ligaments, sometimes . . . What was that? It seemed to be dark as iron, and massive. A manacle and chain?

Ambrose watched me, his canny green eyes in a young man's face bright with interest. "Did You see it?"

"Are you . . . chained, in some other place?" I felt a bit absurd guessing it, but his face lit with pleasure, as if a prized pupil had solved a difficult problem.

"Indeed I am. For quite some time, I'm afraid."

"Who is holding you captive?" I asked, wondering at the might of that wizard.

"It's my own doing," Ambrose replied ruefully. "And not easily undone."

"So you are shackled in a prison in some other reality, but able to move around freely in this one?"

"Not exactly freely, as You observe. The restrictions that bind me govern me in a number of ways."

I considered that. "You're not able to speak of it, unless someone asks you questions."

He tipped his finger to his temple in a salute. "And even then I must be careful what I say, lest I alert those who would be . . . distressed to learn how I've eluded certain restraints."

"Can you be freed?"

He grimaced. "That remains to be seen."

Hmm. "Is there a place in this world that corresponds physically to where you are chained?"

Brightening, he nodded. "An excellent question, Your Highness. Very clever."

"I assume it will do no good to ask where."

"There are clues," he suggested.

"Not helpful, Ambrose." Then I laughed, imagining Con's frustration if he heard this conversation. "Is it important for Me to know?"

He mulled that over. "It might well be. It depends."

"You must leave the riddle for the moment," Mother said without looking back at us. "As we have arrived and Your Highness has a more immediate problem to solve."

I looked around, perplexed. We seemed to be in yet another bend in the tunnel, not anywhere in particular. I thought of Con sardonically expressing disappointment at the lack of fantastic elements at the cave entrance to the temple, and had to admit to a similar feeling. "Right here?" I clarified.

Mother glanced around. "This isn't good enough for You, Queen Euthalia?"

"I don't mean to seem that way. I'd just expected . . ." something that would give me more of a clue as to what I should do. I turned to Ambrose. "Do you sense Merle here?"

"Here and not here," he answered, looking as perplexed as I felt. "Perhaps Your Highness should open a door? Or a window would do," he added helpfully.

I tried looking with different levels of vision, seeing only the tunnel encircling us. Mother watched expectantly. I was missing something . . .

Oh. I'd been so determinedly walling out Calanthe's raging that it had become a reflex. Even now, knowing I must, I hesitated, afraid to make contact with the monster in myself. So much for truth.

The waters of truth had shown me that I'd been cowardly, shirking my more difficult responsibilities, and now it was time to step up.

More than nervous, I reached for the dreamthink. Once a boon to my troubled mind, the state where I could revel in Calanthe and my connection to Her, the dreamthink felt heavy, fraught, and prickly. Full of death and the screams of the suffering. People, animals, plants, soil, the sea— all fouled with violence and despair. And worst of all, Calanthe hungering with avid greed for more.

I flinched from it, from my own guilt and from the pride that had me shunning any sign of weakness, from asking for and accepting help. And I faced my own greed, the craving for control that led to the lust for power, the blood hunger that devoured, uncaring what it killed. I'd felt this, drinking Con's blood. I wanted to dance, to run and be free. Not to be captive, serving as a rock for the parasites that crawled over my skin.

I flailed against the bonds that held me, seeing myself strapped down as the wizards had confined me, bound to their altar of stone, bleeding me dry. I would not be contained! I roared my defiance, my determination to escape and break free. The wizard in purple pushed back his cowled hood, his beak curved and sharp, amber eyes bright with intelligence.

"Merle," I breathed. "Merle, help me."

Merle, with a very serious and concerned expression— though how I could see that on his raven's face, I didn't know—inspected the bonds restraining me. I pulled at them, pouring strength into it. The table under me cracked, and it seemed I felt the world tilt on its axis. Merle spread his wings wide, the cloak falling away, and the giant raven threw himself over me, pinning me down.

I flailed, determined to escape, but also confused. Was I supposed to help Merle?

The wizard in blue robes approached, funneling magic to Merle. The bonds grew stronger again, though I managed to free a hand—not a hand, it was a cluster of twigs? Oh yes. I remembered. But I had the orchid still, and I used that power to fling them away from me. Both wizards went flying, one taking flight on black raven's wings.

"Lia," the wizard in blue yelled to me. "You must take over for Merle. Remember what you are here to do."

Ambrose's voice? In my confusion, I stopped fighting, and the bonds coiled around me again. No, no—I wanted to be free. Magic surged through the orchid, rich and redolent, the sheer force of nature pouring out. All the might of wind over water, the erosion of stone over time, eons of life, the finality of death, the most unstoppable power of all.

I was too powerful and they could not bind me any longer. Roaring my triumph, I broke the last bonds, leapt from the table to the floor, but it crumbled beneath me. People screamed, shrieking as they fell into the sea.

Then Con stood before me, face serious and full of love. He held a crimson ribbon in his hands—and I remembered with a rush the excitement and unexpected freedom of being bound. "It can be good, too," he said, in his low voice. "You liked it. You wanted it. You still want it. Trust in this."

That was true. Truth. Yes, I had agreed to accept the bonds, to lie down in this world and allow my children to live and prosper. "You fed Me blood," I told him.

"And always will," he replied. "Will you accept the bonds?"

"Yes, because I love you."

"I love you, and so I put my bonds upon you."

And then I was binding myself, weaving the ribbons around my limbs. Careful so they'd be comfortable. Firm so they couldn't be broken. I smiled at myself, feeling that love and trust. "I do this for you."

"I know. I love you, too."

As the bonds tightened, as I allowed them to comfort and restrain me, I fell into an easy sleep, dreaming of the orchids that would bloom from me. They didn't have to live on their own, because they had me.

"Love you, my daughter," I murmured.

"I love you, Mother."

I came back to my fleshly body with a start.

We stood in the tunnel, lit only by Mother's lantern. She watched me curiously, and warily. Ambrose stood straighter, a cheerful grin on his face, his gaze roving over me with patent delight. And Merle sat on his shoulder.

Ambrose and Merle, there in that chamber. Helping me to tame and bind Calanthe, who was also me. "I am too many people at once," I murmured, and Ambrose's smile widened.

"I know exactly what you mean," he confided.

"Calanthe is at rest," Mother declared, then bowed deeply to me. "Thank You for Your sacrifice, my queen and my goddess."

Not sure what to say, I inclined my head—and felt the silken slide of cool vines over my bare shoulders. Startled, I put a hand to my head, finding myself not bald anymore, but with luxuriant growth flowing over my shoulders. Scooping it up, I brought it round to see: a wealth of fairy-thin vines, delicate as human hair, but rich with small leaves and blooming with tiny blossoms in every color.

"It's quite remarkable," Ambrose assured me, and Merle croaked in approval.

"And as it should be," Mother added reprovingly. "No more shaving it off."

"No." I smiled at her, feeling radiant with it. My own

hair, as I'd never imagined it could be. Then I realized . . . "My hand!"

It had completed the regeneration, the orchid back on my ring finger. I flexed my fleshly fingers, finding them the same as they'd been before. And my arm no longer looked wasted. I felt like myself again—something I would never again take for granted.

"Thank you, Mother," I breathed, and we all knew I meant Calanthe. I reached for the dreamthink, and She responded with the sleepy embrace I'd been so long familiar with. And no longer minded. Calanthe wasn't meant to be any more awake than this in our realm. Across my island, people and animals bustled, bursting with renewed life. The damage hadn't disappeared, but they were working to fix it. All of us, together, putting things to rights again.

We'd done it. A miracle.

"I'll take You to Tertulyn, Your Highness," Mother said, extinguishing her lantern as we emerged into the light-filled upper caverns of the temple.

"I should go tell Con the good news first," I said, slowing my steps, my good spirits falling.

Mother didn't pause, turning down a tunnel I knew led to the private residential areas and clearly expecting me to follow. "I believe Your wolf will be occupied for some time yet."

"He drank the water?" I hurried to catch up, quite easy in my bare feet and leggings, with my body humming with renewed vitality. I glanced back. Ambrose seemed to be gliding along without too much trouble. Merle had his head pressed into the wizard's golden curls, Ambrose replying softly from time to time, as they carried on the conversation they'd been having the entire walk back.

"Both Conrí and the Lady Sondra partook of the waters."

I didn't doubt she would know, but it still surprised me that Con had. Sondra, yeah. I could see her curiosity overcoming her cynicism, not to mention that she could never resist a dare, but Con? I'd been just certain he'd fight it all the way, and I said as much.

Mother chuckled. "Oh, he fought all right. But his inner self wanted the truth badly enough that he succumbed."

Ah. Now, *that* sounded like my Con. "And he's still under the water?" Surely we'd been gone for hours. Hard to say. Time moved differently in the temple.

"He fought himself for a *very* long time," she replied with wry amusement.

Hmm. Hopefully the truth wouldn't wound him too much. But Con was strong. He was much better at facing ugly realities than I was. If none of the terrible events of his young life—and the trials since—had broken him, I doubted anything could. Still, I very much wanted to go to him. This worrying over someone wasn't something I was accustomed to. Until recently I'd only ever truly fretted over Calanthe. And now that I understood I *was* Calanthe on some levels, that seemed terribly self-absorbed of me.

"Mother, I have a question," I said quietly, glancing back to make sure Ambrose still lagged by a considerable distance and remained absorbed in the conversation with Merle. Though the wizard might understand this better than I did. Still, it felt private. Personal.

Mother glanced at me. "Ask, daughter. The wizard will not hear."

"How is it that I'm an extension of Calanthe, both Her and yet not?"

She smiled in sympathy. "I wondered when You'd receive that truth. I suppose You needed to see that in order to subdue the monster in Yourself."

I nodded. All so very odd to wrap my mind around. *Monster.*

"You are not so different," Mother reassured me, seeming to know I needed it. "We all battle ourselves. Witness Your Conrí, at war with himself in any number of ways."

That was Con, most assuredly.

"We are all spirits taken flesh. Your flesh is simply created somewhat more deliberately than the rest of us, fashioned from a blend of materials."

"Flower made flesh."

"Or flesh made into new flesh. Our spirits descend, occupy our bodies for a while—as we live the life of the body—and then return from whence they came. Most of us cannot know the nature of the spirit we spring from, but You are unusual in that You do know."

"Calanthe."

"Yes."

I frowned. "I still don't understand how I can be both."

"When our spirits animate our earthly forms, we don't descend entirely. Part of that spirit remains in the other realm. What we are in these bodies is an extension of the spirit."

An extension of the goddess. "So I'm a walking piece of Calanthe? Like a puppet?"

"Euthalia," she scolded gently. "You can hardly be a puppet of Yourself. We are all spirits living lives in this reality, with parts of those spirits remaining in the astral realm to guide and learn from our human experiences. Some of those spirits have other manifestations in this world. The island we know as Calanthe is one of Yours."

"Thank you, Mother. I will think on this."

"You and philosophers throughout history." She smiled at me kindly. "Don't overthink. If we were meant to know everything while incarnate, we would." She stopped at a closed door. "Tertulyn is within. I shall leave You now."

Ambrose had caught up to us. "Would You like Merle and me to remain, Your Highness?"

"I would love your company, but I fear I must do this alone." I glanced at Mother, who did not disagree. "Do I knock?"

She shook her head sadly. "She will not respond. Good-bye, my Euthalia. Visit us again soon."

"I will, Mother." I embraced her, and she held me tightly.

She released me, arranging my hair around my face. "My beautiful, powerful girl. Remember that You are Yourself. Don't get caught up in the rest of it. This is Your life to lead as You wish." Brushing tears away, she laughed softly. "I grow sentimental in my old age. Come along, wizards. I shall escort you out. We appreciate your assistance in our time of need, but you have much territory to cross before you can be trusted. I'll be happier with you out of my temple." With that they walked off, disappearing around a bend.

Taking a breath, I pushed the door open and stepped inside. Like all the residences in the temple—like the one I'd had before I went to live in the palace with my father—the room was more garden than chamber. A bed and sitting area nestled under a rock overhang, then progressed into a tangle of vines, flowers, shrubs, and trees. A fishpond occupied a large terrace, bright shapes darting within.

Tertulyn sat on a bed of violas at the rim of the pond, dangling her fingers in the water, apparently absorbed with her reflection. With her simple shift and long hair spilling around her, she might've been a sculpture in her stillness. *Nymph at the Pond.* She didn't seem to hear my approach—or if she did, she ignored me. I walked right up to her and she never moved.

"Tertulyn?" I ventured.

She looked up and pasted on a bright smile, nothing of herself in it. "Oh look," she said in mocking singsong. "If it isn't Lia's pet dogs. His Imperial Majesty Anure, Emperor of All the Lands, regrets to inform you that he had an urgent engagement elsewhere, with his new prize. I hope you're not too fond of Euthalia. You lose, Slave King."

And she went back to gazing at the water.

"Tertulyn, it's Me."

She looked at me and smiled. "Oh look. If it isn't Lia's pet dogs. His Imperial Majesty Anure, Emperor of All the Lands, regrets to inform you that he had an urgent engagement elsewhere, with his new prize. I hope you're not too fond of Euthalia. You lose, Slave King."

I crouched beside her. "I *am* Euthalia. It's Me. Your . . . friend. Remember?"

Tertulyn looked up. "Oh look. If it isn't Lia's pet dogs. His Imperial Majesty Anure, Emperor of All the Lands, regrets to inform you that he had an urgent engagement elsewhere, with his new prize. I hope you're not too fond of Euthalia. You lose, Slave King."

This would get old very quickly. I put a hand on her shoulder, thinking physical contact might remind her of our long relationship. It did—but not as I'd hoped.

She exploded into movement. Like one of Con's vurgsten bombs they'd buried in swamps and fields, to touch them was to set them off. Wizard magic blew over and through me.

Tertulyn flung herself at me, her face a rictus of rage, fingers curled into claws that fastened around my throat. She hurled me onto my back, the breath thudding out of me. I'd fallen into a trap, baited especially for me. Her hands tightened on my throat until I couldn't draw breath.

But I could reverse her viciously expelled energy and

that coiling wizardry. Inhaling the scent of the orchid ring as it funneled Calanthe's deep magic through me, I repelled both. Tertulyn bounced away, falling to her back, and I followed, pinning her there with her own struggling attempts to attack again. The wizard magic, untethered, furled around me, seeking a target. Drawing on Calanthe's wards, I bundled the wizard magic and flung it into the teeth of the ancient enchantments. They chewed, strange otherworldly shrieks echoing, then all went silent.

Tertulyn went limp. I looked into her blank face, the empty eyes vacant of the warm affection they'd once held—or pretended to hold. I wasn't sure what I'd expected from seeing her. Maybe a part of me had hoped she could be reclaimed. Mostly I'd wanted to ask if she'd betrayed me deliberately, if everything had been a lie. I'd wanted resolution and now it seemed I wouldn't ever have it. Shadows slimed behind her smile, her face holding nothing of the woman I'd known, the girl who'd been my friend.

I sat there a moment longer, coming to terms with losing her, that I'd lost her long ago. My friend and lover had died when they wiped her mind. I thought of what Mother had said, about the spirit extending to live awhile in Tertulyn's body. Was it there still, trapped in flesh that lived on mindlessly? If so, it deserved to be freed.

I hated to do this, and yet I refused to be the coward and leave it to another. I'd given execution orders before—more times than I liked to contemplate—and I'd observed those executions, taking that responsibility on myself as queen, as my father had taught me to do. But never had I carried out a death sentence with my own hands. Truly, I never guessed I had this ability. It came to me, though, offering itself, and I pulled at Tertulyn's physical vitality, draining the life slowly from her body. She weakened, then went boneless.

Her eyes drifted closed and her face relaxed dreamily as I let her life sift softly into Calanthe's soil.

Finally she collapsed into herself, a puppet with her strings severed, the last of her body's life gone. Wiping the tears from my face, I arranged her limbs into a peaceful posture, brushing her hair from her face with the old tenderness that had lived between us for so long. Maybe it had never been real for her, but it had been for me. I'd choose to remember her that way. My childhood companion. My fellow student in those first shy joys of the body. I folded her limp and boneless hands, cold and damp from the water, on her breast. In her rest, her face looked familiar again.

"It's time to sleep now, old friend." Tertulyn wasn't a child of Calanthe, but she would become part of us anyway. I could give her that. The orchid hummed gently on my finger as I drew on it, the violas rustling as they burgeoned. Stems wound over Tertulyn, filling in as leaves and blossoms billowed into verdant life. Calanthe, answering my request with a warm embrace, took Tertulyn into her soil. Within moments, there was no sign of her body, except for the lavish mound of flowers. Violet for mourning.

I sat there a while longer, letting the tears fall. "I loved you well, Tertulyn," I finally whispered. "Rest in peace."

When I rose to my feet and turned, Mother stood there. I hastily wiped away my tears, wishing my guilt could be as easily hidden. Hoping she hadn't seen how easily I could take a life. "I thought we'd said goodbye."

She shrugged a little. "I thought this decision might be easier for You if You believed that. I suspected this might be the outcome."

"Do you disagree?" I asked, realizing that it was far too late to ask that question.

"Would I disagree with my queen?" she returned with a sad smile.

"I would hope so," I returned immediately, though I also knew that might be too much to ask.

"For what it's worth, Your Highness, I don't disagree." She gazed at the bed of flowers. "This war has killed many, and Tertulyn was a casualty of that terrible wheel. We can't save everyone."

"That doesn't mean we don't try," I replied, hearing the echoes of Con and myself saying those very words to each other at different times.

"Then go save the rest, my wild daughter." She came and kissed me on the forehead. "We'll wall off this garden to be Tertulyn's resting place, so the others might visit and pay their respects to her memory."

The others. Blessed Ejarat—what would I tell my ladies? Of course they wouldn't question me, but . . . I took a deep breath, mourning the loss of their trust and affection already. I'd executed one of their own, and there was no taking that back. "I must go. If Con has finished?"

"He has. And is pacing, impatient for Your return."

I smiled, despite the ache in my heart. That absolutely sounded like him.

~ 14 ~

"I thought Mother Ascendant said Lia would be out soon," I griped to Sondra. Lia's ladies and a bunch of other Calantheans, priests and priestesses and folk who'd come out of the woodwork, were all dancing in the mossy meadows, flinging petals and singing songs. Mother had said they were celebrating Calanthe's return to balance. Certainly the ground had stopped shaking. So that meant Lia had succeeded.

I'd never doubted that she would. Still, if she was done, why hadn't she come out yet?

Sondra rolled her eyes at me and took the stick Vesno brought her, throwing it for him again. "It hasn't been *that* long."

I eyed the cave mouth, considering going to look for her, took a few steps that way, then paced back again. "I worry about what she's up to, is all."

"Hmm. Good point. Maybe she's doing the nasty with some of the temple maidens," Sondra agreed, then grinned cheekily. "Maidens no more!"

"You are not helping," I growled at her. "And why are you so fucking cheerful?"

"I told you. Water of truth is cathartic. Don't you feel lighter?"

"No." I paced toward the cave mouth, turned back to find Sondra giving me a sympathetic grimace.

"The truth hurt, huh?"

"Not like that." Vesno brought me the stick this time, so I threw it for him. "I talked to my mother."

"Whoa." Sondra looked appalled. "Like your actual mother? Queen Rynda?"

"If I have another mother, I don't know about her." At Sondra's look I relented. "She seemed to be the real thing—knew stuff my mother knew—and said she watches over me."

"Ouch." Sondra rubbed her hands on her pants. Vesno did have a spectacular amount of slobber. "I kind of want to ask how she is, but that seems all kinds of wrong."

I bit out a laugh. "She seemed . . . good. Happy. Are the dead happy? I dunno. At peace, maybe."

"Yeah, well. I didn't get any conversations with the dead." Sondra sounded relieved, and I didn't blame her.

"Did you get clarity?" I ventured.

"Hmm. No, but I didn't expect clarity. I got . . . ideas, maybe. Some stuff to work on, to think about. Be a better person, blah blah blah."

"Yeah." That made sense.

"Remember what we talked about at Cradysica, when we went to see that whirlpool for the first time?"

"I guess?"

She made a snorting sound of disgust. But hey, we'd talked about a lot of things—I wasn't going to take the chance of stepping in shit because I guessed wrong.

"I said that it would be nice if we could have paradise, settle down here, but it wasn't for us, that we'd lost that chance a long time ago."

"I remember." And it reminded me uncomfortably of

Lia's words. *You would be forever second place here on Calanthe, a land that isn't Yours.*

"I think I was maybe wrong about that."

"About what?"

"Are you even listening to me, Conrí?"

I tore my gaze from the cave mouth and focused on Sondra. "Yes."

She shook her head and threw the stick for Vesno. "I'm just saying—and I'm still working this out—but maybe we've been going about this wrong. Obsessing about the past, vengeance, instead of fixing things. You know, maybe we should be rebuilding instead of destroying."

That sounded uncannily close to what my mother had said. "Do you mean Oriel?" I asked carefully, wondering if this was more of the message.

"Maybe. Like I said, I'm still pondering. And I guess I wondered if maybe Queen Rynda said something like that to you, too."

I didn't want to rehash it. "Not exactly."

"Well, obviously you don't have to talk about it if you don't want to. I'm just . . . trying to be a friend."

Vesno nudged my hand with his head, the very large stick whacking me in the thigh. I still wasn't even sure what my mother's point had been.

"And there they are," Sondra proclaimed. "Uncomfortable conversation is over, thank Ejarat."

I scowled at her and she grinned back cheerfully. Turning, I spotted Lia, copper dress bright in the sunlight, crown once again glittering on her head as she emerged from the cave with Ambrose beside her, Merle back on his shoulder. I squinted, wondering if a trick of the light made her . . . "Lia," I breathed, running up to her and taking her by the shoulders. "Look at you."

"My hair grew," she confided in a hushed voice, like it was a secret.

"Yes, and I—hello, Ambrose." I shook my head. "Glad to see you found Merle."

"He found himself," the wizard corrected amiably, though the raven cawed at me with harsh displeasure. "But we are indeed happy to be together. Lady Sondra, shall we observe the dancing?"

"Sure," Sondra agreed. "And you can tell me more about this magic walking stick." She unhitched it from her belt and held it up, Ambrose and Merle both ducking.

"I suppose we'd best discuss it, if we can't persuade you to give it back," Ambrose said ruefully, and Merle croaked agreement. They walked off, Vesno going with them, carrying his own stick.

I returned my fascinated attention to Lia. "Your hair is gorgeous. More than I imagined it would be." Her bright, jeweled eyes—one green, one blue—sparkled back at me with her former good health. Though still delicately boned, her face and body had filled out more, her flawless skin glowing. And her hair—it flowed like a river of blossoms, otherworldly and ethereal. More than ever, she reminded me of the painting of the elemental in the book Rhéiane had read to me when I was a boy. "You are so unbelievably beautiful," I said. "You always have been, but now . . ."

She smiled, uncertainty in it, a shadow of grief in her eyes. "I'm still the same person. Vanity, arrogance, and self-absorption intact."

I laughed, the sound hoarse and uncouth. "What about obstinate and prickly?"

Her smile deepened, relief in it. "That, too."

"I understand you tamed the beast," I ventured, not sure if I was supposed to ask about it.

"The beast in Myself, indeed," she replied cryptically.

I waited, but she didn't say more. "All right."

Her lips quirked and she raised a brow, tiny flowers in it. "You're not going to try to bully more out of Me."

"Nope." I grinned at her perplexed frown. "I'm a changed man."

She snorted in a most indelicate way. "The waters of truth have wrought a miracle, then."

I sobered, then nodded. "It was something."

"I'd bet Myself that you wouldn't do it."

"Yeah. I wasn't going to, but the place made me do it." I told her about the time bubble and how I resisted—leaving out making an utter idiot of myself swinging the bagi-roca at thin air. "You could've warned me that the magic would force me to drink," I finished up crankily, recalling my earlier annoyance with her.

She'd listened to the story with interest, and now she smiled, laughter in her eyes. "I didn't warn you because there is no such compulsion. No one is forced to drink and witness the truth inside themselves. We make ourselves do so."

"Uh-uh." I shook my head vigorously. "You weren't there. Something forced me to do it."

"Yes." She raised a hand to my cheek, her caress silky on the skin over my beard. "*You* did. You made yourself do it."

She was definitely amused by this—but she wasn't lying to me. I felt sure of it. "You're saying some part of me wanted to drink the waters and overpowered the part that didn't."

Pursing her lips, she considered that, then nodded. "That must be what happened. Everyone responds to the waters differently. You're a complex man and a natural rebel, an iconoclast, so naturally you came up with something new."

I decided not to ask what "iconoclast" meant. I'd get someone else to tell me.

"Despite your battle not to, are you glad you drank the waters?"

A good question. "Not glad, but . . . yeah, I learned some things."

She searched my face, then seemed pleased by whatever she saw. "I'm glad to hear that. If it's all right with you, we should return to the palace. No more damage will occur to the island, but the havoc already wreaked won't fix itself."

"Don't you want to deal with Tertulyn while we're here?"

She dropped her hand, her gaze going to her ladies, who circled in a dance nearby, singing gaily. Ambrose, Sondra, and a politely seated Vesno watched them—Sondra handling the wizards' walking stick far more carefully than before.

Lia's mouth flattened into an unhappy line. "I already 'dealt' with Tertulyn. I executed her Myself and will forever carry her blood on My hands." She lifted her hands, long and lovely, staring at them with revulsion.

I took Lia's one hand in mine, remarkably restored, the orchid lavish and large on her ring finger again. "I would've gone with you. You didn't have to do that alone."

Lifting her gaze to mine, she sighed. "I did have to do it alone. She was Mine, and I needed to take responsibility for the damage she caused us all."

"If it helps, I would've done the same thing."

"Would you?" She gave me a speculative look, chewing on her lower lip with teeth tamely rounded again, no sign of the sharp feral fangs. Then she laughed a little. "Well, I suppose you, the brutal and ruthless conqueror, *would*—and has."

The sting of that shouldn't have taken me by surprise. "Yes, I have. Countless times. I warned you a long time ago not to romanticize me. I'm not a good man."

Lia studied me with a canny expression. "By that logic, you believe that I'm no longer a good person."

"No," I burst out. "You're queen, and we both know that means making the hard decisions to protect everyone."

"Just as you have done, Conrí, as a king." Her eyes sparkled with a hint of mischief as I groped for a reply. She'd neatly boxed me into that one. "Now to tell My other ladies. They may not be so understanding."

"If they don't understand, dismiss them from your service," I advised.

"A ruthless stance," she murmured, but not rejecting the idea outright.

"That's what I bring to this marriage," I acknowledged, then realized my misstep. "I mean—"

She laid a finger over my lips. "Don't say it."

Moving my lips over the delicious softness of her finger, I wasn't sure what that meant. Had she relented? Perhaps she'd seen something in the water. "Not talking about it doesn't make the future go away."

"No, but it allows us to live in the moment. I saw some truth new to Me, but . . . I need some time to think about what to do about it." Dropping her finger, she withdrew her other hand from mine, then slipped it into the crook of my arm, turning to stand beside me. "I shall take your advice, Conrí." She spoke formally, but I heard a hint of her wicked sense of humor in her voice, which heartened me, even though I really doubted the wisdom of her solution to the problems between us. "If only because you were right about Tertulyn, and I don't ever want to go through this again. Ladies," she called.

The five of them immediately left the group of dancers. Skirts gathered and unbound hair streaming, they ran to Lia with cries of joy.

Lady Calla stepped forward. "You are restored, Your Highness, and we are so grateful for Your intervention on our behalf. Calanthe is saved and we rejoice!"

Lia's fingers tightened on my arm, but she remained otherwise perfectly composed. "Rejoice for Calanthe, yes, but today also calls for mourning. Your sister in service, the Lady Tertulyn, has gone to Yilkay's embrace."

"Tertulyn is . . . dead?" Calla questioned, seeming unable to quite understand.

"Yes. She betrayed Me, betrayed Calanthe, and all of us."

"But Your Highness," Calla burst out. "It wasn't her fault! Anure's wizards cast a spell on her. We expected You to undo it, not . . . murder her."

"Rightful execution by one's queen is not murder," Lia replied crisply. If I didn't know she'd doubted it herself, I would never have guessed she was anything but utterly at peace with her actions. She relented a little, saying, "What was done to her could not be undone. Don't doubt that I will mourn her loss deeply."

Calla bowed her head but said nothing. I felt Lia sigh, but she gave no outward sign of it. "You all see that I have decided to no longer hide Myself under makeup, wigs, and gowns that take three of you to lift." She smiled, but only Ibolya smiled back. The rest seemed to be in a state of shock. "Thus I no longer require the services of so many ladies," Lia continued, her voice cooling as she forced herself through what had to be painful for her. "If you wish to be released from My service, I'll grant your request now."

"Are you . . . letting us go, Your Highness?" Lady Orvyki asked, clearly stricken.

Lia's smile warmed as she gazed on the young woman.

"Not unless you want to be released. If you stay, however, your duties will change. In some ways they'll be lightened. In other ways, I'll require much more of you." She glanced up at me, her gaze holding secrets. "First and foremost, I'll need true loyalty from you."

Calla's head snapped up. "We have all been loyal to You, Your Highness."

"Have you? Then why was Ibolya the only one who accompanied Conrí to Yekpehr to rescue Me?" Lia replied, her voice going cold.

The other ladies looked at one another. None seemed to have an answer. Lia's hand weighed more heavily on my arm, as if she grew weary. "You all swore to serve Me, to protect Me to your utmost ability. I needed My ladies, and in My hour of greatest need, where were you?"

None of them could meet her eyes. "Your Highness was gone from Calanthe," Nahua said finally. "What could we do?"

Lia nodded, as if confirming something to herself. "For a long time Calanthe was all the world to us, but no longer. The world has reached out to Calanthe, and I am not the queen I was. Perhaps you served Me because it was a job you were given, or because of the status it conveys. The why doesn't matter. The pretty playacting is over now. If that's all you were here for, I don't want you." Several of them flinched. "I don't intend to be cruel, but I—" Lia's voice faltered, and I squeezed her hand. Ambrose and Sondra had drawn near, quietly listening, and Lia's gaze went to Sondra. "I have learned something of loyalty, of courage in the face of adversity," Lia continued, speaking to Sondra. "I won't settle for anything less again."

They all bowed their heads sniffling. "Take some time. Come to Me, if and when you are ready," Lia finished, not unkindly. "Conrí, Ambrose, Sondra, Merle, Ibolya—are you all ready to return to the palace?"

We mounted up and rode down the Pilgrims' Path a sober group.

"I didn't intend to put such a damper on the celebrations," Lia said quietly, riding beside me. Vesno raced ahead, delighted to be on the move again. I knew how he felt.

I shrugged. "You did what you needed to do."

She raised a brow at me, shaking back the flower-laden glory of her hair. "You would've done the same?" she asked in a gruff, stern voice that was clearly an imitation of me.

"Well, yeah." I made my voice even deeper and gruffer as I scowled meanly. "You don't get a rep for being the terrifying and ruthless razer of cities by being nice."

She laughed, the clear bell-like sound much better. "I see I shall have to work on my 'rep,'" she replied.

"You don't need to," I replied very seriously. "I've never seen a ruler whose people loved them more than your people love you."

Looking sorrowful, she grimaced. "Do they? I don't know anymore. Or maybe, I wonder who it is they think they love."

"Too much truth?"

"Could be." She picked up a long lock of flowering hair, examining it. When she looked up at me, her gaze was soulful. "I thought My ladies loved Me. And now I feel like I was blind to so many things. Things that maybe I didn't want to know. I've drunk the waters of truth long before this. Why didn't I see more clearly before?"

I pondered that. "Why drink the waters more than once?"

"Because our truths change over time, as we gain experience, live life, hopefully mature—ah, I see your point."

"Yeah. Your ladies do love you, but maybe you need a different kind of love from them now. It makes sense that your expectations would change. The queen you are now needs a different kind of support than the one you were before all this."

She nodded thoughtfully. "I didn't even realize I was so angry and disappointed with them until I saw them at the temple. They acted like nothing had changed, like I was the same as I'd always been, as if I hadn't suffered what I did and we'd just go back to the same life. Like little girls playing at being queen."

"I guess nothing *did* change for them, right?"

She eyed me. "I see things very differently than I did before. Losing everything . . . it changes you, doesn't it?"

I met her gaze and smiled ruefully. "I think it does—though I don't have much basis for comparison."

"I wonder why you married Me," she said, almost conversationally.

"What?" I shook my head. "I thought you didn't want to discuss this."

"Not the future. The past."

"You know why I married you."

"Yes, the prophecy and all." She waved that away. "But you had to hate Me, and everything I represented, long before I took you prisoner and threatened to execute you." She fluttered lashes at me that looked like new ferns.

"I didn't even know you existed until Ambrose showed me the stuff about the Abiding Ring at the tower of Keiost," I pointed out.

"And what did our wizard tell you about Me?" She glanced over her shoulder at Ambrose apparently discussing Sondra's walking stick. Ambrose was showing her something on its surface, while Ibolya brought up the rear this time, Merle perched on her horse's shoulder harness, tipping his head as she stroked his feathers.

"You know," I replied evasively, "the basic stuff."

I didn't fool her, though. "And you hated Me."

"I disliked what you represented," I corrected. "None of that matters, because I love you now. Once I got to know the woman, you, my Lia . . ." I shrugged, wishing I had a gift for pretty words. "Well, I love everything about you. I'm sorry if you don't believe that or don't want to hear it."

"It's not that I don't want to hear it," she replied quietly. "I'm . . . moved that you love Me, and I do believe in it. I think that's part of what's changed for Me, personally. Now that I know what it's like to be truly loved—and I think you might be the only person alive who sees Me, the person, no matter how My appearance changes—now that I know what real love feels like, I can't abide the false versions."

"There are a lot of different kinds of love," I offered, after a lapse of silence. "Different doesn't mean fake or wrong."

"Such the philosopher," she noted with a slight smile. "All true. I'll think about that." She shook her hair back. "I shall cease dwelling on morose subjects that aren't important anyway," she declared loftily. "I intend to be grateful for My many blessings—as instructed." She gave me a nod. "And I shall concentrate on our very important planning for your mission to Yekpehr. When do you plan to leave and how may I assist?"

15

I hadn't exactly lied to Con—I *was* anxious to get back to the business of running my realm. I felt good physically, and there was so much to do to put Calanthe to rights again. More important, I had no desire to spend any more time on my own emotional flailing. Personal feelings weren't relevant, as my father would say. The only feelings of mine that deserved attention were those regarding the throne.

My job now was to rebuild Calanthe and give Con the best chance at rescuing the captive royals. The more I buried myself in my duties and responsibilities, the easier it would be for me to continue that way once Con returned to Oriel. I refused to let this man who'd walked into my life only weeks before leave a hole when he left. Because leave he would, and I doubted he'd be back.

As we neared the palace, I made mental lists, arranging and rearranging the order of priority of the areas of Calanthe with the worst damage and greatest need of attention first. Taking refuge in logic and order soothed me, and I was ready to put ideas into action.

However, we returned to a festival in progress. Before we even reached the palace grounds, raucous sounds filtered through the usually quiet forest. When we emerged into the gardens, well . . . it seemed half of Calanthe had come to the palace, the party raging at full steam and apparently growing larger by the moment as people streamed into the gardens from all directions.

Con had his bagiroca in hand and Sondra brought her horse up to flank my other side, her sword drawn, before I fully processed the scene. "What is this?" Con growled.

"Not an attack," Sondra answered doubtfully, "as it looks to be all Calantheans."

I looked between the pair of them, incredulous. "It's a party," I explained, drawing the word out to imply they might not be familiar with it.

They pinned me with identical glowers. "Did you plan this?" Con demanded, still suspicious.

I managed to keep a straight face. "I believe it may be *spontaneous*."

"Why aren't your guards putting up barriers, controlling the crowd?" Con asked.

Restraining a sigh of exasperation, I waved a hand at the gardens, which gave way to the tiers of houses gracefully cascading to the harbor below. "This belongs to everyone on Calanthe. Except for a few places that require security, we don't bar anyone. Really, it's fine." But I let go of the idea that I'd get any work done that evening. "Everyone deserves a bit of celebration, yes?"

"Seems like that's about all the Calantheans do," Con replied. They both relaxed somewhat, though neither looked particularly pleased. "News travels fast," Sondra commented sourly.

"Yeah," Con said. "I get how the temple people knew you'd fixed Calanthe, but how did these folks know?"

I shrugged cheerfully. "They felt it."

Sondra muttered something about creepy landscapes, and Con flashed her a grin. By then, my people had spotted us and surged forward, shouting tributes and praise.

"Please don't bash anyone over the head," I said to Con.

"I thought you said this was a party," he complained. "How is that any fun?"

Even Sondra laughed, though she still surveyed the surging mass of rowdy celebrants with glittering suspicion. To forestall further argument, I dismounted, springing lightly to the gravel path and ignoring Con's curse at my making myself vulnerable. Bright Ejarat, but it felt wonderful to have my body healthy and strong again. I even moved speedily enough to dodge Sondra's grab for me, holding out my arms to the crowd.

It wasn't long before I sensed the pair of them at my back, my stalwart protectors. Nearly overwhelmed by my ebullient people, I paid Con and Sondra little attention, giving one person after another the opportunity to bow over the orchid ring, inhale its fragrance, all of us offering praise to Calanthe.

It did my heart good, truly, to walk among my people and share in their joy. Maybe Con was right that there were different kinds of love. Perhaps it had been selfish and greedy of me to long for more. I'd been born to duty—created deliberately for it—and my personal happiness didn't matter. There was work ahead, not just for Calanthe, but to restore the world if Con and his people succeeded. I needed to focus on that.

This is what matters, I told myself. *This love is all you need.* I walked among them for quite some time, passing along orders to bring out food and wine, enjoying the spontaneous revelry.

After a while—and after it seemed that every one of the thousands present had greeted me—Ibolya appeared at my elbow, offering me an iced wine. I took it uncertainly, though I'd grown exceedingly warm and was terribly thirsty. The sun, though lowering quickly to sunset, blazed in the cloudless sky, making it stiflingly warm in the gardens thronged with people, well away from the cooling coastal breezes.

"Just try a sip, Your Highness," Ibolya urged, "to see if You can keep it down. If so, I'll bring You actual food."

I smiled with gratitude and chagrin. Silly of me to imagine Ibolya hadn't known exactly how much I had—and hadn't—been eating. "Thank you."

For privacy, I moved to a bench under a flowering tree, the shade cool and lovely, the rosy panicles falling all around like a gentle rain. Sondra kept an eye on me while Kara spoke with Con, Vesno flopped at his feet, tongue lolling. Reporting on their ships, no doubt. I sat with a grateful sigh. At least the boots, though high-heeled enough to give me some height, didn't hurt to stand in for long periods. I sipped the wine, light and icy, perfectly refreshing. Ibolya watched me carefully, and I waited for my stomach to react, but I seemed to be restored. "It's excellent, and I think I'll be fine."

"Allow me to fetch Your Highness something to eat then." Ibolya turned to go.

"Not just yet. Sit with Me." She obediently joined me, though with an odd hesitation in her manner. I eyed her. "Are you angry with Me?"

Her dark eyes flew to mine in shock before she demurely lowered them again. "It's not my place to have feelings about You one way or the other, Your Highness."

They were so like my father's words—and so clearly misguided—that I experienced a flash of unease before putting it firmly away.

"Oh, fuck that," I replied tartly, shocking her again. "Let Me apologize to you, for putting you on the spot with your sister ladies-in-waiting. Being singled out for favor can be very difficult."

"I don't mind that, Your Highness," she rushed to say, fingers fidgeting with her skirts. "Well, everyone was shocked that You were so severe, but I think that, once they order their thoughts, they'll be here to appeal to You."

"Then what is bothering you?" I asked gently. "Speak freely and be honest. If you would prefer not to continue to serve Me, then you may go with My blessing and good-will. You've already done far more than most."

"I don't wish to leave Your service," Ibolya said with perfect sincerity.

"Perhaps a holiday? I will be recruiting more ladies, re-gardless of what the others decide, so that none of you need shoulder the entire burden of tending Me."

"It has been no burden, but an honor, Your Highness." She smiled uncertainly. "These last days I've felt truly more useful than ever before. I mean," she added hastily, "not that tending to You was ever trivial. It's just that I—"

"I understand," I interrupted gently. "Better to just say what's on your mind."

"I hesitate to pry, but—I believe Your Highness does not intend to travel to Yekpehr with Conrí on the rescue mission?"

The smell of smoldering vurgsten seemed to fill my nose, my throat choking on the foul smoke, the sick sen-sation of my lifeblood draining away. "I cannot," I man-aged to say. I cleared my throat, feeling very like Con. He heard me, giving me a questioning look. I waved him off. "I cannot leave Calanthe again."

"I did not intend to suggest that Your Highness should," Ibolya hastened to say. "But—if Your other ladies return in time—I'd like to request to go on the rescue mission."

My turn to be shocked. I gazed at her, quite unable to summon a response. "You wish to go with Conrí and the others?"

She lifted her pert chin and nodded. "Lady Agatha is determined to go, and there will be Lady Rhéiane to tend. And many others perhaps. I could be useful to them."

"You are useful to Me," I said softly, and she flushed.

"I appreciate that You find me so, and if You do not wish me to go, I won't."

I *didn't* want her to go. Of all my ladies, Ibolya had earned my implicit trust. Even should the others return, I wouldn't feel the same way about them. But her eyes shone with determination and a hint of that same ferocity that drove Con, Sondra, Kara, and even Ambrose and Merle. Ibolya wanted to do more than dress and bathe people, and who could blame her? I certainly wouldn't be so small as to thwart her out of selfishness.

"You realize this will be very dangerous, this mission," I cautioned, and she started nodding before I even finished. I held up a hand to stop her. "More so than rescuing Me. That effort succeeded out of sheer audacity and wild luck. Anure and his wizards will be prepared this time. The same strategy won't work twice. I don't know how this will be accomplished, but there will likely be casualties. It could be that none of you will return." I swallowed against that fear, the hollowing sense of loss that Con might die—something I hadn't allowed myself to think about too much. He was still watching me, a line between his dark brows. I smoothed my expression, missing my heavy makeup, if only for that. "You should also know: Your abilities won't work there. I lost Mine."

"I know, Your Highness," she replied softly. "I felt that as soon as I left Calanthe's waters, even though my magic has never been very strong. I can't imagine how terrible it was for You, on top of everything else."

I nodded, not trusting myself to reply. Her bravery shamed me.

"I want to learn to do without that magic," Ibolya continued. "Lady Sondra is a force without it. If the mission is successful, then there will be a great deal to do in the larger world. They might need my help, and I'll have to do that without magic. I can't help make this a better world by staying here on Calanthe for the rest of my life."

I decided not to mention that assisting me in ruling Calanthe did help make at least our small corner of the world better—and that I had plans to extend my reach, if possible. "Then of course you have My permission to go," I said instead.

"Only if Your Highness has other ladies to attend You."

I waved that off. "I'm not an infant who requires constant care," I said with some irritation. "I won't starve in My bed because no one came to wake Me." A bit too apt, that metaphor, as I'd nearly done exactly that. I would be left alone, without Con, or even Sondra's acerbic company. Never mind that—I would be far too busy setting Calanthe to rights again to have a moment alone, much less unwanted solitude. After all, I'd lived that way for years before Con set boots on my soil. I would be fine.

"Of course, Your Highness." Ibolya bowed her head, chastened.

"I appreciate the thought, however," I added and she smiled. Harmony between us restored, I told her to send some food via a servant and sent her off to enjoy the party, with strict instructions not to show her face to me before morning.

Sondra went off with Kara, and Con returned to me, sitting where Ibolya had, extending his long legs. Vesno flopped onto his belly and scooched under the bench, releasing a happy sigh. "What was that all about?" Con asked.

"I imagine Vesno is hot and tired, with all that running around and excitement."

Con gave me a look. "With Ibolya."

"Girl talk," I replied coyly, laughing when he scowled at me.

"You were upset," he said, taking my hand and lacing my fingers with his. "More about Tertulyn and Calla?"

I decided not to ask how he knew I'd been upset. My masks never had worked as well with him as I'd have liked. "Ibolya requested permission to go with you to Yekpehr."

"Why?" He glanced over sharply. "You haven't changed your mind about coming along, have you?"

"What would you say if I did want to come?" I asked, mostly out of morbid curiosity.

"I'd talk you out of it," he replied promptly. "You're safer here on Calanthe."

Perversely that made me want to insist on going. "If I decided to go, you would *not* be able to talk Me out of it."

He narrowed his eyes at me. "So if I don't want you to come along, I should try insisting that you're going to, like it or not."

"Oh, I am not that bad," I huffed.

"Pretty damn close." He grinned and lifted my hand, kissing the back of it.

A group of servants swept up, producing a small table and array of food, all arranged with elegant speed and efficiency. Con looked at the food and back to me, a smile spreading slowly across his face. "Good," he said, leaving it at that.

"There's plenty for both of us." I put some fruit on a plate, and fresh bread with honey, nibbling slowly.

"You should eat more than that," Con said, helping himself to a generous helping of lobster pie.

"I'm pacing Myself," I replied tartly. "Don't push."

He ran a hand down my arm in apology. "I'm sure it's

not easy to get used to food again." For his part, he wolfed down that portion and took another.

"Indeed, but I could hardly plan to feed from you forever."

"You could, you know." He gave me a somber look, his face expressive of that artless love he offered so effortlessly. I envied his courage in that, as in so many things. "I would, if you needed it."

"I know." And I couldn't help the heavy sigh that followed.

"That shouldn't make you sad, Lia," he said gently. "I just want you to know that I'm here for you. That's a good thing."

But he wouldn't be there for me. He'd be gone to Yekpehr, and then to Oriel. And even if I used his feelings—for me or, worse, for our child—to bring him back to me on Calanthe, I'd feel like the stone around his neck. Ambrose had put it well, that Con was the hero who captained the ship we rode on. A great destiny lay before him, and I'd been a stepping-stone on that journey. It was lowering to realize that I was only the witch on the island the great hero visits, just one episode of many in his epic story. The best and bravest thing I could do would be to let him go.

"It is a good thing," I told him with the warmest smile I could generate. "But I'm glad that I'll be able to eat while you're off on the grand rescue mission."

"Yeah." He frowned thoughtfully. "So, you were saying that Ibolya wants to go?"

Having eaten as much as I could, I set my plate aside. "She does. I think she has some idea of being a hero. She admires Sondra. And apparently Agatha is determined to go, which contributed to Ibolya's decision."

Con raised a brow at that. "Agatha, huh? I hadn't heard that yet. I'm surprised. Yekpehr was hard on her."

"The place has that effect." At my dry tone, Con took my hand, stroking the back of it with the fingers of his other hand, very lightly, as if testing the texture of my skin.

"It does, which is the main reason I agree you shouldn't go. I don't want you to have to see that place ever again," he said, voice rough with emotion.

I hated the creeping sensation that if I weren't so weak, such a fragile flower, so easily crushed, that if I had more real spine and courage, I would go. "I gave Ibolya My permission," I said, "though, naturally, the final decision is yours."

He nodded thoughtfully. "Of course I'll take her help. I want a small strike team, but she could be useful, depending on our final plan."

"What did Kara have to say?" I asked, changing the subject. I'd seen Percy in the crowd, drinking iced bubbling wine and regaling a group with some tale that had them roaring with laughter, but he hadn't approached me. Clearly still sulking.

"The *Last Resort* is ready to go. We also have a few smaller fishing boats that are more or less seaworthy—or will be in another day."

"How much less than more?"

"Probably a critical amount," he admitted.

"But you don't want to delay for further repairs," I said, not a question at all.

"I don't think we can afford to." He stroked the back of my hand thoughtfully, tracing the bones with one rough fingertip. "I also chatted with Ambrose some."

"Did you? I missed that."

"You were busy receiving the adulation of your besotted subjects."

"Be nice." I narrowed my eyes threateningly.

"My middle name," he assured me somberly, but his dimple winked into existence.

"Ha to that. Anyway, Ambrose said . . . ?"

"He seems to think that the work you did with Calanthe will alert the wizards that you're still alive," Con was saying, not noticing my distraction. "Something about it resonating through the alternate realms of magical reality blah blah blah."

"Ah, yes, I see." I nodded very seriously.

"All joking aside," Con continued, "Ambrose and Merle—which still makes my head hurt to picture him as more than a bird—want to make a plan with you to defend against potential attack by the wizards while we're gone. Just in case. I don't think you need to be too worried, but it's another reason for you to stay on Calanthe, as your magic is strongest here."

I nodded in agreement. Not just strongest, but existing at all. "All right," I said mildly. "We can discuss further as we sort out the particulars of the plan."

"That was too easy."

"I happen to have come independently to the same conclusion," I informed him. The work I'd done with Tertulyn, too, had to have alerted them—and already those questing needles of wizard magic had resumed, testing the wards embedded in Calanthe's boundaries by generations of my ancestors. For now they held, but I would have to strengthen them, and soon.

"I guess that's a good dodge around agreeing with me," he teased, smiling. "Still, I don't think anyone will be concentrating on unpleasant business tonight, but maybe tomorrow you could convene one of your famous early-morning breakfast strategy meetings?"

"Famous?" I arched a brow. "I thought you hated that I set those meetings so early."

"I did, but I—" He stopped, gave me a sharp look. "You did that on purpose to piss me off?"

"No!" I protested, but I blew it by laughing. "Just to yank your chain a bit," I confessed.

"I can't believe you." Putting a hand behind my neck, he pulled me close for a sudden, intense, and very deep kiss that heated quickly to flash point. Applause and cheers rose around us, and he let me go, both of us acknowledging the crowd somewhat sheepishly.

"Just for that," he informed me, "I expect those almond pastry things."

"Obviously. One can't plan to overthrow an empire without almond pastry things."

He grinned at me. "Obviously." Standing, he pulled me to my feet. "Let's go check out the dancing."

"Dancing?"

"A hot new fashion. I hear it's fun, and the queen enjoys it."

"Well, if the queen approves, then how could we fail to emulate Her?"

"Indeed," he replied in a fake posh tone, pulling me along.

"I'm not really dressed for it," I pointed out. I still wore my wrap gown, leggings, and boots, having never extracted myself from the celebrating crowd so I could go change.

"Does it matter?"

"No," I decided, "it doesn't." All that mattered was enjoying the little time I had left with the love of my life before I nobly gave him up to his great destiny.

Con was gone from our bed when I woke at dawn, though I hadn't heard Ibolya fetch him. He was no doubt off making plans, fired up to begin his mission, to pursue his delayed vengeance. I'd slept soundly and peacefully, blessedly free of nightmares, so I shouldn't feel this listlessness. I definitely didn't want to start missing him now, because soon I wouldn't have him at all.

To dispel the clinging depression, I reached for the dreamthink—and Calanthe answered immediately, with rich sensory detail. The animals sang to me of their nighttime adventures and the freshness of morning. Flowers bloomed, fruit ripened, and people slept still or went about their activities. Though the damaged places around the island still felt like bleeding wounds, they also itched with healing energy—and called to me for attention.

Spurred into a sense of purpose—and feeling better for it—I threw back the covers, drew on my silk robe, and went to the outer chambers. Ibolya came from the bathing rooms, smiled and curtsied. "Good morning, Your Highness. The realm welcomes the sun of Your presence."

"An appropriate adaptation to changed circumstances," I replied, eyeing her attire. She'd left her hair loose and natural, though more studded with flowers than before. She'd also gone with an unstructured and more revealing gown. Emulating my fashion and setting one for the court, as a good lady-in-waiting should do.

"Thank You, Your Highness. Your bath is prepared, and I've set out several possible gowns for today. I wasn't sure how You would want to dress Your hair." She canted her head to look, and I obligingly turned in a circle. "It doesn't appear to need washing or combing."

"Like magic," I agreed. "One less chore for you."

"Tending You has never been a chore, Your Highness," she protested.

"I misspoke. I apologize."

She rolled her eyes in exasperation, and I found myself smiling back at her. Somewhere along the way, it seemed we'd become actual friends—and I'd learned to value that. An irony there, that I'd finally made some real connections with people, and they would all be leaving me.

Lest I fall into self-pity again, I hastened to bathe and dress. I wanted to visit the map tower before the breakfast strategy meeting, and I needed to do what I could to reinforce the ancient wards. Once I was ready for the day, which looked to be a long one, I tasked Ibolya to put things in place and send messages to everyone to meet in an hour.

Despite her protests, I went to the map tower alone. I needed the quiet to work, and to make myself accustomed to aloneness again. I'd visited the map of Calanthe with Dearsley the morning before, but even so it distressed me to see the changes to my beautiful island.

The map, tiled in loving detail over the wide floor of the circular tower, lay mostly in shadow with the sun barely tipping over the horizon, but here and there the gleaming tiles glittered. Magically maintained by a dedicated team of artisans, the map reflected the current state of Calanthe with unflinching candor.

I paced the circumference once, reaching for the dreamthink and putting my attention to a place somewhere between the magic that continuously updated the representation of the land and my sense of the island itself as it spoke to me.

On that first circuit, I concentrated on the enchantments protecting Calanthe. They responded to my will with ease, as if I'd been manipulating them all my life, accepting the intentions I layered in. I added elements of granite from my bedrock, the yielding yet eroding power of water, the tensile strength of plants, the ferocity of an animal defending its den. I'd told Con and his people that the layers of defenses couldn't keep out a vurgsten attack, but they could prevent magical ones. The wizards would not be using magic against me. Not easily.

On the second circuit, I created a barrier of another kind, this one temporary and all my own. No birds would fly off Calanthe until I allowed free passage again. I had no doubt that plenty of Anure's spies still infested my court. Tertulyn might be gone, but countless others—mostly cheerfully cavalier opportunists—remained. I couldn't excise them all, but I could keep them from reporting on our plans to Anure.

On the third circuit, I extended myself into the physical landscape of the island, seeking out the damages. I flinched from those aching wounds, and had to exercise my will to stay focused on them, like holding my hand to hot flame while it burned me. It was one thing to hear the stories, to read the list of damages, to observe the changes on the map, and another to feel them for myself.

Once lovely Cradysica still smoked in places where the forest had burned. The hillside temple, the docks, and so many other once gracious buildings were in rubble. But they were no longer the worst off. I studied the low marshlands on the western side of Calanthe, where flooding continued unabated, several villages perhaps permanently consigned to the sea. At least eight of the smaller islands off the northern shore had vanished under the waves. And I made myself look long and hard at the eastern cliffs—fortunately sparsely populated—which had sheared off entirely, leaving a raw wound of a new and jagged coastline.

This is what you wrought, I reminded myself—both me the queen and my larger self of the island. *This is the price we paid for our role in the revolution*. It would be up to me to do everything I could to ensure that the price bought us a world worth having.

Kicking off my heels, I knelt down to splay my hands over the eastern cliffs. They were unstable still, with huge boulders shuddering down, and slowly drying mudslides settling into villages in the valleys inland.

The orchid ring fluttered, acting like a smaller extension of my mind, allowing me to reach into that part of the land. I found the weakness in the rocks, where they slid in different directions, perilously close to shearing off in greater chunks, and with careful attention, I knit them together again.

It felt like healing my own body, mending the break, sending the healing energy to stabilize and strengthen. Satisfied, I knelt up, pleased to have done at least one small thing to fix my realm.

"Your Highness?"

I turned to find Ibolya waiting, noted the sun had risen quite a bit. "Am I late?"

"Not quite yet, but the others are already congregating in the Sand Salon."

"Understood." Standing, I slipped on my heels again, Ibolya kneeling to lace them for me.

She glanced up at me, tentative. "Your other ladies have returned and seek an audience."

I hadn't expected them so soon. "All of them?"

"Yes, Your Highness. They await Your pleasure. Would You like to interview them?"

"No need. They may escort Me to the Sand Salon." I would make use of them, and I would be wiser in the doing of it. I only wished it didn't hurt my heart so much to contemplate how short-lived their affection for me had been. The lesson I was to learn, apparently, the depths and shallows of love and loyalty. Besides which, their presence would liberate Ibolya, who deserved that opportunity. "I'll meet with them later to discuss their expanded duties."

"Them, but not me, Your Highness?" Ibolya asked.

"You are released from My service," I told her with an affectionate smile. "I expect heroic tales."

"Oh, I doubt it will be anything like that, Your Highness." But her eyes sparkled with excitement, and I envied her a little.

16

I'd just come up from the shipyard and was wandering the palace looking for this meeting place mentioned in Lia's message when I heard the fanfare of her approach. Excellent timing, as I'd been close to asking a page to take me to the Sand Salon—whatever under Sawehl's gaze *that* might be. Sounded like a beach. Knowing Calanthe, it could well be.

Lia rounded the corner, accompanied by all five of her ladies. Interesting. It was also surprisingly good to see her back to her usual pageantry—ironic, as I'd chafed over it so much before. But hearing the music, the people calling out salutations to their queen, and seeing Lia strolling elegantly through her palace, so clearly in her element . . . Well, it was good. It was how things should be.

She'd dressed up, kind of a combination of what she'd done before. The gown caught my eye first—it was hard to miss—as the skirt part fell around her like the closed wings of a butterfly. The uneven hem billowed around her slender legs, making her seem like she could take flight. It looked just like one of Calanthe's giant butterflies, too, with the black lines that bordered panels of intense color. I'd seen butterflies like that in the gardens, with pinks and purples near the center, merging into deep blue, then pale blue, with green and a tinge of yellow at the tips.

The top part of the dress had the same colors and pattern, but wrapped around her slim waist and cupped her bosom with flares of black, leaving her shoulders bare, though her arms glittered. As she drew near, I saw that she wore sleeves of jewelry, strands of golden vines from her upper arms to her hands, with leaves made of green gems and jewelry butterflies seeming to flutter within, the orchid ring reigning supreme over them all.

"I'm guessing today's theme is butterflies," I said to her, bowing.

She smiled, amused. "It seemed apt. And yours is . . . brutal conqueror? So last season, Conrí."

I grinned at her. "Never goes out of style."

"Not while Anure rules," she agreed, sobering.

"Shall we?" I offered her my arm, and she took it, the others falling back to follow us. They'd pulled her glorious hair into a loose braid that somehow made it look like a cascade of color studded with flowers. "I like the hairstyle."

She slid me an opaque look, subtly guiding me down another hall. "And what have you been up to so early in the morning?"

"I wanted to check out the ships for myself, give Vesno a bit of a run."

"Ah, I wondered where he was."

"I left him with some of the carpenters. He gets bored in meetings."

"As all good wolves do," she replied mildly, her expression so bland I knew she was enjoying poking at me.

"Where are we going?" I asked, deciding not to take her bait.

"The Sand Salon. Didn't you get My message?"

"Yeah, but that doesn't mean I know what or where that is."

"Just through here," she said, then gave me a real smile. "I think you'll like it."

She looked so pleased with herself, almost mischievous, that I didn't grumble about the needless mystery. We turned a corner, entering a large room. Open to the outside as most of them were in the palace, the salon held none of the tables, chairs and seating areas I'd expected of a salon. Instead, what looked like toys were stacked against the walls, and a large table took up the center of the room.

Everyone else awaited us—including Ambrose and Merle, which surprised me—eating pastries and sipping from pretty cups. Sondra and Kara stood together studying the table. The other members of the Defense Council, Percy, Brenda, Agatha, Dearsley, all bowed and exchanged greetings with Lia. Percy ignored me with a lift of his elegant nose. Unperturbed, I grabbed an almond pastry from a platter, went to the table, and peered at it, trying to figure out why the thing looked weird.

It wasn't really a table at all—or not the normal sort— because there wasn't a solid surface. It was more of a box, with a smooth, rounded rim and filled with fine, shifting . . .

"Sand," I said.

"Thus the name," Lia said, coming beside me, that pleased glint in her eyes. "I apologize that it's so low. It's built for children and there wasn't time to raise it and still have it be stable enough, so we'll have to make do."

Children. That's why the toys. "We're in a playroom?" I asked, looking around for any kids.

"Don't worry, Conrí. I asked that the children take their classes elsewhere this morning. None will pop out from under the table to gnaw on your ankles."

"You think you're funny," I growled under my breath, and she smiled serenely. "And we're looking at sand because why?"

"I thought it would be helpful, for planning." She waved a hand over the table and the sand shifted and stirred, following along. Pinching her fingers, she drew her hand up and the sand followed, building itself into a tower. As it took shape, I recognized one of the towers at Yekpehr.

She waved a hand and began detailing a coastline, our companions bursting into excited chatter. "I don't have magic, though," I said, surprisingly disappointed that I couldn't do it, too.

"You don't need it. The sand is enchanted, so anyone can use it." She put her hand over mine, the delicate jewel butterflies fluttering, the golden vines twining between her fingers, too. "Picture what you want it to look like," she instructed, guiding my hand, showing me how my gestures shaped the sand.

I tried it, and the sand swirled, responding to my movements, building itself into that long wall around Yekpehr that seemed to grow out of the craggy rocks of the daunting coast. Feeling kind of like a kid again—but in the best way—I added details of the crenellations along the top, then grinned at Lia. She smiled, well satisfied with her surprise.

"It responds to the image you have in mind," she explained loudly enough for everyone to hear, "so the more clearly you envision what you want to create, the more detailed it will be."

"All right, people," I said, "let's re-create Yekpehr."

"When we're done, can we blow it up?" Sondra asked.

"Absolutely," Lia replied with a lethal smile. "I'd expect nothing else."

*   *   *

I consulted with Dearsley, the two of us settled at the teacher's desk and going over lists while the others worked at the model. They spent hours at it, each taking a section and building it, then critiquing what others had wrought, adding details, making modifications. Being right there allowed me to watch some of the smartest, most talented and creative people I'd ever met play like a bunch of kids at the sand table.

For even though their intent was deadly, the planning critical, and their focus on executing a dangerous, if not impossible rescue, they were having fun. Uproarious laughter broke out now and again with exclamations of chagrin and consternation. They also argued vociferously, and I caught even Agatha's usually quiet voice rising adamantly on some point or another. Ibolya joined in, too, and it was good to see her expressing herself.

Pages, messengers, and my other ladies came and went, casting curious glances at the strange sight of weapons propped among the toys, and adults arguing about towers. Dearsley and I had our own debates, sorting our own rescues around Calanthe into order of priority as more information came in, redistributing aid to the parts of Calanthe in most need, setting a schedule to rebuild. I kept another list, a private one, of land I'd go in and repair myself. Soon we'd have the memorials for those lost, which meant I should consider a real tour of the island—not a false one of distraction—to make the appropriate solemn speeches. I didn't look forward to that duty of grief, especially as I'd have no Con to keep me company.

Every now and again, Con looked over to check on me, but mostly he remained absorbed in the exercise. Once they'd created the exterior of the citadel and immediate coastline, they'd divided into teams, building smaller models of various interior rooms.

I was deep into debate with Dearsley on whether I was favoring Cradysica's rebuilding overmuch—I confess I carried a weight of guilt there, so he could be correct, but they'd also been damaged first—when Con came over and laid a hand on my shoulder.

I glanced up, my smile fading at his serious expression. "What's wrong?" I scanned the room, looking for trouble, but everyone remained involved in their tasks—except Sondra, who stood by one corner of the table, giving me an apologetic grimace.

"Nothing's wrong," Con quickly assured me. "It's just . . . Sondra could use your help remembering the throne room."

The memory of pain welled up, accompanied by black nausea, and I had to swallow hard against it. Con's hand tightened on my shoulder. "Never mind. It's too much to ask. I can—"

"No," I said, standing and smoothing my butterfly-bright skirts. I'd felt like a butterfly in the gorgeous dress, remade and renewed. But apparently my shadows chased me still, the cocoon of the corpse I'd been still waiting to be entirely shed. "Of course I can help."

I went with him to the far end of the table, looking with interest at all they'd done so far. Much of it I didn't recognize, as I'd been either unconscious or locked into one of two sets of rooms for much of our tenure there.

"Why do you need the throne room, in particular?"

"We might not," Con said, so blandly that I knew he was lying, "which is why, if it's too difficult for you to re-visit in memory, we can—"

"I said it wasn't," I interrupted tersely. What was he up to?

"Don't bite," Con replied mildly, setting a hand on the small of my back as if he knew I needed the support.

"We're simply constructing every part of the citadel that we can, in case it's helpful to our plan. You and Sondra are the only ones who've seen the throne room in years."

"And my memory is shit," Sondra explained, making a woeful face at the rudimentary model she'd started on. "I'm not embarrassed to admit I was more worried about seeing You get hacked to bits—sorry—than about where the throne was and how many people the room could hold."

"Only two bits came off," I corrected, producing a smile to cover the shudder of remembered horror. I didn't see a model of the wizards' workrooms where I'd been experimented upon. Though I didn't particularly want to envision them, I asked Con if he needed those, too.

"No," he replied immediately. "There's no reason for us to need to go there again."

"I thought you were constructing every part of the citadel that you can," I pointed out, needling him to determine the boundaries of the lie.

"Not those. Still, if you don't want to think about the throne room, we—"

"Stop." I said it softly but looked up at him so he'd see the resolve in my face—and thus I glimpsed the relief in his. He wanted this more than he was saying. Ejarat take me, he better not be thinking about going after Anure still. But I'd give him the rope. If he hung himself with it, so be it. "Let's do this. It will be therapeutic," I said to Sondra, and she gave me a crookedly halfhearted smile. I examined what she'd done so far, and found it not at all close. "Fortunately—for this project if not for my peace of mind—I have a crystal-clear memory of that room."

Con's hand twitched on my back, and a sound like a low growl rose from deep inside him. "Lia, if—"

"Go supervise someone else," I said, not happy with

him. He grunted but moved away, going to Percy and Agatha who were arguing over some point.

Turning my attention to what Sondra had started, I curled my fingers and adjusted the proportions of the room, allowing my memories to build in the details. The orchid ring assisted, lending its magic to focus the extension of my thoughts, much as it had done with repairing Calanthe. I detailed Anure's towering throne, trying to recreate its illusion of intimidating height while maintaining the correct dimensions. I even added the treasure hoard to the steps, and the figures of the wizards, arranged as they had been that day.

That was where I'd stood, where they'd brought out the block to lay my hand on, to sever first my finger, then my hand. Phantom pain throbbed in my wrist, and the orchid responded, soothing me. It helped to see my hand at the end of my arm, fully restored and myself still in possession of the ring. They'd done their worst to me, and I'd survived them. In a way, it helped to revisit that space, those dark memories. Con had once told me that if you spoke about nightmares aloud, the visions lost their haunting power. This seemed much the same.

When I finished, Sondra whistled low. "That's amazing. It's perfect—as far as I can tell."

"Seared into My brain, apparently," I replied drily, looking over what she'd been working on: an exact replica of the rooms we'd been kept in.

"Agatha thinks the odds are good that the royal captives are kept in similar rooms and towers," Sondra explained. "They were before, and it makes sense that the citadel staff would've classified us as the same sort of prisoner. Any adjustments?"

"No." So odd to see those walls that had contained us

all those days, if only in miniature. "It looks exactly right to Me. I'm impressed."

She shrugged that off, seeming slightly embarrassed at the praise. "I had a lot of time to stare at those walls while You slept."

"I'm very sorry for that."

She frowned. "For what, that You slept? I was glad of it. At least then I could see You. Now, when they would take You away . . ." She shook her head. "You think you've gone through the worst things possible, and then something new happens."

"Are you going back?" I asked softly, so Con wouldn't hear. He was participating in his own argument now, with Ambrose and Agatha, while Brenda and Percy had their heads together with Kara on something to do with the citadel walls.

"Not even a question," Sondra replied with a frown. "Where Conrí goes, I go."

"You could stay here. You'd be welcome."

"It would make me crazy to stay behind, kicking my heels," she answered with a wry grimace. I managed to conceal my wince that I would be doing exactly that. "Besides—if that is our Rhéiane there, she was my future queen. And, well, she was my friend. My first and best friend. That's something special, you know? I owe it to her—oh shit, Lia, I'm sorry. That was thoughtless of me and—"

I held up a hand to stop her. "I know what that kind of friendship means, even if Mine turned out to be only an illusion."

"Do You know that for sure?" Sondra asked, recovering enough to employ the honorific again.

"I don't. I'd rather hoped for that closure, but I think I'll never know. And then I wonder—which is worse? If she was truly the friend I thought and either turned on Me or was turned, or if she was false all along."

"Yeah." Sondra idly swirled some sand, not looking at me. "Some things we don't need the answers to."

"And some answers we simply can't have. I'm making peace with that." I gestured to the model of the throne room, glancing at Con to make sure he was still absorbed. "Here's a question I'd like the answer to: Why does he really want a model of the throne room?"

She looked to Con, too, then back. Sondra wouldn't lie to me. "Because that's where he's likely to find Anure."

I nodded, unsurprised. "Then he still plans to kill Anure."

Sondra gazed back steadily with regret and understanding. The short hair set off her elegant bone structure but ruthlessly revealed the stained and pitted skin of her face, particularly stark in the bright morning light. But her eyes, shades of blue with darker flecks and lavish gold lashes, retained all the beauty of her life before Anure. "Did You really think he'd be able to let that go?"

I'd hoped that it would be enough for him to destroy Anure's hold on the land, to rip his empire out from under him. Foolish me. "What is he planning?"

"Maybe ask him?" Sondra sounded uncertain, as she almost never did.

"I'm asking you, as your queen," I pressed, using that edge ruthlessly, even if I did stop short of royal command.

"That's really unfair, You bitch," Sondra muttered, eyes flashing with irritation.

I nearly laughed—only Sondra could call me a bitch while using the honorific—but I managed to keep a straight face, even narrowing my eyes in regal menace.

She blew out a breath. "I don't know this from him, all

right? But Brenda told me that when Con came to rescue us, he also brought a vurgsten weapon. Agatha made a trigger for it, so he could carry it around inert, then take it to the throne room and set it off personally. The only reason he didn't do that was because he had to carry You out."

That sounded so like Con. "I'm surprised he didn't go back," I murmured, studying the throne room model, "thinking Me dead."

"He tried," Sondra said bluntly. "He would have, but Ambrose stopped him. The trigger—maybe it's changed, but I understand it's pretty much suicide to use it."

I processed that, unsurprised on some level, and also deeply disturbed. Imagine if I'd risen from the dead on the yacht to find Con had, in his grief thinking me lost forever, killed himself trying to take out Anure. It sounded like a tragic ballad.

"Thank you for telling Me." And yet it seemed our story was doomed to tragedy regardless. Con planned to risk himself anyway, despite his protestations of love for me.

As if sensing my thoughts—or my gaze on him—he looked up and grinned wolfishly, violence and vengeance glinting in his golden eyes, that sparkling anticipation he got only when contemplating destroying his nemesis. Nothing else meant as much to him. I'd be a fool to delude myself otherwise.

"All right, everyone," he called out, silencing the room. "I think we can solidify this plan."

Lia asked Ibolya to have adult-sized chairs brought in. Ibolya stayed, apparently officially transferred to my service—which felt weird, but that was how Lia did things—and Dearsley begged off on the discussion, going to execute the plans he and Lia had been so intensely discussing. We pulled our chairs up to the sand table, which

put the models of the citadel more on eye level. I don't
know about the rest of them, but I had a crick in my neck
from bending over the thing. We still loomed too high, but
it was better. I ended up pacing as I talked, anyway, noting
Lia's amused half smile as I did.

Caged wolf, I heard her say in my head. Yeah. That
was me.

Now that we made real plans to return to Yekpehr, to finally and completely destroy Anure's foul regime, victory
seemed possible again. I thought I'd set aside the craving
for revenge. I'd figured it crushed under the weight of my
mistakes and failings. But no. Finally I saw a way to re-
deem myself, to live up to the promises I'd made to so
many.

I would rescue Rhéiane, liberate the others, and rip Anure's empire to shreds, and then I'd look into the false
emperor's eyes when he realized he'd lost everything that
mattered to him. He'd know how it felt to have your world
shattered, to be defeated and broken. Then I'd kill him,
even if I had to kill everyone in the room with him. They
were all complicit. Those courtiers had stood aside and
watched the show when those wizards had butchered Lia.
They all deserved to die. Every one.

And it would be sweet indeed. A real victory this time,
all the sweeter for having been delayed.

"We're agreed that we can't go in by stealth again," I
said, laying the groundwork for the plan that had come
to me. The one the prophecy predicted, I was sure. I had
the key now. "They'll have learned and will be checking
anyone who tries to enter the citadel, even via the Slave
Gates. That leaves either a full assault or some other kind
of trickery."

"A full assault is right out," Kara put in, staring fiercely
at the reproduction of the wall around the citadel. "Anure's

navy might be decimated, but he's no doubt rebuilding at all speed, and his ground forces are largely intact. The fixed defenses on the outer wall and the walls of the citadel itself are formidable. Even if we had an unlimited supply of vurgsten—which we don't—we don't have enough people to place the charges, and neither weapons nor people to cover them while they do it. They're in a position to dump anything they like on our heads and bring up soldiers behind us to pick us off. Against that wall, we'd be trapped."

He paced over to the wall, pointing to the guard towers on the crenellations. "These are manned, night and day. Plus, every bit of all the walls—outer and inner—is lit by vurgsten. Any attempt to scale them would be instantly spotted, and the vurgsten probably exploded in our faces."

"And here I thought the Imperial Toad was just showing off with that excess," Lia murmured, shifting to cross her legs, one elegantly heeled foot kicking in the air, the only betrayal of her internal agitation. I'd like to tell her she didn't need to be here for this, but she wouldn't listen—especially if she thought I was trying to coddle her. Besides, it was important to her to feel like she had input on this plan. Whatever would help set her mind at ease was fine by me.

"His wizards," Ambrose put in. He'd worn his court wizard of Calanthe robes and perched in his chair, Merle on his shoulder for the moment, wearing a decorative chain around his sleek black neck. "I feel it's important to make the distinction," Ambrose added when we all looked at him. "The wizards are keeping the vurgsten perpetually burning, not the man."

"I don't see why that's important at—"

"No, Con," Lia broke in, giving me a quelling look, her eyes like faceted jewels, cold and sharp. "Something

I noticed during My . . . audience with Anure, and subsequent conversations with the four wizards, is that I don't think the emperor is fully running the show."

Merle croaked, bobbing his head, and I didn't miss that Ambrose looked satisfied by Lia's observation.

"What did you notice?" I asked.

She lifted a hand, fluttering her fingers dismissively. "It's difficult to explain. As a person who's spent many years sitting on a throne, holding court, making decisions, and guiding the flow of events, I have a feel for how a person in power behaves. One pays attention to the atmosphere of the room, to the important players. Minute details can betray what a petitioner's true agenda might be. Some courtiers wield more influence than others, and there is constant jockeying to gain more power through information or other means." Her gaze rested briefly on Percy, who fluttered his jeweled nails and simpered at her.

"Anure wasn't doing that," she continued. "He was . . . embroiled in his own thoughts and needs."

"Not a leader in any way," Agatha said, and Lia nodded.

"And the wizards?" Ambrose queried, an unusual tension in him. Rarely did the wizard seem invested in answers, but this one held something important to him. And that, I realized, was partly what Lia meant about observing a room.

"The wizards wanted the orchid ring," Lia replied, fanning the fingers of that hand to display the lavish blossom, which had taken on tones that matched her butterfly gown today. "When I tried to bargain with them, to dissuade them from—" She took a breath and smiled, waving her hand in elegant dismissal, not fooling me for a moment. "That is, when I threatened them with the emperor's displeasure should they . . . damage Me beyond recovery, they were unconcerned. I am quite convinced that the wizards hold Anure's leash, rather than the other way around."

"Or they wanted the orchid ring more than they feared Anure's displeasure," Sondra pointed out.

"The wizards want that ring badly," Kara agreed, his dark gaze on me.

"We are not using Lia or the ring as bait," I announced, glaring around the room severely enough that they would all know I wouldn't discuss it. "Never again," I added, this time to Lia, who smiled tremulously. Time to bring everyone around to the plan I had in mind. I braced myself for the arguments to come when they, inevitably, didn't like it. "We don't need to use Lia as bait, because I have something better than I can take to them. I will offer Anure Lia's hand—with the orchid ring—in trade for my sister."

17

The room erupted in questions and protest, and I managed my own outrage with the familiar ritual of observing the people and noting who didn't protest. Ibolya kept her counsel, revealing little. Ambrose watched Con in canny silence. Merle cocked his head with an oddly similar expression.

And myself, of course. I wasn't happy, but I wasn't surprised.

I gave Con a cold glare for keeping the unveiling of this aspect of his plan from me. I knew him well enough to have followed his manipulations as he appeared to let everyone give input to a strategy he'd already settled upon. He attempted a cheeky grin for me—patently manufactured to charm me, as the dimple never appeared. I tightened the leash on my rising temper. Maybe Con had learned from the past, and I now suspected him unfairly. I would wait to see if this so-called plan improved with explanation.

Though I doubted it would.

Without answering anyone's questions and accusations— many of the others didn't know Sondra had carried my severed finger and hand out of Yekpehr—Con retrieved a bag he'd brought, extracting a wrapped bundle and laying it on the wide rim of the sand table, as far away from me as possible. I watched in fascinated horror as he unwrapped it. The others, one by one, fell silent.

With an apologetic glance to me, Con undid the last layer, revealing my dead hand and finger. Ibolya cast me a distressed look, and Sondra put a reassuring hand on my shoulder. I produced a calm smile, grateful in that moment for the many years of practice controlling my expressions.

"Gracious," I exclaimed into the horrified silence, nearly adding a frivolous giggle. I decided against it as the chances of it going hysterical were too high to risk. "My hand looks remarkably well preserved, all things considered." It did look much the same as when it had been attached to me. The skin was smooth, though sunken against the fragile-seeming bones, marble pale with death. Had I looked like that when they found me? An unsettling thought.

The long jeweled nails I'd been wearing that day gleamed scarlet as fresh blood, gold tips glittering. I'd liked that look, had felt fierce and ready for battle. It seemed I viewed my hand—and the severed finger, in its proper position, but limply detached—from a strange distance. I considered that the sense of dizzying remove could be a warning that I might faint. I'd have once said I wasn't the fainting sort, but that was before they cut my hand off.

"Breathe," Sondra advised under her breath, and I did—finding that the black sparkles in my vision receded with it.

"You *kept* it?" Percy gasped in horror, the first to speak. "What kind of monster does something like that?"

I was likely the only one who saw that epithet hit the mark—and Con's mostly internal wince—because Con met Percy's gaze levelly. "A monster like me," he said. "Make no mistake that the Slave King has done far worse.

And now this will be our entrée into the citadel. Anure, and his wizards," he added with a glance at me, "will be unable to resist this prize."

Brenda cleared her throat, bracing her hands on her knees. "I feel compelled to point out that they're likely to notice the absence of the orchid ring."

Con shrugged that off. "We take some fresh orchids and tie one on right before we get there. It doesn't need to survive close examination—just get us in the door. *Claim the hand that wears the Abiding Ring, And the empire falls*," he quoted. "The prophecy foretold that this would be our key to winning."

Nobody said anything for a moment, the silence stretching with tension.

"I am right," Con bit out. Then he looked to Ambrose. "Aren't I?"

The wizard shrugged cheerfully. "It's a prophecy. Like poetry, it's subject to interpretation."

"I never did like poetry," Con muttered. "I take the hand that wore the Abiding Ring to Yekpehr and use it to lure Anure out of his hole. He won't be able to resist."

"And why won't Anure simply slaughter you where you stand and take the hand and ring anyway?" I asked in a coolly polite tone that should've alerted Con to my grave doubts about this plan. Of course he didn't take warning, because he was galloping heedlessly down his path of vengeance, too wrapped up in his hatred and thirst to fight to think clearly. Fear for him sucked at me, pulling me relentlessly toward the maw of devastating grief. He'd get himself killed for this vengeance. The wolf, biting at my hands as I tried to free him of his chains. I'd been warned.

"Because I'll imply that I have knowledge about you," Con returned. "Sondra told me how you led Anure to believe you hated me and that I'd run off with your wealth. I'll turn it around and offer intelligence on you, confirm the rumors that you're not really dead. Maybe offer a deal to collude to capture you again, string him along that way."

Terror struck my heart. Con had told me repeatedly that Anure's gift was seeing what someone cared about. He would see Con's love for me—everyone could see it— along with Con's reckless thirst for vengeance. He would use both to destroy Con. "This is too risky," I said. "It's not well thought out."

"I *have* thought it out," he insisted. "Besides, that's not the whole plan. We won't all knock on the front door. I'll go alone, and the rest of the team will infiltrate the township and be ready for me to admit them to the citadel. While I have the emperor and his wizards distracted, you all can rescue the captives."

Everyone exchanged glances for a moment, then several people spoke at once, Agatha overriding them. "I have to agree with Her Highness, Conrí. This plan is full of holes."

"It's a good plan," he snapped back. "It gets us inside, then we improvise. That's where I rely on your knowledge. You were indispensable last time, Lady Agatha." He produced a semi-charming grin, but the look she flashed him was decidedly uncharmed.

"Uh-huh, I see what you're up to, Conrí." Brenda pointed a stubby finger at him. "You plan to take that vurgsten bomb into the throne room, hoping to kill Anure and his wizards in one blast, then rely on the confusion to allow us to spirit the royal captives out of the citadel. And you figure if you get yourself killed, well, that's the price you'll pay."

Con looked a little surprised—and more than a little sheepish—then shook his head. "No. Not . . . exactly."

Yes, exactly. I would not stand by and watch Con self-destruct. I stood, drawing everyone's attention, letting the silence settle into unease. Fixing the coldest glare imaginable on Con, I said, "You lied to Me."

He actually sputtered, everyone turning their heads to look at him. "What? No. What are—"

"You *said*," I interrupted, the group looking back to me, "that we'd plan this mission together, that you would take My cooler-headed approach into account this time."

"I am!" he snapped back, gesturing at the table, the sands hissing as they reacted to the movement, which he quickly snatched back. "Obviously, I have been. What do you think all of this is?"

"*This*," I said, stabbing a finger at the model, but restraining my intention so the sands didn't move, "was an elaborate charade, largely for My benefit."

Con set his jaw. "You're wrong, Lia."

"I don't think so. Tell Me, what did you learn from us re-creating the citadel—besides the dimensions of the throne room?"

Everyone looked at him expectantly. "There's the tower rooms," he said, the answer tentative.

"Why do you need to know the layout of those rooms?" I shot back.

He floundered, groping for an answer I knew he didn't have. I laughed, letting it be bitter. "That's right. You don't. The only piece of information you really wanted was the throne room. You already had a plan when you walked in here, the same fucking plan you've had all along, *Conrí*," I spat, letting my fury rise. "All you care about is killing Anure. Worse, you don't care if you die doing it."

"That is *not* true," he roared back at me. "I care about rescuing Rhéiane, too. I can do both!"

I folded my arms, the butterfly jewelry tinkling. "What

about what we discussed? Rescuing all the royals, returning them to their lands, undermining Anure's power so that the fraud of an empire he created falls apart in his hands?"

"We can still do that *and* kill Anure," he snarled.

"With this *plan*?" I loaded incredulity into the question. "It's not even worthy of the word. You're just lunging at your chain, waiting for the moment it breaks so you can devour your enemy." Our fascinated audience snapped their heads back to him for his retort.

"And what if I am?" he shouted at me across the table. "I want this for you, too, Lia. Don't you want them all to suffer like you suffered?"

"No!" I shouted back. "Because nothing that happens to them will change My pain. Adding suffering to suffering doesn't equal zero, Con—it only adds up to more suffering."

"Well, you know I never learned much math," he replied with blistering sarcasm, "since tutors were scarce in the *mines* where I was *enslaved* for most of my life."

"You've apparently learned nothing since then, either," I informed him, slicing to the heart of it coldly. Someone hissed in a breath at the point scored.

"I *have*!" He thumped his fist on the table, and the tower near him shivered into a heap. "I'm not using you this time, am I? I promised you'll be safe, and you will be. No more using anyone else as bait."

"Just yourself," I said with pointed softness.

"It's my life to use," he snarled back.

"This craving for vengeance will destroy you, Conrí." I dusted my hands together. "It eats everything else, making all your words into lies."

"I drank your waters of truth, didn't I?" He threw up his hands.

"Seeing the truth doesn't force you to act upon it. That part is up to you."

"What have I said that's a lie?"

Our audience looked back to me. Fine. "You said you loved Me, wanted to marry Me and build a life here on Calanthe."

He reeled back as if struck, baffled. "I do, but you won't—"

I held up a finger to stop him. "Can't you see? If you truly wanted that with Me, you wouldn't contemplate this suicidal plan for the sake of vengeance."

"It would be *after* that," he offered, far too tentatively. "Once Anure is dead, then—"

"Then what?"

He stumbled, golden eyes flashing with frustration, and he raked a hand through his long black hair, hitting the tie and furiously yanking it out. "Then I come back here."

"What about Oriel?"

"I mean, Oriel first, then back here."

"What about the other forgotten kingdoms?"

"Them, too. I don't know, Lia! We'll figure it out when that happens."

I shook my head, sorrow and frustration warring in my heart. "You don't know because you can't even conceive of a life after Anure. You're a broken man, Conrí, living for one thing only. Which is why you don't care if you die doing it."

"I told you I was broken," he grated out. "I haven't changed."

"No, you haven't. And that's the problem. An insurmountable one. Therefore, I am *done*."

He stared at me, stunned. "Lia, what . . ."

"Done," I repeated. "Done with you, done with this

farce of a strategy session." I waved a hand and sent the model sliding into a featureless surface again.

"Damn," Sondra muttered. "I thought *I* got to blow it up."

"I apologize to all of you that your time and energy was wasted today. You may continue to assist Conrí in his self-destruction or not. It's entirely your choice."

"Does this mean the *Last Resort* is de-commandeered?" Percy asked, glancing up from the notes he'd been taking in order to share the gossip.

I looked to Con, who stared at me in flabbergasted silence. He leaned on the table, hair hanging wildly around his face, looking like a man who'd had his feet cut out from under him.

"Whether you donate your yacht to Conrí's doomed venture is entirely up to you," I replied, and Percy did a chair dance of joy, flashing a triumphant look at Con.

"Lia." Con growled my name with ominous temper. "What do you mean you're done?"

"*Done*," I spat, letting the fury warm my cold and aching heart. "Done with you. Done with your vengeance. Get what you need and go. Get off My island and never come back. *If* you even survive. You are not welcome on Calanthe and I will never marry you."

"Whoa, wait." Sondra stood, bewildered, looking between us. "You're already married, like forever."

I gazed coolly at Con, who looked pained. I'd been willing to keep the truth quiet, but I was also done going along with his pretenses. "No, we're not. When I died, the marriage bond dissolved. Our brief liaison is nothing but a footnote in Ambrose's history. There." I gestured to my severed hand. "The trophy you needed, duly claimed. Take it and go."

Holding on to my composure with the last thread of my

control, I spun and strode out of the room. Over the furious clicking of my heels on the tile, I heard Sondra's voice. "Oh man, did you fuck up."

Ibolya tried to follow, but I waved her away. My other ladies were off taking care of assigned tasks, not expecting me to leave the strategy session so soon. I snorted to myself, muttering, "*So-called* strategy session."

Con would never learn—and apparently neither would I.

I likely should consider convening court, since I wasn't going to be wasting time watching Con pretend to take advice. But I couldn't bear the thought of maintaining my poise in front of everyone—much less attempting to make coolheaded decisions—not when I felt so terribly raw.

I might be healed physically, but internally I remained a shattered mess.

So, knuckling away the traitorous tears and walking at a brisk pace, I entered the main hall and turned toward my chambers, needing to just be alone for a while. Maybe I could spend some time in the dreamthink, gain some clarity and calm that way. Startled nobles and courtiers flashed me curious glances as they quickly bowed before my furious passage. I tried to convey the impression that I was hurrying to an important engagement rather than running away.

"Lia!" Con's voice thundered from some distance behind me, echoing through the graceful hall with coarse, dark threat.

Against all reason, I picked up my pace.

"Don't you run from me!" he roared.

Aghast faces became a blur as I ran indeed—at least as fast as my towering heels would allow—practically leaping up the stairs before racing down the hall to my chambers. It made no sense, but I held on to the goal of simply reaching my rooms and barring the door against him.

There weren't guards on my doors since I wasn't within, but they were closed. I skidded to a halt and lost precious seconds twisting the handle open. I threw myself inside, turning to thrust the door shut and lock it—only to find Con *right there*, golden eyes blazing, hair streaming like a thunder god's. He hit the door with his hand, throwing me backward with the force of it, and I teetered on my heels, flailing for balance.

Until he caught me around the waist, kicked the door shut, then—holding me fast—paused to turn the lock.

"Put Me down, you crazed brute!" I practically shrieked, flailing to be free.

"No." He sounded eerily calm.

"I told you to put Me down this instant."

"If you were serious, you would've hit me with that magic whammy." He strode across the sitting room and carried me through the next sets of doors, into our bedroom, then tossed me onto the bed. Folding his arms, he scowled at me. "We're going to talk."

I made a great show of looking around at the bed. "This is *talking*?"

With a growl he went to close the bedroom door, sliding that bolt home, too. "They won't interrupt us in here if they think we're having sex."

He had a point, though that just pissed me off further. "I am *not* having sex with you," I spat, sliding off the bed and pacing a good distance away.

"I know that, Lia." He sounded sorry and weary, and rubbed his hands over his face. "When I said we needed to talk, I meant it."

"There is nothing to discuss," I informed him crisply. "We've said everything that needs to be said."

He dropped his hands and studied me. For once he didn't have the rock hammer on his back, and I realized he must have left it behind in the Sand Salon to chase after me. What a spectacle we'd made of ourselves. Between Con chasing me through the main hall of the palace, bellowing, and the very public argument that Percy was no doubt spreading even now to capitalize on the exclusive and titillating news, the gossip would be blazing.

"You do that so well," Con said, in an almost wondering tone, and I had to think back to what he could possibly mean. "You just declare what you will and won't discuss. You deliver your edicts and then refuse to listen to—"

"To listen to lies and foolishness!" I shouted.

"To any opinion that's different from yours," he roared over me. "You cut me out of your life, tell me you're *done*, and banish me from your precious realm with less compassion than you'd give a stray dog."

"Because I am queen here," I shot back, trembling with righteous fury. "It's My responsibility to protect Calanthe and—"

"Yeah, yeah. Protect Calanthe, blah blah blah," he snarled, closing the distance between us. "This isn't about the throne or Calanthe, and you know it, Lia."

I did want him gone—if only to end this roiling surf of up-and-down emotions. He was determined to kill himself; nothing I could say would stop him.

Unless I told him about the baby.

Did I dare use that lever against him? And what then, if it worked, where his love for me hadn't? I might not survive that blow. "I know no such thing," I spat, but I lacked conviction.

"Liar." He reached for me and I scrambled back, barely evading him. He only followed. "This is about you, Lia.

The woman. Now what in great green Ejarat is going on inside your head?"

"My personal emotions aren't relevant," I replied stiffly. *The only feelings of yours that deserve attention are those regarding the throne.*

"The hell they aren't." He reached for me again. I backed up—and hit the wall. A glint of victory in his eyes, he took me by the shoulders.

"Drop your hands," I warned, "or I will hit you with a 'whammy' that will put you out for three days."

He searched my face, smiled thinly. "Do it then."

I summoned my magic, ready to fell him like a tree, but there was nothing to push against. I couldn't reverse the violent intention if he didn't have any. Curling my lip at the discovery, I glared in impotent fury instead. "Very clever, wolf."

He looked grimly satisfied—and deeply unhappy. The wolf, kicked on his tender muzzle. He flexed his hands on my shoulders, searching my face, searching for words. "How could you say those things to me, Lia? Don't you care for me at all?"

I wanted to tell him no, that I did *not* care, not a whit. The words assembled themselves in my brain. *The sex was great. It's been fun. Thanks for saving My life. Good luck storming the citadel. Go ahead and get your fool self killed for all I care.*

But none of them reached my lips. Instead, without warning or sense, I burst into tears.

"Oh, Lia." Con's arms came around me. "No, Lia. Don't cry. Yell at me, but don't cry."

"I *hate* you," I sobbed.

"I know." He picked me up, again carrying me to the bed, but this time he sat on it, holding me on his lap. "I'm sorry, Lia."

I caught my breath, viciously wiping the tears from my face. "Fuck me—all I do anymore is cry."

His chuckle rumbled under my ear. "Barely at all. And only in front of me, which is allowed."

Was that true? Bright Ejarat—it was. Tears were a sign of weakness, I'd thought, but . . .

He tipped up my chin so I'd look at him. "You should be able to trust me with your tears. Besides, you get a pass, considering what you've been through."

"*You* never cry," I accused, more querulously than I'd wanted.

"I do. I have. But mostly I rage and roar and make stupid choices." He brushed the last tears from my cheeks. "I really am sorry. I wasn't thinking. I got caught up in . . ."

"Vengeance," I finished bitterly.

"Yeah." He smoothed the wild strands of blooming hair from my damp temples. "Is it so terrible that I want Anure dead? That I want to destroy those wizards for what they did to you, so they can never do that to anyone again?"

"No," I admitted. "I understand that this is how you deal with an unjust world. It's your nature to bash and destroy your enemies."

"You make me sound like a savage." He kissed me, not savage at all, but infinitely gentle. "And it's your nature to control everything with icy logic, keeping all your feelings bottled up inside."

"True," I admitted. The man did know me well.

He kissed me again and smiled sadly. "Lia, I *have* to try to rescue Rhéiane. You even agreed, and then you said we needed to rescue all of the royal captives."

"I know that," I bit out, pushing against him, against my own irrationality.

"Shh. Stay with me. Then what's the problem?"

"Exactly what I said. What Brenda said," I fired back.

"You're not listening to anyone else. You're not taking a team on a rescue mission. This is a lone-wolf thing in your mind. I know why you wanted that detailed model of the throne room—so you can take that bomb in there and kill everyone in the room, including yourself."

"There's a trigger," he argued. "And I'm fast. I could run out in time."

"No, you couldn't. More relevant: You wouldn't if it came to a choice between saving your own life and killing Anure."

His smile faded, replaced by grim intensity. "Wouldn't it be worth it, Lia? My life isn't worth much, but if I could sacrifice it—"

"How can you say your life isn't worth much?" I ground out, his casual reference to sacrificing his own life pushing me beyond carefully reasoned words. "What about Me? Don't you have any idea what you're worth to Me?"

Studying my face, his was a canvas of contrasts, desolation warring with hope, bafflement giving way to dawning realization. "No," he said slowly, "I don't know. Because *you* have never told me. In fact, you act like you can't see the back of me soon enough. Just now you said you were done with me and ordered me off Your island." He finished that on a growing growl of frustration, using the honorific mockingly.

"I mean it, too!" I threw at him. "Go, already. Leave Me alone here, never come back. I was fine before you came here and I cannot wait for you to be gone from My sight."

Abruptly, he grinned. "You're in love with me."

"Ha to that!"

"Why didn't you tell me?" he demanded, pushing me back onto the bed and pinning my wrists as he straddled me on all fours. His dark hair rained around us, his eyes effulgent as afternoon sunlight. "I've been pouring my heart out to you, miserable because you only seemed to want to be freed of me, thrilled to shake me loose. Why keep it a secret?"

"I did tell you," I said, hearing the defensiveness in my own voice.

He narrowed his eyes. "Uh-uh, crazy lady. I'd remember that for sure."

"Not in so many words," I admitted, "but I told you that, when I was . . ." *Dying.* One day I'd be able to think of it without crumbling. "I only thought of you. Not Calanthe. You. That you were first for Me."

Huffing out a humorless laugh, he shook his head. "Only you would think that's the same thing."

"It *is* the same thing," I insisted, struggling a little, but he held me fast.

"No way, you're not going anywhere. This is a grand and glorious moment for me, and I'm going to savor every drop."

I groaned, letting my head drop back. "You don't get it, wolf."

"I don't get what?"

"It doesn't matter how much I love you, because that strands Me on the shore alone when I'm not first for you."

"The hell you aren't," he growled, lowering his head to kiss me. I bit his lip, and he jerked back. "Fuck! What was that for?"

"You're not listening to Me!"

"Fine. I'm listening." He gave me an exaggeratedly patient look, a bead of blood welling on his lower lip. The same place I'd wounded him before.

"You can't put Me first *and* put revenge first," I explained. "Math. Two different things can't be number one."

He frowned. "Real life doesn't work that way. I can kill Anure and then come back home to you. And do whatever else needs to be done afterward in whatever order you want to do it," he added.

"What if I ask you not to kill Anure?"

Searching my face for the trick, he shook his head. "You wouldn't ask me that. You want him dead, too."

"Conrí. I am asking you, right here, right now: Please don't try to kill Anure."

"What?" Complete bewilderment had him sitting up and letting me go. "Why would you ask me that?"

I sat up, brushing at my silk skirts, hopelessly crushed and wrinkled. "Because if you'll give up trying to kill Anure, then your focus will be on getting the captives out— and you'll actually have a chance of coming home to Me."

He darted me a surprised look. "You just called Calanthe my home."

"Oh, Con." I lifted a hand to his cheek, but he seized it in both of his, pressing his lips to my palm, the blood smearing there like the mark of a vow. "Of course Calanthe is your home, if you want it to be. I'm sorry I said otherwise. It was cruel of Me. I was trying to . . ."

"Drive me away," he murmured, lips moving over my palm. "It nearly worked, too."

"I can be savage, too," I whispered.

"Very sharp thorns," he agreed, tongue stroking over my palm and making me gasp. Then he lifted his head, gazing at me, stark emotion in his face. "Do you really love me, Lia?"

"I do," I admitted it with resignation, like a confession. "I love you with everything in Me. I'm not sure I could survive losing you." There. I'd given him my bleeding heart on a platter. May he feast on it.

"Love isn't a weakness, my flower," he said, drawing

my hand behind his neck and tucking a strand of escaping hair behind my ear.

"You've called it a vulnerability," I insisted. "Anure uses what we love against us. It's a chink in the armor, the thin skin over our hearts easily penetrated by the slightest of arrows."

He frowned. "Maybe both things are true. Love can be a strength, too, instead of a wound."

I wanted that to be true. I was afraid it wasn't. "If it's not a wound, then why does it hurt so much?" I tried to smile and failed.

"Maybe because we haven't been doing it right," he said ruefully. "It hurts me, too. We seem to have a knack for screwing things up together. That's probably some math, right? Add the two of us and we get something even bigger than the sum of the parts."

I actually giggled, maybe from the emotional release. It hadn't been easy to keep from telling him how much I loved him, and now that I had, it felt as if a dam had burst, allowing the waters to flow again. "Some kind of math, anyway."

"I have a confession to make," he whispered.

"Oh?" I braced for it.

"I don't have a better plan," he said. "I really wasn't trying to lone-wolf it so much, but that was the best plan I could come up with. Everyone is counting on me to come up with some kind of strategy and I . . . just don't know. Ambrose pointed out that my plan to rescue you was terrible—that only luck and his intervention saved it from disaster. Lia, what if I can't do this?"

"Oh, my Con." I breathed out the tension, then cupped his face in my hands. "That's why you have other people. That's one of the first rules of being in charge: You don't have to do everything yourself, you only need to gather good minds together. You have an eye for choosing people. Use them."

He made a sound, a kind of disparaging laugh. "I don't know. Doesn't sound very brutish and iconoclastic. I found out what it meant, by the way."

I smiled at that. "Who did you ask?"

"Sondra. It's not such a bad thing."

"It's not, and you could've asked Me."

"You could avoid using words I don't know."

"What's the fun in that?" I kissed him—and he seized the opportunity, deepening the kiss with dizzying speed. My head spun with the swift sexual hunger, the fire blazing between us as if fed by the brutal argument.

"You are a cruel woman," Con said when he broke the kiss for us both to draw in gasping breaths. He pushed me back on the bed, slid a hand up my thigh under the silk petals of my skirts. "And I love you for it, Sawehl help me."

"I love you, too, Con," I said, still feeling the rawness of that exposure. "I didn't want to, didn't imagine it could happen—but it's done now and there's no going back."

He stroked my thigh, sliding his rough fingers ever higher. "Done?" he asked with a smile.

"Done," I breathed on a gasp as his hand brushed my sex, my hips lifting in the pure wanting and fiery love that had taken my mind so long to catch up to.

"You're so wet, Lia," he murmured, sliding his callused finger into my tender folds. "Do you want me still, even after everything?"

"I always want you. I can't seem to help Myself." I slid my hand to his cock, pressing hard against his leather pants. "The same for you?"

"Yes." He shook his head, golden eyes full of chagrin. "There you are, screaming that you hate me and I'm hard

thinking how gorgeous you are when you're pissed at me
and how badly I want you."

"I don't hate you," I whispered.

"I know." He brushed his lips over mine, a smile curving them when I moaned as a finger slid inside me. "I *am*
a broken man, and I do lose my perspective. I'm sorry for
that. I promise I won't make killing Anure a priority."

I stilled, reaching for his wrist to move his hand away
from my sizzling sex, so I could think while I searched
his face for the truth. "That's not a promise not to kill him."

"No." He shook his head slightly, hair spilling over his
shoulders. "If I can find a way to kill him without risking
my life, I will. But the priority will be getting the captives
and everyone on the team, including myself, home to you.
Is that good enough?"

"A compromise." I considered it.

"I hear people make them," he said, raising a dark brow,
humor in his eyes.

"Imagine that." I supposed I could try.

"I'm trying to be honest with you, Lia—and that's the
most I can promise," he said more soberly.

"All right, I can accept that. But in that spirit, I should
tell you something also."

He stopped resisting my grip, stilling and watching me
warily. "What is it?"

I hesitated, aware of the drag of the crown on my hair,
his big body taut above me. This would change things between us. *The one truth we can count on is that things
will change.* "It's early days yet, but I've conceived a child."

He didn't process the news immediately, then a wondering smile spread across his face. "The other night—
when I fed you?"

I nodded, surprised. "How did you know?"

"I felt . . . *something* then." He pushed up my skirts

THE PROMISED QUEEN 273

fully, sitting back to splay his big hands over my still-too-concave belly.

"You won't be able to see anything yet," I laughed.

He glanced up at me, sheepish, but eyes sparkling gold with delight. "I'm going to look anyway. Every day. When I get back," he amended, remembering and sobering. "Is that why you're telling me now—so I'll be careful?"

"It occurred to Me," I confessed. "But I'm also terribly selfish, and I wanted you to want to live for Me, not just for the child."

"Oh, Lia," he murmured, lowering his head to kiss me thoroughly. Then he gazed at me steadily. "Everything is for you. You call me broken—but that's a step up from what I was before you. I was dead inside. You are my life. Never send me away."

"I wish I could ask you to never leave Me," I breathed, shocked at myself for confessing that.

"Only for this. I wouldn't go for any other reason." His hand flattened over my belly, and he leaned his forehead against mine.

Not only for this, I thought, because he would have to leave me for Oriel, too. But I would face that day when it came. I was tired of grieving for a future that had not yet arrived. When it did, I'd wish I'd appreciated this time while I had it.

"Even if I can't go with you, I can help you craft a logical strategy. Speaking of, we should get back down to the Sand Salon and resume planning. *Real* planning."

"They were taking a break for lunch," he replied, sliding his hand over my mound to stroke me, so I arched in helpless pleasure. "We have time."

"Yes, but—" I convulsed when he plunged two fingers into me. "Oh, *Con*."

"Yes, my love?" he asked innocently, brushing kisses

over my collarbones, then the upper curves of my breasts. "Did you need something from me?"

"Yes." I writhed as he tormented me. "You."

"Tell me you love me."

"I love you," I agreed, quite willingly.

"Tell me again."

I narrowed my eyes at him, then lost my focus as he pressed the spot inside me that sent me wild, his mouth closing over one nipple, hot and intense through the silk. I writhed, then found my voice. "I love you."

"Sweet indeed," he murmured hoarsely. "One more time."

I laughed, full of surprisingly intense joy that had nothing to do with the sexual pleasure—or only a little to do with it. "I love you, Con."

"I love you, too, Lia." And he proceeded to demonstrate exactly how much.

18

"This is a charmingly new experience," Lia muttered to me under her breath, sounding anything but charmed as she walked beside me, hand looped through the crook of my elbow. "Returning to a strategy meeting in a different gown than I left in."

"You change dresses twelve times a day anyway," I teased.

"I do not, you oaf." She poked me with her pointy elbow and flashed me a glittering glare, which lacked her usual punch given that her lush mouth was swollen from kisses and her skin flushed still from pleasure. A scattering of petals imprinted into her skin flowed over her long throat and over one breast. A nearly naked breast.

She'd declared the butterfly dress beyond salvaging without considerable cleaning and repair, and had changed into another gown. On this one, the sheer fabric seemed mainly to function as a see-through scaffolding for silk flowers. It clung to her like a second skin, only the scattering of flowers keeping her from being entirely naked—and those didn't cover much. Lia looked breathtakingly sensual, like Ejarat as maiden in springtime. Lia had claimed she'd picked the dress because she wouldn't have to call her ladies to sew her into it—but I figured she knew it would torture me to see her in it, a little payback for all the ways I'd teased her into quivering submission.

Totally worth it.

"Twice, maybe three times a day," she allowed, "depending on My formal and informal engagements. With this costume change, however, they'll all know what we've been doing."

"I'm pretty sure they know we have sex," I said, grinning down at her.

She produced a sharper glare, almost completely managing to keep her lips from twitching into a smile. "How long have you been waiting to throw those words back at Me?"

"Since you said them to me," I replied cheerfully, turning us down the short hall to the Sand Salon. "Let's see who came back."

All of them. We turned into the room, and our council of misfits all stood, offering a polite round of applause, like courtiers at some arty entertainment. Lia actually blushed, then glared round the room. "All right," she declared. "I concede that the joke is on Me. Have your fun."

"Well, yeah," Sondra replied with a smirk. "Since you two obviously did."

"Ha ha," Lia retorted, but she also smiled, rolling her eyes. "Are we ready to get back to work?"

"I don't know, Your Highness," Percy drawled. "Are You *done*?"

"Blessed Ejarat," Lia said under her breath, "I should have them all pitched off the cliffs into the sea."

"Can I watch?" I asked in the same voice.

She gave me a brilliant smile. "This is why I love you."

"The only reason?"

"One of many," she amended with that smile I'd come

to think of as only for me. Despite the circumstances, the dire problems before us, I towered in my joy that she actually did love me.

"All right, people." Sondra raised her voice, making me realize I'd been stupidly grinning at Lia. "Now that Mommy and Daddy have made up, let's figure out an actual, workable plan that won't get everyone killed. At least not on Anure's doorstep. If I'm going to squander my life, I want to do it *inside* the citadel."

"Let's go back to the beginning," Kara said after glancing at me for permission and then clearing his throat. "What are our first steps?"

"We need to rebuild our model," Brenda said, stepping up beside him.

"Ah," Lia said. "Allow Me." She waved a hand over the table and the model appeared as it had been, even including the tower I'd shattered when I'd lost my shit and pounded the table.

"Thank You, Your Highness." Brenda gave her a slight bow. "Saves us some work."

"I retained the mental map of it," Lia explained, sounding abashed as she gestured to her temple. "I apologize, to you all, that I lost My temper."

"It's about the only thing that gets our Conrí's attention," Sondra replied cheerfully.

"Sometimes the irresistible force benefits from an encounter with the immovable object," Ambrose agreed. "As for the plan, at the risk of drawing the ire of our esteemed royal host," he added, nodding to Lia, "I feel I must say that aspects of Con's concept aren't entirely awful."

That got my attention. Not because it vindicated me somewhat—though that was nice for once—but because Ambrose so rarely weighed in with specific advice. Like never. "Does that mean my idea is the correct use for Lia's severed hand?"

Ambrose waved a hand at me, shaking his head so his golden curls bounced. "Correct? What is correct? This isn't a math problem with a single solution."

Lia swallowed a laugh and I decided to let that go. "But it's not an incorrect application. The subterfuge could potentially work, is what you're saying."

"It could," Ambrose replied, stroking Merle's feathers, sounding vague. "If Her Highness agrees. It *is* Her hand, after all, claimed by you or not."

Everyone looked at Lia like she might be a vurgsten package about to explode. She huffed, extracted her arm from mine, and paced to the table. "I'll agree it's not an entirely awful plan for entrée to the citadel. Nor is setting off vurgsten in the throne room a bad plan for creating a distraction from our *true purpose*." She slid a keen glance at me. "Suicidal gambits are right out, however. The game belongs to us for the moment, so let's set it up to our best advantage. I want contingency plans in place—and I want contingency plans for our contingency plans. We should figure out all the ways things could go terribly wrong and plan for them. Then there's no room for emotion to drive decisions in the heat of conflict."

She pinned me with a knowing glare, and I bowed my head in contrition.

Acknowledging that, she continued. "I suggest that we begin with the desired result: extracting the captives and removing them to a safe location. That is the thrust of our strategy. Everything else is secondary. Get in, get the royal captives, get them out." She looked around at everyone, waiting until they agreed.

"Get them to where?" I asked. "Not here."

"Why not? Calanthe is closest."

"But is it safe?" I asked. "You'd be putting Calanthe in jeopardy, especially if Anure's wizards pursue."

"True. I say it's a risk Calanthe should take. I realize this is a change in My policy, but what point is there in having retained our sovereignty if we can't use that to help restore the other kingdoms?" She gave me a rueful smile of her own, and I nodded in appreciation for her concession to our long-standing argument.

"Also," she continued, "I'm learning more all the time. This morning I strengthened Calanthe's wards. The wizards can try their tricks, but they'll find it much more difficult."

"I can verify that," Ambrose said with a smile. Merle croaked an unhappy sound.

Lia looked abashed. "Ambrose . . . it didn't occur to Me that you two would be affected, because you're already on Calanthe and so—" She cut herself off, giving him an odd look.

He smiled back, the two of them exchanging some kind of understanding. "You made it uncomfortable for us." Merle flapped his wings in indignant agreement. "The wards are excellently woven, so I think any other wizards would be hard-pressed to penetrate Your defenses. And, if they escalate their efforts, You would know in time to take steps."

"Thank you," she replied, still seeming bemused, then drew herself up. "So we sail the captives to Calanthe. Unless someone has a magical method to fly them over the ocean . . ." She trailed off, and we all looked at Ambrose.

Merle cawed in indignation, and Ambrose gave us all a disbelieving look. "Seriously? After all this time, I'd think you'd understand that is *not*—"

"Not how magic works," we all chorused with him.

Merle flipped his wings to his back and Ambrose huffed. "Well, it's not."

"With that settled," Lia continued gravely, though her eyes were lively with humor, "we should agree that the limiting factor to our plan is putting the captives on a ship in the first place. Indeed, given new information, we'll need several ships, depending on their capacity."

"They'd have to be fast ships," Kara said. "Unless we manage to extract the captives in total secrecy, we'll be pursued by more than wizard magic. Even with the bulk of Anure's fleet decimated, we cannot outfight his remaining ships. We'll need speed."

Everyone very carefully didn't look at Percy, but he threw his hands up with an exclamation of disgust. "*Fine*," he hissed. "Take the *Last Resort*. She's the fastest thing we've got—but *do* try not to wreck her this time." He leveled a mean look at me, and I did my best to look grave and not triumphant.

Lia held up an elegant finger. "Thank you, Lord Percy. Your generosity will be remembered. However, the *Last Resort* will not be enough." She turned the finger to crook it at Ibolya, who hastened over, extracting a folded envelope from a pocket of her gown and handing it to Lia. "I have not been entirely idle." She gave me an arch look, but I only raised my brows expectantly. "We have an idea now of how many people we need to rescue. There are more than we thought, I assume in part because the royals have companions, such as My own ladies." She raised a brow at Agatha, where she'd been hanging back behind Kara.

She stepped forward, looking drawn and thin—well, she always had, but more so now—and I really wondered at the wisdom of her returning to Yekpehr. "They do, Your Highness," she answered in her whispery voice. "These are loyal companions and servants who've attended them for many years. The companionship among them runs deep. If You wish to extract the royal captives without noticeable fuss, then I advise planning to rescue all of them. They will not betray one another."

"But *you* escaped," Kara said to her, partly in question. "Alone. Ah, not that I mean to accuse, but—"

The look she gave him was bitter enough to cut him off without a word from her. "Yes, Kara, I am a traitor to my former comrades. I seized an opportunity to escape, and in doing so I betrayed those I left behind. Don't judge them by my failures, Kara. Not everyone is as faithless as I."

Kara looked aghast at his misstep, and Agatha turned her face away to stare out the open gallery—a scene that might've been the bleak and empty landscape of Vurgmun, judging by her expression, rather than the riotous and verdant gardens of Calanthe. Oddly enough, it was Percy who stepped in to break the awkward silence.

"You're not faithless, Agatha," he said, with none of his usual drama or flamboyance. "Every one of us here has done terrible things to survive. You did what you had to."

"We all have," Brenda agreed.

"Yes." I went to Agatha and put a hand on her shoulder, understanding now why she felt compelled to return to Yekpehr, no matter how painful it might be for her. "I've killed, and worse, so I might live—and I'm not proud of it. But with this mission, we have the chance to right some wrongs. Because you escaped, you had the knowledge to get Lia and Sondra out. Because you escaped, you can tell us how to get the rest of them out."

She tipped her face up to me, the hollows of grief and

guilt making shadows under her papery skin. "Thank you, Conrí," she said softly. "And Percy, all of you."

"All right," I said. "How many people will we be rescuing?"

Lia grimaced. "Ninety-seven."

Percy whistled long and low, while everyone else murmured unhappily. "The *Last Resort* can't hold more than two dozen," he noted with regret.

"So we need to get ninety-seven of them, plus six of us—me, Agatha, Brenda, Ambrose, Ibolya, and Kara—back to—"

"Seven," Percy clarified. "I'm going."

"All right," I nodded, surprised, but not unhappy about it.

"Eight, counting Merle," Ambrose supplied, when the raven croaked and flapped his wings.

"Nine, then," I said, "counting Vesno, too. This problem is easily solved," I said, "using tried-and-true techniques of the Slave King's rebellion." Sondra and Kara grinned back at me. "We need a ship to carry a hundred and five people back to Calanthe, but we only need to take nine of us there. We'll sail the *Last Resort* to Yekpehr, then steal one of Anure's fastest ships of appropriate size and speed to return."

Lia gave me a real smile. "Brilliant."

"What would be even better," Brenda mused, twirling her finger over the smooth sand that imitated the harbor, making it swirl, "is if we could somehow get Anure to load those captives onto that ship himself."

"Yesss . . ." Sondra paced to the towers Agatha had helped detail, studying the replicas of the rooms where the royal captives lived. I refrained from giving Lia a triumphant look that—*see?*—that part of the model *was* useful. "That is a diabolically clever plan. It would remove the most difficult and dangerous aspect of this rescue—getting to the royals and getting them out of their imprisonment. No way are we hustling a hundred people out from under the guards' noses without them smelling a problem."

"But if the guards themselves are moving the people . . ." I said, moving up beside her.

She gave me that flesh-eating grin of hers. "And they load them onto the ship for us . . ."

"Then we steal it and sail away," Kara finished. "I like this plan."

"*If* we can figure out how to get them to do it," Brenda qualified.

I stared at Ambrose, who returned my gaze expectantly. "When we were stuck at the Slave Gate at Yekpehr, Ambrose appeared, looking like a lord of the citadel. Exact enough to convince the guards."

"A combination of illusion and coaxing them to believe what I wanted them to," Ambrose conceded. "That *is* how magic works."

"Can you make people believe you are Anure?" I asked, hope battling in my chest, Lia's face dawning with a similar light.

"More effectively, I can appear as one of Anure's wizards. As Her Highness has noted, they hold as much power as the false emperor, if not more. I can create a plausible excuse, and between Merle and me, we can manage a deception for a short time. However—and this is critical—there cannot be any cognitive dissonance. Any interruption and the illusion will cease to be sufficiently convincing."

Perplexed, I looked to Lia. "The actual wizard he's impersonating cannot appear," she explained, "or people will realize the trick. And no one else, like the emperor, can arrive to countermand the order."

"That's exactly what I said," Ambrose complained, and Merle croaked an agreement.

"That brings us back to distracting Anure and the wizards," I said, mostly to Lia, "so they won't interfere."

She gave me a wry look that clearly communicated she suspected me of being happy with this turn of events. "So you think that if you have an audience with the toad, you'll be of sufficient interest to distract him *and* his four wizards long enough for a full removal of the royal captives, moving a hundred people to a stolen ship in the harbor, and sailing it out of reach."

"Leave the stealing to Brenda and me," Kara said.

She nodded. "We can do that while the rest are infiltrating the citadel."

Lia studied them a moment, then nodded. "The timing is still a problem, even if you're ready to set sail. How long does it take to travel from the citadel to the harbor?" She flicked a glance at Sondra. "I remember our journey from Anure's ship to the gate we entered taking more than an hour."

Sondra frowned and went to the table. "It was more like two hours. You're right—that's a problem."

Agatha drifted up to join them. With a thin finger, she traced a route from the harbor through the township outside the walls, then through the massive main gate, and then through the winding streets between the walls and the towers of the citadel. "Does that seem like the route you took?"

Lia, looking pained, shook her head. I put a hand on the small of her back. She leaned into my touch, her trust telling me more than any words could speak. "I'm no help with that," she said. "I was . . . not in a good frame of mind."

"That's the route we took," Sondra said. "I counted the turns, in case we had a chance to escape and had to retrace our path." She grinned at Lia. "My memory went to shit *after* that."

"Smart," Lia murmured. "It didn't occur to Me to pay attention to turns."

"Yeah, well." Sondra shrugged. "When you've escaped one prison, you learn a few life-preserving habits."

"They took you on the formal procession route," Agatha said. "It does take nearly two hours. There's a shorter route." She pointed to another road from a side gate. "This is a supply road. It goes directly to the harbor, to expedite transfer of supplies from ships to the citadel storerooms."

"Better." Lia raised her brows. "How short?"

Agatha pursed her lips. "A quarter hour to get from the walls to the harbor."

"And to get from the royals' tower rooms to the walls?" Lia prompted.

"Figuring that you're herding along recalcitrant people suddenly uprooted from their dwellings? Another quarter hour, at best. Probably more, depending on how much trouble they give us."

"And they will give you trouble," Lia said, not really a question.

Agatha inclined her head in wry agreement. "They are not long on trust, any of them."

"Not surprising. We're calling it an hour, total," Lia decided. She pinned me with a sharp look. "How are you going to make this audience with Anure last at least an hour?"

"I'll find a way," I assured her.

"Not good enough, Con." Lia's voice was ice, her face sharp. Amazing how those lush and tender petals could reveal wicked thorns in an instant. "You had an audience with Me when you arrived on Calanthe. How long did it last?"

"Not long," I admitted with remembered bitterness.

"Exactly. Do you know why I kept it short?"

"You're a busy woman?" I ventured.

She smiled mirthlessly. "Ibolya?"

The lady-in-waiting who'd been keeping surreptitiously to the background glided up and curtsied. "Your Highness?"

"What's the answer?"

Ibolya considered. "Your Highness keeps all audiences in formal court brief. You control the interview, not the petitioner."

Lia's smile warmed. "Exactly. Now, we can assume that Anure is less practiced at this. He wasn't trained to manipulate and contain formal court as I was, as I've previously noted. But Anure is also not stupid. Every moment a petitioner receives attention is a tiny bit more power yielded to someone not on the throne."

"All right, all right." I held up my hands. "I get your point."

"An hour is a *long* time, Conrí," she pressed. "Too long."

"Doesn't that mean setting off the vurgsten is a good idea? No more worrying about long audiences."

Lia stared at me, brow truly furrowed. "Lady Agatha," Lia said, "tell Me about this bomb and the trigger you developed."

"It's not ideal, Your Highness," Agatha answered. "I wove a length of twine, treated with wax to burn slowly, like a candle. After a delay, the fire reaches the vurgsten, and the package explodes. However, there's a risk of the twine ceasing to burn, especially in the airless confines of a bag. The longer the fuse, the greater the chance of the fire smothering. I experimented with a number of lengths and finally determined the greatest chance of the flame reaching the package with sufficient heat to explode it requires a fuse that is quite short." She held up her thumb and index finger in demonstration.

"How long between setting the spark and the explosion?" Lia inquired.

"Less than a minute," Agatha admitted.

Lia's eyes sparkled with anger, and I was hard-pressed not to look chagrined. "Can a man outrun an explosion in that amount of time?"

"Yes," I said.

Sondra smothered a snort of derision. Kara gave me a pointedly bland look.

"I could," I insisted. "I'd have to set the spark and beat hell out of there, but I could do it."

"And if you're restrained by guards?" Lia inquired coolly.

"I'll bash 'em with my rock hammer," I replied with a grin she didn't return. "Fine. If I don't have a clear shot at running, I won't set the spark until I do."

"Conrí," Agatha said, "we all know your lungs aren't good for running." She said it with enough neutral compassion that I couldn't very well take insult.

"For a short distance, I'm good," I assured her, and Lia—who watched me with her jeweled eyes full of canny patience I didn't trust.

"All right," Lia replied smoothly. "Let's say you could. Explain to Me exactly how this will work. You've obtained the audience with Anure, using the subterfuge of My hand and a false orchid ring—which I feel compelled to point out will be immediately detected as non-magical by the wizards." She paced over to her model of the throne room and indicated a wide area in front of the throne. Even in replica, Anure's throne looked crazy and obscene, heaped with treasure. If anyone else had told me about it, I'd say they exaggerated, but I knew Lia had been exacting in her detail. "You will likely be here," Lia continued, "and in Anure's court, the courtiers all stay well back, forming a semicircle in the far third of the room."

"Out of the range of Anure's spittle," Sondra inserted sardonically, and Lia threw her an appreciative glance.

"Indeed. The overwhelming feel of the court is that they are all terrified of Anure, with the exception of the wizards."

"The wizards are not entirely exempt from that fear," Ambrose corrected.

Interesting. Lia cocked her head at Ambrose, waited a moment, but he said nothing more. "So we set our scene," Lia said, waving a finger over the model of the court, creating a figure that had to be me, flanked by guards. Featureless figures sprang up to ring the back third of the room. "Let's pretend you get lucky, Con, and the guards don't chain you, don't disarm you. How are you going to open the sack, light a fuse, and then run away with no one hindering you in any way?"

I stared at the model, both to avoid her accusing gaze and hoping some answer would offer itself. She was right that I hadn't worried about all of this before because I'd figured I only needed to get close to Anure, light the vurgsten, and die with him.

"You've been to My court, Con," she continued remorselessly. "You know how far you got trying to attack Me. How far do you imagine Anure's guards will let you get if you reach for your sack of vurgsten—I assume it's a substantial size?" When Brenda nodded, Lia continued crisply. "And that is *if* they even let you keep it."

"I'll think of a way to trick them," I insisted. I'd dragged that sack around the citadel before, after all.

"What trick?" she demanded.

"These things can't always be planned," I insisted, aware that I sounded defensive. And stubborn. "You can't control the whole fucking world," I gritted between my teeth.

"This is your *life*, Conrí," she shot back, "which you just promised to safeguard for Me at all costs. Come up with a better plan."

Everyone looked from Lia—slim and delicate, unflinchingly staring me down—to me. Was she the irresistible force or the immovable object? I raked my hand over my scalp. "I will."

"*Before* you leave."

I took her hand and kissed it. "I promise."

"Something to figure into your scenario," Agatha said into the quiet lull, "is that the royal captives sometimes attend court." She made a bracket of her fingers, measuring from my figure to Anure, then back from "me" to the front row of courtiers. "Any vurgsten package powerful enough to reach the Imperial Toad—if we're trying to kill him and not just create a distracting boom—would also possibly kill the very people we're attempting to rescue."

"Give me ideas, people. How do we make sure the royal captives are in their rooms and not in court?" Lia asked the group.

"I have an idea, Your Highness, Conrí," Ibolya said, then seemed abashed when we all looked at her. "If it's not impertinent to interrupt at this point."

"I asked for ideas, so you're not interrupting," Lia told her gently. "What is it?"

"If some of us infiltrate the citadel before Conrí's audience, we can pose as servants and warn the royal captives.

That would also give us time to explain what's going on. They'll cooperate when it's time to move because they'll know they're being rescued. Conrí won't need a full hour."

Lia smiled. "Good thinking."

"Yes," Agatha said. "Very smart. Some of them might even be helpful in the effort."

Ibolya smiled back, hesitant, then more widely. "I know something about serving royals, so I volunteer to be one of those people who sneaks in to talk to them."

Lia's smile faded, the specter of horror darkening her eyes. "I hate to ask that of you. And you wouldn't know how to find them."

"You didn't ask, Your Highness; I offered," Ibolya replied. "This is my idea and I want to do this."

"I can guide Ibolya, Your Highness." Agatha gestured to the model. "As of our last visit, however, the royal captives were lodged in three separate towers."

"If I go in at least the night before," Ibolya said, "I can make sure no one leaves early for a breakfast meeting or some such before court. I could make my way to all three towers in the course of a night."

"A new lady-in-waiting moving among all three towers?" Agatha shook her head. "That would be noticed. Too suspicious. I'll take two towers, and you take the other."

"Better, three of us go, each taking one," Sondra said, not looking at me. She brushed a hand over her shorn hair. "I knew I cut this stuff off for a reason. I can't pull off elegant lady-in-waiting, but I can be slave girl."

I eyed her tall, muscular form, the fierce gaze of a warrior, and thought there was no way anyone would mistake Sondra for a simple slave girl. She caught me looking. "I can do it, Con. I've lived it, remember? My way of holding the torch. Besides, I memorized all the old royalty, back in the day. I can be useful."

"All right," I said, both to her and to get the room's attention. "How do we get Agatha, Ibolya, and Sondra into the citadel?"

"We'll need papers," Agatha said, "and to look like servants and slaves of no note. More surreptitious is better. We three will work on that."

Brenda tapped the table. "I'll help Conrí with designing a bomb he can smuggle in and still escape from. While you all have been off waging battles and executing heroic rescues, I've been experimenting with vurgsten. Since I only had small amounts to work with, I found ways to purify and condense the stuff. I can make a smaller bomb powerful enough to clear that throne room—and maybe disguise it as something else."

"And here I thought you'd been composing sonnets," Percy observed.

Brenda lifted a silver brow. "I have. Tinkering with chemistry is excellent for allowing the mind to wander through poetic composition."

"We should go in two groups then," Kara put in. "I can pilot one of the Hertaq fishing boats and take it into the harbor the night before to drop off our infiltrators. Then Brenda and I can scout a target ship to steal. Conrí and Lord Percy can take the *Last Resort*."

"And what?" Lia twirled elegant fingers in the air. "Sail it into the harbor in broad daylight and request an audience?"

"We could do exactly that," Percy said quietly. "We'll dock in the nobles section of Anure's harbor. I'll request the audience and the Imperial Toad will receive us both. Our shared history will get me that far."

We all stared at Percy, Lia as baffled as the rest of us. "Is there some information you'd like to disclose, Percy?" she asked, all velvet-covered steel.

Percy shrugged, pouting dramatically. "I might be Anure's cousin."

Nobody said anything. Only Ambrose seemed unsurprised. Percy looked around at the shocked faces. "I didn't tell you because I foolishly thought you might not like me anymore." He sounded uncertain, even a little sad.

"Don't be ridiculous, Percy," Brenda said drily. "We never liked you."

He stuck his tongue out at her but smiled, relief in it. Then he gave me a pointed glare, lifting his nose. "The story will be that you and I became friends—perhaps even lovers—during your time on Calanthe, Conrí. Between us we decided to bring the orchid ring to Anure, to curry favor."

"Fine." I nodded, then looked to Lia. "If Lia agrees."

She rolled her eyes somewhat but nodded. "Fine. Fill the holes. I have an idea for making an orchid ring that seems magical long enough to fool them."

"I may have something that will help with that," Ambrose said, patting down his robes absentmindedly. "Now, where did I put that? Oh yes." He raised a hand and reached out—the hand oddly warping, then disappearing in midair. I blinked, my brain not quite grasping what I'd seen, and his hand reappeared with a rolled parchment. Ambrose handed it to Lia, who took it gingerly.

"It stinks of magic," she noted, looking like she'd rather not be holding it.

"Yes, yes. Take a look." Ambrose gestured at the thing genially.

My nose itched, and even before Lia unrolled it to reveal the vivid illustration of the orchid ring, I recalled the nosebleed I'd had in the Tower of the Sun in Keiost at the first sight of it.

"An image of the ring," Lia said, then frowned for her obvious statement but found nothing more to say. The orchid on her finger billowed like a sea anemone.

"An alchemical reproduction," Ambrose corrected with a delighted smile.

Comprehension dawned on Lia's face. "Aha. Yes. Yes, I can use this." She looked to me. "They won't suspect a fake until close inspection, I think."

"Thank you," I said to her, hoping she understood all the ways I meant it.

"You're welcome," she replied in a wry tone. "Pay Me back by figuring out how you're going to set off this smaller, more powerful bomb without getting yourself killed."

Lady Calla stepped into the room just then. "I beg Your pardon, Your Highness," she said. "Lord Dearsley asked me to remind You of the meeting this afternoon with the regional heads?"

Lia looked to the clever spring-wound clock on the wall, all glittering copper wheels. "Blessed Ejarat, I'm late. I have to go." Her gaze rested briefly on me, worry in it.

"We know what we need to work on," I told her, then addressed the rest of the group. "Let's fill in those holes."

"Remember, Con: contingencies for the contingencies."

"I remember," I promised. "We'll hammer it out."

"There's no fallback position from this one," she warned me. "No Ambrose to suddenly appear to save your ass. I won't be able to do anything to help you, not even via Vesno."

"We won't need it. This is going to work, Lia."

"I've heard that before," she replied, but some of the

worry relaxed from her face. "You know where to find Me should you need anything,"

"Yes. Go be regal. I'll see you later."

She smiled a little at that, then swept out the door.

19

By the time I finished meeting with Dearsley and the regional heads from throughout the island, hours more had passed. Naturally every village and region regarded their problems as the most pressing—and just as naturally, they wanted more aid and support than they'd already been given. Calanthe was fortunate in Her prosperity—even after feeding Anure's insatiable hunger all these years—but even the largesse of my realm only went so far.

Still, by dint of rational problem solving and even more meticulous diplomacy, we had them all sorted by evening. At least the headache of it all had kept me from dwelling—overmuch—on all the things that could go wrong with Con's strategy. It was a slightly better plan than it had been, though that did little to comfort me. I supposed I had to accept that Con would always rely on improvising in the moment—which admittedly had kept him alive so far—and that I wouldn't be able to change him.

There was also no sense in dwelling on everything else in our future that I couldn't control or change.

"Lia!" Con called to me from the end of the hall I'd turned into. I paused, expecting him to catch up with me, but he beckoned to me. A number of courtiers loitering in the hall began whispering to one another at the sight of the queen being summoned—and pulling out paper to take notes in case of another dramatic fight in the halls— but I found I didn't much care. Con would soon be gone, perhaps never to return, and I was happy to see him. So I turned my feet and walked his way—albeit with regal poise, to make clear I chose to go to him.

He had Vesno with him, and he carried a basket. I raised a brow. "What's this?" Stroking Vesno's silky head, I received an impression of exciting smells and a lot of the shipyard, nothing helpful.

Con grinned, all mischievous boy. He took my hand, tucked it in the crook of his elbow, and started walking in the opposite direction. "A surprise. This way."

"I'm to attend a formal dinner for the regional heads," I informed him, digging in my heels.

"Not anymore. Ibolya is arranging for it to be moved to tomorrow night. At my behest," he added in a posh tone, spoiling it by slanting me a wicked smile.

"Conrí. You cannot simply rearrange My schedule and—"

"But I *can*." He steered me out through the gardens and toward a path that led over the ridge to the next bay. "It's amazing. I give orders and they obey. I should've tried this out long ago."

"See what you missed by pacing My gardens and sulking?" I slid him a narrow look. "*I*, however, do not simply obey."

"You did in the Night Court," he reminded me in a sultry growl—which had me immediately blushing.

I cleared my throat. "If that's what you have in mind, then you're going the wrong direction."

He shook his head. "Tempting, but not tonight. There's something else I want to do with you. And I'm asking,

Lia." He slowed, giving me a hopeful look, golden-brown eyes wide. "It could be my last night alive, after all."

"Oh, you did not attempt to leverage Me with that threat," I gasped.

"I blame Sondra," he hastened to say. "She said guilt would pry you out of your responsibilities if nothing else did."

I would have words with Sondra.

"It'll be fun," he coaxed, then stopped, turning me to face him. Vesno circled back to us, concerned at the lack of progress. "I only want to spend this time with you, Lia. We've had so little of it when we haven't been pretending with each other. But if you are certain this dinner is critical to have tonight, then I'll go put on fancy clothes and we can do that together instead."

Critical. No, it wasn't critical to have it that night. I'd been reacting out of habit, hating to have my schedule changed for me. Was he asking so much? No, of course not. I gestured to my gown and heels. "Am I appropriately garbed?"

He grinned, victorious and delighted in one, the dimple showing in his left cheek as it did only when he smiled with genuine happiness. Just as it had been captured in the portrait of the royal family of Oriel, when he'd been only a mischievous boy with a wild streak, his skin and heart unscarred. "It won't matter," he declared mysteriously, "though you might be happier going barefoot. It's a bit of a walk."

Curiouser and curiouser. I slipped off my heels, and Orvyki appeared to take them from me. I handed them to her, not terribly surprised to find that she'd been surreptitiously keeping an eye on me. My ladies had all received the message that I no longer cared to have an extensive entourage at all times, and they seemed to have worked out a system where at least one stayed nearby in case I needed anything. I wasn't sure I loved that system, but we would see. We had yet to settle into a new normal.

"I'll be out for the evening," I told her. Considering, I unpinned my crown and gave her that, too. I supposed having them around could be useful. "Please pass the word that I'll be with Conrí and you all may spend the evening as you wish. I'll see you in the morning."

Orvyki curtsied, then carried off my things with subdued reverence. I watched her go, a delirious sense of playing hooky on my responsibilities lightening me.

"Have you worked things out with your ladies?" Con asked as we resumed walking.

"Yes and no," I replied, musing on how much attention Con paid to the trivial matters of my personal life. "They all wish to continue serving Me—and they are doing so with perfect etiquette, as you observed—but there is a coolness between us now."

"I'm sorry to hear that, Lia. I know how much you rely on their company."

I shook my head a little, realizing that it felt good to be free of the crown's weight, slight as it was. "It could be that the distance was always there and I simply didn't realize it." I squeezed his arm and smiled at him, feeling a bit shy and exposed. "I have a new understanding of what it's like to be truly intimate with someone."

He covered my hand with his. "Me too." After a moment, he added, in a low, gruff voice, "I never imagined I could have this, with you, so thank you."

I burst out laughing. "It's not a gift to thank Me for."

He didn't laugh, or even smile, simply gave me a very serious look. "Your heart is a gift, and I should be grateful for it. No matter what happens, Lia, I want you to know this has been the best part of my life. I know that's not saying much, but it's been . . . everything. I'm not good with words, but if I don't survive Yekpehr, I—"

"Don't even speak it," I said, cutting him off, feeling superstitious and not caring a whit. "Those words are more than enough."

We walked on quietly, passing out of the outer gardens and following the path that led eventually to the harbor.

"I'm trying to be smart about this," Con said after a while. "Coolheaded and calculating, like you are."

I slid him a side-eyed glance, but didn't comment.

"I know Anure will try to manipulate me, so I'm thinking through the possibilities. Contingencies for contingencies."

"That's all I ask," I said, restraining a sigh of resignation. I could not control this, so I'd let it go. As best I could. We'd turned away from the harbor path and followed a narrow foot trail through a grove of flowering trees. The setting sun filtered through the delicate, trailing bracts of the scarlet blossoms, giving them an otherworldly glow. In the quiet, the nearby surf rolled in steady rhythm, and a few nocturnal songbirds trilled their first calls. "Where on blessed Ejarat are we going?"

"You don't know?" Con teased. "I thought you knew everything about Calanthe."

"I know where I am, but I can't imagine what your destination might be. This path doesn't go anywhere but to the next cove, which is only a . . ." I trailed off in realization.

"A swimming beach!" Con finished triumphantly.

"You're going swimming?" I replied faintly, trying to form a real response.

"We both are. Ibolya says you've never been, as far as she knows."

"My life has not been one that lends itself to swimming. I don't know how."

"There's not much to know. We won't go deeper than you can stand with your head above water anyway. I taught myself, when I was a kid. There was this lake—so perfectly still it mirrored the sky—and I would sneak off to it and swim all day."

"Eluding your tutors."

"Exactly." He grinned unrepentantly. "They never could find me there. No one could. I was free to do as I pleased."

"You were the crown prince of Oriel," I pointed out. "Do you really think they'd let you disappear for an entire day with no knowledge of where you'd gone?"

His smile faded, and I felt bad for saying something, but then he shook his head in astonishment, a light of affection in his golden eyes. "You're absolutely right—and that never occurred to me. My parents let me do that, didn't they?"

"It seems likely," I offered tentatively. "It wouldn't have been difficult to have you watched from a distance."

"I remember being scolded," he said in a musing tone, "but never punished. They let me go do that," he repeated with some wonder. "Probably my other escapes, too."

"They loved you," I said, shrugging. "Children need to be able to play and stretch their wings."

"You never did," he pointed out, and it was true.

"I want to say that I was never a child," I said slowly, "but of course I was—just not the normal sort."

"What is normal?" he mused quietly. "Neither of us have had anything like a peaceful life, but we have this." We had emerged from the winding trail onto the dunes, following Vesno as he blazed across a set of wooden bridges and onto the soft sand, and Con waved a hand as if he'd created it. The beach was entirely empty, with no one in sight, not even a boat on the water. "Paradise," he said, dimple flashing in delight. "And all to ourselves."

"More of your doing?" I asked.

"Yes. I spotted this beach on the map in the tower. It will be romantic. We're going to swim naked, and have a picnic on the beach, just you and me."

"And Vesno," I noted as the wolfhound barreled glee-fully into the gentle surf.

"He never gossips," Con replied in a confiding tone. "There's no currency for it in the world of wolfhounds."

I giggled at that image, surprised to hear that sound emerge from me.

Con's grin widened. "Race you to the water?"

"Naked first. I'm not ruining a second gown in one day."

"Like you don't have thousands more."

I snorted at him, pulling off my gown and laying it on the blanket he spread on the sand, then removing the rest of my jewelry. It felt strange to be naked out on this open beach—odd, since I was well accustomed to nakedness, especially with Con—but also wonderful. Freeing, as he'd said.

He took more time than I had, wrestling off his boots, shedding his weapons, then his other clothing—so I took off running. Ignoring Con's shout of protest, I ran to the water with a glorious *whoop!* Vesno, radiating delight, dashed up to circle me and plunge into the surf also.

The first wave took me by surprise, tumbling me over and filling my mouth with sand and salt. Calanthe's sea filled my heart and mind also, the water carrying to me the myriad thoughts and sensations of all the ocean denizens—and their memories. It was the dreamthink magnified, and I wondered why I'd never tried this before.

Con seized me, catching me up in his strong arms. "Cheater!" he accused, acting horrified and astonished.

"It's not cheating when you win," I informed him. "I like to win."

"Do you know what happens to cheaters?" he growled. Before I could answer, he launched me into the air, sending me flying and then plummeting into the sea. I came up sputtering and spitting water, and he pointed at me and laughed.

"You'll pay for that!" I shrieked and threw myself at him.

We played like that, like kids yelling and splashing in the surf. And then not like children at all, as our touches grew hot and hungry, the teasing kisses lasting longer, going deeper and welling with both newfound tenderness and the anticipation of goodbye.

We made love on the blanket in the sand, the warm tropical night enfolding us, an exhausted Vesno sleeping in the sand nearby. And then we ate the picnic by the light of a candle, drinking wine and watching the glitter of stars on the water.

It was romantic, fun, and carefree in a way so few things in my life had been. And when Con whispered to me that I'd given him as many reasons as the stars to want to live, I only hoped that I wouldn't be the weakness Anure would use to strike him down.

We returned to the palace in the early hours before dawn, Con and I parting to prepare for the day. Since Ibolya was off preparing for her own journey, my other ladies assisted my bath. None of them commented on the sand they washed out of my hair. Ibolya would have, and I already missed her gentle amusement and steadfast presence.

I selected my gown carefully. So many times my courtiers had traded analyses of my gowns, how they reflected my mood—and predicted which direction their petitions would go. While I had little desire to return to the elaborate scaffolding of my previous wardrobe, I also felt this occasion required a sense of ceremony. My brave adventurers deserved a send-off from their queen worthy of the risk they took. If I must stay behind on my island while they sailed away, I'd remain in style.

Nahua and Zariah laced me into the corset the gown required, along with the curving panniers that would support the heavy skirts. The bodice sported high epaulets that stood up on their own, and the metallic gold frontispiece molded over my breasts in a sunburst. Sculpted gold plates over my hips gave way to a fall of golden silk, shimmering and flowing, while a panel of patterned pieces draped down the center of my skirts.

Overall, the gown gave the impression of a golden statue of a warrior queen come to life—and once upon a time, I would have donned a gold wig and painted my skin with metallic gold paint. As it was, I had my ladies pile my own wild hair of vines and blossoms into an intricate coronet of braids, my new crown of diamonds and gold nestled in them.

Some touches of gold glitter to my lighter makeup palette completed the look. I examined myself in the full-length mirror. Ejarat gilded by Sawehl's sun. It would do—and it would help make up for the fact that my own personal sun would soon sail away.

I walked down to meet them at the docks just before sunrise, my ladies with me, but no one else. Though I'd continued to make sure no birds had flown to Yekpehr with messages to betray our plans, it still seemed wiser to keep as much secrecy as possible.

Ambrose appeared along the way, walking easily, his

staff barely touching the ground, Merle riding on the faceted emerald topping it. He gave me a nod of greeting with a raised brow, and my ladies fell back at my gesture to give us privacy.

"So, wizard," I said, "is all going according to your master plan?"

He slid me a canny look, the ancient forest in his gaze. "Your Highness is presuming both that there is a master plan and that I am the originator of it."

"Yes, and?"

Laughing, he shook his head. "I told You before, like You, I am a passenger on this ship captained by Conrí. Will he sail us to our longed-for destination or run us aground on the rocks? It remains to be seen."

Ambrose had spoken of Con that way before, back at Cradysica, before the battle. *Conrí has the courage and determination to set sail, the willingness to take the chances that You and I flinch from, because we can see all too well how difficult the journey will be.* Not at all a reassurance that Con would succeed.

"But you have seen aspects of this, in the prophecy," I pressed. "You knew he'd need My hand."

"Aspects, yes." He turned the staff thoughtfully, Merle picking up one foot and then the next to remain facing us, listening with a cocked head. "The future is difficult to predict because it hasn't happened yet," he confided.

"This is exactly what I've always said," I replied, though I'd have liked a different answer.

Ambrose shrugged cheerfully. "It's like looking down a raging river and spotting a boulder that divides the current. The boulder might be more or less fixed, but a great deal else can change by the time you reach that location."

"I keep feeling like there's something more I need to do, more than donating a body part to the cause."

"That's hardly all You've contributed." His very bland-ness sharpened my attention.

"So is My part in the tale over?" I pressed. A side note in the hero's epic journey, the lonely witch queen left to the island she could never leave.

Ambrose didn't say anything until we'd nearly reached the docks. Finally he shook his head, sliding me a rueful look. "The trouble with attempting to nudge the future in a particular direction," he confided, "is that so much depends on the motivations of the people involved. I trust that You will follow your heart and do . . ." Merle cawed and Ambrose nodded. "Yes, whatever You think best."

"People always make that sound like a simple decision," I complained, "and it never is."

"Nothing is ever as simple as 'people' make things sound," Ambrose observed.

The *Last Resort* and the fishing vessel from Hertaq sat side by side at the end of the dock, the former outshining the latter like a jewel beside a rock. If I hadn't been informed—by my own people, not just Kara—that the fishing ship was seaworthy enough to make it to Yekpehr, I'd have seriously doubted. As it was . . . it didn't inspire confidence.

I didn't see Con anywhere. Ambrose, Merle, and my ladies all wandered on down the pier, inspecting the ships and meeting up with some of the others. Kara, no doubt seeing my frown, leapt off the deck of the fishing boat and, landing on the dock before me, bowed deeply. "Don't worry, Your Highness—it sails far better than it appears."

"I know," I replied, tearing my gaze from the ship, which seemed to list ever so slightly to one side. Should it do that? "I asked a few of My people to verify," I added.

He smiled, a narrow and humorless slash in his dark face. "You still don't trust me?"

"I believe in being thorough," I replied. "Though I do trust you, if only because Con does. Can I charge you to do your utmost to make sure he survives this mission?"

Kara's smile twisted into a grimace. "You can ask, and I can promise—but we both know Conrí follows his own path. I tried at Cradysica, you know. Or maybe You don't." He hesitated. "Conrí is a man possessed by a powerful idea."

"I know that." And I did—and it wasn't something I could change. "I also realize it's brought him this far."

"It's brought all of us this far," Kara corrected gently. "Without Conrí . . . well, I don't think we'd be in a position to attempt this at all."

"There's something to be said for being bullheaded," I remarked with a rueful smile, an expression Kara reflected.

"Talking about me?" Con asked, catching me around the waist and speaking into my ear.

I managed not to jump, but just barely. For a big man, he could move as silently as a cat—and now that I'd seen his surprisingly playful side, I knew full well that he enjoyed sneaking up on me. "As a matter of fact, yes," I said. "However did you guess?"

With his hands on my hips, he turned me to face him. "I seem to recall you were likened to the other bull in the small pen we occupy."

"I never denied the metaphor," I replied. "Brenda has a gift for them."

I looked him over, seeing he wore the court clothes that I'd had made for him—the black with silver trim—though he'd forgone the crown and wore a sword instead of the rock hammer. "No crown is a good call," I noted, as Anure wouldn't appreciate the Slave King pretending to actual royalty, "but I'm surprised you gave up your rock hammer."

He scowled in disgust. "Blame Sondra for that. She thinks the sword is more 'impressive gentleman' and not so 'escaped-slave-from-Vurgmun.'"

"She has a point."

"I left it in our rooms," he confided. "So you can keep it for my return."

I blinked back tears, moved by this small gesture that meant so much. Never mind the bitter voice that whispered he'd be more invested in returning for the rock hammer than for me. "I will."

With the excitement of taking action, the sheer glee of going after his long-held goal sparkling in his eyes, Con looked taller, charismatically imposing, vividly and fully the man I loved. "I have a favor to ask," I said. "Keep Vesno with you."

He raised a brow. "You want me to bring a wolfhound into Anure's throne room?"

"Yes. It's not so unusual that the guards will balk, as well-behaved as Vesno is. And I'll be able to watch, perhaps." The one advantage of being a witch queen: I might be confined to my island, but I had ways of looking beyond it.

He nodded, considering. "I'll do my best to keep him with me. You look amazing," he said in a lower voice. "Like a golden goddess."

"Thank you." I tried to think of something else to say, but all that came to mind were cautions and questions. Not how you sent off a hero who charted his own course through the raging seas of doubt and stacked odds.

He seemed to be searching for words, too, also coming up empty. "I love you, Lia," he finally said, and I understood in that moment why people liked to say those words to each other. They held a wealth of other, unspoken and unspeakable thoughts and feelings. A kind of a gift, a token that symbolized so much more.

"I love you, Con," I told him, infusing the simple words with all my hopes and wishes for good luck. He smiled, dimple winking into existence like the first star of evening.

Then his gaze lifted over my head, looking beyond me. "Everyone is assembled, ready for Your Highness to address them." For once he employed the honorific with total sincerity.

I hadn't meant to make this farewell that sort of event, but he was right—when I turned, they'd all gathered expectantly. Besides, I'd dressed for the part, hadn't I? Naturally an address fell to me, queen of Calanthe. I'd come to think of myself as Lia among most of this group, people who'd become friends, who teased me about fighting with and loving Con.

I looked them over: Con, tall and itching with anticipation, the predawn breeze catching and whipping his long hair, Vesno, noble profile raised to sniff that breeze, sitting at his heel. Kara, dark-skinned and somber, leanly relaxed. Brenda beside him, square and silver-haired, solid determination in the set of her jaw. Agatha, wrapped in a shawl, thin face pale and eyes distant. Ibolya stood just behind her, black hair gathered into a braid, eyes on me with trust and loyalty. Sondra, off to the side, always a bit on her own, golden hair shorn brutally short, wearing a slave's dull garb and twirling the walking stick she'd found in Yekpehr. Percy stood with Ambrose, both of them in glittering garb. Ambrose wore his court wizard of Calanthe robes and leaned on his tall staff, the emerald topping it a dull green under the pinkening sky. Merle, large and glossy as obsidian, sat on his shoulder, returning my gaze with a canny glimmer in his eye, a much larger being visible in the layers of alternate realities beyond him. As for Percy, he'd dressed as his version of a sea captain, in nautical colors, plenty of braid, long pleated skirts and a jaunty cap on his head.

I'd miss them all, I realized suddenly, and their departure would leave me more alone than I'd ever been in my life, because I'd never known before what it was to work with a team like this. I also, with sudden and acute regret, wished I could go with them.

I even considered, in the impulse of that terrible loneliness of being left behind, that I *would* go with them. What would Anure do if I knocked on his door with Con and faced him down?

Turn me over to his wizards, that's what. And I'd be powerless, an orchid severed from the stem, wilted and dying by stages. A liability to them all.

Con tipped his head, studying me, and I realized I'd been silent too long.

"Farewell and calm seas," I said, beginning where I'd meant to end. I gathered the frayed edges of my thoughts. "You all take with you our dearly held hopes. The world will celebrate your deeds, your bravery, and your selfless determination to right the many wrongs done. When you return, you may ask of Me anything you wish. If it's within My power, I will give it to you."

They stirred, a few whispering among themselves. Even Sondra, though she narrowed her eyes in habitual suspicion, looked interested.

"Farewell and calm seas," I repeated, and the bookending sounded purposeful, like a poem.

They all saluted, bowed, curtsied, or nodded, according to their natures. Then the larger group boarded the slower fishing boat. In short order, they threw off the lines and pushed away. I helped them along with some gentle currents, while Percy and Con made the *Last Resort* ready.

Then Con, leaving Vesno aboard the yacht, came back down to the dock while my ladies wandered discreetly away some distance.

"Do I get a kiss goodbye this time?" he asked, with a wry half smile for the last time he'd asked, just before the Battle at Cradysica, when I'd refused him.

"I suspect it would be bad luck not to," I conceded.

"Exactly," he replied, gaze wandering over my face as if memorizing it.

Since he didn't move, I stepped closer to him, sliding my hands behind his neck and tipping up my face. Though he put his hands around my waist, nearly able to span the width of it with his big hands, he still didn't kiss me.

"No matter what happens, Lia," he said, softly enough that I couldn't have heard him if we weren't so close, "remember that you are the reason I want to live. For someone like me, that's a miracle. And it's truth."

I parted my lips for a reply, but he stole the words and my breath, mouth moving over mine with devastating thoroughness, as if he tried to drink me in. The sun tipped over the horizon, spilling golden light through the tangle of his hair, and I trembled with need and emotion.

He wrenched away, giving me one last blazing look with his eyes so like the sun, steadied me on my feet, and walked away. Striding aboard the *Last Resort*, he pulled up the gangplank and threw down the final ropes before looking my way again, like he didn't trust himself to see me until he'd forced their departure.

Con raised a hand and I returned the gesture. We stood there, our hands up in a frozen wave, a kind of salute to so many things between us. My remaining ladies gathered behind me, respectful in their quiet, and we all watched the yacht sail into the sunrise, my guiding currents beneath to send them on their way as far as I could reach.

They cleared the barrier reef before the sun rose high enough to heat me through. When they disappeared from sight, I finally lowered my hand, finding it had gone numb from being held aloft so long. The rest of me had gone numb, too, as if Con had taken my heart with him.

Which, I supposed, he had.

But I still had the rest of myself. Along with all that I had learned and grown into.

I turned to my four ladies, the formal distance between us bruising with its awkward edges. We were as private as we'd ever be. So, while the end of a lonely dock seemed like an odd place to have this conversation, it was also fitting in a way. New approaches to handling our changing world. Calanthe and I—and all my people—had been in stasis for so long. Living in our delicate bubble, one that depended on us not breaking it from the inside.

I studied their familiar faces, awaiting any indication of my wishes with alert eyes and carefully sweet smiles. I sighed mentally for the last. I'd like to tell them to only smile when they felt it sincerely, but that would be asking too much.

"I mentioned that I'd be asking more of you than I have before," I said, noting the wariness creeping into their serene gazes. "You all are practiced at defending My person. I'd like you to expand your efforts to defending all of Calanthe."

They gazed back at me, with varying levels of comprehension and confusion. Calla frowned slightly but took the initiative. "Using the same techniques, Your Highness?"

I smiled, pleased with her quickness. "Yes. If you envision Calanthe as a larger embodiment of Myself, then the magic should naturally follow."

Orvyki's face cleared, lighting with interest. "A violent attack on Calanthe can be reversed just as a violent attack on Your Highness would be."

I nodded. "That's My theory exactly."

"Your Highness is expecting magical attacks by Anure's wizards," Nahua put in, not quite a question. "Ibolya told us everything."

Good. Thank you, Ibolya. "Yes. They've been using various magics to test Calanthe's wards—to Me they feel like needle jabs or splashes of hot water, other similar odd sensations—so I'd like you four to spend today attuning yourselves to that probing and being alert for escalation."

"Do we know *how* to do that, Your Highness?" Zariah asked tentatively. "I want to do this, make no mistake, but . . ." She trailed off, her demurely interlaced fingers gripping one another tight. She clearly worried about being dismissed, but—by the way the other ladies threw her grateful glances—they all harbored the same concern.

"I'm asking you to try," I said, trying to speak to them as the friends and companions I'd like them to be. My new team of warriors and confidants. "I'm trying new tools, too, magical techniques I'm not sure I know how to do, either. I'm hoping we can all learn together."

They relaxed at that, smiling back at me with hesitation, then increasing warmth. Genuine smiles. They were all so young, I realized. All younger than I, except for Calla who was my same age. And look how much I'd grown in just a few weeks. We'd been frozen in time, in our seemingly eternal youth. Now it was time to grow up.

"It will be a challenge for us all," I proclaimed. "I think we'll be brilliant."

"Do You intend to convene court today, Your Highness?" Calla asked, raising a brow. "If so, then I advise one of us should remain with You, while the other three practice this new task. We'll take turns."

"Then you're all willing?" I asked, with some surprise.

They exchanged looks and nodded, breaking into excited smiles. "Ibolya is not the only one who'd like to do something more," Nahua said staunchly. "But I agree with Calla: One of us should be with Your Highness at all times."

"We won't abandon You again," Orvyki declared fervently.

"Besides," Zariah added with a quirk of a smile, "it will be nice to do something besides sit by the throne all day. Taking turns sounds lovely."

"Thank you," I said, tremendously moved. "Let's get started."

Walking together, we returned to the palace, ready to begin a new way of life.

20

I didn't know if Lia had picked that dress because it would shine so brightly, but with the rising sun hitting all that gold, she glittered like a beacon of all that was good in the world, a brilliant star visible until we sailed well past the barrier reef—and she was lost from sight.

Feeling the stab of loneliness like a gut wound, I ruffled Vesno's head. The wolfhound, who'd been sitting patiently beside me, holding vigil, too, lifted his chin and licked my hand, like he knew I needed comfort. It could be Lia sent that gesture of affection through the wolfhound, a silent reminder that her thoughts went with me.

For she didn't fool me with her reassurances and poise: She wished she was going with us, would have come along if she could withstand being severed from Calanthe. But no one wanted her to go through that lethal separation again. *An orchid can't live on its own.* I was frankly relieved to leave her safely on Calanthe. No matter what happened to us, Anure would never have her again—and that set my heart at ease, at least on that account.

Percy came up beside me, not to look on disappearing Calanthe, but turning to lean against the rail, giving me a long, and appraising stare.

"Shouldn't you be steering the boat?" I asked mildly.

"Not necessary." He flicked his glittering nails. "Her Highness has Her hand on the currents, guiding us through Calanthe's waters. Once we pass the boundary, then it won't be such smooth sailing." He rolled his eyes, a dramatic gesture with his long, jewel-tipped lashes. "Metaphorically, too," he added pointedly.

I dragged my thoughts back to the conversation. "So you're Anure's cousin, huh?"

Percy pursed his mouth, carefully lipsticked in navy blue, covering that I'd surprised him. "Did you think I lied previously, Conrí?"

"No, I'm curious."

He shrugged huffily. "Then ask."

"How are you a lord if Anure was a commoner?"

Percy laughed gaily, tipping his head back, the cap miraculously staying in place. "*This* is his first question."

"Seemed like a place to start."

"Yes, well." Percy looked off to the side, giving the appearance of thinking, but he gripped the rails with enough tension to whiten his knuckles. "You know how Anure became a landholder in Aekis—granted that minor title that gave him legal rights to it?"

"Kind of." I remembered my parents talking about it, but I'd had little interest in their boring political conversations.

"*My* land," Percy confided, laying a finger alongside his nose and winking. "My title."

"Ah." It was more of a grunt than Lia's breathed sound of neutral interest, the one where you couldn't be sure if she was letting you continue because she might be interested—or because she was waiting for you to hang yourself with your own rope.

"My father and I didn't get along," Percy continued. "The Robho family was a patriarchy from way back, setting great store in masculine values. I was not the son my father hoped for, but I was the only one he got. I didn't care, because I'd never been much interested in government anyway, so when my father made my cousin Anure his heir, my heart wasn't broken—and neither was anyone else's." He glanced at me and away again. "And Anure, he was ambitious even then, clever, determined to prove himself. We were companions in our youth, growing up together in Valencia. It was a small, rural corner of Aekis, where very little of interest ever happened. We shared certain interests. I viewed him as my savior from a life of dull governance, and he was grateful that I didn't resent him. We were the best of friends."

He looked to me, defying me to judge him for that. "People change," I said.

Percy blew out a breath, shaking his head. "Yes. Two things changed, as it happens. As Anure took over management of the lands, it became clear that he had no talent for it, no intuitive ability. Despite his studious application, he lacked something."

"No blood connection to the land? Oh. He wasn't truly your uncle's son," I filled in. It happened often enough.

Percy painted a point for me in the air. "Much consternation and gnashing of teeth. My faithless aunt—a woman of common blood herself—was executed for her betrayal." He slid his gaze to me. "Did I mention my father's family tended to be intolerant and unforgiving?"

"I gathered," I replied drily.

"Anure . . . He was devastated. He'd been close to his mother. Losing her that way ripped his heart out—and sent him into a black rage. He wanted his father dead for it, and mine, too, for disinheriting him. He lost everything that mattered to him in the space of a few days, the one person in our horrible family who'd loved him and his one ambition in life. He became someone I hardly recognized."

"Do you feel sorry for him?" The old, dull hatred roiled in me, ready to flare into fury.

"Down, boy," Percy said. "Not now—but I did then. I'd already been disinherited—and I flatly refused to cooperate when they nattered about making me lord again. Anure was so . . . full of grief and anger that I wanted to help him. I wanted my friend back, so I did help him."

"With vurgsten," I guessed.

Percy nodded unhappily, staring into the middle distance of regret. "I was clever, too, in my way. I helped Anure take my family's land despite our fathers. I'd been fond of my late aunt, also—and frankly didn't blame her for seeking affection from a man less brutal than my uncle. In the arrogance of my youth, I saw our conniving as an act of revolution, dealing justice to my father, who greatly deserved to be deposed, and my uncle, who deserved much worse. I helped Anure murder his father and mine, created vurgsten devices for him to use. What did I care? Naturally, we didn't believe in magic or the blood connection to the land. Or rather, I didn't."

"But Anure did."

"Have you heard this tale before?" Percy laughed, a shrill edge to it. "Anure took over the family lands and eventually, through the diligent application of treachery and devious cunning, we put Anure on the throne of the kingdom of Aekis itself. We lived well, too, and he rewarded me lavishly. I congratulated myself on our victory over our oppressors," he finished bitterly. "I was young, gorgeous, wealthy, powerful—everything a stupid, selfish boy could want."

"For a while," I put in.

"Yes. Not a long while, because the source of our ill-gotten wealth, the land . . . it began to fail again. All over Aekis, the crops didn't flourish, lambs were born dead or twisted, horses and cattle failed to quicken. I put it down to a few bad seasons, but the failures enraged Anure. He found a wizard to help him. Or the wizard found him. I don't know, as Anure kept him secret until they seized me for their experiments. The wizard taught Anure how to use me to control the land." His lips trembled and he pressed them flat, his face going hard. "They kept me prisoner in a tower in Valencia and milked me for my blood, using it to coax the land into obedience."

I nodded, understanding. If I hadn't gone through all I had with Lia, I'd have been confused, but not now. "I'm sorry, Percy," I said gruffly, putting a hand on his shoulder.

He looked at me, eyes bright with tears. "Sympathy, wolf? I expected teeth."

"I need you to get to Anure," I replied, baring those teeth.

Laughing a little, he wiped his eyes. "Fair enough."

"How'd you escape?"

"What makes you think I did?"

"You're here, with a fancy lifeboat, not chained in a tower in Valencia bleeding royal blood."

He huffed a bitter laugh. "It's ignominious. They forgot about me. I'd been Anure's first experiment, but once he had a captive to control Aekis overall, he didn't need me for poor Valencia—which he hated anyway and let rot. One day I filled my pockets with what treasure I could—I had been wise enough to squirrel some things away over the years—and simply wandered away. When no one came after me, I kept going."

"And came to Calanthe."

"Yes. To while my days away in lavish entertainment, as is my greatest talent."

I considered that. "Why tell me all this?"

"So you'll know why Anure will accept an audience with me. He won't be able to resist. He'll be shocked to hear from me—and concerned. I know his secrets."

"I see." I stroked Vesno's ears, wondering what else.

"Also." Percy took a deep breath. "I'll crawl into my cousin's lap and set off the bomb if it comes to that. Call it a last attempt at redemption."

I understood how Lia felt, listening to someone else offer suicide to solve a problem, no matter how nobly intended—and I wondered what she'd say. "Vengeance isn't necessarily redemption."

Percy didn't laugh as I'd expected. "No, but if redemption isn't possible, then at least I won't have to live with myself any longer. And you can return to live happily ever after with Her Highness, who deserves that much more than I."

"It doesn't matter," I said. "Our plan will work. No one has to die."

"Hmm. I'll reserve judgment." He gave me a wry, funny smile, then trailed a finger over my biceps. "I don't suppose you'd be interested in killing some time with me. Long, boring sail. Verisimilitude for our tale of being secret lovers."

"Thanks, but no. I'm staying faithful to Lia."

Percy raised a brow at me, the jewel at the tip winking. "Even though you're not married anymore?"

"She might not be, but I am." When he frowned, I shrugged. "I made a vow and I intend to keep it. I don't care what Calanthe's magic and marriage bonds dictate." *Does Sawehl's sun cease to shine if Ejarat's earth ignores him?*

"I don't think Her Highness views it the same way."

I bared my teeth again, my grin friendlier this time but no less determined. "I plan to change her mind about that."

Percy laughed and gripped my arm. "If anyone can do it, wolf, you can."

At the end of the day—all of my duties to Calanthe dispensed with as well as they could be for the moment—I changed into a simpler gown, took myself to the map tower, and dismissed all my ladies but Zariah, who was taking her turn to watch over me. The tower provided seclusion, quiet, and also made me feel closer to Con to be in that place, where we'd once made love with such shattering intensity and intimacy that my eyes had revealed their true colors for the first time in so many years.

Besides all that, the tower boasted the longest view. That, along with the ambient magic of the map itself, should assist with the enchantment I hoped to employ. I was beginning to understand from Ambrose—and Con would laugh heartily at this—how magic truly worked. Taking advantage of a place already accustomed to revealing distances, to making the faraway clear to the eye, would ease the way for the enchantment I had in mind.

I also felt more than a little nervous at attempting to extend my magical influence beyond Calanthe, though my ladies had reported enthusiastically on their own practice that day. Their glowing delight at flexing their abilities helped to counter my nerves. And it came as a relief to know that someone besides myself was able to sense the wizard attacks—and that they'd had some success repelling them. I wasn't alone in this.

I paced to the sand table set up on the side of the tower facing Yekpehr. It wasn't the one from the Sand Salon, as we'd deprived the children long enough. I had, however, helped myself to some of their sand. As I'd asked, a smaller replica of the Sand Salon table had been set up, the magic-infused sand a smooth, nearly glassy surface in the moonlight.

Zariah had doused the lanterns and torches for me. That was going entirely on intuition—though most of this was— but I wanted nothing nearby to distract me from seeing the distant. In the gentle, tropical shadows, the Night Court far enough away that no music or sounds of revelry made it to my quiet tower, I waved a hand over the unblemished surface of the sand. It sifted musically in response to my will, the orchid ring wafting the sweet scent of Calanthe's native magic. My realm's magic and my own. Instead of asking the sand to build a model of anything, I instead formed the will to see what occurred far away.

I started with Vesno, a familiar extension for me, touching the wolfhound's mind as I already had many times that day. Vesno greeted me with absolute joy. I had to laugh—no matter how many times I'd reached out to him, his enthusiasm remained as great as the first time. I returned the greeting, sending love. It had been a comfort to me throughout the long day of meetings, and the interminable formal dinner with the regional heads—the dinner Con had cleverly evaded having to attend—that I'd been able to see Con aboard the *Last Resort* through Vesno's eyes, and know he was safe still.

Though when that inevitably changed, it would be the opposite of a comfort, I knew. If things went terribly wrong, I'd only be able to watch and do nothing. Still, I'd rather know than be ignorant.

Holding on to Vesno's mind, I tried lifting my mind's eye away from his. I wanted to be able to see and hear at will—not just where the dog ended up going. Despite my assurances to Con, I wasn't at all sure that Ambrose would allow the wolfhound into his throne room.

As soon as I moved beyond Vesno's perception, however, I lost the connection. So much for that idea. I'd rather suspected it wouldn't work, but it had been the easiest path and worth attempting first. I'd always been able to connect to the denizens of Calanthe, to feel through their lives, large and small—but I'd also always skipped from one to the next. Fish to bird to mouse to flower to bee to tree to sea to soil. For this, I wanted a higher perspective, a disembodied one. If I could do that.

I hadn't told Con of my plan to try to watch over them from afar—besides via Vesno—for this very reason: in case I failed. If only I'd spent some time actually practicing magic over the long years of doing nothing useful while pretending to be Anure's fiancée. Though I supposed I'd never really understood before recently that I could actively wield magic, instead of just being created by it.

All right, next I'd try connecting via Ibolya. As with Vesno, I could touch her mind through Calanthe's connection to Her children. Ibolya had been born on Calanthe, and so she was Mine on that level beyond thought or physical limitations. Though she'd granted my request that I look through her eyes on the mission—something I'd asked her to keep secret—I also treated that permission with great care. Ibolya would hardly refuse her queen, even if she'd prefer to.

I slipped into her mind quietly, like the scent of a night-blooming flower, not enough to alert her to my presence, just enough to anchor myself to the place she occupied. Not wanting to startle her with any sort of greeting—especially as that might give her away—I found that she was sleeping anyway. I sensed the rocking of the boat and the smell of fish that had permeated it. They'd thought they might

have the best chances of sneaking into the citadel unde-
tected late at night, so that aspect of the mission clearly
had not yet commenced.

I tried lifting myself from her mind, but met with the
same obstacle. I could leap from her to Vesno—who
greeted me again with the same enthusiastic joy—and
back again to Ibolya's sleeping mind, but I couldn't *go* anywhere else.

Hmm. I withdrew my mind's eye back to the quiet
tower, the smooth sand gleaming before me. If nothing
else, I could follow through those two. But I wanted more.

Time for my last gambit, which felt risky on a number
of levels.

Show Me Ambrose, I murmured mentally, waving my
hand over the sand to help the vision along. I'd decided to
try for the wizard if nothing else worked, as his magical
profile should make him stand out in the planes between
realms like an iceberg floating in the sea—visible no
matter from which angle I came upon him. I flung my intention outward, feeling as if I'd tossed a garland of flowers onto the waves in hope of catching a fish. And very
much like that, I came up with nothing.

Ejarat take it. Maybe this wouldn't work after all.

In that case, I'd have to reconcile myself to observing through Vesno's eyes—or Ibolya's, in a pinch—but I
couldn't shake the foreboding that I needed to be able to
do *more*. Just in case. Con would likely say that was me
trying to control everything, and he wouldn't be wrong.
Still, Ambrose's last words to me kept circling my mind. *I
trust that You will follow your heart.* My heart urged me
to find a way to see, perhaps affect events.

The stakes were high, so I wouldn't give up easily.

I tried going back through Ibolya, as Ambrose should
be on the same boat with her. But short of waking her

and making her go look, I couldn't find the wizard that way. Besides, I didn't sense him anywhere near her, which seemed odd. Ambrose's magic shone brightly, and it seemed I should be able to detect him. Withdrawing to the tower and the immaculate surface of the sand, I mulled the problem.

Probably I was hitting a block because I was trying to go from a physical body in this reality—Vesno's or Ibolya's body—to an astral realm. My connecting to them via Calanthe went from a physical body to the astral realm and back to physical. To find Ambrose, I should try to keep to the astral side.

The orchid on my finger stirred, petals unfurling to larger and lusher extravagance, nearly glowing in the starlit night, its sweet scent stronger than ever. Taking my cue from it, I allowed my consciousness to open, to bloom in the gentle nourishment of darkness and dew. Letting the wind and water carry me, I flew over the curve of the world, looking for the iceberg of Ambrose's power.

I found him, a beacon of green solidity that indeed spanned a number of dimensions. I recognized the feel of his magic, like the sacred silence of an ancient forest. I had done it! In my eagerness and excitement, I raced forward, barely managing to skid to a halt as I became aware of three other presences.

One, like a pyramid of translucent obsidian, loomed over the others, so immense I couldn't quite wrap my mind around it. Though it looked in shape like a pyramid, with five points, it also projected into other realms, almost like a starburst. Seen from another dimension, it flattened to a pentagram. It didn't seem to notice me, so I eased back, feeling much like a bee carefully extracting herself from an orb-weaver's complex web.

Another presence, this one like a sphere of old blood,

spun in space and time, ripples of expression crossing its globular face. With a volume far exceeding its surface, it seethed with power, the occasional bubble burping up from deep within. The way it spun slowly in place, it seemed to be turning to look my way. I pulled back. Before I got far, a tentacle of red something snaked out to seize me.

I struggled against it, extracting one part of myself, only to find another part ensnared. It swarmed closer, examining me, a rotten scent of unholy avarice choking me to unconsciousness. I knew this presence, also. It had held my hand as it ushered me into death, smiling kindly and asking what it was like to feel my body die around me.

Panicking, I thrashed in its grip, only sinking farther into its influence as its ponderous attention turned to me. I knew on a level beyond conscious knowledge that I'd only tripped over part of its awareness—that it was largely focused elsewhere—but that once it concentrated more fully on me in this plane of reality, I'd be fucked sideways, as Sondra would say. Hearing her dry assessment in my head helped to steady me.

But it didn't help me to break free. I'd foolishly—like the naive amateur I was—stumbled into depths I couldn't swim. Con would kill me for this.

Though if I couldn't extract myself, he wouldn't have to.

Then a blaze of purple light, jagged as lightning, fast and feathered, *zoomed* through the tentacle holding me, severing it and setting me free. Where the pyramid and the sphere were ponderous monuments, this presence was all roaring flight, shards of purple ricocheting around in prismatic light, anchoring and protecting me. I knew this presence, too. I'd been in an astral plane with it before. Calanthe's verdant inner heart.

I withdrew back to myself—but careened headlong into the green I'd first recognized as Ambrose. Like a tree, his

astral presence had a solid trunk, with branching roots
and limbs extending through various realities.

Not back to Your body, Euthalia, his presence communicated to me, my name an image of the good and true
blossom. He showed me how those malicious presences
could follow if I retreated to my physical form. Then
he drew me into the leafy branches, hiding me there as
the purple presence zoomed a distracting display. The
bloodred, seething sphere slowly turned away again, for-
getting us.

The purple lightning landed on a nearby branch, the
shards coalescing into feathers.

Merle? I wondered, and both presences agreed.

Ambrose asked what I'd been trying to do and I tried
to wordlessly communicate my desire to follow the team
to Yekpehr, to watch and be ready. His understanding
flooded me, and the tree self of Ambrose shivered, leaves
turning inside out, until we stood on a glass surface.

No, not glass—ice. The pond I'd showed Ambrose in
Cradysica. Where we'd traded questions and answers.
Ambrose stood before me in his usual, human-seeming
form, leaning on the staff with the emerald atop it. His
shriveled leg seemed to extend into some other distance,
not fully in this reality. Another human-shaped person
joined us, a tall figure with flowing black hair and glossy
dark feathers. He had a long, nearly gaunt face, with a
large, hooked nose—and the amber eyes of Merle's canny
face.

I looked between them, and Ambrose smiled, a world
of apology in it. Understanding all at once, I said, "You
are two of Anure's wizards."

Ambrose winced and Merle made a soft negation, the
echo of a raven's caw in it. "We are not his," Ambrose

corrected gently. "We are our own wizards, but we are also not free."

"Those other wizards—the black pyramid and the red sphere—those are the black-and red-robed wizards," I realized.

Merle and Ambrose exchanged glances. "They do not appear to our perceptions in the same way, but You are a child of a different magic, so it makes sense You see them differently."

"Let's try this," I said, gathering my anger around me, layering the hurt of betrayal and incipient rage tightly around my heart so it wouldn't break. "In my usual reality, the one where I was a prisoner to be tortured, you wore a blue robe, Ambrose, and Merle wore purple."

Instead of denying or protesting, they both sank to their knees, pressing their foreheads to the watery, magical ice. Below us, birds flew through an infinite sky.

"We do not beg Your forgiveness," Ambrose said, "for we know we do not deserve it. But we do ask Your forbearance. Neither of us had the power to free You from the other wizards. If we had that ability, we'd have freed ourselves long since. We could not offer You comfort, or aid You in any way, lest we be discovered too soon. We could only do what we did: help You escape to live again."

"You pretended to be our friends." It was all I could think to say. All those times Con had wanted to throttle Ambrose. If only he'd known this . . .

They both knelt up, keeping their heads bowed and nodding solemnly. "We were doing what we could," Ambrose explained. "We could not act directly against Anure or his wishes, but we found a . . . loophole, if You will."

"By aiding Con and his people."

Ambrose looked up, haunted shadows in his green gaze.

"And You, Your Highness, though dropping hints and clues only goes so far. We could not act directly."

"Merle acted," I pointed out. "You preserved Calanthe for My return."

Merle met my gaze with his amber one. "I wasn't there for mosst of what happened to You at the citadel," he said in a deep voice, an accent twisting some of the words oddly. "Only the thinnesst sslice of my attention was required to appear to be present. The rest of myself sstayed with Calanthe."

I nodded, still working my way through understanding, then turned to Ambrose. "That's why you seemed to disappear after Cradysica—you had to concentrate your presence to Yekpehr."

Ambrose smiled, a gaunt version of his usual cheer. "I counseled Anure on how to handle You as best I could, diverting his attention as much as possible. I couldn't stop them from all they did to You—but I could keep them from taking the ring, and stall until Con arrived to rescue You."

"And you helped Con get Me out." I focused on his leg. "This is part of how you are shackled there. You with that tether, and Merle with the raven form?"

"That's close enough to the correct metaphor," Ambrose agreed. "The other wizards do not know of our defection. We are not as powerful as they are. Should they discover we are aiding You . . ."

"They would stop you?"

"Worsse." Merle's caution echoed and spiraled like feathers caught in a dust devil. "They would correct the loophole that allowss uss to do thiss—and they would force uss to aid them againsst you."

"It's been a dicey gambit," Ambrose confessed. "We needed to know enough about You to help, but if they tighten our leashes sufficiently, we might have to give up knowledge we've so far withheld."

"You asked Me for the secret of the ring's transference," I said to Ambrose. And I had trusted him.

"Yes." He returned my gaze somberly. "And You will recall that I did not share what I knew with the others. I had to know the truth, so I could misdirect them. I couldn't risk that they'd stumble upon the secret."

I supposed that was true. "Oh, stand up already." Their penitential mien did nothing to appease my anger at the trick they'd pulled on us. They had such potential to destroy us utterly. It seemed so close to betrayal that I couldn't see how the scales balanced. Had their assistance been worth more to us than the great risk they posed? I could just imagine Con's ire at hearing this. "Was it worth it?"

"It was worth it to uss," Merle hissed, a black feather wafting down to settle on the ice, floating with regret.

"What Merle is saying is that we made the choice out of selfishness, at its core," Ambrose said, meeting my gaze like a prisoner ready to accept a sentence of execution. "We admit that, but we have also attempted to balance that self-interest with altruism."

"We lacked the power to free oursselves," Merle agreed.

"And though we deeply regretted our role in Anure's conquest and reign," Ambrose said slowly, adjusting his grip on the staff, "we'd also originally entered into that cabal of our own free will. Neither of us deserves rescue— or we didn't, to begin with—so all we could do was leverage circumstances to arrange our rescue, and attempt to deliver enough value to be worth the rescuing in the end."

"Con doesn't know any of this," I said, not really a question, just clarifying. "Did you influence Me to rescue the royal captives just to free yourselves?"

"No." Ambrose said that firmly and clearly, Merle shaking his head earnestly. "The royals must be freed to return to govern the lands. Once that's accomplished, we can begin to redress what we've done."

"Why tell Me now?" I asked. "More to the point, why didn't you explain this up front?"

Ambrose gestured to the icy pond that didn't truly exist. "We are in a safe bubble of space. We couldn't speak of these things in a non-astral realm at all. This place is one of our fabrication, where the others cannot find us. We had to wait for You to find Your way to joining us."

"You could have taught Me," I pointed out. "That would've been direct."

Ambrose smiled ruefully. "No, I couldn't. You had to find Your own way, Euthalia. And You wouldn't make this risky venture into the unknown without the proper motivation."

"Fear?" I asked.

Merle hissed a laugh, and Ambrose shook his head. "Love."

Oh. *I trust that You will follow your heart.* Perhaps I wouldn't have tried this if not for Con, who'd found my heart and taken it with him. "I suppose we have to proceed as planned," I finally said.

They both pressed hands to hearts, bowing to me.

"We help as our bondss allow," Merle told me. "That hass not changed."

"Good, because a great deal rests on you. If you betray us . . ." I trailed off. I didn't know what threat I could level against them. "I will do everything in My power to destroy you."

"At the risk of being trite, Your Highness, that has been a contingency plan for us, all along," Ambrose confided. "A fail-safe, if You will. We wanted You involved so that,

if all else failed, someone with Your power would be mo-
tivated to destroy us, rather than letting us continue down
our current path."

I didn't even know how to take that. "You wanted
Me to love Con enough to destroy you in retribution if
he fails."

Ambrose spread his hands. "Would Your Highness have
been moved by less, thinking back to Your life before Conrí
came to Calanthe?"

I didn't have to think. Or rather, I'd been thinking
about nothing else these last days, how I'd been before
Con, with my frozen heart and my endless stalemate. I'd
dressed every day for a battle that raged far beyond my fertile shores, never digging deeper into my own nature or
what more life might hold.

"Was there really a prophecy?" I asked. I'd meant it to
sound like a demand, to call them out for dishonesty and
manipulation, but the question came out nearly plaintive,
like a child discovering a favored story was entirely fiction.

"Yes and no," Ambrose conceded. "The vision of the
future was true—a focal point of forces in perfect align-
ment that could lead to the shattering of Anure's power,
the boulder in the river, if You will—but we crafted the
words. It's not easy, You know," he said, warming to his
subject with his more normal ebullience, "to create a solid
prophecy. It's got to contain a lot of information in a mem-
orable way."

"Sshort," Merle qualified.

"Yes, concise, so nothing gets forgotten. Every word
and phrase needs to contain numerous meanings. This is
where You come in."

"Oh?"

"Indeed. Now, let us teach You some tricks, Your Highness." Ambrose folded his hands together. "You wanted

to be able to observe, to project Your presence to Yek-pehr. I advise against astral form. The other two did not expect You in that plane, so they were slow to react—and I believe neither is consciously aware that was You; those were automatic defenses—but a renewed visitation will pique their interest. You are very bright in this form, Eu-thalia, as is the Abiding Ring."

I glanced at my hand, rather astonished to see the orchid as something entirely new and other. The petals extended with furls and flourishes into other realms and planes of existence. It seemed the very embodiment of life, radiating the purest essence of it. "Orchids can't live on their own," I whispered in wonderment, uncertain why that came to mind just then.

"Because they draw life symbiotically from others," Ambrose replied.

"Conssentrating it," Merle agreed. "A focuss."

"Only You, a true daughter of Calanthe, could wield the ring in the way that will be necessary."

"Can you teach Me how to use the ring?"

"Of course, Your Highness," Ambrose said, inclin-ing his head as Merle bowed. "You have but to ask." He smiled, more of his genuine warmth and humor in it.

"Why now?" I asked. "And don't give Me the fancy sidestepping that I didn't ask the right questions before."

"Without seeming to sidestep, Your Highness," Am-brose replied very seriously, "You hadn't fully embraced Your nature until recently, and so couldn't understand what we're going to show You."

I supposed I had to grant the truth of that, as I'd been thinking to myself that very thing, that I hadn't thought of myself as someone who could wield magic. Did I have to die to be born again? I supposed it didn't matter. I had done both.

"And the timing is right," I said, watching them both for reactions.

Merle inclined their head and Ambrose smiled ruefully spreading his hand. "We are at the true endgame, the moment we had foreseen."

"But you couldn't have known I would find My way to this place, to have this conversation."

They shook their heads. "Indeed we had despaired," Ambrose said, Merle nodding sadly. "We thought we had failed to point You in the correct direction."

"Yet here You are." Merle bowed.

"All right." Recriminations could wait. "Teach Me what I need to know."

21

The *Last Resort* easily outpaced the slower, shabbier fishing boat from Hertaq, so Percy took us on an oblique course to Yekpehr. We needed the rest of the team to reach and infiltrate the citadel first—but we also wanted to be nearby if they needed a quick extraction. That was one of the contingency plans we'd developed—and I had to admit it was a good idea—since Percy's yacht was the only one with a fighting chance of outdistancing any of Anure's fleet.

It went against my grain to be planning to fail that way—and then I'd reminded myself that my going all-in at Cradysica had nearly destroyed us. Still, part of me—the restless, pacing wolf—wanted only to move forward and kill. I didn't much care for this mature, account-for-all-contingencies approach to conquest, but I supposed that's why I had Lia.

Percy had fallen into thoughtful silence, speaking only when necessary, as we took turns through the night keeping watch and avoiding the legitimate shipping traffic—and keeping an eye out for Merle. He was to come warn us if the other groups encountered trouble. But the night passed peacefully enough—Percy located an anchorage well outside the busier shipping lanes—and the morning found us, if not rested, at least relieved to be taking action.

When Percy emerged from below, I did a double take, for a moment thinking I saw Lia. He paused, then struck a pose, nose and nails lifted in the air.

"Striking," I offered, for lack of a better word, earning a glare for my weak praise. If nothing else, we'd blind Anure into insensibility—though I was at least smart enough not to say so.

"I've saved this outfit for a long time," Percy informed me, looking down at himself and adjusting the fall of the skirts. "It's based on the traditional garb of the Aekis royal family. I thought it would be a lovely way to tweak Anure's nose."

I studied the white fitted jacket, lavishly embellished with braid and diamond-bright buttons. The tight sleeves finished with belled cuffs embroidered with flowers that enveloped Percy's hands, with the same design on the full skirts that ended at his knees, revealing ivory leather boots. "Smart," I told him. "You'll remind Anure of his illegitimacy, that you are what he can never be. It will put him off balance."

Percy deflated slightly. "Even after everything that rat bastard has done, I don't like playing that card. Being born on the wrong side of the blanket isn't anyone's fault."

"No, but what Anure chose to do with his lot *is* his fault," I reminded Percy without remorse. "Shitty things happened to us, too, but you and I aren't ravaging the world, enslaving people to fill our treasuries."

"Too true, Conrí." Percy turned and surveyed the jaggedly ugly outline of the citadel looming above us. "Though I've hardly lived an admirable life."

"Neither have I." The smoke from the burning vurgsten on the walls darkened the sky, creating a gloom in the previously fresh morning light. I might have mined those very rocks with my own hands. As my lungs tightened from the stink, my throat closing in a reflexive clench to shut the noxious stuff out, I missed Calanthe's fragrant air with a pang of nostalgia. *When did you start thinking of Calanthe as home?*

I still wasn't sure of the answer to that, except it had happened sometime after Cradysica, when Lia had been taken and I'd been left to sort through the rubble, to give the orders she would have. I'd felt a connection to Calanthe then—probably a thin shadow of what Lia felt—but I'd had a love for the land in those days, when I had nothing else.

"You've done better than most of us," Percy was saying. He lifted a brow at my inattention. "At least doing admirable things."

"I've done terrible things," I corrected, keeping my gaze riveted on the citadel. I'd once thought killing Anure would be the atonement for my many crimes. Now I might have to walk away and let him live. That would please Lia, but would it be enough to silence the ghosts of the angry dead, to expiate the many sins I'd committed in the name of vengeance? I could only hope.

"In the name of good," Percy reminded me. "Whereas I've been petty and selfish for no other reason than because I could. And because I lacked the courage to do otherwise."

"Except for now."

"Yes. Except for now." He sighed, a releasing of tension, no drama in it. "Here comes the harbor guard. Are you certain you can handle this?"

I wasn't sure at all, but after what Lia and Sondra suffered, I could hardly shrink from bringing up a few bad memories. Holding out my hands in front of me, I pressed my wrists together. "Do it."

Percy smirked as he clapped the heavy manacles on my wrists, binding them tightly together. "When I fantasized about this, it was much sexier," he said, fluttering his lashes and earning a hoarse laugh from me. I appreciated his effort to distract me, as the clasp of heavy iron sent my heart pounding. "All right?" Percy asked, peering at me with keen insight.

"Yeah." Mostly. I'd sworn I'd never wear chains again, but the world had a way of making us taking back those sorts of reckless vows.

"At least the beads of cold sweat will lend realism to the ruse," Percy noted, placing the glass case in my hands and attaching its chain to my manacles. He and Brenda had crafted the box with the help of the palace glassblowers. Metalworkers had constructed the heavy base, the two pieces fitting together with Calanthe's trademark artistry. Lia's severed hand rested within on a black satin pillow designed to set off the pale, dead skin—and the large and lavish orchid Lia had attached to it, breathing into it some kind of magic that had kept it fresh and lush all this time. Magic she'd learned from those scrolls we'd taken from the tower of Keiost.

I concentrated on the orchid's steadying loveliness, and the memories of Lia it evoked, as Percy attached a chain from it to encircle his wrist, then the heavy bag to my belt, draping the fuse to dangle in clear sight.

The two smaller ships came straight for us—against the wind and with considerable speed. Smoke blew behind them, and I narrowed my eyes. "They're using vurgsten to power those boats," I observed.

Percy leaned over the rail to see better, then nodded. "A clever application."

"Hail, yacht!" a voice boomed through an amplifying horn. "Who are you and what is your business?"

Percy waited a deliberate moment, studying his nails, then picked up a similar horn. "Inform His Imperial Majesty Anure, Emperor of All the Lands, that Lord Percival Robho of Valencia, his beloved cousin, has brought him a gift."

A pause ensued, with some clustering and shifting among the guards on the deck of the boat that had hailed us. They'd drawn up closer to the *Last Resort* in the interim, flanking us. Vesno growled, and I tended to agree. "No one here has heard of you," they finally shouted back.

"Ah, the fickle nature of fame," Percy muttered, then lifted the horn again. "I assure you that my imperial cousin has heard of me and will want to see me—and the gift I've brought to honor him." He gestured to me, as if he'd conjured me from thin air. "Behold: His Imperial Majesty's enemy, the Slave King. He's brought something very special with him in homage, a tribute to His Imperial Majesty. Let's call it a unique and sweetly scented piece of jewelry. He'll know."

"Give them to us," called the captain, close enough now that no amplification was necessary. "You can stay here and await His Imperial Majesty's decision."

Percy leaned his elbow on the rail, cupping his chin in one hand so he framed his face with his long nails. "Aren't you adorable? But no. I'm not stupid. Escort us with an armed guard if you must, but I'll negotiate with my cousin in person—or not at all."

"Our armed guard will confiscate the prisoner and the box, and you can await His Imperial Majesty's pleasure in a prison cell," the captain replied without hesitation.

"One day something will happen that Lia didn't accurately predict," I grumbled, and Percy threw me a mirthless smile.

"Oh, Conrí, darling. You *are* an idealist. But Her High-

ness isn't infallible, She is simply very good at predicting
the toad. Let's see if Her Highness was also correct that
the wizards will be watching for this." From his volumi-
nous skirts, Percy produced a sparker, holding it up so the
guards could clearly see it. "I believe this gift is of considerable interest to His Imperial Majesty. This bag con-
tains vurgsten sufficient to incinerate the Abiding Ring,
and I can light the fuse in a moment. One wrong move and
I'll do it."

More discussion, and I watched them keenly. "You'd
kill yourself, too," the captain pointed out.

Percy smiled thinly. "Possibly, but I have little left to
lose. Regardless, it *would* kill the Slave King, and destroy
the ring. I'm certain His Imperial Majesty would be most
unhappy to have lost out on both prizes, and only because
his guards were too stupid to know better. As I recall, my
imperial cousin is not tolerant of incompetence in his service. I wonder what he would do to you?"

A younger soldier ran up and spoke to the captain with
every appearance of conveying an urgent message. The
man nodded, eyeing us the whole time. "All right," he
called. "We'll escort you in."

"Delighted to accept the invitation," Percy called back,
then turned to me. "Another point for Her Highness."

I learned what Ambrose and Merle thought I most needed
to know, though I couldn't practice the trick without revealing my newfound power to the other wizards. I was
also frankly terrified to do it—and I'd try only if I had to.
Hopefully it wouldn't come to that. Though I was quite
sure it would.

I spent the rest of the night looking through Ibolya's
eyes. Using that familiar technique allowed me to rest what
felt like entirely new muscles—which I would need in

the morning once Con and Percy were on the move—and monitor how that team was progressing. If they needed help, I wanted to know immediately.

They sailed the fishing boat into the trade quadrant just after midnight. Ibolya, standing at the rail, a rough cloak covering her garb as a Yekpehr lady-in-waiting, was surprised to see that part of the harbor as busy as in broad daylight, and lit by lanterns and torches to be nearly that bright. Chains of laborers unloaded ships, passing barrels, crates, and other packages up to the township and the citadel, while horses and oxen pulling wagons laden with goods waited patiently to load the ships again.

Anure was doing a brisk business, which made me want to growl like Con would, over the exorbitant tithes the Imperial Toad had extracted from Calanthe. Never again.

"You sure you're up for this?" Sondra asked, and I had to stifle the impulse to reply, taking a mental step back from Ibolya's senses.

"Yes," Ibolya replied firmly. "Stop asking me that."

Sondra grinned at her, the lamplight casting harsh shadows across her face, undaunted. She wore a plain tunic and carried only her walking stick. With her shorn head and the dirt she'd smudged over her face, she looked convincingly like a slave girl—except for that flesh-eating smile. "If it bothers you to answer the question, then maybe your resolve isn't there."

Ibolya glared at her. "Maybe some of us have enough resolve that we don't need to constantly revisit it." She felt instant remorse as Sondra's smile dimmed. "I apologize. I didn't mean to—"

Sondra held up hand to stop her. "Hey, it was a fair point. Don't muck up a well-aimed retort with an apology." She turned to lean on the rail, giving the high walls of the citadel a dour stare. "And yeah, I'm asking myself the same question. Fuck me, but I hate this place. You're right, though: The decision has been made." She scanned the busy harbor. "Not like any of us can stay aboard the boat with this level of activity. And there won't be any coming back to it."

"There certainly won't," Ambrose replied. "As if Lord Ryder would allow his servants to shirk their duties." He sniffed with convincing arrogance, posing in his fancy clothing, the emerald-topped staff looking like an elegant cane. "I see you're bringing your prize along, Sondra."

She twirled her knobby, ugly walking stick. "Yep. Can't carry a blade in this outfit, and this is at least a weapon."

"One you don't know how to use," Ambrose pointed out.

"Well, you taught me how to *not* use it, so I figure if things go south, I'll stop being careful with it."

Ambrose looked pained but said nothing more. The ship came to a halt at anchor in a darker and quieter part of the harbor. Brenda and Agatha joined them. "This is where you get off," Brenda announced. "Take the skiff to wherever looks like a reasonable spot for Lord Ryder to appear with his servants, then it's up to you. Any word from Merle?"

"Yes," Ambrose replied. "All is quiet within, and he's confirmed the current location of the captives."

Brenda nodded and pulled down her sailor's cap to shade her face. She looked scruffy enough to blend in with the other dockworkers. "Kara and I will shop for a ship to steal. Send Merle to us in a few hours to find out which one we picked out. Good luck, all."

They climbed down the rope ladder to the skiff, and Sondra rowed them to the dock. Then Ambrose took the lead, strolling with arrogant purpose along the dock, Ibolya and Agatha just behind him, and Sondra humbly bringing up the rear—and carrying their bags, her stick strapped to one.

They earned curious glances that turned into dull disinterest when Ambrose glanced their way, and made it to the harbor Slave Gate with little trouble. As predicted, entrants to the citadel were stopped and questioned, and Ambrose gave a convincing display of impatient boredom at the delay.

When they reached the head of the line, the guard blinked at Ambrose, confusion turning to suspicion. "And who are—?"

"Lord Ryder," Ambrose replied haughtily, "and servants. I'll have your name for impeding my progress."

"Papers, syr," the other guard inserted, "no matter who ye are. Orders of His Imperial Majesty."

Ambrose sighed mightily but flicked his fingers at Ibolya, who pulled the faked documents from her skirt pocket, curtsying deeply as she handed them over. Agatha kept her face well shaded by the hood of her cloak while the guards scrutinized the papers long enough that Ambrose had to snap at Sondra to quit her restless stomping.

"We don't have a Lord Ryder on our list of guests or residents," the first guard finally said.

"Are you certain?" Ambrose asked. "Look again. You likely spelled it wrong. It's right there, before Lady Rysong."

"Oh, huh. Go figure. Sorry, syr."

"Why is a fancy lord like you coming through the Slave Gate?" the other guard asked, not at all convinced.

Ambrose flipped back his curls, considerably longer, glossier, and more golden than usual. "Have you seen the mob at the main gates?" He shuddered delicately. "Besides," he added in a conspiratorial tone, "I don't wish for a certain lover to know I've been out tomcatting. Iris, darling, give the gentlemen a gift for their service."

Ibolya had the coins ready and slipped them into the guards' palms with smooth sleight of hand as if she'd been giving and taking bribes for years. Perhaps she had.

Ambrose produced an elaborate yawn. "I'm exhausted. May I go to bed now, gentlemen? My *own* bed," he clarified with a wink.

The guards waved them through, and Ambrose kept to his genteel pace until they were well out of sight. "They may be onto us," he informed the others. "That should've been easier."

"The guards?" Ibolya asked.

"No—the wizards. The guards shouldn't have questioned us so much."

"What should we do?" Sondra had unslung her stick and carried it again.

Ambrose shook his head at her. "Nothing. We're in. Just be aware. And . . ." He hesitated, then seemed to come to a decision. "If I disappear or seem distracted in some way, don't be alarmed. Proceed as planned without me."

"Yeah, like that behavior would be anything new," Sondra muttered sardonically, then gave Ambrose a sunny smile. "Lead on, Syr Ryder."

They wended their way through back hallways, Ambrose unerringly making turns in dimly lit corridors as if he knew them well, until they came to a shadowed intersection where Merle joined them. Ambrose and Merle conferred, Ambrose relaying information to Agatha, who nodded. "So far, so good," she said.

"It seems so," Ambrose agreed, Merle giving an answering croak. "But I'll be happier when you're in the towers."

"We're beneath one," Agatha said. "Either Sondra or Ibolya can take this one, then I'll lead us to the next closest and take the farthest."

"I'll take the one with Rhéiane in it," Sondra declared.

Agatha shook her head. "She is in the farthest tower—which means I'd have to take you there and then retrace my steps, putting us all more at risk."

Sondra glowered. "She was—is—my friend and—"

"And it will be a shock for her to see you," Agatha interrupted sharply. "You'll see her on the ship."

"What if you don't make it?" Sondra demanded.

"Then none of us make it," Ambrose inserted. "We get everyone or no one. This is a onetime attempt. We won't get a second chance."

They were all quiet a moment, processing that, then Sondra nodded reluctantly. "Which do you want, Ibolya?"

"I'll take this tower," Ibolya replied immediately, "since I'm the least experienced at this sort of thing. Cuts down on risk for us all," she added, and Sondra smiled thinly.

"The tenth, eleventh, and twelfth floors," Agatha told her. "Three rooms on each floor."

"I'll send Merle with you," Ambrose said. "He'll get you in the doors if you have a problem doing it on your own. If he seems to disappear or if, ah, someone *else* appears, don't worry. The black feather will be the sign. Good luck."

Merle spread his wings and hopped the short distance to Ibolya's shoulder, his talons sinking into her flesh but only lightly pricking her skin. It felt odd to have the big bird perched there. Not heavy exactly, but a definite weight, his glossy feathers brushing her cheek. He bobbed his head, chucking softly like ravens did to their young, likely intended to be soothing.

Feeling not nearly so brave as she had been, Ibolya

climbed the servants' stairs to what felt nearly like the top of the tower before Merle clicked his beak, halting her. He pointed his beak at the door, cocking his head to gaze at her with an amber eye, an encouraging gleam in it. Moving quietly, Ibolya reached for the doorknob, knowing from the models in the Sand Salon that an antechamber lay beyond it, with locked doors to the rooms behind. And guards with weapons.

The weight on her shoulder vanished, and she faltered, then straightened her spine. She was a lady-in-waiting to a queen and she knew how to get her way in the name of another. Stepping through the door, Ibolya didn't allow her stride to falter as she walked toward one of the three doors.

"Halt," said one of the guards, tipping his lance to cross the doorway. "I don't know you."

"I'm a new lady-in-waiting, syr, just now arrived. I'm expected."

"In the middle of the night?" the other guard asked, not exactly suspicious, but definitely wondering.

Ibolya shrugged, lifting her hands at the vagaries of nobles. "I just go where I'm told. It doesn't pay to ask questions," she confided.

The guard scoffed knowingly. "Ain't that the truth?"

"You got the key then?" the first guard asked.

Ibolya stilled, heart accelerating—then felt something in her palm that hadn't been there before. A black feather. Smiling, she held it up. "Right here."

The guard with the lance nodded and stepped aside. Ibolya inserted the feather in the keyhole, and the door swung open. *Thank you, Merle*, she whispered in her head.

It took Ibolya most of the night to visit all nine chambers in her tower. After the first, entrée to the next became easier as she carried specific notes from one denizen to the next, or claimed to run an errand for yet another. The royal captives might be prisoners, but they'd also formed a tightly knit society complete with a complex barter system, carefully cultivated mutually beneficial relationships, and a network of information sharing that nearly put the courts at Calanthe to shame.

Once she overcame her fear and anxiety, Ibolya fitted herself almost seamlessly into their midst, finding those waters as familiar as the ones she'd swum in all these years. She did visit all the rooms that were "hers," though she didn't need to. Once she explained the reason for her presence—and convinced the captives of her sincerity, largely by citing Her Highness Queen Euthalia, well known for granting asylum on Calanthe and more recently famous for defying Anure rather spectacularly in court—the lords and ladies sent their own messengers to the other captives, alerting them to Ibolya's mission.

By the early morning, all the nobles in Ibolya's tower had prepared messages canceling meetings and appearances—and had assembled their belongings for escape. She'd only had to argue with a few of them about what they intended to bring along. Most of them were grimly excited to escape the citadel with their skins intact and nothing more. Still, Agatha had been correct: They all absolutely insisted on bringing their servants and attendants.

Finally, in the dark predawn hours, they settled in to wait for Con and Percy to have their audience.

22

As Percy had promised, we parked the *Last Resort* at a slip reserved for nobles in favor with the Imperial Toad, conveniently close to an ostentatiously magnificent bridge to the main gate. Nice for getting in, but terrible for getting out again. Even if we could evade capture long enough to escape the citadel, we'd never make it to the *Last Resort*—or get the yacht out of the harbor.

Which Percy had to have known when he suggested the tactic. His last sacrifice, for sure. The guards balked at Vesno coming along, but no way was I leaving the wolfhound behind, since we wouldn't be back to the yacht. To deal with the guards, Percy pointed out—at blistering length—that they were not the ones to be attempting to negotiate such a piddling issue, especially when my affection for the dog acted as another leash on my good behavior. They finally capitulated, maybe out of sheer exhaustion.

It was definitely a faster entrée to Anure's stronghold than the Slave Gate had been, the phalanx of guards escorting us past the long line awaiting entry, through the massive maw of the main gate, then down the dark stone hallways. I studied the walls and branching halls and stairs, attempting to place myself from my previous visit, but I didn't recognize much. Or rather, everything looked the same and thus far too familiar. I could only guess that there must be markers indicating the various towers—Agatha had seemed to know the system—and I hoped our other team had all infiltrated their towers and had the captives ready to evacuate as we began our distraction. Ambrose had been confident he and Merle would know of our movements, but I hadn't caught a glimpse of either of them.

As we drew nearer the throne room, I was able to place it from Lia's re-creation on the model. We stepped into the huge hall, and I imagined myself on that sand table. The small figure of myself—sadly without the rock hammer I'd left with Lia, or even my sword or bagiroca, as Percy had taken possession of those—being marched by a child's hand through the encircling ring of courtiers. I resisted searching their faces to see if I could spot Rhéiane. If all had gone as it should, my sister wouldn't be in the room. Ambrose and Merle should be already posing as Anure's generals, moving the captives out to whatever ship Brenda and Kara had decided was best for stealing.

So many moving pieces I knew nothing about. I began to understand Lia's frustration at being out of control. There was something to be said for lone-wolfing it.

Just outside the throne room, the captain of the guard halted at the closed doors. His men swiftly surrounded Percy, relieving him of the chain to the fuse, and detaching the bag from my belt. The captain grinned at Percy's dismay. "You didn't really believe we'd let you carry a bomb before His Imperial Majesty, did you? We're not idiots."

Percy protested that it wasn't a bomb. I concentrated on looking mean and stoic. The guards laughed and marched us in—one taking the bomb away, the fuse unlit.

They deposited us on the wide apron at the foot of the imposing throne. I'd been grateful that Lia had pushed herself to re-create the throne room for us because we needed the information. Now I found myself glad in a way I hadn't expected that I'd seen Lia's model of the throne itself, and heard her and Sondra discuss the optical illusion of the thing. If I hadn't known, I might've been intimidated by the vast scale, the awesome height, and the piles of treasure mounded on the steps. As it was, I had been braced for the sight of Anure seemingly so far above me—and I could smile inside at the ridiculousness of a man so desperate to feel superior.

Also as Lia had described, the four wizards stood on the steps of the throne. The one in black stood nearest Anure, only two steps down, the two in blue and purple midway down on each side, and the one in red nearly at the bottom.

The guards retreated a few steps behind us, blocking our retreat. Percy bowed gracefully to Anure while I—true to my expected character—refused. Returning Anure's stare without flinching, I put all my disgust and hatred on display. *Make him think all you care about is defying him.*

"I should declare this an imperial holiday," Anure said in his smoothly cultured voice. "My prodigal cousin returns to Me and brings Me two gifts: the wretched rebel Slave King and something else of note. A special piece of *jewelry*, I understand?" The avid greed leaked into his tone, his fingers twitching in his longing to grasp and take.

At his words, the red wizard tipped back his cowl to reveal black eyes in a curiously smooth face. He should be able to sense the magic of the case and Lia's enchantment on the orchid, but the spell wouldn't stand up to close inspection, she'd said, not for long. He didn't look at the case, though. Instead the red wizard stared long and hard at me, then smiled, not at all nicely. Snapping his fingers, he summoned a page and bent to whisper some message, sending the page off again.

"Your Imperial Majesty," Percy had been saying during this little scene, oozing obsequious charm, "I greet you. It has been too long since the joyful days of our youth."

"I thought you were dead, Percival," Anure said, sounding unpleasantly surprised to discover he was wrong. "I can't imagine why you aren't—nor why you're here."

Percy shrugged. "Aekis was boring. I helped you before, and you shared your wealth and position with me. I want that again. So I brought you gifts to demonstrate my sincerity."

Anure's lip curled, and he tapped twitching fingers on the arm of his obscene throne. "And you, Slave King, I'm astonished you didn't kill yourself rather than be dragged to face justice in my court, given all you've stolen from Me."

I laughed at that, loudly and heartily, for once not self-conscious at the harsh burr of it, like a dog choking on its collar, even enjoying how the courtiers in my peripheral vision flinched at the sound.

"Do I amuse you, dog?" Anure sneered.

"Well, yeah." I tipped my chin at the treasure dripping down the steps of the throne. "It's pretty fucking funny to hear a thief sitting on a pile of stolen jewels accuse someone *else* of theft." I couldn't help scanning the hoard, wondering if the crown of Oriel lay in there somewhere, if I'd even recognize it after all these years. "I'm also surprised you can even say the word 'justice.' Did it burn your tongue on the way out?"

"I could have you killed where you stand for such insolence," Anure shouted, thumping his fist on the arm of his throne.

I glanced around, raising a dubious brow at his guards. "I *am* chained and unarmed," I noted. "So you might have a shot at it. I'm sure you realize that's the only way you could beat me—since I've defeated you in every other battle."

People behind me gasped and muttered, a hint of titillation in their voices. Anure ignored them as beneath his notice, and I finally got Lia's point about the false emperor being lax about his court. Lia would've played to their reactions. As it was, Anure had lost that opportunity and I was going to snatch it up.

"What about Cradysica?" Anure retorted, a greedy smile devouring his face. "It seems you lost there, Slave King."

"Really—*that* is what you call a victory?" I snorted in disbelief, glancing to a cluster of courtiers at the edge of my vision, shaking my head and inviting them to join in my incredulity. "You lost more than two hundred ships, the best of your fleet—we're not sure how many since most of them are at the bottom of the sea. Thousands of your best sailors and soldiers died. And we successfully repelled you from Calanthe, which is now forever beyond your reach. I'm not clear on how you figure victory, but we must have different definitions."

Anure leaned forward from the edge of his throne, precarious in his perch, clawed fingers hanging on to the arms of the chair as if loosening his grip would pitch him headlong down the steps. "I won!" he gritted out. "I captured the only prize worth having, and everyone here witnessed that. Queen Euthalia, so celebrated and honored—your *wife*—humiliated and broken right where you stand."

"You didn't manage to keep her long, though," I pointed out sympathetically. "Her escape must've stung, huh?"

Anure stilled, and I worked hard to look casual, not

holding my breath. "Her Highness is My prisoner," Anure declared. "When she has reconsidered the error of
her ways, I might readmit her to My presence. Of course,
since you so foully raped an untouched blossom, I can no
longer marry her, but perhaps she will be pleased to see
her abuser tortured."

Beside me, Percy relaxed, just enough for me to
notice—hopefully imperceptible to anyone else. The wizards didn't so much as twitch, but I liked to think I'd
made them nervous. Lia might be right that they held Anure's leash, but the guy sitting on the throne still gave the
orders.

"Are you sure of that?" I asked, making it clear he
shouldn't be. "Because I just saw Queen Euthalia on
Calanthe. I even kissed Her Highness goodbye, after fucking her all night. You missed out on a prime piece there,
Anure." My deliberate crudeness sent renewed murmuring through the court. The black wizard made a complicated hand gesture, turning his face in the direction of
Calanthe.

A high whining sound skittered off the marble walls,
silencing everyone, a rime of fear stilling all movement.
"*Lies*," Anure hissed, the acute pitch nearly painful. "I
shall make you suffer, Slave King. You might have raped
and defiled My beloved fiancée, but I rescued her from
your unclean hands. She is Mine now. You'll never touch
her again."

I made a face of dramatic regret. "You're wrong, Your
Imperiousness. But let's make a bet. Send for Her High-
ness. If you can produce her, I'll give you the Abiding
Ring." I held up the glass case in demonstration.

"We can take it anyway, just as we divested you of
that bomb." Anure sat back, considering. "Besides, I see
through your trick. You hope to deceive Me into releasing

Her Highness from My prisons in an attempt to recover her. You must care about Euthalia very much." His keen gaze rested on me, seeing into my heart.

"My spoils of war belong to me and no one else," I replied. "I already recovered what you attempted to take and weren't strong or clever enough to keep. Look closer at this," I said, allowing a smirk of triumph as I held the case aloft for all to see. "The hand and finger you severed in this very room. When I reclaimed my bride, I took those, too. Along with the Abiding Ring."

The black wizard descended the steps to confer with the red wizard, both eyeing my trophy. The other two wizards seemed oddly still. I kept an eye on them, most of my attention on Anure. "Queen Euthalia hasn't been your guest for some time now." I tipped my head meaningfully at the wizards. "Maybe these guys lied to you?"

Anure looked to the wizard nearest him, the blue-robed one, gesturing impatiently. The blue wizard suddenly stirred, bowed, and spoke to Anure at length, but quietly. The purple wizard seemed not to notice anything, the red and black wizards still in their private conversation, occasionally glancing my way as if trying to see the contents of the case better.

Then the blue wizard's words apparently penetrated Anure's thick skull. As if his fuse finally burned through, Anure exploded. "Dead?!" he thundered. "Why wasn't I informed?"

The red wizard tore his gaze from the case I held to assess Anure. "Your Imperial Majesty," the red wizard said, bowing deeply. "Her Highness, the queen of Calanthe, did indeed perish of blood loss from the injuries You ordered done to Her. But the Abiding Ring remained blooming and fresh. The ways of magic are mysterious. We had preserved Her corpse in the hope of resurrecting Her. If She has indeed been brought back to life, this is cause for celebration, indeed."

Anure wasn't mollified. "This is akin to treachery! Explain yourselves to Me."

The black wizard opened his mouth, but the red wizard held up a hand to silence him. "Perhaps Your Imperial Majesty will accept some information as an apology. This Slave King is someone you know."

Anure swung his attention to me, all temper vanished, that penetrating intellect focusing. "I knew it. Who is he?"

"Conrí," the wizard said with some satisfaction. "Former crown prince of former Oriel, son of your old friend King Tuur."

Shit. This wasn't good. But I held my head high, hiding all reaction.

Anure smiled as if he'd won a great prize. "Is that so? I have someone you might like to meet, Slave King. Summon Lady Rhéiane."

"Your Imperial Majesty," the red wizard replied with a like smile. "I already have."

"Good." Anure steepled his fingers together. "Now that all the stakes are on the table, we can discuss the terms of our bargain."

In the early morning, I left Ibolya to her tense waiting and—somewhat disoriented from spending so much time in someone else's head—I returned to my rooms, walking with Zariah and discussing my wardrobe for the day. I needed to look impressive, just in case. My other ladies were waiting for us, so I sent Zariah off to sleep, demurring at their suggestions that I rest also. Though I'd been awake all night, I knew that sleeping at all would only make me groggy, taking my edge off.

I was going to need that edge by the end of the day, I

suspected. Everything had gone well so far—and I could only hope it had gone that well for Sondra and Agatha, too—but the trickiest parts had yet to be executed.

My natural hair didn't do regal well. It better suited looking like a dryad emerged from a forest pool, as Con had noted. But I also wanted my nature, fully embraced, on display for all to witness. I had my ladies leave my hair down, Orvyki pulling some of it back from my face to be pinned under the crown, then coaxing the increasingly long fall of it into rolling waves.

Otherwise, to create a regal impression, I went with jewels. Nahua found a collar of diamonds, fastening it around my throat and adding successive strings of pearls and diamonds, covering my bare breasts and draping to the top of my pubis. Calla added epaulets of more diamonds and pearls affixed to my shoulders. Suspended from those, strings of jewels brushed my arms where the patterns of barks, leaves, stems, and flowers roamed over my skin with growing abandon.

A girdle of sapphires and emeralds draped low over my hips, the larger jewels hanging in thicker panels that thinned to dangling strands of glittering gems that swirled around my thighs. Zariah had returned, refreshed and in a new gown, declaring herself unable to sleep. I suspected she simply wouldn't take rest if I wouldn't. The heels she found for me were jewelry in themselves—made of strands of silver chains studded with diamonds.

By the time they finished, I wore a good portion of Calanthe's treasury—and was more weighed down by it than I had been by some of my old gowns.

I'd canceled court for the day, so I'd be free to do what was needed, and I returned to the map tower along with my ladies. It took two of them to carry Con's rock hammer for me, Nahua and Orvyki nearly staggering under its weight, but they protested so fiercely when I suggested a guard could carry it for me that I acceded.

Once we reached the map room, I had them set the rock hammer gently in the center of the map, where I'd once lain spread open, naked to my soul, and vulnerable to Con. It had been a beginning of sorts for us, and I would use that connection, since I no longer had the marriage bond.

"You may go," I told my ladies once I was satisfied with the hammer's placement. "I have no more need of you for the time being."

Several of them exchanged glances, then all curtsied deeply and Calla stepped forward, curtsying also. "I beg Your pardon, Your Highness. We have no wish to disobey You, but it's clear that You intend to embark on some sort of personal battle in the next hours. We failed Your Highness in the past by not staying to protect You. We've all been practicing, as You asked, and while we are not yet as proficient as we'd like to be, we beg leave to remain, to guard Your back and Calanthe, as is our sworn duty."

I regarded her with some surprise, seeing the same resolve on all their faces. The blossoms of the Flower Court, displaying their thorns in fine style. Emotion moved through me, fine and sweet. I'd perhaps learned something about not rejecting the love offered to me, like a child flinging away a toy that proved less shiny than initially thought.

"Please rise. I welcome your protection and support," I told them. "Thank you. Though I cannot vouch how this particular battle will appear to you. It may be quite strange."

Orvyki smothered a giggle, and Calla smiled with genuine humor. "We are rather growing accustomed to strangeness, Your Highness."

I smiled back. "No doubt. If you would each take one

of the cardinal directions out on the balcony." They hastened to oblige. Instead of going to the sand table, I went to the center of the map of Calanthe, smiling wryly at myself for lifting my weight off my heels so as to tread lightly. I'd observed to Con in the past that it amused me to see how tentatively visitors moved over the glittering mosaic, though we had no such qualms about treading on Calanthe Herself. Even I was not immune from the nicety, however.

Standing in the midst of Calanthe, my foot touching the haft of Con's rock hammer, I gathered the dreamthink to me, simultaneously stretching my senses to the vast circle that was my realm, from her boundary waters to the geographic heart of the island—and into the sleeping mind of Calanthe, my mother goddess. She murmured dreamily to me, and I soothed Her. I wouldn't need Her might. Not just yet.

I checked with Vesno first, the wolfhound greeting me with overwhelming joy. Con and Percy were still aboard the *Last Resort*, the citadel looming closer so that the smoke increasingly obscured the bright morning light, but they were some distance away yet. So I went on to Ibolya's mind, finding her amid a bustle of preparation. The atmosphere in the tower room was tense, a grim determination in the faces around her, with a sharp edge of hope.

They wouldn't move until Ambrose came for them— when Con reached the citadel—so I went back to Vesno. I ended up pacing in circles as I watched their interaction with the harbor guard, and the gambit with putting Con in chains. "Idiot wolf," I muttered at him.

I wasn't surprised he hadn't told me about that part of his plan—as I would've argued strenuously against it, along with the incredibly foolish tactic of actually chaining himself to the bomb—but I also marveled at his courage. I knew well of his vows never to be chained again. Except for a brief time when I'd taken him prisoner, he'd managed it, too.

"Never again, my wolf," I murmured to him. "After this, never again." *If he survives.* I banished the traitorous doubts.

It took some time for them to sail into the harbor and negotiate with the guards to bring Vesno, then to travel to the throne room, so I checked back with Ibolya. Just in time, too.

A knock at the door had them all scurrying to hide their preparations as a guard opened the door and stuck his head in. "Syr Wizard here to see you. Behave yourselves now."

A tall wizard in a deep purple strode into the room. Ibolya tried to hide herself from his view, her heart climbing into her throat with acid fear, but his amber eyes fastened on her. Tipping his hood back, he gave her a narrow smile, the granite cast of his long face altering very little, but lighting his eyes. He reached up into his long black hair and withdrew a raven's feather, twirling it briefly and letting it fall—and Ibolya breathed a sigh of relief.

"By order of His Imperial Majesty, Emperor of All the Landss," Merle declared to the group, "you are to be moved to a place of safety. You will be peaceful and compliant."

A few of the nobles looked nervously at Ibolya, but she nodded reassuringly, then turned to Merle. "We will comply, Syr Wizard."

With a nod to her, Merle commanded the guards to round up the captives. They extracted the occupants of the other two rooms on that floor, then descended in a closely guarded queue to the next floor, and the next. With thirty-two captives, plus Ibolya, Merle, and six guards, they paraded down the main stairs of the tower. Each set of guards that challenged them were recruited by Merle to guard the evacuation of the captives.

At the intersection of hallways where they'd parted company hours before, Ibolya's group reunited with Agatha's. They had a similar number of captives and guards, and Agatha nodded in confirmation of their success— though she looked tense and anxious. Ambrose wore his blue wizard's robes instead of his Lord Ryder guise. He looked somewhat the same as he had on Calanthe—and not. Not so youthful, but worn down, aged and gray, leaning heavily on his staff.

He instructed the guards to count heads and prepare the prisoners to be moved to a ship in the harbor, then he and Merle briefly conferred. Ibolya sidled near, and Ambrose beckoned her to come closer. "We have a problem with Sondra's lot," he said quietly. "They were fine when I left them, but there's been a complication."

"I knew I should've taken the far tower," Agatha noted, joining the conversation with a grim face and shadowed eyes.

"I thought you did," Ibolya said, and Agatha grimaced, shaking her head.

"I let Sondra talk me out of it. Her dedication to Rhéiane is fierce—and she persuaded me against my better judgment."

"The Lady Sondra is formidable that way," Ibolya commented quietly.

"Indeed," Ambrose said. "Your Highness, we need Your assistance."

"Her Highness?" Ibolya asked, startled. "But I don't know that—"

"She is lisstening now," Merle informed her gravely, setting a hand briefly on Ibolya's arm to soothe her. "Be not alarmed."

"Oh," Ibolya breathed. "Her Highness said She might listen through me, but I thought I'd feel it."

"In time, with practice, perhapss," Merle replied. "You have much native magic that you can train to use." Ibolya smiled, pride and excitement filling her.

"For now, Your Highness," Ambrose said to her, to me, "would you go to Sondra? We dare not release this group from our control. We'll move them to the ship, then one of us will return to assist you. Can you stall them?"

23

Yes, I said in my head, though I'd never done this before. I didn't expect anyone to hear. To my surprise and Ibolya's, she spoke the word aloud at the exact moment I thought it.

That's not deeply unsettling or anything, I thought to myself, feeling Ibolya's chagrined agreement—and so I quickly withdrew from her head.

Taking a deep breath and steadying myself, I prayed to Ejarat that this would work. Drawing on Calanthe's stabilizing, granite-deep and life-giving magic, I channeled it through the orchid ring and concentrated as Ambrose and Merle had shown me. Loosening my grip on my physical form was disorienting, but I held to the connection with Calanthe, drawing from Her with intact roots. I formed a clear image of Sondra in my mind, then reached for her physical location. For a moment it seemed as if I viewed all the world, swooping over it like a bird, then narrowing to Yekpehr, the citadel looming large and smoky—and to Sondra. Fortunately, I seemed to stop before actually entering her head. I didn't want to invade her mind, and I greatly doubted she would want me there.

Sondra had apparently extracted all the captives from their tower rooms and they'd made it down several levels—no doubt why Ambrose had thought their situation well enough in hand to go aid Agatha—but they'd encountered a brace of guards ascending, a captain of the guard at their forefront. Back luck, that. Sondra, trying to look like a humble slave and not succeeding very well, lurked near the back of the group. She stood with a tall woman, whose dark hair was braided severely back from a face lined with fear and sorrow. Thick stripes of snow-white streaked from her temples to the coronet of braids, winding through the black coils like silver frosting. Tawny brown eyes dominated her face, the color—very nearly gold—so very familiar to me. Aged beyond her years, yes, but otherwise unmistakably Con's sister. Rhéiane of Oriel.

Now that I'd arrived, I wasn't sure how I was to assist them—only that I knew I must. I couldn't face Con having again failed to save his sister. Calanthe's magic welled through my blood but remained with my body. I could see and hear but not affect anything physically. I might as well be a ghost.

"An evacuation?" the captain of the guard repeated incredulously to one of the tower guards. "His Imperial Majesty ordered no such thing. I would know."

The guard looked confused and anxious, casting a glance over the group, looking for backup. No help was forthcoming. "Captain Jan, syr, we received orders," he protested, though weakly.

"Orders." Captain Jan made the word into a curse. "*I* give the orders, or His Imperial Majesty does. I know *I* wasn't here until a moment ago. Are you claiming the emperor stopped by to chat?"

"No, syr," the guard answered, flushing.

Jan, anger rising, shoved the hapless spokesman aside. "*You*, I will deal with later." He confronted a regal woman at the front of the group, who lifted her chin and stared the captain down. "Consort Ibb, what is the meaning of this?"

Lady Ibb gave him a cool look and a disgusted wave of her hand, encompassing all of her contempt for the clearly slipshod bureaucracy. "Your guards commanded us to evacuate. We complied. Isn't that our primary responsibility, to obey without question?"

Captain Jan set his teeth. "His Imperial Majesty expected You to attend him in formal court this morning, Consort. They have already convened and You are late. His Imperial Majesty sent me to retrieve You." His gaze roamed suspiciously over the group, settling on Sondra, frowning when he didn't recognize her—and looking from her to Rhéiane with dawning suspicion. Frustration burning through me, I tried channeling magic and managed only to stir some dust motes. Hmm. Ambrose had explained this, but actually doing it was more difficult.

"I sent a message that I would not attend this morning," Lady Ibb sniffed in disdain. "I am unwell."

"How distressing, Consort," Captain Jan replied, sounding anything but distressed. "You don't appear to be ill. Tell me Your symptoms and I'll relay them to the healers, so they may attend You."

"A woman's complaint of some delicacy," she returned with a steely smile. "I simply require rest."

"You should return to Your bed."

"I will, since this drill appears to have been for naught." She turned, her ladies following behind, Rhéiane going with them.

"Not so fast, Consort. Lady Rhéiane," Captain Jan called. "I was also sent to fetch you to court."

Rhéiane halted, paling so dramatically I worried she might pass out. Sondra took her arm to support her, and Jan's jaw firmed as he noted it. *Shit.* Anure would only be summoning Rhéiane out of the blue if he knew Con's real identity—and planned to use Rhéiane against him.

"Is there a problem, Lady Rhéiane?" he asked silkily, prowling toward her, the group parting like birds scattering at a hawk's shadow.

"Ah . . . no, Captain Jan," she stammered, averting her gaze. "But surely there must be a mistake—I am never summoned to formal court."

"Apparently today is your lucky day," he replied, grabbing her arm and ignoring the difference of rank between them, along with her flinch of pain at the hard grip. Sondra stiffened, her knuckles whitening on the walking stick, as Jan yanked Rhéiane close.

"Quite the coincidence, isn't it," Jan continued, raising his voice to the group. "Consort Ibb attempts to skip formal court on the flimsy excuse of an undefined ailment on the exact morning that Lady Rhéiane is summoned to court *and* that my guards also receive a clearly false command to evacuate all of you? Something is going on—and I think you know what it is." He gave Rhéiane another shake and Sondra very nearly lunged at him, barely restraining herself.

Rhéiane didn't attempt to wrest her arm from his grip. She didn't seem to have the physical strength for it. She didn't lack for spine, however, and I recognized Con's ferocity in her fiery glare. "The confusion, lack of discipline, and sheer idiocy in your chain of command is hardly within my control, Captain."

Casually, he slapped her, still retaining his grip. "Watch your attitude, slut," he replied pleasantly, then looked to the guard he'd first interrogated. "Where were you to take them?"

"Captain, syr, to a ship in the harbor, syr. The *Emperor's Pet*."

Jan's eyes widened in patent disbelief. "Well, Lady Rhé-iane. You are correct at least in that I am surrounded by idiots. Nir!" He pointed to one of the guards he'd brought with him. "Sound the alert. We have an escape attempt under way and—"

I'd been poised to stop the messenger on the stairs—in any way I could—but Sondra couldn't know that. Swing-ing her heavy walking stick and ululating in an ear-piercing shriek, she charged the captain. With unfortunate presence of mind, he yanked Rhéiane in front of him, drawing his sword. The downward blow of the stick hit the edged metal with a thud that had Sondra bouncing off. She used the momentum to spin and come around, narrowly missing Rhéiane's skull as Jan held the slight woman between them as a shield.

"Guards!" Jan yelled. "First squad to me." He blocked another blow of Sondra's and lunged—fortunately ham-pered by his struggling shield, and missing Sondra's heart as she danced back. "Second squad, circle the prisoners. Take them back. Lock them in."

Sondra changed tactics, lancing the stick straight for Jan's eye, glancing off his forehead as he jerked his head to the side at the last moment. "Nir, why are you still here?" he bellowed.

The guard appointed to give warning raced down the steps, and Jan released Rhéiane just long enough to wrap his forearm around her throat with brutal force. She choked as he crushed her larynx. He pointed his sword at Sondra. "I don't know who you are, slave, but you're killing her."

The guards began rounding up the captives, shouting and shoving. Sondra narrowed her eyes, assessing the scene. Yes, we needed to eliminate Jan and then take ad-vantage of the guards' confusion and lack of leadership. As if she'd heard me, Sondra nodded minutely, then held up her hands in a gesture of surrender, the stick high over her head.

"Drop the stick," Jan ordered.

Sondra smiled. "Sure." She dropped it—and the concussion flattened everyone in the room, including Sondra. Wonderful.

Taking advantage of the temporary détente, I flew my attention down the stairwell, catching up to the hapless Nir. He raced at top speed down the steps. If I could stir dust motes, I could affect stone. Density shouldn't matter.

I flew down a turn of the stairs before him, pressed my mind against the stone, suggesting to it that it wanted to be like dust motes. Nir thundered down—and his foot passed through the step as if it weren't there. He fell hard, breaking his leg with a *snap!* His skull thudded with an ominous *crack* against the stones as he went deathly still.

Well then.

I flew back to Sondra—and to a room full of unconscious people. All right. At least the guards were out of the equation. I simply needed to resurrect the rest. Hmm. I went to Sondra, touching intangible fingertips to her temples, feeling very much like some story of a fairy flitting about while the heroes lay fallen.

Whatever the stick had done, it had sent her life energy deep inside. At least I knew something about manipulating that. Carefully, I reversed her energy, changing it so it flowed out to her limbs and brain again. She woke with a start, bright-blue eyes staring blindly through me.

"Lia?" she whispered.

Well, go figure. *Yes*, I said, and her eyes widened. *Hurry*, I thought at her and she pushed up to a sitting position, crawling to the unconscious Rhéiane. I woke Rhéiane next, then moved on, going from person to person—starting with Lady Ibb and avoiding the guards—waking them one by one. It grew easier with practice, and I felt even more like some creature from an old tale. I supposed the stories had come from somewhere.

Sondra got Rhéiane on her feet and followed behind me, marshaling the querulously waking captives into a line, managing them with a combination of reassurance and crisp orders. "If You can hear me, Lia," she muttered under her breath, "we're facing a problem walking them out of here without guards. The ruse won't work without that cover."

I agreed, but I didn't know what else we could do. We had to get them out of Anure's reach, especially if Anure was onto Con. If he was able to get Rhéiane to the throne room, we'd be facing disaster. Knowing Con, he'd probably cut his own throat at the toad's request if it meant saving Rhéiane at last.

I'd really expected—and now viciously hoped—that Ambrose or Merle would've arrived by now to assist. The fact that neither had was a bad sign, too. They'd be dividing their presence between their required stations in the throne room and moving the prisoners out. Something had gotten complicated in one place or the other. Or both.

I was terribly afraid it had to do with Con.

So desperate to know something, I took a precious moment to click to Vesno's vision—which snapped me back to my body in the tower. Clouds had gathered ominously, black as a sheet of obsidian, and white lightning forked out of the sky. A bolt stabbed for the tower, and Calla raised her hands, pushing back. Reversing, the lightning recoiled into the cloud and lit it up from within, a *boom* resounding and rolling over the island. Nahua, the next station over, seemed to be funneling energy in a continuous stream to hold off something else. *Good for them.*

I had no time to help them—or say anything—so I looked through Vesno's eyes long enough to confirm that Con still lived, as did Percy, and they were mid-audience with Anure. Then, though my heart cried for me to stay with him, I forced myself to go back to Sondra. We nearly had Rhéiane out—along with the others. After that, we could pull out all the stops to extract Con and Percy.

By the time I returned to Sondra, she was leading the captives down the servants' stairs—the best choice for moving without the cover of guards. Still no sign of Ambrose or Merle, Ejarat take them. I went back to Ibolya—and breathed a sigh of relief to find her with Kara and Brenda, aboard the *Emperor's Pet*, which looked to be a well-favored sailing ship. They were all anxiously watching the gate for the third set of captives, discussing what steps they should take. Agatha and Brenda seemed to be on the verge of going after them.

Though I hated to do it, I couldn't afford to have any of them back in the citadel, so I spoke in Ibolya's mind, hoping she'd hear me. Far better than using her mouth to speak.

"I apologize, Ibolya. This is Lia. Tell Brenda and Agatha to stay put. Sondra and the others are on their way." Hopefully she wouldn't detect the prevarication in what I'd told her.

Ibolya sighed with relief. "Her Highness is here," she said, and passed along my message.

Brenda and Kara exchanged frowns, regarding my former lady-in-waiting with consternation and disbelief. "Ibolya," Brenda said gently, "wishful thinking can—"

"She's not crazy," Agatha interrupted. "Ambrose and Merle said in the citadel that Her Highness is here and helping us. Message received," she added. "We will wait as long as possible."

"Once that group is aboard, go," I told her. *"Do* not *wait for the rest of us. We'll find another way."*

Ibolya dutifully passed that along, and they assented, though unhappily.

"Hopefully it won't come to a battle," Kara commented dourly, and Brenda rounded on him with a protest.

I left them to their arguing and returned to Sondra. They'd made it to the bottom of the tower, all of them bunched up and huddled in the narrow stairwell. Sondra peeked through a crack in the door, observing the busy daytime bustle of the main hall outside. They were trapped there, unless we found help.

Wait, I told her. And some tension left her shoulders.

"We're sure not going anywhere," she muttered softly. "Tick tock, Lia."

Yes—every moment they waited meant increasing chances of discovery—not just of this group, but of the entire enterprise.

With no other option, I reached for Ambrose and Merle, delicately seeking their auras while skulking around the looming presences of the red and black wizards. Merle responded with a quiet purple crackle of a question. I showed him an image of Sondra and the captives in the stair.

Resignation—and worry—flowed from him, and with a sigh of acknowledgment, he flew off. I didn't want to go with Merle—I wanted to stay with Con, try to help—but I apparently had no choice. He pulled me with him, and I was snatched away.

They were bringing Rhéiane to the throne room. At any moment, the guards would drag my sister into the room and I'd lay eyes on her for the first time since that horrible day so long ago.

And they would hurt her.

They'd hurt Rhéiane to hurt me. And it would work.

The red wizard, though, had said that he'd already sent for Rhéiane—and I knew right when he'd done it, too. He'd taken one long look at me and sent the page on an errand, but they hadn't brought Rhéiane yet. Maybe she was already away. On the ship, or even sailing to Calanthe without us.

Bright Ejarat and Sawehl, I hoped so.

I shrugged, as nonchalantly as I could. "Sure, let's bargain. That's why we're here. Though I don't know who this Renee is."

Anure nearly rolled his eyes at me. "You're no idiot, Slave King of Oriel. You remember your sister. Unless working in My mines poisoned your brain into stupidity. I hear that happens, along with other, terrible physical tolls. Tell Me—how's your father? Oh, wait, I do believe he died on Vurgmun." He grinned at me with cruel delight.

I clamped down on every vile and raging part of myself, refusing to let the howling, wounded wolf in me rise to the bait. *He's poking at you, figuring out what you really care about.* "I wouldn't know. I haven't been there myself in a long time." I bared my teeth. "I pardoned myself, just like I've been helping myself to anything I wanted, including the Flower of Calanthe."

That worked to distract him—some fruitful testing of my own—and Anure jerked with rage. "You will give Me what is *Mine*," he shouted. "And it is *all* Mine!"

"Not this," I replied easily, showing him the case still chained to my manacles. "If you want this—with or without Queen Euthalia—you'd better offer me something more than idle threats."

Anure made a sound of disgust. "You weary Me. Take the ring."

The black wizard came close enough to reach for the case, but I held it well out of his reach. I topped the old guy by at least a head, and I'd have felt a bit like a bully playing keep-away if the stakes hadn't been so high. I also knew, though, that the fragile-looking elder swallowed in his cowled black robe wasn't anyone to be taken lightly. If I'd learned nothing else from Ambrose—and Merle—it was not to make assumptions based on appearances.

"It is definitely Her Highness's hand and finger," the black wizard called back to his brethren, eyes glittering as they fixed on me, like a snake measuring its striking distance.

"And the ring?" the red wizard inquired.

"It is the magic of the Abiding Ring, but . . . I need to inspect it more closely." The black wizard smiled at Percy. "Lord Percy, you may undo the chains. I'm sure you'll be pleased to be relieved of this responsibility, as you were of so many others in your frivolous youth."

Percy pulled a key from the pocket of his full skirts and turned to me.

"No!" I snarled. "I won't give it to them."

The black wizard only shook his head. "You will. Lower your arms, please. I'm sure they're terribly tired."

My arms *were* tired. The strength fell out of them like water falling to the earth, draining them. They dropped of their own deadweight. I wasn't surprised—I'd been warned—but it was deeply unnerving. Lia could reverse intention, but this . . .

Percy unlocked the chain that attached the case to my manacles—simultaneously slipping the pin that held the manacles together—and removed the chain leash. As he did, he flicked the sparker embedded in the bottom of the case, starting the fuse on Brenda's smaller, more potent bomb. The countdown had begun. We had ten minutes—or less—before Agatha's new, slower-burning fuse, nicely housed in a ventilated case—set off the bomb. Percy and I would both be counting, and I hoped to blessed Ejarat between the two of us we'd get it right and be gone before it went off.

If they did bring Rhéiane into the room before that . . . It didn't bear thinking of.

"Hand me that case, please," the black wizard instructed. I made a show of resisting but gave it over. "So obliging." He carried the case to the red wizard, both of them bending their heads over it.

"An orchid ring," the red wizard announced, "and one touched by Her Highness's elemental magic. Along with something else quite intriguing." He looked back at the blue wizard, who stood unmoving. "Her Highness's living essence has recently come in contact with this, which confirms that She lives. A clever facsimile, but this is not the Abiding Ring."

The black wizard curled his lip, released his grip on the case, and let it fall to the marble floor where it shattered, sending fragments skittering as far as my feet. The heavier base containing the packed vurgsten thudded intact, and it was all I could do not to flinch in anticipation of it going off.

But it didn't—Brenda had crafted it well, and the metal compartment stayed intact—so I moved on to the next worry: that the fuse had either gone out or never sparked. If it had sparked: nine minutes left.

Lia's severed finger had bounced a distance from the hand, the orchid's petals crushed. The hand itself fell palm down, a withered and dead thing, and the wizard in black gave it a little kick, sending it farther from him. I had to viciously rein my temper at the sight of them treating her with such disregard.

"Of course that's not the Abiding Ring," I sneered. "That ring is still on Her Highness's finger, where it will stay until she passes it to her heir. You lose, False Emperor."

"You'll suffer for this," Anure ground out. "Where is Lady Rhéiane? You will watch us torture her, Slave King, and then you will die."

Percy yawned elaborately, fanning fingers over his mouth in an elegantly polite gesture, holding up three, then five of them. Yeah, that was my count, too. Eight minutes until that bomb blew.

A guard came running into the room, out of breath. Then snapped to attention, bowed deeply, straightened—and hesitated. He brought bad news he clearly didn't want to speak, but in our favor or not?

"Captain Jan?" Anure inquired silkily. "What is the meaning of this?"

"Your Imperial Majesty. Honored syrs." Jan bowed to Anure and the wizards. "There's been an escape attempt. Lady Rhéiane is gone."

This time Anure didn't blow. He went white and still, his hard gaze fastening on me. "Where are they?"

I shrugged, nearly giddy with relief. "How should I know? I've been here with you."

"You will die for this," Anure snarled. "Executioner!"

Finally. My brief hope that we'd be sent out of the throne room for execution died as a large figure in scarlet leather from head to toe—including a full face mask with slits for eyes and a few holes around the nose for air—stepped out from behind the throne, carrying a large double-bladed axe. Handy to have an executioner so nearby. Not so handy for us, when we'd been counting on being removed from the throne room, for imprisonment, torture, or execution, it didn't matter what, so long as we weren't near that bomb. Seven minutes to get out of here.

The figure strode toward us, and I eyed his axe, liking the look of its heft and balance. Maybe I could get it away from him. Risky, though.

"If you kill us," I said in a loud, carrying voice, "you'll never get to Euthalia. Your wizards know they can't penetrate the enchantments of Calanthe. Lord Percy and I are prepared to offer you a deal—but the first stipulation is that our heads remain attached to our necks."

Anure studied us, looking from one to the other, then to the false orchid ring lying among the glass fragments. Enraged, impetuous, greedy, self-involved—but not stupid, I reminded myself. We'd pretty much played this out. Lia was right as usual: We'd never have spun this audience to an hour.

Ten minutes sure went fast, though.

"If you can offer Me that . . ." Anure said slowly. Much too slowly. I reined in my anxious impatience. "Then why try to trick Me with this fake flower?"

I shrugged nonchalantly, baring my teeth in an insulting grin. "I thought you might be stupid enough to fall for that. Better for me, if I could get away with it."

"A miscalculation, Slave King and worthless cousin of Mine."

"I wasn't so worthless to Your Imperial Majesty once," Percy crooned, bowing with an elaborate twirl of his hands. "I care not how you handle this beastly rebel, but I could be of service to You, as I once was. I beseech You to end my exile. The bargain we have still to offer Your Imperial Majesty is enticing indeed." From the depths of his obeisance, Percy slid me a wide-eyed look, placing five fingers against his cheekbone. Yeah, right. We needed to go or be blazed with the rest of them.

Anure shifted restlessly on his throne, ignoring Percy,

glaring at me. Pursing his lips as he thought, trying to see through the trick he sensed.

Time ticked away and I looked down at Vesno, waiting quietly at my heel. Could I risk sending the wolfhound out of the room? If he'd even go. Likely not, with his steadfast loyalty. I sent a silent apology to Lia. She wouldn't forgive me for getting myself killed, but I wanted to offer it anyway. I also greatly regretted that I'd never see Rhéiane again. Never see Oriel. Never know if this gambit succeeded.

At least Lia would be safe, and she'd have our child. I would've given her something for all she'd done to show me what it was to live, and love.

"What could either of you worthless curs possibly offer Me?" Anure finally asked, his greed getting the better of him.

"Queen Euthalia, herself, with the Abiding Ring on her finger, obedient to your command and willing," I said, though the words felt like glass in my mouth. "I can deliver her to you—for a price."

Anure considered, tapping his fingers on the throne. Percy slid me a glance from the corner of his eye, gave a slight, rueful shrug. Yeah, we could only buy time for the bomb to go off now. No way were we getting out of here in time to escape the blast.

Vesno yipped, rising from his haunches slightly and giving an excited wag of his tail. I set a hand on his head, quieting him. It took everything in me not to look at the square holding the vurgsten bomb.

The wizard in blue leaned to say something to Anure. The emperor considered, then chopped a hand impatiently. "I weary of talking. And of the stink of you both. Execute them. Starting with my cousin." Anure smiled

thinly. "I should have done this long ago, you presumptu-
ous, arrogant ass."

The guards seized Percy, and he grimaced at me in resignation. Would he lose his head before the bomb went
off? Either way, we were both dead. I opened my mouth
to at least taunt Anure—

Then came a blinding flash.

24

Merle moved with mind-battering speed—dragging me with him faster than I could consciously follow—and stopped us with a metaphysical *bang!* that knocked the breath from my lungs in my faraway body. I caught up mentally and surveyed Sondra and the other captives where they anxiously hid in the stairwell. A guard lay prone and bleeding sluggishly. Two servants had been tied and gagged, propped more gently in a corner. So they'd had company—and had handled it. Merle manifested, appearing before Sondra as the part man, part raven I'd met in the astral realm, wearing the purple wizard's robes.

Sondra reacted faster than thought, recognizing him immediately as one of Anure's wizards from the throne room that day, and swung the stick to lash him with it. Merle didn't move to stop her.

And I understood why Merle had forced me to come along.

"No," I told her, and in my panic, I stopped her hand. She froze in disbelief—both that I had, and that I could.

"Lia?" Sondra scanned the air in my general vicinity. "Don't stop me! Look at him! This is one of—"

"I know, but it's also Merle, our friend. Trust Me. Follow him."

I felt it, the moment she made the reluctant choice to trust me, and I released her.

"Con?" she asked.

"Alive. I'm going to him now. When you get the captives to the ship, set sail," I added. *"That's a royal command."*

Merle inclined his head, then pointed me in the direction of the throne room. Casting a purple glow over them all, he opened the door and strode out. After a bare moment of hesitation, Sondra took Rhéiane's hand. Exchanging a solemn look, they followed Merle, the rest of the captives trotting behind like trusting ducklings.

Hoping against hope that they'd make it, I flew back to Con.

I didn't bother with subtlety this time, and Ambrose felt me enter the throne room, his blue-robed figure familiar to me from that nightmarish time before. As with Merle, he looked unlike himself as I knew him on Calanthe—but that ancient forest feel to him hummed beneath, like distant music. He gave me a slight nod of acknowledgment. Vesno also lifted his head, giving a yip of welcome, and Con quieted him.

Con, who was chained before Anure. A large and menacing figure, dressed in scarlet leather from head to toe and carrying a large double-bladed axe, loomed over Con and Percy. Anure's executioner no doubt. I would yell at Con later about his stupid plan.

Ruthlessly shoving down my panic—if ever I needed my icy calm, it was now—I quickly assessed the rest of the scene.

The wizard in purple seemed to be there but stood immobile, a placeholder for Merle who was risking himself to evacuate our captives. Fifteen minutes to get them to the ship. The false orchid ring lay among glass fragments, the square base that held the real vurgsten bomb beside it. I touched it with my mind and found it moments from exploding. Bomb or execution—Con was going to die.

Unless I stopped it.

So stop it I would. I snuffed out the spark, leaving the bomb inert.

Noting my action, Ambrose spoke quietly to Anure. The black and red wizards, standing together, seemed to sniff the air, as if sensing my presence. A lance of glasslike obsidian sliced in my direction. I ducked it, a move I'd practiced during that long night with Ambrose and Merle. As I did, Anure spoke, and the guards seized Percy, the executioner moving into position. Merle remained immobile, not yet returned to this body, which meant the captives were not yet safe.

It was up to me to save Percy and Con—and I couldn't do it as a ghost with minor magics.

Resolved, I narrowed myself back into my physical body, the map tower coming into focus around me. I could do this. Moving my foot, the jewelry heels tinkling musically, I touched the solidity of the rock hammer. Gathering the power of Calanthe, I stepped through the physical distance, bringing the rock hammer with me, and manifested in Anure's throne room with a clap of sound and light, the laws of our reality shuddering in protest.

Con gaped at me. Everyone did, except Ambrose, who grinned with youthful exuberance. He lifted hands, miming a silent round of applause. I kept an eye on Merle, who remained motionless. They weren't clear yet. *Come on.*

"Lia?" Con asked tentatively, a confusion of reactions on his face. "Are you really . . . here?" Vesno bounced to me, licking my hand.

"In the flesh," I replied wryly. I toed the rock hammer, giving Con a slow smile. "I believe this is yours."

He grinned, his dimple winking into existence like the sun through storm clouds. Popping the manacles apart, he hefted the rock hammer and swung it at a raft of guards that, finally recovered from the shock of my appearance, advanced on me with swords pointed. The guards fell before Con's mighty swing like wheat before a scythe.

He wheeled on the executioner, who'd paused, double-bladed axe poised. "You'll want to put that down," Con growled. "And *not* on Percy's neck." The executioner hastily obeyed, setting down the axe and raising his hands in surrender. The guards holding Percy released him and Percy regained his feet, straightening his clothes, then bowed deeply.

"Your Highness," he said with reverence that, for once, I felt I deserved.

Look at what I can do.

Anure had slowly risen, staring at me with astonishment—and glittering lust, whether for me or the jewels I wore. Behind me, waves of reaction muttered through his court. Shock, awe, and . . . hope?

I turned to face them, giving Anure my back in contempt, raising my voice. "I am Her Highness Queen Euthalia of Calanthe. Conrí of Oriel and I have come to release you from your service to the interloper. Today the false empire falls." They all shifted, murmuring, watching me with wide eyes and tense expressions—and noticing my glittering costume, more wealth than they'd seen on anyone but Anure in ages. "You don't want to be here," I added gently. "I advise you to go. Now."

For a frozen second, no one moved—then they fled, some sending up inarticulate cries, others moving with the sly stealth of professional sycophants. I turned back from the wave of their frantic exit and glided forward, pausing at Con's side. Percy stepped behind and to the side of us.

"Lia," Con said out of the side of his mouth. "The bomb is . . ."

"Handled," I replied just as quietly. Merle still hadn't moved. How long had it been?

Anure sat again, attempting to pull his cloak of Emperor of All the World around him, but to my eye his confidence had taken a blow, the holes in his composure growing larger as fear shredded it. "What is the meaning of this uncouth display, Euthalia?" he sneered. "Prancing about in your jewels and frightening My court with petty tricks worthy of a street magician. You will pay for this. Guards—seize her."

The guards started for me again, and Con swung his rock hammer, taking out three at once. I blew a kiss at the ones approaching my side, sending them tumbling until they lay still. I leveled a cold stare on Anure. "You were saying?"

He opened and closed his mouth like a fish, then pointed at his wizards. "Deal with her!"

The red and black wizards had been conferring. They gestured for Ambrose and Merle to join them. Ambrose gazed back, standing very near Anure, and shook his head slowly. The red wizard hissed a command and the black wizard started up the throne's steps, stopping at Merle, seizing his arm. Or the spot where Merle's arm should have been. The purple robe shivered, then fell into an empty puddle of cloth. Confounded, the black wizard stared at it, then turned back to me, expression contorted in a rictus of rage.

The red wizard glided toward me, his smooth face mild, black eyes glittering with venom. "What have You done, Your Highness?" he asked with soft menace.

"What you only dreamed of," I replied in the same tone. "What I was born to do—and what you will never be able to do, you hack thief and humbug."

I crouched, laying the hand with the orchid ring against the cool marble. "Observe."

The tendrils of my consciousness spun down into the earth, the orchid reaching for the spirit of the land sleeping beneath the hulk of the citadel. It rumbled in reply, coming awake with vigor, answering my call in a very different voice than Calanthe's.

"It seems You've learned some things since last we met." The red wizard smiled thinly, expression calculating, the glint in his eyes acquisitive. "But Your Highness is a rank amateur, and You meddle at Your peril. This is scratching the surface of what You can do. Work with me and I can teach You. I have the knowledge You will need."

The connection to Yekpehr established, I stood slowly, making sure the thread from the orchid ring to the land stayed strong. I gazed back into the mild and cruel eyes of my chief torturer, his ruthlessly cold savagery veiled with an academic's manner. Beyond him, Ambrose remained near Anure, a restraining hand on Anure's shoulder, gaze on me and not on the raging black wizard, who'd climbed the steps to shout at him, gesturing wildly. Anure looked stunned, staring at me as if he'd never seen me before.

"No, thank you," I replied, pouring the living vitality of Calanthe into Yekpehr, prodding the monster. "I've tasted your brand of tutelage and I don't care to again." Facing him like this, I found I wasn't afraid, that I could touch those memories and they didn't weaken me. I was no longer his prisoner and plaything. I tickled Yekpehr and the ground rumbled beneath us, a stone falling from the ceiling to the floor with a *boom!* Small stones ricocheted from the impact, and dust filled the air.

Something flickered in the red wizard's gaze, and he signaled to the black wizard. Nerves? "You're a reckless fool. You have no idea how difficult it is to hold a land one has acquired."

"Don't I?" I asked softly, noting how the black wizard picked his way down the steps toward us. "I think I know far more than you ever will, you with your stolen blood and pretensions to power." Yekpehr rumbled in agreement, several windows shattering.

The red wizard winced. "You can't hold two lands at once. You need someone of the blood or You'll doom us all."

I didn't show my dismay, but he was right on that. Already I could feel Yekpehr shaking off my leash. It knew I had no right to it—and it roared for one who did. I should've thought to ask if any of Yekpehr's royal line remained among the captives. Surely there must be someone, since Anure had tamed it.

A raven flew into the room. Shedding purple sparks and black feathers, he zoomed to land on the black wizard's shoulder, beads of blood welling up from where Merle's suddenly wicked talons pierced the wizard's flesh. The red wizard made no move to help his colleague; he watched the orchid ring with rapt fascination.

Agatha and Sondra ran into the throne room, following after Merle, and skidded to a halt at the sight of the enormous room empty but for unconscious guards, shards of glass and stone, and the few of us. Though I was happy to see Sondra, I shot her a glare. "I thought I told you to set sail with the captives."

"What?" Sondra yelled, as if hard of hearing. She banged the heel of her hand against her ear. "Did You say something?"

I did my best not to laugh. The yearning of Yekpehr

stretched that direction, reaching—not for the ship in the harbor with the captives—but for Agatha.

Ah. Several pieces settled into place.

"Bring Agatha to Me, Con."

He did, without question, offering Agatha his arm as if at a formal event and escorting her to me. Crouching again to place my ring hand on the marble floor, I held out the other for Agatha. Anure screeched and was silenced. The red wizard watched with narrowed eyes, unmoving otherwise, pinned in Merle's grip.

"Behold the power of the Abiding Ring," I told him as Agatha slipped her cold, spindly fingers through mine. The world seemed to spin as I connected Agatha to her land again, handing over those pulsing reins with relief.

Yekpehr groaned mightily, like a lover reunited with the beloved thought dead, and Agatha seemed to swell with that vigor, her papery skin taking on a glow as the sharp bones of her face softened, gaining fullness of life like a wilted plant finally watered.

"Nooo!" Anure howled, and I released Agatha, standing again. I swayed, dizzy as Calanthe rushed in to fill the hole Yekpehr left in me, and Con caught me with a strong arm around my waist. I looked up at him and he grinned down at me, fierce and proud.

The red wizard backed away, staring at Agatha as if she were something monstrous. Then at me, with wonder. "It's true," he whispered. "You are the promised queen."

"I've had enough of prophecies, quite frankly. Regardless, I can do what you never will. Choke on that."

Face contorting with rage, he grew in size, his presence reaching into multiple dimensions, the dense bloodred sphere of his being truly frightening to behold—and anchored to our reality by only a flimsy strand of a flesh-and-blood body. With a sharp thought, I seized that slim physical connection, holding him fast so he could not escape. "Hit him," I told Con.

Without hesitation Con swung the rock hammer, crushing the wizard with a single blow. He crumpled, leaving barely a red smear on the dusty marble. The black wizard shrieked, lunging for Sondra, Merle clinging to his shoulder—grabbing for the walking stick she yanked out of reach. "That is mine," he snarled.

"All right," Sondra replied with her flesh-eating grin. "Catch!"

"No!" he screamed as she threw it at him. He dove to catch it. Merle vanished in a cloud of purple shards. The stick hit the floor just as the black wizard did, a bilious cloud rising up. When it cleared, he'd vanished, leaving only a bit of ragged black cloth behind.

"Save Me," Anure shrieked to Ambrose and Merle. "Do something, you idiots."

Merle in raven form circled, then came to land on Con's shoulder. Anure gaped, then turned his pleading to his one remaining wizard. Ambrose, hand still on Anure's shoulder, gazed down at him with something akin to compassion. "You are destroyed," he said softly.

"Anure Robho," I said in a clear voice, the one I used for delivering a sentence of execution, though I would not be the one to decide his fate, a burden I was happy to hand over, "you are nothing but a sad, pitiful excuse for a human being. Look around you. You are alone. The lands you stole are slipping from your grasp. They will be returned to their rightful bloodlines, just as I have returned Yekpehr to Queen Agatha's care." I bowed to her and she inclined her head regally, then turned her gaze on Anure.

"Get off My throne," she said.

Merle flew up into a cawing spiral. Ambrose gave Anure a shove. He tumbled down the long steps, falling in an ignominious heap at the bottom, weeping and protesting. Cutting his hands on the shattered glass, he held them up to first Con, then me—showing us the blood as if we might take pity.

"Please," Anure sobbed, "have mercy. I never meant for it to get so . . . large. It was the wizards! They put a spell on Me to want more and more. I only wanted Valencia. For My mother who loved Me and was cruelly used. I only sought justice, and what was supposed to be Mine. Percy! You remember, how it was in the beginning."

"I do." Percy gazed on the sobbing mess with true pity, perhaps seeing him from long ago. Con met my gaze, a promise there of a story to be told.

"Help Me, cousin," Anure pleaded. "I'll give you Valencia to rule, as we both know it should've been yours all along. I'll give you Aekis! Or more. Whatever you want. You helped Me, so I'll help you. We were always as brothers."

"We were," Percy agreed sorrowfully. "But I disavow all relation, all affection. You are nothing to me." Percy looked to me. "Can You restore Valencia to me, as you did with Agatha—if that is the boon I ask of You?"

"I can, and I will," I promised. "But I will because it belongs to you by right of blood. You may ask another boon of Me."

Percy shook his head. "I only want Valencia, so I can take responsibility for my land, as I should have done to begin with. Perhaps by reversing that first, terrible mistake, I can take one step in a long journey to make amends." He turned and walked away from Anure.

Con stood over the crumbled and sniveling heap that had been the false emperor, fingers flexing on the rock hammer. He glanced at me, eyes gold flames in his dark face, black hair hanging wild, and he shook his head a little, as if clearing it. "Rhéiane?"

"Safe," Sondra told him, then clapped him on the shoulder. "And reasonably sane. Anxious to see you, so I'm glad you're not dead, Conrí."

"Thanks." He snorted. They both turned their gazes on Anure, bonelessly sniveling at their feet. Indeed, the man had been reduced to less than nothing. "Here we stand," Con said, "after all this time."

Sondra nodded. "Not quite how I pictured this moment."

"No torch," Con commented, and she grinned at him. They both glanced at me as if asking permission.

"Go ahead," I told them. "Kill him if you need to."

They exchanged a long look, and Sondra held up her hands with a sigh. "I think this is enough."

Con let out a breath, too, and set down the rock hammer. "Yeah. You're right, Lia. This is enough. And this decision belongs to the ruler here." He glanced to Agatha. "That *is* You in the portrait hall at Calanthe, isn't it? Your Highness," he added.

Agatha smiled wryly. "Long ago—and now again, it seems. Thank You, Your Highness," she said to me.

"See if You still thank Me after a few days of all the work You have to do, Your Highness," I replied drily, and she laughed. I ended up smiling back—and I realized that I'd never had this. Agatha would be a peer, a colleague of sorts. I was no longer alone.

"I'll leave Anure to You, Your Highness," Con said with a slight bow, and Agatha nodded.

"This is going to get confusing fast," Sondra complained, "with so many queens about."

Con turned to me. "Thank you for coming to my rescue."

"Well," I offered with a regal nod, "I owed you one."

"The 'promised queen,' huh?" He raised a brow, uncertainty in it, so I cupped his face in my hand and gave him a long kiss.

"Who knows? I'm still me."

Emotions crossed his face like rapidly moving clouds, but he firmed his jaw, then kissed me back. "Yes," he replied, as if I'd asked him something else entirely. "You always are. Let's get out of here."

"First we must free Ambrose," I told him.

He looked confused, and I indicated Ambrose still up on the steps, Merle in raven form perched on the arm of the throne. Con's expression darkened. "Ambrose?" he said, finally putting it together in the aftermath of all the furor. His fingers flexed. "He's one of Anure's wizards?"

"And Merle," I confirmed.

"I'm going to strangle them both, those fucking traitors."

"No," I said, stopping him with a hand on his arm. "It's a long story, but it's not what you think. Trust me."

Con gave me a long look, hearing that I'd asked him as the woman, not the queen. Slowly, he nodded. "As you wish, Lia."

Love burst through me. "Bring your rock hammer." Taking his hand, I led him to the steps of the throne. "Suffice to say," I added as we climbed, picking our way through the scattered treasure from so many forgotten kingdoms, "that Ambrose and Merle have been prisoners of Anure and his wizards as much as anyone. And we would not have succeeded without them."

"That's not precisely true," Ambrose called cheerfully. "There's not a direct, linear relationship between my intervention and the ensuing events. You could argue that—"

"Ambrose," I interrupted, "better to stop while you're ahead."

"Excellent point, Your Highness." He cocked his head at Merle. "I told you."

Merle cawed in reply.

Laying my hands on Ambrose, using the same technique that I'd used to tether the red wizard long enough to sever his physical attachment to this world, I made the manacle tethering Ambrose's leg show itself. Con frowned at it, perplexed. "How did Ambrose—"

"Please don't get him started," I cautioned, and Ambrose beamed angelically. "Just break it?"

Con swung his hammer on the chain, and it dissolved as if it had never been. Ambrose sighed like a person relieved of a tremendous weight. "It really is a long story," he assured Con.

"I don't care," Con snarled. "You come near me or mine again and I'll kill you."

"As for that," Ambrose replied cheerfully, "I think I'll call in that favor you promised when I saved Her Highness's life."

Con stared at him in fulminous realization. He glanced at me and I shrugged. I'd warned him not to make cavalier promises to a wizard. "You can't make me forgive you," he shouted, swinging back on Ambrose.

The wizard held up his palms, sorrow in his face. "We don't ask forgiveness. Only your forbearance." He looked to me, nodding in confirmation that they'd asked the same of me.

"What will you do now?" I asked.

Ambrose and Merle exchanged a long look, the raven cawing softly. Ambrose nodded. "Our erstwhile colleagues are fled, but not destroyed. We have much to do." The air folded around him, and he manifested in a green robe, looking young, his staff topped by the emerald. Merle flew to it. "We'll see you again someday, Euthalia, Conrí."

"Don't count on it," Con grumbled. I lifted a hand, able to see the threads of their transmutation to another reality . . . until they were cut off, and Merle and Ambrose were gone.

Con turned down the steps, kicking and picking through the treasure, looking for something. I knew what it was—perhaps they all guessed, for everyone waited patiently. At last he bent down and retrieved a crown, glittering with fat rubies.

"The crown of Oriel," I said on a sigh.

He nodded, grief and satisfaction giving him an almost relaxed mien. "Let's find yours."

I shook my head, indicating the crown I wore. "I have one. I don't need more than this."

"We'll catalog everything," Agatha said, surveying the immensity of the job with some dismay. "As Your Highness restores the other bloodlines to their lands, they'll be wanting their crowns—and no doubt funding to rebuild."

"Good thinking," I told her. "We'll stay in communication?"

"Of course." Agatha studied the pile. "I suppose mine is there too, somewhere."

"Do you want help looking?" Sondra offered.

"No." Agatha gave us a sad smile. "I think I need some time alone, to . . . equilibrate."

Nodding in understanding, I inclined my head. "Best of luck. Call on Me for anything at all. I still owe You a boon."

She spread her hands at the ruined throne room. "This is more than enough, Your Highness. You've given

Me something I never thought to have again." Emotion threaded through her voice.

Having known the agony of separation from Calanthe, I understood. "This was Your due. And You won't have an easy road ahead. You'll think of something You need. When You do, ask."

"Thank You, Euthalia."

I smiled at the sound of my name from her. My peer and companion. Con cocked his head at the exit. "Ready to leave this place?"

Yes. Yes, I was.

25

The *Emperor's Pet* had set sail as soon as Sondra and Agatha had bolted for the citadel to rescue us—at least Kara and Brenda followed Lia's orders—so we went to the *Last Resort*. The citadel and harbor were in utter chaos, and Percy sailed us out of the harbor with little trouble and all speed. Vesno and Sondra stood with Percy at the wheel, leaving Lia and me to recline on the couch under the awning. Already the smoke was clearing from the sky, the vurgsten on the walls petering out into wisps without the wizards to sustain the blaze.

For a while we just held each other—and I wondered if she was as surprised as I to be with me, in the flesh. "You're really here," I finally said.

"Apparently so," she replied in a dry tone.

"And what exactly aren't you wearing?" I asked, tracing her warm, velvety skin between two cool, diamond-studded chains.

"I needed to put on a show, just in case I didn't have access to magic when I arrived," she answered. "I wasn't at all sure how it would go, as I'd never tried that before."

"Then you didn't have a plan." I made sure to look shocked and horrified. "Tell me it's not so!"

"I was improvising," she confided, then laughed. "Can you believe it?"

"No." I shook my head. "I don't even know what you did. How are you here—and with Calanthe's magic?"

"The orchid ring," she replied, eyes dancing. "It allows Me to connect to Calanthe—to preserve My roots there—no matter where I might go. I didn't know how to do it before, but I do now."

"Then you can survive anywhere?" I said, realization dawning.

She followed my thinking easily. "For short times, anyway. I can't live on My own, but I bring Calanthe with Me. Con . . . I know what you're thinking, but I'll still have to spend most of My time on Calanthe. Besides, it's My sacred—"

"Duty," I finished for her.

"Love and responsibility," she corrected. "I love you, Con, with everything in Me—but I am Calanthe and She is Me. I cannot separate the two."

"I don't want you to," I told her, lifting her hand and kissing her delicate fingers. "But you can travel some . . . to the other kingdoms?"

"Yes, and I will have to. I can awaken the inherent spirit of any land, connect it to the rightful blood again, as I did with Agatha and Yekpehr."

"Can you—" The sharp hope caught in my throat, and I had to clear it. "Can you restore Oriel?"

"Yes." She laid a hand on my cheek. "We'll go to Oriel first and I'll return your throne to you."

I turned my face and kissed her palm. "Not to me. To Rhéiane."

"Con, you don't know that—"

"I'm going to find out," I said. "If Rhéiane can't rule,

then I'll find a regent. We'll go to Oriel, but on our honey-moon." I laid a hand over her flat belly, the jewels an edged contrast to the soft heat of her body. "I want to be a father to my child, a husband to you. On Calanthe. Lia, will you marry me?"

I'd flustered her, and she searched for words. For once I wasn't glad to have gotten the advantage of her, I was so impatient for her reply. "Con—"

"Sails ho!" Percy called.

"Sorry to interrupt you lovebirds," Sondra added, "but the *Emperor's Pet* lies ahead."

I got up and gave a hand to Lia. "We'll discuss this more."

"Yes," she muttered ungraciously. "We certainly will."

We took the skiff to the *Emperor's Pet*, everyone crowd-ing the decks at the sight of us. Kara bent over the rail, hauling me up and into a back-pounding embrace. Then he grasped my shoulders and grinned at me, the rare joy in it nearly splitting his sere, dark face. "You did it."

"Lia did it," I corrected, helping her onto the deck.

"*We* did it," Lia corrected, a wide smile on her face. "All of us."

Percy followed up the ladder, then Sondra, carrying Vesno over one shoulder. Brenda grinned and waved, her arm linked through another woman's with the same jaw-line. Looked like she'd found one of her Derten relations. I waved back, giving her a gesture of congratulations. Lia nudged my arm, pointing me at the dark-haired woman ap-proaching.

White wings striped her black hair from the temples, but even without having looked at her portrait, I would have known her anywhere. I could lay the fears that I'd for-gotten her to rest. "Rhéiane," I breathed, my voice hoarse and lungs tight—though, under the clearing blue skies, not from vurgsten.

She flung herself into my arms, and I held her, careful of her birdlike bones. Tall as me, but so thin. Tears clogged my throat as she leaned back to frame my face with her hands. "Little Conrí," she said, tears streaming freely down her face. "Look at you. You're taller than Father was. Wider in the shoulder, too."

That's what Mother said, I thought but didn't say aloud. I hoped they were watching as she'd said. "Rhéiane, I am so sorry that—"

She stopped me, eyes so large in her lined face. "No apologies." Then she smiled. "It's so good to see you."

"Yes." I cleared my throat, then released her and held out a hand to Lia. She floated to me, a vision of sparkling jewels, shining like the sea.

"Rhéiane, this is my wife, Lia. Queen Euthalia of Calanthe."

"Your wife?" Rhéiane looked at Lia, taking in her ostentatious costume, then focusing on her mismatched eyes and extraordinary blossoming hair. Then Rhéiane looked at me, her expression full of wonder. "Con. . . . she's like the girl in that book we read—remember? The flower fairy princess."

"I do remember." I nodded. "I forgot a lot of things over the years, but I remember you reading that book to me, showing me that illustration."

Rhéiane gave me an odd half smile. "You said you were going to marry a girl like that someday."

That halted me. "I did?"

"Yes," Rhéiane breathed. "It's just like magic."

"Not just like it," I corrected, "it is magic."

"Where are my manners?" Rhéiane took Lia's proffered hands and held them as she gazed at her, then she curtsied deeply. "It's beyond wonderful to meet You, Your Highness."

"Likewise," Lia replied. "We're relieved to find you again. You're all Con has thought of, once we knew you were alive."

"Thank You, Your Highness," Rhéiane replied gravely, "for freeing us."

Lia extracted her hands and patted me on the shoulder. "I'll let you two talk alone."

We watched her stroll over to Brenda, the sunlight glinting off her jewels so brightly it hurt to look at her. "My baby brother's wife," Rhéiane repeated, as if still trying to make sense of the words. She looked at me again. "Somehow, though I knew that you must have grown up—if you'd lived—I still saw you in my head as a little boy."

"I know the feeling," I said. "You haven't changed, though."

She didn't smile, her mouth twisting. "I have. I've aged, grown brittle. There's so much . . ."

"I know," I said, wishing there was more to say.

She surveyed me. "You've suffered, too, judging by the scars. I know Mother died in Oriel, but Father?"

"Died on Vurgmun," I told her bluntly. "I was with him, but . . ." I blew out a breath for those old sorrows and hopelessness. "There was nothing I could do."

She raised her tawny eyes to mine, sharing that grief. "But there was, and you did it. I've been hearing the tales. You led a revolution and tore down Anure's empire. My brother, the hero."

I almost couldn't choke the words past the emotion. "I'm no hero. You're the one who survived all the . . . I can't imagine what . . ."

She laid a finger over my lips. "We have time now, to shed all the tears, to tell the stories." She smiled then, dropping her hand to poke my arm. "Like how you married the Queen of Flowers."

We both turned to look at Lia, the ocean breeze tugging at her long hair, a few flower petals detaching to dance away. "It's another long story," I said, "but I'm going to have to marry her again."

Rhéiane considered me. "What of Oriel? I thought you did all of this to win your throne back."

I shook my head. "I did what I did for a lot of reasons, but none of them so noble as that." Taking a breath, I met her gaze. "The throne of Oriel is yours, if you're willing."

Searching my face, she hesitated, then nodded. "Yes. You don't have to ask twice. Rebuilding Oriel is . . . It will be good for me. That dream has kept me alive."

Relief flooding me, I opened my arms, and she fitted herself against me. "Whatever I can do to help," I said hoarsely, "I'll do it. I'm better at destroying than building but . . . I've gotta learn sometime. We'll make it right."

"Yes." She squeezed me tight. "We will."

I let her go. "Now I just have to talk Lia into it."

Rhéiane laughed, sliding her gaze to Lia's dazzling form. "Will that be difficult?"

"No," I replied, giving her my cockiest grin. "She has a weakness for me."

Winking at my sister, I went to woo my wife.

26

"You make a beautiful bride, Your Highness," Ibolya said, dark eyes sparkling with delight and warm affection. My other ladies agreed, standing in a circle, beaming at the result of their labors.

They'd had some time to come up with this gown—days instead of hours, anyway, unlike my first wedding—while we sorted Anure's erstwhile captives and gave them the time and peace they needed to adjust to their greatly changed circumstances. Calanthe welcomed them in, Her tropical loveliness a balm to the scarred spirits, the pleasures of the Flower Court—and, for some, the Night Court—providing the joys and catharsis so desperately needed.

I wore white, because Con insisted that we follow tradition, no matter how untraditional our path to get here. He'd been insistent about a lot of the wedding details, seeming determined to set us firmly on that other time line, to create the world we would have had if not for the twists of fate that created the monster Anure, and the wizards who came to feed on the devastation he wrought.

Besides, he'd said, I had a reputation to uphold—and a responsibility to wear a gown worthy of the event of the century. He thought he was funny, bringing up the words I'd used to stall Anure so long ago. He had something of a point, however. We were launching a new era, and our wedding would be the long remembered as the first celebration following the defeat of Anure and the demise of his horrible empire.

The gown was dazzling, the skirts belling out in frothy layers that draped and scooped, light as clouds, scattered with crystals that caught the light. The bodice, made entirely of more crystals, rose from a trim waist to flare over my breasts. I'd experimented and learned to guide the patterns of leaves and blossoms on my skin, coaxing them into delicate fronds of orchids in shades of ivory and blush pink, accented with pale-green leaves. They flowered over my bosom, throat, and collarbones, then wound down my arms.

My hair, also blossoming with pale orchids, tumbled down my back in a waterfall. Diamond clips held a veil of spider silk lace to the back, with diamond strands draping between.

Sondra handed me my bouquet—an elaborate fall of more orchids, in hundreds of shades—and gave me a wry grin. "Nahua offered me one of Your wigs," she said, running a hand self-consciously over her cropped golden hair, "but I figure, who are we kidding? Unless You want me to wear one?"

"I think you look wonderful as is," I told her sincerely. Sondra had put on a dress and heels for me and that was enough. She and Rhéiane wore matching gowns of watered silk that shifted in shades of color from sapphire to ice blue. Simply made, the dresses complimented their tall, lean bodies, high-cut slits showing off long legs and scarves streaming from their shoulders adding drama. My ladies wore gowns in the same style but each in a single jewel-bright shade, and each carried a bouquet of orchids in matching colors.

The blossoms of the Flower Court, with Sondra and Rhéiane as honorary members, stunning in their loveliness—and their hidden thorns.

"Dare I ask if Conrí is ready?" I asked Rhéiane.

She shook her head in exasperation. "If Your Highness means, is he dressed, yes. Is he in position at the altar? No."

"I know he can't have cold feet," I said with a raised brow. Con had wanted to have the ceremony days ago, with the same insistence that he'd wanted a grand event for the history books. I told him he couldn't have it both ways and he'd agreed, if with ill grace.

"Should we delay, Your Highness?" Calla asked. "I believe everyone is assembled."

"Let Me see." I reached out to Vesno—who greeted me joyfully—and saw he was indeed with Con, both of them jogging toward where the ceremony would be on the cliffside. "He's nearly there now," I informed them. "Shall we?"

We stepped out of the tent I'd used to dress and into the bright sunshine of Calanthe, the crowd sending up a roar. Everyone who could had traveled to the palace for the ceremony, which worked out well because we were sending them home with wagonloads of supplies for the more distant and destitute corners of the island. Might as well take advantage of their travels. We paused on the apron held clear by sentries. I held on to my bouquet with both hands, but my attendants all waved to acknowledge the cheers. Even Sondra, I noted, followed instructions to smile. I called in clouds of butterflies to swirl around us and land on the bouquets we carried, bringing them alive with more color.

The aisle to the folly on the cliff opened up, and we began a sedate stroll through the calling people. Musicians played, and I encouraged the birds to sing along in harmony, so the melody filled the skies. At the folly, Con slid into place, saying something to the waiting Kara that had the somber man grinning and shaking his head. They, along with Percy, wore midnight blue edged with silver and gold. I'd been surprised that Con wanted Percy to stand up with him, but he'd said it made sense to him. They'd bonded on that journey in some way, and I wouldn't question it.

As we drew close, I saw that Vesno, sitting at Con's heel, wore a matching wreath of deep-blue orchids with silver and gold ribbons. It made me laugh, and I wondered who'd thought of it. As I raised my gaze to Con's, to his dimpled grin as he witnessed my reaction, I knew it had been him. He sobered then, eyes blazing golden as he took me in, his smile turning half wistful as his gaze went to Sondra and Rhéiane, flanking me a step behind. Likely he'd never imagined a day like this.

In all truth, neither had I.

I stepped into the shade of the folly, turning my shoulder to the sea, facing Con. He wore his black hair loose, brushed to a glossy sheen, and the breezes lifted the ends, toying with them playfully. Neither of us wore our crowns. Though this was an affair of state—and an event to be shared with our people, of Calanthe, Oriel, and all the scattered kingdoms—we'd wanted to marry each other as ourselves.

Con held his hands out to me, a challenging glint in his eyes. I handed my bouquet to Sondra and put both of my hands in his. Big, rough from wielding his rock hammer, forever stained from working the vurgsten mines, his hands were as familiar to me now as coming home.

True to his word, Ambrose had not reappeared, nor had Merle—an absence that Ibolya in particular fretted over. We could've had Mother marry us, but I could invoke the magic just as well, and it seemed right for Con and I to make our own vows, of our own accord this time. "Ready?" I asked him quietly.

"Always and forever," he answered with a broad grin, his dimple appearing, a star to guide me.

"We stand here on Ejarat's body," I began, allowing my voice to carry to the now quiet assembly, "here on Her sacred isle of Calanthe."

"Beneath Sawehl's loving gaze." Con took up the ancient words, the burr in his voice sensual. "We embrace the gift of their union, to bring two together into one. Do you, Euthalia, enter into this union of your own free will, with an open heart and no other obligations?"

"I do," I replied with a smile. The first time I hadn't been sure if that was true. Now I felt that truth shining from my heart like a beacon. "And you, Conrí?"

"I do." Con grinned. "As many times as necessary."

I laughed at that, a ripple of laughter echoing through the crowd.

"As Ejarat claimed Sawehl," Con said, sobering, "unlike Herself and yet like, do you promise to take into your being the entirety of myself, with all my flaws and virtues, ugliness and beauty, weaknesses and strengths, including my obstinate and hotheaded nature?"

He'd added that last, amusement sparking in his golden eyes at surprising me. "I do," I confirmed, "along with your loving and generous nature, which is the sunshine that allows me to blossom."

Con squeezed my hands, tears adding a glimmer to the gold, and he nodded, overcome.

"As Sawehl claimed Ejarat," I said, "unlike Himself and yet like, do you promise to take into your being the entirety of myself, with all my flaws and virtues, ugliness and beauty, weaknesses and strengths, including my obstinate and controlling nature?"

He grinned, shaking his head a little. "I do—along with your radiance that allowed me to live again when I was nothing but ash."

Oh. My turn to get weepy. I cleared my throat, watching him, as this next part we'd say together. "We promise to nurture and shelter each other, to protect and support, to shed our light so that we might find our best path in life."

The binding sizzled into place, connected between the palms of our hands. The orchid ring waved, seeming to grow larger, spilling a spectrum of light. Con released my hands, taking the silver blade Kara handed him. I held my right palm up in perfect trust, loving the look of concentration on Con's intent face as he carefully sliced my skin, blood springing to the call. He winced with me at the bright pain, then gave the blade back to Kara, holding his palm out to me. I drew the tip of my finger along his skin, calling the blood to emerge. Con gave me a wry, appreciative smile for my new skill—though it hurt him just as much as a knife would—and wrapped his bleeding palm against mine, the contact immediately soothing.

I understood something then that I hadn't the first time, how this aspect of the ceremony symbolized the pain we'd sometimes cause each other, and that we'd mend those wounds in this way. Our hands clasped, blood mingling, Con looked into my eyes—and I knew he'd always be there to salve my hurts. I'd do my best for him, also.

"One flesh, one blood, one mind, one heart," we intoned together, and the marriage bond snapped back into place as if it had never been severed. It rippled throughout Calanthe and farther, through all the forgotten kingdoms, the orphaned lands waiting to be restored, and through

other realities. They kaleidoscoped through my mind, all
the times and places that were and that might have been.
Somewhere out there, Ambrose's deep forest presence replied, like summer leaves in an afternoon breeze, Merle's
purple shards of feathers fluttering in good wishes.

Con's face showed shock and wonder as he felt it all
through me.

"As Ejarat cups you in Her hand," Sondra, Rhéiane, and
my ladies said together.

"And Sawehl showers blessings from above," Kara and
Percy added.

"Share the first kiss of your married union," they all
chorused, sounding not at all serious, but voices threaded
with laughter.

Yes, far from our first kiss, but as Con's lips settled over
mine with a hunger and feeding as old as time and as fresh
as the morning dew, it was a beginning. We'd come a full
circle, with sorrows and painful endings between us. Now
we'd begin anew.

And begin the world anew with us.

~Acknowledgments~

I started this book at the beginning of February 2020, when the COVID-19 global pandemic seemed like something that would stay on the other side of the world. I finished the first draft at the end of April, while we in New Mexico were in the fifth week of a two-week stay-at-home order that would end up lasting until mid-May. By the time I was tackling developmental edits, it was mid-July and the state was shutting down again to prevent the ever-increasing spread of the virus. As I write this, after reviewing copyedits, we are in the last few days of December 2020. Hope is in sight as the vaccine is distributed, but the impact has been staggering beyond anything most of us imagined. I suppose all this makes *The Promised Queen* my pandemic-year book. When it releases, it will be May 25, 2021. I imagine the world will again look very different. I'm not quite sure why I put this message in the Acknowledgments, except that I feel I should acknowledge the enormous upheaval of this year, and the way we have come together to rise above. The ways that the pandemic changed our lives leaked into this book in many small ways. It's fitting that this trilogy, which first took shape in my mind in the wake of the disastrous 2016 U.S.

election, finished for me with the 2020 U.S. election that came as a much-needed triumph—but also the first steps in another long battle. The books echo this.

So, I acknowledge all of you out there who went through this, too.

Many thanks to my editor Jennie Conway, who is a hugely talented editor and forever a delight to work with. To the rest of the team at St. Martin's Press: thank you for working so hard on behalf of this series.

Much love and gratitude to my agent, Sarah Younger, who helped bring this trilogy into being.

Many heartfelt thanks and love to my writer friends who are always there for me at the other end of the phone, internet connection, or Zoom meeting, as we adapted to this year: Amanda Bouchet, Grace Draven, Jennifer Estep, Darynda Jones, Katie Lane, Emily Mah, Jack Mitchell, Leslye Penelope, Kelly Robson, Jim Sorenson, and Sage Walker. I'm really looking forward to seeing your actual, IRL faces again.

Special thanks to Megan Mulry and Charlie Whittock for socially distant outdoor cocktails.

As always, many thanks to my professional writers organizations, the Science Fiction and Fantasy Writers of America (SFWA) and the Romance Writers of America (RWA)—especially my local RWA chapter, the Land of Enchantment Romance Authors—for being a port in the storm, a rising tide that floats all boats, and fellow travelers on the sea of publishing. Special shout-out to the SFWA Slack chat for daily advice and nonsense.

Hugs and gratitude to my fantastic assistant Carien Ubink, who always provides the perfect combination of efficiency and snark.

Love always to my mom. Thank you for wearing your mask.

Finally—first, last, and always—love to David, who is there every day. I'd totally survive any pandemic with you, but let's not do this again, huh?